D0267590

000000254097

How the Soldier
Repairs the Gramophone

How the Soldier Repairs the Gramophone

SAŠA STANIŠIĆ

Translated from the German by Anthea Bell

Weidenfeld & Nicolson

LONDON

First published in Great Britain in 2008
by Weidenfeld & Nicolson

Wie der Soldat das Grammofon repariert © 2006
by Luchterhand Literaturverlag,
a division of Verlagsgruppe Random House GmbH,
Munich, Germany

English translation © Anthea Bell 2008

All rights reserved. No part of this publication may be
reproduced, stored in a retrieval system, or transmitted,
in any form or by any means, electronic, mechanical,
photocopying, recording or otherwise, without the prior
permission of both the copyright owner and the
above publisher.

The right of Saša Stanišić to be identified as the author
of this work has been asserted in accordance with the
Copyright, Designs and Patents Act 1988.

The right of Anthea Bell to be identified as the translator
of this work has been asserted in accordance with the
Copyright, Designs and Patents Act 1988.

This book is a work of fiction. Names, characters, places and
incidents either are the product of the author's imagination or
are used fictitiously, and any resemblance to actual persons
living or dead, events or locales is entirely coincidental.

The translation of this work was supported by a grant from the
Goethe-Institut that is funded by the Ministry of Foreign Affairs.

This book has been selected to receive financial assistance
from English PEN Writers in Translation programme
supported by Bloomsberg.

A CIP catalogue record for this book
is available from the British Library

ISBN 978 0 297 85298 8 (hardback)
ISBN 978 0 297 85299 5 (trade paperback)

Typeset at The Spartan Press Ltd,
Lymington, Hants

Printed in Great Britain by Clays Ltd, St Ives plc

Weidenfeld & Nicolson
An imprint of the Orion Publishing Group
Orion House, 5 Upper St Martin's Lane,
London WC2H 9EA

www.orionbooks.co.uk

For my parents / Mojim roditeljima

Contents

How long a heart attack takes over a hundred metres, how much a spider's life weighs, why my sad man writes to the cruel river, and what magic the Comrade-in-Chief of all that's unfinished can work

Grandpa Slavko measured my head with Granny's washing line, I got a magic hat, a pointy magic hat made of cardboard, and Grandpa Slavko said: I'm really still too young for this sort of thing, and you're already too old.

So I got a magic hat with yellow and blue shooting stars on it, trailing yellow and blue tails, and I cut out a little crescent moon to go with them and two triangular rockets. Gagarin was flying one, Grandpa Slavko was flying the other.

Grandpa, I can't go out in this hat!

I should hope not!

On the morning of the day when he was to die in the evening, Grandpa Slavko made me a magic wand from a stick and said: there's magic in that hat and wand. If you wear the hat and wave the wand you'll be the most powerful magician in the non-aligned states. You'll be able to revolutionise all sorts of things, just as long as they're in line with Tito's ideas and the Statutes of the Communist League of Yugoslavia.

I doubted the magic, but I never doubted my grandpa. The most valuable gift of all is invention, imagination is your greatest wealth. Remember that, Aleksandar, said Grandpa very gravely as he put the hat on my head, you remember that and imagine the world better than it is. He handed me the magic wand, and I doubted nothing any more.

It's usual for people to think sadly of the dead now and then. In our family that happens when Sunday, rain, coffee and Granny Katarina all come together at the same time. Granny sips from her favourite cup, the white one with the cracked handle, she cries and remembers all the dead and the good things they did before dying got in the way. Our family and friends are at Granny's today because we're remembering Grandpa Slavko who's been dead for two days, dead for now anyway, just until I can find my magic wand and my hat again.

Still not dead in my family are Mother, Father, and Father's brothers – Uncle Bora and Uncle Miki Nena Fatima, my mother's mother, is well in herself, it's only her ears and her tongue that have died – she's deaf as a post and silent as snowfall, as they say. Auntie Gordana isn't dead yet either, she's Uncle Bora's wife and pregnant. Auntie Gordana, a blonde island in the dark sea of our family's hair, is always called Typhoon because she's four times livelier than normal people, she runs eight times faster and talks at fourteen times the usual speed. She even sprints from the loo to the wash-basin, and at the cash desk in shops she's worked out the price of everything even before the cashier can tap it in.

They've all come to Granny's because of Grandpa Slavko's death, but they're talking about the life in Auntie Typhoon's belly. Every-one is sure she'll have her baby on Sunday at the latest, or at the very, very latest on Monday, months early but already as perfect as if it were in the ninth month. I suggest calling the baby Speedy Gonzales. Auntie Typhoon shakes her blonde curls, says all in a rush: are-we-Mexicans-or-what? It'll-be-a-girl-not-a-mouse! She's-going-to-be-called-Ema.

Or Slavko, adds Uncle Bora quietly, Slavko if it's a boy.

There's a lot of love around for Grandpa Slavko today among all the people in black drinking coffee with Granny Katarina and taking surreptitious looks at the sofa where Grandpa was sitting when Carl Lewis set the new world record in Tokyo. Grandpa died in 9.86 seconds flat; his heart was racing right up there with Carl Lewis, they were neck and neck. Then his heart stopped and Carl ran on like crazy. Grandpa gasped, and Carl flung his arms up in the air and threw an American flag over his shoulders.

The mourners bring chocolates and sugar cubes, cognac and schnapps. They want to console Granny with sweet things, they want to comfort themselves with drink. Male mourning smells of aftershave. It stands in small groups in the kitchen, getting sozzled. Female mourning sits around the living-room table with Granny, suggesting names for the new life in Auntie Typhoon's belly and discussing the right way to put a baby down to sleep in its first few months. When anyone mentions Grandpa's name the women cut up cake and hand slices round. They add sugar to their coffee and stir it with spoons that look like toys.

Women always praise the virtues of cake.

Great-Granny Mileva and Great-Grandpa Nikola aren't here because their son is going home to them in Veletovo, to be buried in the village where he was born. What the two have to do with each other I don't know. You should be allowed to be dead where you really liked being when you were alive. My father down in our cellar, for instance, which he calls his studio and he hardly ever leaves, among his canvases and brushes. Granny anywhere just as long as her women neighbours are there too and there's coffee and chocolates. Great-Granny and Great-Grandpa under the plum trees in their orchard in Veletovo. Where has my mother really liked being?

Grandpa Slavko in his best stories, or underneath the Party office.

I may be able to manage without him for another two days. My magic things are sure to turn up by then.

I'm looking forward to seeing Great-Grandpa and Great-Granny again. Ever since I can remember they haven't smelled very sweet, and their average age is about a hundred and fifty. All the same, they're the least dead and the most alive of the whole family if you leave out Auntie Typhoon, who doesn't count – she's more of a natural catastrophe than a human being and she has a propeller in her backside. So Uncle Bora sometimes says, kissing his natural catastrophe's back.

Uncle Bora weighs as many kilos as my great-grandparents are old.

Someone else in my family who's not dead yet is Granny Katarina, although on the evening when Grandpa's great heart died of the fastest illness in the world she wished she was and wailed: all alone, what's to become of me without you? I don't want to be all alone, Slavko, oh, my Slavko, I'm so sad!

I was less afraid of Grandpa's death than of Granny's great grief crawling about on its knees like that: all alone, how am I going to live all alone? Granny beat her breast at Grandpa's dead feet and begged to be dead herself. I was still breathing fast, but not easily any more. Granny was so weak that I imagined her body going all soft on the floor, soft and round. On TV a large woman jumped into the sand and looked happy about it. At Grandpa's feet, Granny shouted to the neighbours to come round. They unbuttoned his shirt, Grandpa's glasses slipped, his mouth was twisted to one side . . . I cut things out in my mind, the way I always do when I'm at a loss, more stars for my magic hat. In spite of being afraid, and though it was so soon after a death, I noticed that Granny's china dog on the TV set had fallen over and the plate with fishbones left from supper was still standing on the crocheted tablecloth. I could hear every word the neighbours said as they bustled about, I heard it all in spite of Granny's whimpering and howling. She tugged at Grandpa's legs and Grandpa slid forward off the sofa. I hid in the corner behind the TV. But a thousand TV sets couldn't have hidden Granny's distorted face from me, or Grandpa falling off the sofa all twisted sideways, or the thought that I'd never seen my grandparents look uglier.

I'd have liked to put my hand on Granny's shaking back – her blouse would have been wet with sweat – and I'd have liked to say: Granny, don't! It will be all right. After all, Grandpa's a Party member, and the Party agrees with the Statutes of the Communist League, it's just that I can't find my magic wand at the moment. It's going to be all right again, Granny.

But her grief-stricken madness silenced me. The louder she cried, leave me alone! flailing around, the less courageous I felt in my hiding place. The more the neighbours turned away from Grandpa and went to Granny instead, trying to console someone obviously inconsolable, as if they were selling her something she didn't need, the more frantically she defended herself. As more and more tears covered her cheeks, her mouth, her lamentation, her chin, like oil coating a pan, I cut out more and more little details of the living room: the bookcase with works by Marx, Lenin and Kardelj, *Das Kapital* at the left on the bottom shelf, the smell of fish, the branches of the pattern on the wallpaper, four tapestry pictures on the wall – children playing in a village street, brightly coloured flowers in a brightly coloured vase, a ship on a rough sea, a little cottage in the forest – a photograph of Tito and Gandhi shaking hands, right above and between the ship and the cottage. Someone saying: how do we get her off him?

More and more people came along, one taking another's place as if to catch up with something, or at least not miss out on anything else, anxious to be as lively as possible in the presence of death. Grandpa's death had been too quick. It upset the neighbours, it made them look guiltily at the floor. No one had been able to keep up with Grandpa's heart running its race, not even Granny: oh no, why, why, why, Slavko? Teta Amela from the second floor collapsed. Someone cried: oh, sacred heart of Jesus! Someone else immediately cursed the mother of Jesus and several other members of his family. Granny tugged at Grandpa's trouser legs, hit out at the two paramedics who appeared in the living room with their little bags. Keep your hands off him, she cried. Under their white coats the paramedics wore lumberjack shirts, and they hauled Granny off Grandpa's legs as if prising a sea shell off a rock. As Granny saw it, Grandpa wouldn't be dead until she let go of him, so she wasn't letting go. The men in white coats listened to Grandpa's chest. One of them held a mirror to his face and said: no, nothing.

I shouted that Grandpa was still there, his death didn't conform to the aims and ideals of the Communist League. You just get out of the way, give me my magic wand and I'll prove it!

No one took any notice of me. The lumberjack-paramedics put their hands inside Grandpa's shirt and shone a pencil torch in his eyes. I pulled out the electric cable, and the TV turned itself off. There were loose cobwebs hanging in the corner next to the power socket. How much less does a spider's death weigh than the death of a human being? Which of her husband's dead legs does the spider's wife cling to? I decided that I would never again put a spider in a bottle and run water slowly into it.

Where was my magic wand?

I don't know how long I stood in the corner before my father grabbed my arm as if taking me prisoner. He handed me over to my mother, who hauled me down the stairs and out into the yard. The air smelled of mirabelles mashed to make schnapps and there were fires burning in the central square, or megdan. You can see almost the whole town from the megdan, perhaps you can even see into the yard in front of the big five-storey block, practically a high-rise building for Višegrad, where a young woman with long black hair and brown eyes was bending down to a boy with hair the same colour and with the same almond-shaped eyes. She blew some strands of hair off his forehead, her eyes filled with tears. No one on the megdan could hear what she was whispering to the boy. And perhaps no one could see that after the woman had taken the boy in her arms and hugged him for a long, long time, he nodded. The way you nod when you're promising something.

On the evening of the third day after Grandpa Slavko's death I'm sitting in the kitchen, looking through photograph albums. I take all the photos of Grandpa Slavko out of the album. Out in the yard our cherry tree is arguing with the wind, it's stormy. When I've fixed it so that Grandpa Slavko can come alive again, for my next trick I'll make us all able to keep hold of noises. Then we can put the wind in the cherry-tree leaves into an album of sounds, along with the rumble of thunder and dogs barking at night in summer. And this is me chopping wood for the stove – that's how we'll be able to present our life proudly, in sounds, the way we show holiday snaps of the Adriatic. We'll be carrying small sounds around with us. I'd cover up the anxiety on my mother's face with the laughter she laughs on her good days.

The brownish photos with broad white rims smell of plastic tablecloths, and show people with funny trousers that get wider at the bottom. There's a short man in a railwayman's uniform standing in front of the façades of an unfinished Višegrad, looking straight ahead, upright as a soldier: Grandpa Rafik.

Grandpa Rafik, my mother's father, died for good a long time ago – he drowned in the river Drina. I hardly knew him, but I can remember one game we played, a simple game. Grandpa Rafik would point to something and I'd say its name, its colour, and the first thing that occurred to me about it. He'd point to his penknife, and I'd say: knife, grey, and railway engine. He'd point to a sparrow, and I'd say: bird, grey, and railway engine. Grandpa Rafik pointed through the window at the night, and I said: dreams, grey, and railway engine, and Grandpa tucked me up and said: sleep an iron sleep.

The time of my grey period was the time of my visits to the eye specialist, who diagnosed nothing except that I could see things too fast, for instance the sequence of little letters and big letters on his wall chart. You'll have to cure him of that somehow, Mrs Krsmanović, said the eye specialist, and he prescribed drops for her own eyes, which were always red.

I was very scared of trains and railway engines at that time. Grandpa Rafik had taken me to the disused railway tracks, he scratched flaking paint off the old engine; you've broken my heart, he whispered, rubbing the black paint between the palms of his hands. On the way home – paving-stone, grey, railway engine, my hand in his large one, black with sharp scraps of peeling paint – I decided to be nice to railway trains, because now he had me worried about my own heart. But it had been a long time since any trains had passed through our town. A few years later the first girl I loved, Danijela with her very long hair, who didn't return my love, showed me how silly I'd been to protect my heart from being broken by trains.

Peeling scraps of paint and the grey game are all I remember of Grandpa Rafik, unless old photos count as memories. And Grandpa Rafik is absent from our home in general. However often and however readily my family like to talk about themselves and other families and the dead over coffee Grandpa Rafik is very seldom mentioned. No one ever looks at the coffee grounds in a cup and sighs: oh, Rafik, my Rafik, if only you were here! No one ever wonders what Grandpa Rafik would say about something, his name isn't spoken with either gratitude or disapproval.

No dead person could be less alive than Grandpa Rafik.

The dead are lonely enough in the earth where they lie, so why do we leave even the memory of Grandpa Rafik to be so lonely?

Mother comes into the kitchen and opens the fridge. She's going to make sandwiches to take to work, she puts butter and cheese on the table. I look at her face, searching it for Grandpa Rafik's face in the photos.

Mama, do you look like Grandpa Rafik? I ask when she sits down at the table and unwraps the bread. She cuts up tomatoes. I wait and ask the question again, and only now does Mother stop, knife-blade on a tomato. What kind of grandpa was Grandpa Rafik? I ask again, why does no one talk about him? How am I ever going to know what kind of a grandpa I had?

Mother puts the knife aside and lays her hands in her lap. Mother raises her eyes. Mother looks at me.

You didn't have a real grandpa, Aleksandar, only a sad man. He mourned for his river and his earth. He would kneel down, scratch about in that earth of his until his fingernails broke and the blood came. He stroked the grass and smelled it and wept into its tufts like a tiny child – my dear earth, you're trodden underfoot, at the mercy of all kinds of weight. You didn't have a real grandpa, only a stupid man. He drank and drank. He ate earth, he brought earth up, then he crawled to the bank on all fours and washed his mouth out with water from the river. How that sad man loved his river! And his cognac – a stupid man who could love only what he saw as humbled and subjugated. Who could love only if he drank and drank.

The Drina, what a neglected river, what forgotten beauty, he would lament when he came staggering out of a bar, once with the frame of his glasses bent, another time after wetting himself, oh, the stink of it! What a messy business old age is, he wept when he stumbled and fell, trying to hold tight to the river in case he took off. Oh, how often we found him at night under the first arch of the bridge, lying on his belly with his fingers clutching the surface of the water. Swollen, blue hands, half-clenched into fists. He'd be holding flowers in the river, stones, sometimes a cognac bottle. It went on like that for years. Ever since they took the railway out of service, so that there were no more trains running through the town with that sad man switching the points for them, setting the signals, raising the barriers. He lost his job and never said a word about it, he had nothing to do now and nothing at all to say. He was sent into retirement and he drank day after day, first in secret up at the railway station that wasn't a station any more, though the old engine still stood there, and later by the river and in the middle of town, overcome by sudden, stupid love for the water and its banks.

You didn't have a real grandpa, only an embittered man. He drank and drank and drank until he was tired of life. If only he'd loved chess or the Party or us as much as he loved his trains and then his river, and most of all his brandy! If only he'd listened to us and not the deep, unfathomable Drina!

On the evening of the night he died, a driven man, he scratched writing into the river bank. He had drunk three litres of wine, and he used the broken neck of a bottle as his pen to write the river a long letter. We pulled him out of the mud by his feet, and he whimpered and cried out to the river: how am I to save you, how am I to save something so large all by myself?

To think that something so sad can stink like that! We were called when his shouting and his songs got to be more than anyone could bear. Papa carried him home in his arms and put him in the bathtub, clothes and all, and in the bathtub your drunken grand-father threw up twice, in a fury, cursing all anglers: may your weapons turn against your own mouths, he said, poking about in the river's belly like that with your hooks, tearing the fishes' lips – ah, what silent pain! May your skin be flayed with blunt knives, you criminals, may the depths take you along with your boats, your filthy petrol, all your weirs, all your turbines, all your mechanical

9

diggers! A river: a river is water and life and power and nothing else.

Around midnight I washed his hair and his tortoise neck, I washed behind his ears and under his armpits. He kissed my hands and said he knew exactly who I was. In spite of his tears he knew whose knuckles he was patting, he remembered everything: what a jewel Love was, Fate was such a bugger.

I'm your daughter, I told him three times, not your wife, and on that night, his last, he made me three promises: clean clothes, no alcohol, and he'd stay alive. He kept only one of them. His railwayman's cap was found under the first arch of the bridge, his cognac bottle was also found, but he was never found himself. We probed the water near the banks of the Drina for him with pitchforks. Why had he gone out again? What was there left to love on that May night? The bars had all been shut for ages when I tucked him up after his bath, after he'd made his promises. An angler, of all people, found his body in the reeds downstream. His face was under the water, his feet were on the bank – his beloved Drina was kissing him in death, marrying that sad man who kept only one of his promises. He had smartened himself up for the wedding and he was wearing his uniform with the railwayman's badge. He had spent so many nights looking for death, but until then he didn't have the courage to find it, he didn't keep his head under water long enough for the Drina to be the last and only tear he wept.

And when he was to be laid out for the funeral, twelve hours after I'd washed him into making his three promises, I was the one who took the loofah again, the hardest I could find, I was the one who scrubbed his thin torso the way you scrub a carpet, rubbed soap into his yellow, wrinkled belly and brushed his flabby calves. I didn't touch his fingers and his face. Your sad grandfather had dug his hands into the bank, and what kind of daughter would I have been to scrape the earth out from under his fingernails? After he had said: when I die I don't want any coffin? How that sad man loved his cruel river, how he loved the willows and the fish and the mud! You didn't have a grandpa, Aleksandar, only a stupid man.

But you were too little to remember his stupidity. You liked the way he said grey, grey, grey to everything, for some reason you thought it was funny. It was only for his river that he thought up the brightest of colours, he saw the detail of nothing but the Drina, that sad man who could laugh only when he saw his reflection in the water. You didn't have a grandpa, Aleksandar, just a sad man.

I look at my mother with a thousand questions in my eyes. She has sung me the song of the sad man as if she'd been rehearsing it since the day he drowned. She has sung it as if he hadn't belonged to her, as if someone else had written the lines, yet with such loving anger that I was afraid a mere nod of my head might steal him away from her. Now she shakes her head over something I can't see and lays slices of bread out in a row on the table.

I ask only two of my thousands of questions. What did Grandpa write on the bank? And why didn't any of you help him?

My mother is a small woman. She runs her fingers through her long hair, combing it. She puffs in my face as if we were playing. She unwraps the butter. Unwraps the cheese. Spreads butter on the bread. Puts a slice of cheese on the butter. Puts tomatoes on the cheese. Sprinkles salt on the tomatoes with her thumb and forefinger. Takes the bread on the palm of her hand. Puts another slice of bread on top of it. Presses them firmly together.

The cherry tree withstands the storm, whipping its branches about. At first the tapping on our front roof sounds like a few coins dropping into a money-box, then it goes faster and faster; it's hail. After my mother has silently left the kitchen I open the window and put a photo of Grandpa Slavko and me on the sill. The cold wind reaches out for my face, I close the window. In the other brownish photos people are standing about in bathing suits with vertical stripes, ankle-deep in the Drina. There are no such bathing suits any more, the dog and her four puppies probably aren't around either. My young Grandpa Slavko, with his hat on, is patting the puppies, enjoying himself. Which is the last photo of him? How long do dogs live, and do I know any of the puppies? A time comes when there are no new photos of dogs or people because their lives are over. And how do you photograph a life that's over? When I die, I'll tell everyone, photograph me in the ground. That'll be in seventy years' time. Photograph my nails growing, photograph me getting thinner and thinner and losing my skin.

Everything that's finished and over, all deaths seem to me uncalled for, unhappy, undeserved. Summers turn to winter, houses are demolished, people in photos turn to photos on gravestones. So many things ought to be left unfinished – Sundays, so that Mondays don't come; dams so that rivers aren't held up. Tables ought not to be varnished because the smell gives me a headache, holidays shouldn't turn into going back to school, cartoons ought not to turn into the news. And my love for Danijela with her very long hair shouldn't have turned into unrequited love. And I should never finish making magic hats with Grandpa, but go on talking endlessly to him about the advantages of life as a magician in the service of the Communist League, and what might happen if you season bread with dust from the tail of a shooting star.

I'm against endings, I'm against things being over. Being finished should be stopped! I am Comrade-in-Chief of going on and on, I support furthermore and et cetera!

I find a picture of the bridge over the Drina in the last photo album. The bridge looks the same as usual except that there's scaffolding around its eleven arches. People are standing on the scaffolding, waving as if the bridge were a ship about to sail away down the river. In spite of the scaffolding the bridge looks finished. It's complete, the scaffolding can't spoil its beauty and usefulness. I don't mind the gigantic completeness of our bridge. The Drina is fast in that photo and rushes along, the broad, the dangerous Drina – a young river!

Flowing fast is like shouting out loud.

Today it rolls lazily by, more of a lake than a river, the dam has discouraged the water so much – the slow Drina, with driftwood and dirt near the banks as if it's fraying at the edges. I carefully take the bridge out of the photo album. The surface is cool and smooth, just as the once wild, untamed river is today. I put the photo in my trouser pocket, where it will get crumpled and dog-eared.

I want to make unfinished things. I'm not a builder, and I'm rather bad at maths except for mental arithmetic. I don't know how you make bricks. But I can paint. I get that from my artist father, along with my big ears and his constant cry of: not now, can't you see I'm busy! I'm going to be the artist of the lovely Unfinished! I'll paint plums without stones, rivers without dams, Comrade Tito in a T-shirt! Artists have to create pictures in a logical series; that, says my father the spare-time artist, is the recipe for success, he told me about it in his studio. As well as his canvases and paints there are tubs of sauerkraut stored there, boxes of old clothes, and the child's bed I've grown out of. My father spends entire weekends in his studio. A painter must never be satisfied with what he sees – painting reality means surrendering to it, he cries when I knock at the door to say the air's running out of my football again, or the inner tube of my bike tyre. Artists have to reshuffle and rebuild reality, says my father in his beret as he pumps up the football. He isn't really talking to me, he doesn't expect any answer. There are French songs playing in the studio, Pink Floyd late in the evening, and the door is locked.

Logical series are the answer. Other people can fly planes and delouse the pelicans in the zoo, but I'm going to be a footballing, fishing, serial artist of the Unfinished! None of my pictures will ever be painted to the end, there'll be something important missing from every one of them.

I get my painting things, my paintbox, I borrow paper from my father. I put water in a jam jar and soften my brushes in it. The empty sheet of paper lies in front of me. The first picture of something unfinished must be the Drina, the mischievous river before it had a dam. I put blue and yellow on the plate where I mix them; I make the first green brush-stroke on the paper, the green is too pale, I darken it carefully and paint a curve, I lighten it, too cold, I add ochre, green, green, but I'll never get a green like the green of the river Drina, not in a hundred years.

*

The dead are lonelier than the living ever can be. They can't hear each other through coffins and the earth. And the living go and plant flowers on the graves. The roots grow down into the earth and break through the coffins. After a while the coffins are full of roots and the dead people's hair. Then they can't even talk to themselves. When I die I'd like to be buried in a mass grave. I wouldn't be afraid of the dark in a mass grave, and I'd be lonely only because of missing my grandson so much, the way I miss Grandpa Slavko now.

I don't have grandpa any more, and the tears are building up behind my forehead. Everything important in the world can be found in the morning paper, the Communist Manifesto, or the stories that make us laugh or cry, best of all both at the same time. That was one of Grandpa Slavko's clever sayings. When I get to be as old as he was I'll have his clever sayings, I'll have big veins like the veins on my father's forearms, I'll have my granny's recipes and my mother's rare look of happiness.

On the morning of the fourth day after Grandpa's death Father wakes me, and I know at once: it's Grandpa's funeral. I dreamed everyone in my family was dead except me, which felt like being suddenly very far away and unable to find my way back.

Pack your things, we're leaving.

My father wakes me up only when there's some kind of disaster, otherwise Mother comes to kiss my hair. Father doesn't kiss me on principle. It's awkward between men. He sits down on the edge of the bed as if to say something else. I sit up. So there we are now, sitting. Papa, I look at you the way a person looks at someone when you're listening, look, I'm not getting up, it's a good thing for you to tell me everything I already know, explaining what I already understand, because the thing isn't complete until a father has told his son and explained it all. But I don't say that, and Father doesn't say anything either. That's the way we often talk to each other. He goes to work, then after work he goes into his studio and spends the whole night there. He sleeps in late at weekends. If he's watching the news there's a ban on talking. I'm not complaining, he talks to other people even less than he talks to me. I'm content and my mother is happy that she can bring me up on her own, without interference from Father.

Sitting there saying nothing today, my father looks as if he doesn't have any muscles. He's been staying with Granny since Grandpa died. Granny phoned late yesterday and asked how the boy was doing. She thought it was my mother who'd picked up the phone, so I said nothing. We're going to wash Slavko now, she added, and said goodbye. I imagined Grandpa being washed and dressed for his own funeral. I didn't see any faces, just hands pulling Grandpa about. The hands threw all the bed-linen out of the bedroom and boiled the sheets, you do that when there's a dead person in the place. Little veins in your eyes burst from washing your dead father, your hands get smaller and you have to keep looking at them. My silent father sits on the edge of my bed with his red-rimmed eyes, hands on his knees, palms turned up. When I'm as old as Father I'll have the lines on his face. Lines show how well you've lived. I don't know if lots of lines mean you've lived better. Mother says no, but I've heard the opposite too.

I get up. Father straightens the sheet and plumps up the pillow. Do you have anything black to wear?

Not: Grandpa.

Not: Grandpa's dead.

Not: Aleksandar, your grandpa won't be coming back.

Not: Life can never be as quick as a sudden heart attack.

Not: Grandpa's only asleep – I'd resent that even more than the way he opens the window now and hangs the blanket out to air.

I take a black shirt off its hanger. Suddenly I realise that my father is counting on me. He understands that magic is our last chance. We can start right away, I say, I just have to fetch something from Grandpa's apartment first. Something important.

On the way in the car he says: Granny and your uncles have gone ahead. Hurry up, everybody else is already there. 'There' he calls it.

Not a word from him about the funeral, and I don't say that I'm the most powerful magician-grandson in the non-aligned states. Don't worry, step on the accelerator and I'll get my grandpa back for me and your father back for you. I don't say anything because suddenly being a child seems so difficult.

Grandpa's apartment. I take a deep breath. The kitchen. Fried onions, nothing left of Grandpa. Bedroom. I press my face against the shirts. Living room. I sit down on the sofa. That's where Grandpa was sitting. Nothing. I go into the corner behind the TV set. Nothing. The cobwebs are still there. I look out of the window into the yard. Nothing. Our Yugo with its engine running. Father has got out. My magic hat on the glass case. I climb on a chair, carefully fold up the hat and put it in my rucksack. The rucksack! I search it for the magic wand. I was going to show the wand to my best friend Edin, I remember, and for demonstration purposes I was going to break some unimportant bone in our history teacher. He skips almost every lesson with Partisans in it, even though there've never been better battles than the fighting of the People's Liberation Army and Red Star Belgrade's matches. Red Star Belgrade is my favourite football team. We almost always win and when we lose it's a tragedy. Grandpa's death has saved the history teacher for now.

Like all the others I wear black, but wearing black can't be all you have to do at a funeral, so I imitate Uncle Bora and my father in turn. When Uncle Bora bows his head, I bow mine. When Father exchanges a few words with someone, I listen to what he says and repeat the words to someone else. I scratch my stomach because Uncle Bora is scratching his own big belly. It's hot, I unbutton my shirt because Father is unbuttoning his. That's the grandson, people whisper.

Auntie Typhoon has caught up with the pall-bearers and has to be called back. She asks if she can help. Oh-this-slow-creeping-about, she says, it'll-be-the-death-of-me.

Great-Grandpa and Great-Granny walk behind the coffin. Great-Grandpa isn't wearing a hat on his long white hair. When I get to be as old as he is, mine will be longer. I'd like to tell him about my magic plan because he's a magician himself, but I can't find a good opportunity. Grandpa Slavko once told me that long ago Great-Grandpa mucked out the biggest stable in Yugoslavia in a single night because in return its owner promised him his daughter's hand in marriage – today she's my Great-Granny. Grandpa wasn't sure just when it all happened. Two hundred years ago, I cried, and Uncle Miki tapped his forehead: there wasn't any Yugoslavia back then, midget, those were the royal stables after the First World War. I liked Uncle Miki's version because it made Great-Granny into a princess. Grandpa said Great-Grandpa didn't just muck out the gigantic stable, on the very same night he helped two cows to calve, he won an immense sum of money against the best rummy players in town, and he repaired an electric light bulb in his father-in-law's house – which I thought was the most difficult task of all, when you remember that nothing in the world is deader than a dead light bulb. None of it could have been done without magic. Princess Great-Granny said nothing about it, but smiled a smile full of meaning. You should have seen his arms, she said, no one ever had eyes of a colour that suited his arms as well as my blue-eyed Nikola.

I stand beside the grave and I know it can be done. After all, I magically made it possible for Carl Lewis to break the world record. So not all Americans are capitalists, at least, Comrade Lewis isn't because my wand and pointy hat work magic exclusively along Party lines. I stand beside the grave where Grandpa, formerly chairman of the Višegrad Local Committee, is going to be buried, and I know it can work.

Great-Grandpa climbs down into the grave and tears roots and stones out of the earth walls with both hands. Oh, what a sight! he says. My son, my son!

It's hard to imagine Grandpa Slavko as anyone's son. Sons are sixty at the most. In fact almost all the people saying goodbye to Grandpa today are around sixty. The women have black scarves over their hair and wear perfume because they want to drown out the smell of death. Death smells like freshly mown grass here. The men murmur, they have coloured badges on the breast pockets of their black jackets, they clasp their hands behind their backs and I clasp mine too.

Father helps Great-Grandpa out of the grave and stands behind me. His hands press down firmly on my shoulders. The speeches begin, the speeches go on and on, the speeches are never going to end, and I don't want to interrupt anyone making a speech with my magic spells, that would be rude. I'm sweating. The sun is blazing down, cicadas are chirping. Uncle Bora mops the sweat off his face with a pale blue handkerchief. I mop my forehead with my sleeve. Once I secretly watched a funeral where there weren't any long, boring speeches, just a short incomprehensible one. A bearded man wearing a woman's dress sang and waved a golden ball about on the end of a chain. Smoke was coming out of the ball, and death smelled of green tea. Later I found out that the man was a priest. We don't have priests – the people who make speeches at our funerals are sixty years old with badges on their breast pockets. No one tells any jokes. They all praise Grandpa, often saying exactly the same thing, as if they'd been copying from each other. They sound like women praising the virtues of cake. As the dead can't hear any more when they're in the ground, the last thing they hear up here ought to make them feel good. But correct as my grandpa was, he would always put anyone who tried sweet-talking him right. No, Comrade Poljo, he would say, I have not been busy reforming our country every single day, last Friday I did nothing at all to lower the rate of inflation, I slept in late on Saturday instead of going ahead to implement the plan in our regional collectives, and on Sundays I go walking with my grandson the magician. We always go a different way and think up stories, that's the great thing about Višegrad, you never run out of new ways to walk and stories to tell – little stories, great ones, comical and tragical, they're all our stories! And where else would you find a place where a grandson knows more stories than his grandpa? When he was this big, Grandpa would say, raising his thumb, forefinger and middle finger, he thought up stories about the later life of Mary Poppins. Comrade Poppins gets tired of her silly queen, changes her name to Marica, moves into our high-rise building in Yugoslavia and marries Petar Popović the music teacher. He's already married, and allergic to umbrellas, but he plays the piano so well that Marica

18

can't resist him. She enchants him with her singing and her tightly laced boots. Marica flies over the town with her umbrella, she doesn't want to be a children's nanny any more, she gets a job on the assembly line of the Partisan machine-tools factory, whereupon it exceeds the planned production quota twice over, month after month.

But I'm straying from the subject, Grandpa would say, snapping his fingers, I really had something else to say: I don't always have good advice for everyone. For instance, for young people – it's not that I don't know what to tell them to do, *I don't want* to tell them – they have to find out about the world by themselves. And when our neighbours on the second floor put their rubbish out beside the container instead of in it, I am far from being feeling polite about it, Comrade Poljo! I'm a pernickety neighbour! I shout up the stairway: if this happens again I'm emptying my rubbish outside the neighbours' door, that's what I'm going to do! Nor is it true that I carry coals down to some old widow's cellar for her, Grandpa would say, dismissing the notion, I'm not particularly fond of old widows! In one thing, however, you are right, Grandpa would have said, taking Granny's hand and running his thumb over the back of it. I help my Katarina do the dishes, I hoover the apartment, and I love to cook. Katarina has never had to spend all day on her feet, not as long as I could stand on mine! And why shouldn't men cook? Best of all I like cooking catfish for my grandson and my proud wife Comrade Katarina. With lemon, garlic, and potatoes with chopped parsley. And there's one thing I treasure above all others, Comrade Poljo: Aleksandar is the best angler from here to the Danube, his grandpa's sunshine, that's what he is.

I don't know how long I stood, deep in thought, beside Grandpa's coffin. I don't know when I freed myself from my father's heavy hands and ran around the grave with the smell of summer rain rising from it. Or when I put on my hat with its blue and yellow stars turning round the crescent moon, although on the day of the evening when he died a death that proved stronger than any magic, Grandpa had told me that stars didn't turn around moons, moons turned around stars. How long did I point my wand at the five-pointed star at the head end of the coffin; how often did I hit out when people tried to carry me away? What curses did I utter, how much did I cry? And will I ever forgive Carl Lewis for using up all of my magic power on his world record, leaving none for Grandpa? All of it went during those 9.86 seconds on 25 August 1991, the day before the day before the evening when someone on the megdan might not have heard a mother whispering to her son: you had a loving grandpa, and he will never come back. But his love for us is never-ending, his love will never be gone. Aleksandar, you have a never-ending grandpa now.

We made a promise about stories, Mama, the son said, nodding, and closed his eyes as if he were working magic without his hat and magic wand, a very simple promise: never to stop telling them.

*How sweet dark red is, how many oxen you need to pull
down a wall, why Kraljević Marko's horse is related to
Superman, and how war can come to a party*

I can't eat any more, I let myself drop and lie there among the
buzzing sweetness of the crushed fruit. Little flies buzz around my
head, the dark red sweetness of the plums is sticky in my mouth,
around my lips and on my hands, I'm feeding the flies as if they
were birds. We're billing and cooing.

Plum-picking time in Veletovo: Great-Granny Mileva and
Great-Grandpa Nikola have invited us to the village harvest
festival. The whole family are here, some of them still wearing
black in mourning for Grandpa Slavko. Black is the opposite of
summer and so that grudging bastard the sun feels insulted, says
Great-Granny, and burns down on their backs. She wipes the sweat
from her forehead with the back of her hand.

Grandpa's death is the very opposite of summer, the most
opposite of all.

I get my love of plums from my mother. Recently, when she saw
how I was looking forward to the plum harvest, she told me that in
the last months of her pregnancy she did nothing but watch figure
skating and eat large quantities of plums: plums all through the day,
she said, minced meat and chocolate in the evenings, now and then
carrots, and coffee by the litre when I was thirsty.

And a cigarette now and then, right? finished my father, without
looking up from his newspaper.

Father slept through my birth.

I'm like my mother in my fondness for plums and minced meat,
and I've painted a plum without a stone surrounded by minced
meat for both of us. Mother has sweet dark redness all over her face
like a beard too. You'll have to eat some lunch, all the same, she
warns me from up on the ladder, don't eat so fast!

Don't eat so many would have been better advice, because I've just broken the world record for plum-eating, and now I hold two world records for indigestion. I lie there and let the flies buzz around me.

Plums are dusty fruit.

That's the first thing you've laughed at, Aleksandar, said my mother when we were talking about the harvest. She didn't add: since Grandpa died.

These roads are made for an arse, not a car! cursed my father yesterday morning on the way to Veletovo, looking under the hood of our yellow Yugo and shaking his head.

Yugos are made for four, not six, replied Mother, lighting a cigarette.

That's not the trouble, its contrary nature is the trouble! This is not a car, it's a donkey on wheels! Father kicked the wheel rim.

A donkey . . . Mother began to answer back, but then luckily she went away to smoke her cigarette in the company of the flowers by the roadside.

Even on its very first drive our Yugo, which was brand new at the time, had stopped on the winding road to Veletovo with its engine still running, as if it just wanted to take a quick look at the view: the brambles covered with ripe blackberries, the stream under the fir trees, ferns the colour of my mother's bright red perm. Father had taken his hands off the steering wheel and shrugged: stepping on the accelerator didn't work. Ever since then we've always had to walk part of the way to my great-grandparents' house. On the way home the Yugo will start first time. The only one of us who can never get used to it is my father.

Yesterday, while he was busy repairing the engine until his fingers were black, I tried to tell my uncles and Nena Fatima that they didn't have to let me win at rummy.

The days of giving me a toddler's privileges are over, I cried, I'm only pretending I can't cope with fourteen cards at once to lull you into a false sense of security!

I threw my hand of cards down hard on to the middle of the rock around which we were sitting, so as to make a loud sound without raising my voice. My mother was expert at such gestures, she was Comrade-in-Chief of them. She could leave the table with just a shake of her head, she could put her hands on her hips and frown, and the sound was so loud I felt like stopping my ears.

Hey, you, Uncle, I said, tapping Bora's shoulder with my forefinger, if you're going to look at my cards then please hang on to the jack you need yourself, and don't discard it on my behalf, I'm not incompetent!

I know the word 'incompetent' from my father. He uses it when there's something political on TV, or when he and Uncle Miki are quarrelling about something political they've seen on TV. Incompetence means doing something even though you haven't the faintest idea how to − like governing Yugoslavia, for instance. 'Fellow-traveller' is another important term, and several times already it's led to me being sent to my room, or the brothers not speaking to each other for days on end. If I had a brother, we'd be the exact opposite of my father and Uncle Miki. We'd talk seriously to each other, and no one would have to be afraid we'd raise our voices.

Uncle Bora said OK, picked up the cards, shuffled them, and we let Nena Fatima win the next game. Behind us, Father slammed the bonnet of the car down and Bora offered him his packet of cigarettes. We started to walk the rest of the way.

My father was a Veletovo smoker. He smoked the only cigarettes of his life on the way from our stalled Yugo to my great-grandparents' house. He did it again yesterday − two packets in two hours. When we had to take a rest for Uncle Bora's sake, because he was so badly out of breath he couldn't go on, I imagined our Yugo minus its exhaust on the road to Veletovo. Early morning, dew gleaming on the grass, birds twittering, and the rest of our family, whose Yugos never break down, hooting as they overtook us.

I'm doubled up with stomach cramps under a sky full of ripe fruit on bending boughs, and I badly need to go to the loo. Quick, up the hill, across the veranda where Uncle Bora is nailing plastic tablecloths to the tables. This morning, when we were deciding who'd stay here to pick plums and who'd go and put the furniture up on the veranda ready for the party, he was the only man who ponderously turned to go. A-little-tree-climbing-would-do-you-good, Auntie Typhoon called after him, all in a rush. How fast her tongue went! Her words overtook first what she was saying herself, then anyone listening.

It might do *me* good but think of the poor trees, said her husband, dismissing this idea, and he dragged his hundred and fifty kilos up the hill. As if to express his opinion of plums in general he polished an apple on his sleeve and bit into it so hard that the apple broke right apart, and juice ran down both his double chins. Undeterred, the big man made a face and closed his eyes with relish.

This-is-the-end! This-is-the-end! Auntie Typhoon was tearing her hair. Fascinated, we stared at Steamroller and his pregnant natural catastrophe, ah, how delightful love must be, sighed Great-Granny, wiping a tear from the corner of her eye.

My aunt speaks at the speed of a German autobahn. For years Uncle Bora has been pounding tar with a steamroller in Germany to make the fastest autobahns in the world, while Auntie Typhoon is a waitress at a service station. If anyone asks me what my uncle does for a living I don't mention the roller. I say he's a guest-worker. Although it puzzles me that there are places where guests have to work, in our family we don't even let a guest do the dishes, but our neighbour Čika Veselin once called Bora a steamroller, that fat skinflint wouldn't need to use any machine, he'd only have to lie down and roll the roads himself. I asked my mother to get Uncle Bora to go on a diet so that he wouldn't grow any fatter and people would stop saying nasty things about him. She thought she was too fat herself at the time, so she was on a diet of plums and minced meat. People say nasty things, she said, not because Bora is fat himself but because they think he has a fat wallet full of Deutschmarks.

Guest-workers aren't welcome anywhere except in their own families.

Now Uncle Bora is nailing the tablecloths to the tables in slow motion, wheezing like Father's circular saw when it's about to run down. Auntie Typhoon is racing around among the trees shaking their branches: we-don't-need-any-rest-go-on-go-on-go-on!

The cutlery clatters in the plastic bucket that Great-Granny bangs down on the table beside the stack of plates. She plants herself four-square in my way, looking just like her hero the Comrade-in-Chief of all cowboys, Marshal Rooster, although with forks at her hips instead of Colts: where are you going, jailbird? She's even wearing her eye-patch. Every time we visit Veletovo I have to sit with Great-Granny and watch that grumpy drunk Rooster and Mattie Ross quarrelling.

That was how I used to look, just like that, only my skin was pinker, sighs Great-Granny, pointing to Miss Ross. Great-Granny's tears as the final credits roll are followed by High Noon on the veranda. In winter when the grasshoppers don't chirp, Great-Granny takes over from them. She presses her lips together, chirping fit to terrify you. She keeps her finger-pistols low, she's always quicker on the draw than any tenderfoot around. Great-Granny is faster than the wind, and with her eye-patch she can look even more cynical than John Wayne.

Very old people live two lives. In one life they cough, they walk with a stoop, they sigh: oh dear, oh dear, oh dear! In the other life, their eye-patch life, they talk to stinging nettles about the neighbours, they believe they're sheriffs, or they fall in love with deck-chairs or bees.

Where are you going, jailbird? Great-Granny's hand moves down to her hip, her thumb takes the safety catch off the fork. I feint to the right, then storm past her on the left and into the house. Oh wow, Great-Granny! High Noon in my guts! Only seconds to go before I break the world record for an accident in my trousers, out of the way!

The new loo. The inside loo. Great-Grandpa and four oxen demolished half the wall for it, four oxen can do that kind of thing well but two would have been better, then no one would have had to think what to do later about too much hole in the wall and the ripped-out banisters. Great-Grandpa soon found the answer, he fitted the new loo next to the balcony – which is smaller now, but the loo is bigger, and you can get into it from the balcony through a curtain, fresh air thrown in for free, says Great-Granny. At the same time the four-hundred-year-old outside loo was jettisoned, and no one ever had to go standing up again. The first TV set in the village years ago, black and white, two channels, the second channel showing busy little scurrying dots for Great-Granny to watch before going to sleep, now the first inside loo – my great-grandparents were always forty kilometres ahead of the times in Veletovo.

There was a party to inaugurate the new loo. Abroad they think we have parties here the whole time, says my uncle the guest-worker. Which is not entirely right, because we have to spend time clearing up after the parties too. And a party costs a lot, so parents have to go to work in the day. However, it's a fact that my great-grandparents see anything as an excuse for a party. Once they partied through two whole nights because Great-Granny had found a meteorite the size of a man's fist among the carrots. That was an hour after they'd been showing *Superman* on the new TV set. Great-Granny made soup out of the meteorite, three kilos of carrots and seven secret seasonings of her own. The whole village, she cried around midnight, when her eyes were glazed and she was trying to uproot an oak tree with a judo hold, the whole village smells of kryptonite! She failed, because Yugoslavian oak trees are stronger than superpowers.

All the neighbours came to the party for the loo. Even Radovan Bunda from the high mountains, who knew about electricity only by hearsay and who talked to his chickens. By neighbours they don't mean the same in Veletovo as they do in Višegrad. In Veletovo even the Pešićs count as neighbours, though it's half a day's walk for them to visit my great-grandparents. Not because they're too poor to own a car – they *are* poor, yes, but there isn't any road to drive a car on where they live. The grown-up Pešićs are all over two metres tall, including the women and the old folk. Once, long ago, I visited their place. I remember the sourish goat's milk, and the wooden toys, and wondering why they didn't build higher ceilings, with all of them being so gigantic. When a baby is born or someone gets married in the Pešić family or in ours, we exchange visits. The families are godparents to each others' children or witnesses at weddings. My mother says I didn't have a Pešić godparent, though, it has something to do with her and the religion on her side of the family. Nothing bad, says my mother, and she asks: would you have liked to be baptised?

What's that? I ask.

Well, there you are, she says.

Queuing up for the new loo, the neighbours were shifting restlessly about with bladder pressure and anticipation. Great-Grandpa had first go. He was wearing his black frock-coat, he tapped his stomach and he crowed at the top of his voice: haven't gone for four days now! Bong bong, torn torn, bong bong, he beat out a rousing rhythm with the loo lid.

Some people, including me, clapped along. Everyone was in good humour waiting for the inside loo, sixteen spectators, a five-man band to play music, perfect loo weather, I said, presenting the show. Great-Granny gave Great-Grandpa a bottle of spirits as solemnly as if she were handing him the Baton of Youth. He put the shot glass on top of the bottle like a hat and stayed sitting on the loo for forty-five minutes. Outside, the neighbours and relatives began talking in loud voices so as not to hear all the noises inside the new loo. When he wasn't groaning and crying out and clattering like a moped, Great-Grandpa sang. I put my ear close to the door so that I could hear his deep voice. How the door vibrated! My Great-Grandpa sounded like the lowest string of a double bass! In his songs, someone called Kraljević Marko jumped a horse that drank wine across the river Drina and butchered some Turks. So many that I couldn't keep up with the head count. But more exciting than the poor wretched Turks, I thought, was the question of whether all horses who drank wine could fly. When Great-Grandpa came out after forty-five minutes, triumphantly raising his clenched fist, the bottle of spirits was half empty and the shot glass was gone for ever.

Flush it, you idiot! Great-Granny said, loud and earnestly, then she looked down into the bowl and crossed herself for the first time in sixty years. They drank the rest of the good pear schnapps and the five-man band played a waltz. After that the band opened the dancing with gypsy music that no one liked because the fast bit came too soon. We can still lie down without holding on to anything, you amateurs! cried Great-Grandpa, and he couldn't stop dancing.

Now the neighbours had a go on the new loo too, starting with the men. Oh, how my heart is pounding, someone said before closing the door behind him. Radovan Bunda was last in line. He kept on grumbling more and more crossly, holding on to himself in front and behind. When it was nearly his turn he roared out: what an idea, tormenting a man who's come all this way, you tramps with your new-fangled notions! He was rapidly unbuttoning his trousers as he raced off in the direction of the outside loo.

What outside loo, Radovan must have asked himself when he got there, because two oxen had uprooted the little cubicle from the ground like a weed. I don't need any bowl, any flushing mechanism, any tiles! I don't even need a hole in the ground, Radovan would say later, drinking to liberty.

All this comes back to my mind now in the inside loo during the thirty minutes I spend there, almost as long as Great-Grandpa, suffering horribly from my plum world record. I'm out again at last, and here comes Marshal Rooster's finger-Colt prodding me in the back – scrub those tablecloths, Great-Granny orders, scrub them, Redskin! She'd been lying in wait for me behind the door.

Unenthusiastically, I pass the dishcloth over the stains and wonder why everyone is celebrating the fact that Uncle Miki is going away. I'd rather celebrate when he comes back from the army.

Great-Granny's teeth are yellow, and brown at the tips, she laughs and nods: yes, yes. That, she says, pointing to a greenish lump of something, that's kryptowitz – kryptonite with slivowitz. You won't get your hands on that. It made a pile of money but a fearful stink too. Great-Granny winks at me and takes her finger away from the back of my neck to adjust her eye-patch.

Great-Granny doesn't talk to me about Grandpa Slavko. You're all my children, oh, you don't give me an easy time, she told Father when we arrived in Veletovo. No one wants to bury the child she bore. I'm burying my own joy.

Father did not reply.

Great-Grandpa replied by searching around for words.

I miss him too, I say then, quietly, putting the cloth down. Great-Granny takes her eye-patch off. Her big brown eyes. She has a thin hair growing from the mole on her cheek. Her flowered overall above her black dress. I slink away from her bad mood. The sun's shining. I climb a plum tree. Lost to the world, Father is singing a song. Mother is smiling. Nena Fatima takes off her boots: Auntie Typhoon fills bucket after bucket and pats her big belly. Uncle Miki has seized a chicken by its legs and is taking it out into the yard.

There's cured sausage with red pepper and garlic, there's smoked ham, there's smoked bacon, there's goat's milk cheese, sheep's milk cheese, cow's milk cheese, there are fried potatoes with leeks, there are hard-boiled eggs; there are toothpicks sticking in the sausage, the ham, the cheese, the slices of egg; there's white bread and golden cornbread, the bread is always broken, never cut; there's garlic butter, liver pâté and creamy kaymak, there's cabbage soup, potato soup, and thumb-sized dollops of fat swimming on top of the chicken soup, you can dunk the bread in all those soups; there's bean broth (it's horrible!), there are baked beans and bean salad; there's white cabbage leaves stuffed with rice and minced meat, there are peppers stuffed with minced meat, minced meat stuffed with minced meat, minced meat and plums – Mother and I look at each other, she asks if there's any chocolate – yes, there's chocolate, there's chicken, there's cucumber salad (I've never seen any dish go ignored the way that cucumber salad is ignored); there's warm baklava with syrup made from sugar, cinnamon, honey and cloves, it drips from your fingers on to your trousers, on to the minced meat; so sweet, someone cries, oh, so sweet, it's Uncle Bora, he's enjoying the sweet baklava so much that he gets to his feet, so sweet! it's almost more than I can stand, stop it, oh, more! There are plums piled on top of plums, there's plum strudel with vanilla sugar and plum jam, there are baked plums with icing-sugar topping; there are melons, the five-man amateur band takes a break from playing specially for the melons; it's a mystery to me why they've been invited to play again after the failure of their performance at the loo inauguration party, but there they are, falling on the melon slices, slurping, slobbering, smacking their lips, all of them slurping-slobbering-smacking, and the first tune the band plays after their break is 'In Višegrad, that fine old town'. But Great-Grandpa cries angrily, pleasurably: aah! and spits a barrage of melon seeds in the direction of the trumpet, aah! that won't do, you don't play something so tender with melon, you amateurs! Grandpa himself reached the lamb stage long ago – he has a melon boat on his left, a shank of lamb on his right, and is munching them in turn, aah! Yes, there's lamb too, its grey meat piled up on the flowered plates, and any moment now there'll be sucking pig: Auntie Typhoon is turning the spit, pouring beer over the pig's back and wine over the pig's belly, red-cheeked with the heat and the effort, no-no-I-don't-need-a-chair, her blonde hair flying around her head. Auntie Typhoon turns the spit with both hands so energetically that ashes fly up under the sucking pig, turn-it-too-slowly-and-it-won't-roast-evenly. There's rendered, salted, pressed pork dripping with bits of crackling in it, there's fried pig's innards, there are pig's trotters and pig's ears coated with jelly, nothing whatsoever is missing.

I take the bucket of melon rinds off to the pigsty and throw the rinds over the pigs, the pigs don't mind, they have thick skins, they eat the rinds and burrow their soft snouts in the mud. I hit the fattest sow on the belly. She grunts, but she isn't bothered about anything but the rind, my tooth-marks on what she's eating, that's a pig's life for you. Great-Grandpa promised me today, next time we kill a pig I can chase it too, help to get it down on the ground, put it on the spit – you run the spit in at the back, along under the backbone and out through the mouth. And I can scrape and wash the stomach out too, but I wouldn't want to put my hands in where there might be melon rind. I'd rather leave the bit with the knife to my father or my uncles too. Cutting a pig's throat is the best way, says my father, but Uncle Bora shakes his head: in the heart is the best place. Uncle Miki doesn't mind which, as long as the pig ends up good and dead.

If it was up to Great-Grandpa I could do a lot more things anyway, not just pig-killing. I could eat whatever I liked and I wouldn't have to go to school. Great-Grandpa says: boys don't get to be men in town, schools don't teach stupid lads to be fine men. You lose your sense of smell in town and you see two metres less far ahead of you.

Great-Grandpa got no further than the letter 't' when he was at school, because there's nothing important after that. He left his village only three times, twice to go to war, once to win a wife. He won three victories. Proud, robust, always singing, always close to tears or laughter. The family like to tell every guest how last Easter – it is always last Easter – Great-Grandpa seized one of his oxen by the horns, forced it to kneel with one hand, while he picked the first lily of the valley for Great-Granny with the other, and then ploughed his fields in just four days. The ox that a human being can humiliate like that, he's said to have announced, patting the ox's nostrils, doesn't deserve to set hoof on my land. If he's asked his age Great-Grandpa says: oh, I'm still young, I've never yet seen a ship and I've never yet taught a liar to be an honest man.

Some day, when I'm as old as my Great-Grandpa Nikola, I will have set sail in a ship, I'll have met a liar and left him an honest man, I'll have persuaded a donkey to go the way I want, and I'll have sung like Great-Grandpa, with a voice as powerful as a mountain range, a ship, the habit of honesty and a donkey all rolled in together.

Back to the table, because there's coffee, and Great-Granny reads everyone's future in the grounds. She promises me an unfulfilled yearning and three great loves in the next three months. Mother laughs and interrupts: but he's much too young, Great-Granny tells me off for drinking coffee while I'm still so young, and she changes the details to two great loves and one affair – but the

31

affair will be with an uncomplicated woman artist, you never saw such green eyes!

She doesn't need more than two minutes for anyone's future except Uncle Miki's, and she takes thirty minutes over his, rocking back and forth and never ending a sentence; then suddenly there's stuffed pastry börek, there's pitta filled with potatoes, pitta filled with young nettles, pitta filled with pumpkin, there's walnut cake and a sip of red wine for me; the courses aren't served one by one in any special order, there's always someone saying he can't eat any more, he couldn't possibly force another morsel down, hands gesticulate, fending off any more, and no one takes the gesticulations seriously; there's no stopping now, there are hurt expressions if someone seriously threatens to expire after the next half-chicken; the wine will fortify your blood, says Great-Granny, pouring more for me when no one's looking. There's white bread with everything, Uncle Bora puts warm white bread on top of cold white bread: I'm in white bread heaven, he says, and then I'll move on to cider paradise – although that will lead to problems on plum-picking day, as Uncle Bora knows, and he laughs when Great-Grandpa holds a glass of slivowitz in front of his face: how are you going to drink it, then, of your own free will or through the nose? There's beer, there's brandy, there's cognac, ice clinks in glasses. There are never any empty plates. And there's Nataša, that girl Nataša in her flowered dress, with bare feet and red cheeks as if she has a fever. Nataša's been around all evening, chasing me and chasing me and chasing me, come and be kissed! she keeps calling, come and be kissed! She finds all my hiding places. I escape under the table, determined to stay there for a hundred thousand years until she gives up, Nataša with the gap in her teeth and her pouting lips, come and be kissed, come and be kissed! Marshal Rooster, of all people, is mean enough to speak out and give me away: he's under the table, catch him, why don't you? That's town boys for you, they're afraid of us, they crawl away under the table legs! So Nataša dives down and crawls towards me, and the way she crawls makes me think of Petak, Great-Grandpa's sheepdog, falling on the squealing, bleeding piglet today. Come and be kissed, come and be kissed, and the loud trumpet and the family singing and no one there to give Nataša a kick. I retreat, my back's up against my mother's legs when I hear the roaring. A man's voice is roaring, and the music suddenly stops. The singing stops. There's silence.

Nataša freezes beside me. Heads close together, we peer out from under the tablecloth: we can see Uncle Miki's best friend Kamenko putting his pistol in the mouth of the trumpet and shouting until his cheeks are redder than the cheeks of two furious red faces put together and his head swells two sizes bigger: what's all this? Music like that in my village? Are we in Veletovo or are we in Istanbul? Are we decent folk or are we gypsies? You ought to be singing the praises of our kings and heroes, our battles, the great Serbian state. Miki's off to join the army tomorrow, and on his last evening you stuff his ears with this Turkish gypsy filth!

Catching a pig for the spit isn't easy. Because pigs are fast, they swerve well, and pigs follow your train of thought, said my father at the beginning of the party, surprising us with a speech, the longest speech any of us had ever heard him make. The pig sees the sharpened knife and puts two and two together. It says to itself: right, let's get out of here double quick! Does the pig have some kind of vision? asked my father, looking round at us. It hasn't found the way out of its sty for years, why should anything change over the next twenty seconds? It can smell the pig-killers already. Panic and instinct exist side by side in the pig's head. Independent thought blooms sparsely in our communal garden: a bright flower for bright moments. The pig picks one of those flowers, it squeals and runs! The last pig-killer hasn't closed the gate behind him yet. The last pig-killer is Bora. He looks down at the tunnel made by his legs and says: that was never the pig, was it? Yes, brother Bora, it was, and the pig is already out of the farmyard and into the meadows. With us in hot pursuit, the runaway animal is galloping across the meadows to freedom! And guess what? Such a sophisticated pig, such a speedy and elegant pig, a pig with such vision deserves its freedom! Away from collective stupidity and the musty smell of the pigsty, off to individuality! cried my father to his audience, spreading his arms. Ahead of the pig is the forest, so are its wild colleagues, and so is the mountain range above – and here are our meadows; nothing except the river Drina is a healthier green, you feel like kneeling down to eat the grass. The pig squeals, and I can tell you it's a cry of sheer joy! The pig squeals to celebrate its revolution! Bora is the first to stop, or was he ever running after it at all? I soon give up too, only Miki runs on. My little brother Miki, said Father, looking at the place where Miki was sitting. Anyone can see he's going to be a soldier, the pig has a start of fifty, maybe sixty metres on him, but Miki isn't having any of it. I'm not having this! he shouts, so loud you can hear him right across the meadows, into the forest, high up in the mountains. Still invincible in its cunning and speed, the pig suddenly stops. It turns its head to my little brother Miki. Now what? The pig stands there looking at the mountains, at Miki, at the mountains, at Miki. And only when Miki has almost caught up with it does it rush away again, not towards freedom in the forest this time, but back to the farmyard. It crashes in between the stable and the barn and gets stuck where the gap narrows at the back. You saw the rest for yourselves; we had to get a roll of cable and the tractor to uncork it.

My father raised his glass. My father the pig-killer, eyes glazed, cried: to my brother! Everyone drank to Miki. Killing a pig for the spit is no joke! cried Father. Because pigs follow a train of thought, unlike my brother Bora here. Because Bora didn't want to go for the throat, he insisted it ought to be the heart. And because he forgot to tie Petak up. Yet there are only two mistakes you can make when killing a pig: forgetting to tie your dog up when it's going frantic with the smell of all that blood, or missing the spot when you use the knife, so that the pig goes frantic too and takes forever to die.

Until the pain's so great that life is past bearing, I thought to myself.

Uncle Bora had made both mistakes.

Oh, fuck those divine pig's trotters, Bora, you may have hit the kidneys but you never hit the heart! is what Uncle Miki had shouted at his brother, putting his knee on the pig and pushing it down to the ground with all his weight. The blood was spurting in every direction. The barking was coming closer. Petak shot across the yard faster than the sound of his own bark. Bora, watch out! shouted Miki, and then Petak was leaping around the men and the bleeding pig. He wasn't barking now, he was screaming, slobber oozing through his bared teeth and dripping down his muzzle. Miki couldn't let go of the pig because Bora was raising the knife again. Stop it, Petak! Stop! he shouted, my father kicked out at the dog, who howled, and Bora brought the knife down for the second time.

Stop it! Stop the music! That's what Kamenko is roaring now, although the bandsmen aren't playing any more, they're retreating before Kamenko's pistol. Only the trumpeter doesn't move, with the trumpet still where it was at his lips when he played the last merry note, and the last merry note still hangs in the air, only not so merry any more. The barrel of the pistol is resting in the trumpet. Kamenko's arm is trembling, the trumpeter is trembling, a cold wind rises. Kamenko with his roaring and Petak with his barking are sharpening the wind, the way Uncle Bora sharpened the longest knife ready for the pig's heart.

Bark away, bark away, mutters Kamenko, staring fixedly as he slowly takes his pistol out of the trumpet.

Stay down there, whispers my mother, pushing my head under the table. I can see everything all the same, I see Kamenko's arm twitch, there's the shot, there are screams, there's the clatter of the trumpet as it lands on the ground. Nataša falls on my neck, falls into my arms, doesn't bite, doesn't kiss, just whispers: what was that?

Something so loud that even Petak is silenced. Something so horrifying that my mother's legs twitch. Something of such significance that the mountains repeat it, and the echo sounds like distant thunder. His face distorted by pain, the trumpeter holds both hands to his right ear, but he's writhing as if he had been hit in the stomach. The pistol was too close, I want to shout, why so close? Nataša leans her head against my back and hugs me. She doesn't

35

have to do that, I'd like to fight her off, or perhaps she does have to do that just now.

Stop! Stop the music! You'll play what I say now! orders Kamenko, kicking the trumpet. Has our nation won battles so gypsies can shit on our songs?

Only Great-Grandpa's snoring breaks the silence after Kamenko's question. No shot, no barking, no orders in the world can disturb so melodious a sleep. Before Kamenko rose to interrupt the song of Fair Emina, Great-Grandpa was singing along with the first verse. He went to sleep in mid-song, with his head on the table.

Kamenko pushes the trumpeter up against the wall and puts his arm under the man's chin. The leather of his boots is worn right down to the metal. The trumpeter's breath rattles in his throat, and Great-Granny dabs the corners of her mouth with a lettuce leaf, adjusts her eye-patch and plants herself right behind Kamenko. High Noon, cowboy! she calls out to him. She is armed with two forks. I'm going to count to three! One: Kamenko, my sound and healthy Kamenko, did you know I suckled your grandfather Kosta because his mother's milk was too thin? It was my milk made your Kosta tall and healthy. He played with my Slavko and danced at our parties. And when your Kosta wanted a song, he strapped on his own accordion and hit the keys manfully, the musicians just couldn't keep up with him! And two: Kamenko, my handsome Kamenko, you've let your hair and beard grow, you wave that pistol about and you've sewn a badge on your cap – admittedly it's sewn on crooked, but these things can be learnt. But did you know your grandfather Kosta went to war against caps like that and the double-headed eagle on them, did you know he was wounded twice in the same shoulder and twice in the same calf? So three: Kamenko, my trigger-happy bandit, why are you firing guns in our house? We raised it from the ground and up to the sky with these hands, and now you go shooting it right in the throat where its soul lives!

Kamenko pushes the trumpeter away and turns to Great-Granny. Ah yes, the house . . . at once the fathers behind him get

36

to their feet. I'll pay for the mortar in your wall, but who, Kamenko asks, is going to compensate me for the injury done to my ears by these bastards? Kamenko with his pistol pushes in between Great-Granny and the musicians huddled in the corner. Great-Granny's fingers are playing impatiently with the forks in her skirt pocket. Kamenko doesn't stand a chance against Marshal Rooster, the fastest gun in Veletovo. Miki is my blood-brother, his family is my family – all honour and respect to this blood! says Kamenko, turning out his forearm, because when you're talking about blood and brothers you are bound to think of a wrist. Miki stares straight ahead, pulping bread in his closed fist. He has turned his sleeves up, he bites the bread so hard that the muscles in his lower jaw tense. The fathers hurry towards Kamenko, my own father moves fastest – but Kamenko raises his pistol even faster, turns and mimics a shot at each father as they stand in a semicircle. Bang, bang, bang, he says.

I put my hands over my ears, the fathers stand there. My father has stopped in mid-stride, arms bent, leaning forward the way he did when chasing the runaway pig.

But, but, but! Kamenko turns in a second, slower semicircle, waves his pistol as if shaking his head. Each 'but' is for one of the fathers, and the fourth is for Great-Granny: but didn't my grand-father sacrifice his shoulder and calf for his country and his people? While we sit here the Ustashas are plundering our country, driving our people away, murdering them! Didn't my grandfather fight the Ustashas too? He did, Mrs Krsmanović, he did! I'm not having gypsies give me Ustasha songs and Turkish howling any more! I want our own music for our own Miki! Songs from the glorious days that once we knew and that will come again! Kamenko strikes his chest with his free hand. Let's start now! I'm not here to talk or dance. Get on with it!

However, it is not the fat singer who starts performing. Instead, Great-Grandpa wakes up. All of a sudden he raises his head from the table and continues the song of Fair Emina at the very place where Kamenko shot it dead. Loud and sorrowful, as if the vain girl

Emina were standing in front of Great-Grandpa's balcony and won't return his greeting:

. . . ja joj nazvah selam, al' moga mi dina,
ne šće ni da čuje lijepa Emina . . .

Great-Grandpa's voice rings out, and Petak joins in, howling. Bemused, Kamenko looks at the white-haired singer. Emina's hair, worn in braids, smells of hyacinths, she has a silver dish under her arm, in the song she is standing under a jasmine bush but in Veletovo it's under a plum tree:

. . . no u srbren ibrik zahitila vode
pa po bašti dule zalivati ode . . .

Great-Grandpa spreads his arms wide and throws back his head. Kamenko and I both let the song distract our attention, and when I look at him again the fathers have got him down on the ground and my father is kneeling on Kamenko's pistol arm until he lets go:

S grana vjetar duhnu pa niz pleći puste
rasplete joj one pletenice guste . . .

The wind plays in Emina's thick hair. Only one person is heard above Great-Grandpa's singing, Petak's howling and Kamenko's scream of pain when the fathers turn him over on his stomach, face to the ground, and that person is Uncle Miki. Not because he raises his voice, but because this is the first time he's said anything at all since the pistol first went into the trumpet—

zamirisa kosa ko zumbuli plavi,
a meni se krenu bururet u glavi . . .

Emina's hyacinthine hair has my enamoured Great-Grandpa totally confused, and Miki says: let him go at once!

Good heavens, Miki, the man's sick! Nataša's father, an unshaven farmer with bushy eyebrows, twists Kamenko's arm behind his back. My father picks up the pistol between his thumb and forefinger—

38

. . . malo ne posrnuh, mojega mi dina,
no meni ne dođe lijepa Emina.

Emina smells so sweet that you can hardly keep on your feet when she comes close.

I said: let him go! shouts Miki, bending over his friend. Kamenko, you wouldn't really have shot anyone, would you?

But there's no time for questions and answers, the fathers look at each other, pick Kamenko up, hold him against the wall, there's saliva and blood on his chin. Cheek pressed to the wall of the house he gasps: it's OK . . . let go . . . it's OK!

Great-Grandpa needs no music, the amateurs wouldn't be able to sing for him anyway now, they're looking at their trumpeter's ear with concern. Great-Grandpa has risen to his feet, he's singing the last couplet:

samo me je jednom pogledala mrko,
niti haje, alčak, što za njome crko'!

And he's dancing: Emina has nothing but dark looks for Great-Grandpa; she doesn't want his love. Great-Grandpa dances around the table and snatches Kamenko's pistol from my father. He dances to the stables and shoots at the big muck-heap until the shots are mere clicks. Then he pushes the pistol into the muck with his boot until it's out of sight, straightens his back and says: that's it!

There's no explanation for a lot of things, there's the *that's it*; there's a furious Kamenko on a tiny veranda in a tiny village in the mountains above the little town of Višegrad; there's long-haired Kamenko holding his painful arm as they lead him away from the veranda and throw his camouflage jacket on the floor; there's Kamenko breathing heavily as he rummages around in the cow dung for his pistol; there's Kamenko bellowing: I'm rummaging in the shit now, but when our time comes it's the traitors who'll be eating shit! There's a sudden shower of rain, a two-minute summer shower, there's the fat amateur singer wanting double pay from Great-Grandpa Nikola, and he'll get it too if, says Great-Grandpa, with a hand to the fat man's cheek, if you wake my hyacinth tomorrow morning with – and he whispers something in his ear. Great-Grandpa drops a kiss on his hyacinth's face below the eye-patch. Ahead there's the army for Uncle Miki. There was a quarrel in spring between father and son, Grandpa and my uncle, and an order: Miki, this is not the time to go joining the army, we'll have no discussion about it. I was in the next room, and now Grandpa Slavko is gone. I didn't tell anyone about the quarrel, you don't tell tales of your own family. There's been a party, there were threats, there was a brawl, there was a shot, maybe that's how it has to be when someone joins the army; before you even really get there the war comes after you. There's the fear of Miki being sent somewhere they don't just shoot into muck-heaps, there's a sad goodbye to Miki, there are tears for Miki and a slap in the face for Miki: you shameless brat! The slap is because tomorrow's soldier says: Kamenko is right, we don't have to take this kind of thing, it's high time we faced up to the Ustashas and the Mujaheddin; that's the reason for the slap, and there are surreptitious glances at my mother and my Nena Fatima, deaf mute Nena Fatima, who looks around, ashamed and sad, as if she's understood every word, every gesture and every shot. Sides are taken, you belong or you don't belong, suddenly the veranda is like the school yard where Vukoje nick-named Worm asked me: what are you, really? The question sounded like trouble, and I didn't know the right answer.

There's no Kamenko on the veranda now, only his threats are left, he went off without finding his pistol, which Great-Grandpa takes out of his boot, all nice and clean now, as he says to Miki, but what you are doing is not. There's such a thing as shame. I'm ashamed of myself, and not because Uncle Miki says a man who doesn't have all his marbles is right, I'm ashamed of myself on my own account, because I thought it was brave of my uncle to stand up for his friend. But I'm also ashamed because Mother is ashamed, and is stroking Nena Fatima's back as if she were a cat. Across the table Mother says, so quietly that I don't think Miki can hear her: oh, Miki, what's all this . . . ? There's my father, saying nothing as usual, there's the colour of his face – if I looked like that they'd give me a penicillin injection. There are the Ustashas, there's the history book which says the Partisans defeated those Ustashas the way they defeated the Nazis and the Chechniks and the Mussolinis and everyone who opposed Yugoslavia and freedom. And there are the Mujaheddin, they ride through the desert wearing sheets. There was that question from Vukoje Worm in the school yard, I thought it was a threat and I thought my mother's explanation was a joke. I'm a mixture. I'm half and half. There was everyone in the school yard wondering how I could be something so vague, there were discussions about whose blood is stronger in your body, male or female, and me wishing I could be something not so vague, or a made-up thing that Vukoje Worm didn't know about, or maybe something he couldn't laugh at, a German autobahn, a flying horse that drinks wine, a shot in the throat of a house.

There's me, and later I'll paint a party without any pistols. There's Nataša close to me, there's Nataša's flowered dress, there are Nataša's feet with their dirty soles, there are her braids, twined together like Emina's in Great-Grandpa's song; there's Nataša on the trail of a kiss, my hero, she says to me, oh, my hero, my hero, and she closes her eyes, come and be kissed, come and be kissed; there's me sitting in the middle of the buzzing, world-record sweetness of Nataša's kisses, they're humming around my head like little flies, their dark red sweetness on my forehead, my cheek, my cheek, my forehead.

Who wins when Walrus blows the whistle, what a band smells of, when you can't cut fog, and how a story leads to an agreement

After the end of his own career Milenko Pavlović, once a three-point shooter and feared for his scoring prowess, who was nick-named Walrus because of his bristly moustache and drooping cheeks, went off every Saturday to blow the whistle at basketball games in the top Yugoslavian league, getting home the next day in time for lunch. Of the sixty matches he refereed, fifty-five were won by the home side.

That particular Saturday in late April 1991 his son Zoran went to a match with him in Split, and Zoran suggested coming home straight after the bingo. Bingo and beans with pork ribs in the most expensive hotel in town. A hearty helping for Walrus, who had whistled valiantly. After the offensive foul from the away team four seconds before the final whistle the crowd had chanted: Walrus! Walrus! rather than the names of their players. The home team, Jugoplastika, nearly missed out on victory, but Walrus didn't miss out on good winnings at bingo.

I can't be doing with a sleeping passenger, said Walrus, if you drop off to sleep in the car I'll put you out on the Romanija. He licked the fingers that had been holding the pork ribs. Walrus, that diligent referee, had equally diligently gnawed the meat right off the bone. The bill was on the house. The pear cake was on the house. The pear schnapps was on the house. Walrus had tipped his third down the hatch, and over his fourth he and the hotel proprietor drank to Jugoplastika's victory. Walrus! Walrus! Walrus! cried the waiters and the guests of honour.

Walrus! Let's have a song for Walrus! babbled the hotelier, a sturdy Hungarian by the name of Agoston Szabolcs, loosening his tie. A lively accordion tune wound its way out of the kitchen and into the restaurant. The chef kicked the door open and swayed across the room. I'm the band around here! He squeezed the red accordion back and forth over his magnificent paunch, a greasy meat fork dangled from his hip, sweat dripped into his smile. His stubby fingers slipped across the keys, the prelude smelled of beef, of garlic, of metal. Twenty well-fed men took up the song, twenty victorious voices, more seriously smashed, more rapturous, more enamoured with every verse and every shot of spirits. The chef grinned as if under torture. The chef whistled. The chef dripped. The chef put his foot down on a chair to support the accordion. Yoohoo! cried the suffering chef, grabbing the schnapps bottle. He tipped spirits down his throat straight from the bottle, and there was no break in the singing when he took his hand off the keys. I'm the band around here, he gurgled, that's me, the band!

The waiters took orders, always ordering a double for themselves. They twirled trays on their fingertips, hugged one another and swayed in time to the songs, sailors dressed in black.

The eighth, cried Walrus, throwing the seventh glass over his shoulder, the eighth is for my little lad here, only he can't legally drink yet, so I'll just have to manage it for him.

Little means a lot smaller than me, Zoran protested, and he drank the dregs from every glass without making a face. Agoston Szabolcs did the same, only with full glasses, and he went to sleep after the tenth with his elbow in a brimming ashtray. All of you shut up! snarled the chef, and the accordion whispered an emotional csárdás in the hotelier's ear. The men rose to their feet, looked at each other, closed the circle, moving arm in arm. Glasses hit the wall and didn't break, whereupon Agoston Szabolcs stood up as well, joining the dance even before he'd woken up. Milenko joined in, tilting his head back, more wolf than walrus.

Zoran stayed awake for the first hundred kilometres – the way his father was singing, there was no chance of going to sleep. Two hours later he drank the first Thermos of coffee, and just before Sarajevo and after his third packet of glucose he felt a little unwell. When his father woke him up in the Romanija region – look at

43

that, Zoran, fog like cement! – he rubbed his eyes and instantly cried: I wasn't asleep!

No, no, you just closed your eyes for a minute, same as me. We'll both have to replace those eyes of ours, next time the meadows may not save us. The car had stopped a good way into a field, with a steep slope downhill on the right, you couldn't see where it went. Five in the morning, fog like cement, Zoran!

It was night, morning and cold all in one in the Romanija. Father and son got out of the car, the big man stretched and scratched his moustache. Zoran yawned, picked up a stone and threw it into the fog. Dew lay on the grass and their shoes. They peed to right and left of a fir tree, aiming downhill through the foggy cement, both of them whistling, both of them happy. Walrus leaned against the warm bonnet, one hand in his trouser pocket, a cigarette in the other. Zoran picked dandelions and daisies and something pale blue the name of which he didn't know and put them together in a bunch. He unwrapped the remains of the pork ribs and folded the foil around the stems. He didn't think much of flowers, and the bunch showed it, crap was his father's highest praise, but flowers are flowers, your mother will be pleased.

She wasn't pleased. The front door was unlocked, her mother's hair was mussed. She wasn't pleased, she was naked, and why, Zoran asked himself, why fog like cement anyway? Nothing was ever as soft as the fog in the Romanija on the Sunday morning when Zoran and his father Milenko, nicknamed Walrus, arrived home six hours earlier than planned. The door was open, and so was the zip of Bogoljub Balvan the tobacconist's flies.

Zoran is sitting on the steps outside Maestro Stankovski's barber's shop staring at a photo in his hands. Zoran likes the kind of girls who are princesses – they have to have long hair, they have to be pale and slender and proud. Like the woman in the photo. And like Ankica, Zoran's Ankica with her black curls.

I sit down beside him and hand him the bag of sunflower seeds. Zoran is three years older than me, and I get to do things for him

44

now and then. Today I had to go and speak to his Ankica. I had to apologise to her on Zoran's behalf.

Although the shop is closed, Zoran still has to be there today. He has to help Maestro Stankovski pack because he's going on holiday in a few days' time. Holiday – ho, yes, said Zoran when we first met this morning, pulling the skin under his eye down with his forefinger.

Sure, I said, doing the same,

Usually Zoran sweeps up the hair, polishes the mirrors, and cleans the two Panesamig shavers with tiny brushes. Maestro Stankovski claims they're better than Panasonic – sharper and cheaper, and let's be honest, how would the Japanese know what's best for beards?

Doesn't my little Austrian girl look like Ankica? asks Zoran as I hand him the sunflower seeds, and he wipes invisible dust motes off the crumpled black and white picture.

Her eyes seem familiar to me, I say, nodding, and I look more closely at the young woman with the long curly hair and the white dress with a bell-shaped skirt. I've seen the photo before, Zoran always shows it when he waxes enthusiastic about Austria or about girls.

They all look like that, says Zoran, and the princess gazes sternly at us, just think of it – a country where all the girls look like that! Wow!

Tell you what, Zoran, I say, she looks like Bruce Lee . . .

That's right, he replies dreamily, not surprised at all, Austrian women all look like Bruce Lee. But with prettier hair, and that neck . . .

We both sit in silence, just looking at the photo. That neck! Zoran smells the sunflower seeds. It's not difficult to sit in silence with Zoran because it isn't easy to talk to him. He's not interested in anything but books, princesses (first and foremost Ankica), Austria and his father Walrus. There's always a book in the back pocket of his jeans, the jeans are washed out, there's a white star on his trainers.

Grüss Gott, he whispers to the photo, kissing the corner where you can see Hissi or Sissi or something written with a flourish. *Grüss Gott*, kiss-your-hand, lovely lady! Zoran's lips are slightly pursed when he tries talking like an Austrian, pursed for a little kiss. Kiss-your-hand, pretty lady, kiss-your-hand! Kung fu!

Zoran leans back on the steps and narrows his eyes. The sun is low, there's hardly anyone out and about in the street. Another reason why it's easy to sit in silence with Zoran is because I never know how to ask him a question.

What kept you so long? he asks me, spitting the shell of a sunflower seed out in a high trajectory.

I looked in at home. My old folks were quarrelling. I listened at the door.

Whose fault was it?

It wasn't about them. It was about everyone going away, like Maestro Stankovski. And the situation. The situation, the situation, the situation . . . well, what's in the offing, what we ought to do and all that.

Hm. Zoran cracks a seed in his teeth, puts the photo down on the steps and runs a hand through his hair. What *is* in the offing, then?

No idea. My old lady opened the door at that point.

Hm.

When I'm talking to Zoran I call my parents 'the old folks'. We sit in silence again, there's nothing to hear but the cracking and spitting. A sparrow comes down beside the shells.

I went and told Ankica, I say after the silence has turned a little too silent. Zoran blinks at the sun. We were alone, like you said, and I just told her, this is how it is, that's it.

This is how it is, that's it, repeats Zoran.

Well, yes, I said you're sorry. You apologise. It won't happen again . . .

What did she look like?

What?

What was my Ankica looking like?

Hm, well, same as usual, curls and eyes and all that. She said you promised it wouldn't happen again the first two times as well. She said she hates you and she never wants to see you again. She said kindly don't send any midgets round when you want to speak to her, it's almost worse than your temper. I didn't think that was very nice of her.

She didn't really say temper. Zoran shakes his head and flicks a shell away.

She said 'the slap', that's what she said. She's had enough, she said, you don't make her feel good any more.

Zoran has slapped his Ankica three times. His Ankica, because everyone knows that she *is* his Ankica, and Zoran is Ankica's Zoran. It seems that the first time he told her: this is for taking something away from me that I'll never get back again.

You really ought to apologise to her yourself, Zoran, I tell him, and I feel embarrassed having to say a thing like that. I heard it in a film, but it sounded a thousand times better there. The film was about a detective who spent ages hunting for the wrong woman.

Zoran stands up and leans on the handrail relaxed. He looks at the photo again.

Why do you hit her, anyway? I ask. I daren't remind him of his part in the agreement.

After I'm through with school, Zoran tells the photograph, I'm going there, to Austria. And there'll be roses for my Ankica tomorrow. You just remember this, Aleksandar, roses aren't simply flowers. My Ankica will come with me, then I won't need any Austrian girls, they can make Bruce Lee eyes at me all they want. *Grüss Gott* and so long, pretty lady, so long and goodbye . . . He stuffs the photo in his shirt pocket, says: that's how you want to treat your girl from the very start, and then what happened to my father can never happen to you . . .

47

When flowers are just flowers, how Mr Hemingway and Comrade Marx feel about each other, who's the real Jetris champion, and the indignity suffered by Bogoljub Balvan's scarf

. . . That Sunday morning Father and I came home six hours earlier than planned. The door was open and so was the zip of Bogoljub Balvan the tobacconist's flies. My mother was kneeling in front of Bogoljub with her hair all messy as if she'd just woken up, but then at least she'd have had her nightie on. She was stroking the tobacconist's thighs and bobbing her head back and forth like a chicken.

The bunch of flowers was jammed between Father's hand and his sports bag, the stems squashed flat, but flowers are flowers. I looked at him, I wanted him to explain all this to me, the chicken movements and the tobacconist. He dropped the bunch of flowers then dropped his bag on top of them. Mother and Bogoljub hadn't noticed us yet. Father put his ref's whistle to his mouth and blew it. The two of them jumped in alarm, Mother clenched her teeth and Bogoljub shrieked with pain. She moved away from the tobacconist's lap, wiped her mouth and staggered towards Father. God help me, Milenko! she pleaded, with her hair falling over her forehead, and she snatched Granny's crochet tablecloth off the table to cover herself. The vase of flowers on it tipped over and water flowed over the table-top, but flowers are flowers – these were roses from Bogoljub' s tobacconist's shop.

Just a moment, murmured Father, striding towards her. He put out a powerful arm: offensive foul. Thus far and not a step further, his fist showed her. There were two books lying on the floor at Bogoljub's feet. Just a moment, is that Marx and Hemingway lying side by side?

Bogoljub Balvan widened his eyes. Mary, Mother of God, he

whimpered, tiptoeing his way between *Das Kapital* and *The Old Man and the Sea* and tugging at his zip. Holy Mother of God, he squealed, blowing on his crotch where it was still painful, Mary, my soul's salvation, don't let it stick!

But the zip did stick, so Bogoljub cursed the name of God's mother, the holy mother of all zips, and gave Father no option but to bellow at him loud enough for the whole neighbourhood and half the town to hear and never forget it: go fuck the sun, Dragica! Did I build this house with my own hands for you to whore around in it? Did I make those bookshelves and choose the books just for some arsehole of a tobacconist to bring himself off on Comrade Marx and Mr Hemingway? Take that tablecloth off this minute, do you hear? Soiling the work of your own mother's hands! As for you, Bogoljub, have we known each other since we were in the Pioneers for you to break the Pioneer oath of friendship right here in my house, to shame me and madden me by stuffing yourself in my Dragica's mouth, making an adulteress of her? Did I lend you money back then for the tobacconist's shop and never ask for a dinar of interest, just for you to turn all reactionary and religious in my house and land your prick in debts you can never repay? Go fuck the holy mother of all tobacconists! Get out of here! Both of you! And if you value your lives, put those books back on the shelf!

Trembling, Mother picked up the literary classics and collected her clothes. Bogoljub still had his hands too full to help her. He hunched his shoulders and sobbed, barely audibly: I didn't mean to . . . we were only . . .

Just a moment! Father took his shirt off and looked at the flickering TV screen. Our C-64 console was lying on the floor, a jumble of cables, along with two joysticks, salted nibbles, and toothpicks stuck into pieces of cheese on Father's favourite plate, the one with the little basketballs. That just-a-moment had hardly died away before Father turned and Hemingwayed Bogoljub so forcefully that the tobacconist was sent flying against the book-shelves. Tito's *The Party*, Volume 2, and *Thus Spake Zarathustra* fell out; that pair weren't such a tragedy. Mother picked them up too, whimpering, and Father perpetrated a technical foul on the TV set: just a moment . . . were you two playing Tetris?

The list of high scores was visible on screen: Bogoljub had taken over the first three. He had written BOG – God – under his results. Father reached behind the shelves and loaded his shotgun. Have you gone and broken my record in my own home? He closed his left eye and took careful aim. Mother and the tobacconist ran out of the house in panic. Father put the safety catch on the shotgun and leaned it against the bookshelf. He raised his hands in front of his face, turned them around and examined them, as if surprised to find he had such things as thumbs or fingernails or lines of destiny. Then he sat down in front of the TV and played Tetris late into the night, in his undershirt, without saying a word or washing his hands, which he usually did when he came home from a basketball game, even before hugging Mother and me.

I ate what was left of the pork ribs, which tasted of earth. I picked the petals off the flowers: Ankica loves me, she loves me not, she loves me and she loves me. Father didn't answer any of my questions. I set to work on the savoury nibbles and the cheese. Father didn't eat anything, didn't say anything, stacked blocks and now and then polished up his shotgun until the metal gleamed. Around midnight he topped out with a score of 74,360 points – MIL MIL MIL, it said on squares one to three.

God, said Father, is dead.

Bring all the drink here, Zoran, I won't be needing a glass. He stripped to his underpants, and I brought him schnapps, brandy, wine. I watched him for a while – drinking, putting the bottle down, drinking, putting the bottle down. But serious drinking without any singing or company is the most boring thing in the world, so finally I went to sleep on the sofa.

Father drank until the sparrows started twittering. Then he shouldered his shotgun, walked through the street, shot at sparrows in the light of dawn and failed to hit a single one of them. He rang Bogoljub's doorbell, shouting: come out and let's kiss like brothers! But as nothing moved inside the house he shot out all the windows, forced the door open, knocked the bookshelf over and slammed his gun against the TV set, but didn't break the glass. So he plugged in Bogoljub's C-64, laid the gun across his lap, and did better than BOG's highest Tetris score at the first attempt. Then he set fire to Bogoljub's edition of the collected works of Marx, and as the flames rose higher he crapped on the carpet.

The first shots had woken me and I followed Father through town, first alone, later with some of the old men of Višegrad who went out angling at this time of day. They were nibbling salted sunflower seeds and laying bets. Not many were betting on the TV set. I bet ten thousand dinars on my father's talent for Tetris – in her haste Mother had forgotten her purse – and I won forty-five thousand. Just as Father was taking his trousers down and straining over Bogoljub Balvan's carpet, the two policemen – Pokor and Kodro – arrived, sleepy, pale and unshaven. Their uniforms smelled of fried liver and they were smoking. Papa hadn't thought to bring any loo paper, but Bogoljub's scarf proved useful. He wrapped the soiled scarf around the TV and the policemen asked him to wash his hands now, please. This kind of thing won't do. Private property. Wilful damage. Fire. A fine. Come with us.

Father listened to what Pokor and Kodro had to say, leaned on his shotgun, and agreed with them in every particular. But then he told them, sadly and truthfully, what that bastard had been doing in his house, how broken trust hurts worse than broken ribs, how many sparrows he'd left alive because sparrows are tormented so much anyway, and how very badly ashamed he felt, how ashamed he would feel all his life, that his only son had been forced to see these shameful things with his own fair eyes.

The policemen took off their caps, scratched the backs of their necks with the peaks of the caps, nodded, and shook their uncombed heads. Finally Father shrugged his shoulders and showed them the palms of his hands: go on, tell me again this won't do, it's private property! I'll pay any fine you like, but I'm not going with you until I've settled accounts. I'll never get back what was taken from me, not the way it was before. Everything I'm going to take from him can be replaced, so I'm taking plenty.

Pokor and Kodro retreated to Bogoljub's kitchen, had breakfast and consulted together. The anglers unpacked their stools and offered me apple juice out of unlabelled cans. When Pokor and Kodro put their caps on again and went off without a word to drink coffee, the old men nodded approvingly. The policemen had lost their bet – they didn't take Father away.

Bogoljub had guessed what was coming to him. He was a tobacconist through and through, he always wore the same dark red overall, and he could get hold of anything for his customers – instantly, or by the day after tomorrow at the latest. He had salvaged what he could carry and drive away with from the tobacconist's shop. My father cleared out what was left. He knocked the window panes in, threw all of Bogoljub's wares off the bridge into the Drina one by one, down to the very last pen. Drawers, the shelves from the walls, newspaper stands – everything that hadn't been screwed down landed in the river, and later on so did everything that *had* been screwed down. No one stopped him; over twenty men were watching when he finished by tearing the door off its hinges and chucking that into the river too.

Word had gone around town of what had happened to us in our own home. People gave Father schnapps and leeks, Amela brought him warm bread and salt. Amela bakes the best bread in the world. Old men patted me on the head and looked as if they were going to curse and cry at the same time. Drunk as he was, my father took me aside and said: Zoran, I'm going away now. You can stay with Aunt Desa. I'll be coming back, but first I have to get everything new for us: *Das Kapital* for me and a new mother for you. He put two hundred Deutschmarks in my shirt pocket and rubbed the back of my neck by way of saying goodbye. He rammed the car into the tobacconist's shop twice and then drove out of town, hooting.

So now what? I ask Zoran, although I know the answer: Zoran's mother ran off to Sarajevo with Bogoljub the same day as his father went out of town. She left some money for him with his Aunt Desa, but Desa managed the money on his behalf the same way as Zoran's father had managed the pear schnapps meant for Zoran in Split. Zoran was sleeping in his aunt's attic, and beating up his two cousins every day, once after getting up and once before going to bed. Zoran only beats up people who really deserve it: his two cousins because they kept shooting their mouths off, and Edin because he learns ballet dancing, but he apologised for that when he discovered that Edin doesn't have a father. Desa let his parents' house to seasonal labourers working on the dam. She was divorced, and spent a lot of time with the tired men. They always spoke highly of her. Uncle Miki says: Desa is our Marilyn Monroe.

Now, says Zoran, standing up and interrupting my thoughts about his aunt, who always smells of honey, now I can't stand daisies and dandelions – crappy flowers are crappy flowers. My mother preferred those filthy roses. Flowers are not just flowers.

That's true, I can confirm it, Danijela with the very long hair had an alarming fit of laughter when I gave her my daisies.

Zoran takes the broom and sweeps up the sunflower-seed shells in front of the steps. He's lanky like his father, long arms, long legs, sturdy torso. His hair is thick and uncombed above his ears. However hot it is, he never takes off his father's worn old denim jacket. The twigs of the broom scratch over the asphalt, the only sound in the afternoon silence.

Mother and I talked on the phone, says Zoran, sweeping away with the broom. She says she can't come back. Because of people, and what the town would say. She says none of it is true, and she wants me to move in with her in Sarajevo.

What did you say to that?

Zoran, gathers the mucus in his throat with a hard, grating sound, and spits on the ground. I said: right, Mother, OK, but what I'd have to say to you is worse than anything the people here are saying. That's why I'll never move in with you and you'll never move in with me – because I'd be telling you those things every day till the end of my life, and I'd have to see you bobbing your head about like a chicken every day when you answered me.

The bell inside the shop door rings, and Maestro Stankovski's bald patch appears round the door: Zoran, I said take a break, not a holiday!

Comin!, says Zoran, leaning the broom against the handrail. We

53

can hear the clip-clop of hooves. Musa Hasanagić is leading his mare Cauliflower across the square by her reins. Zoran and he shake hands. Musa takes off his top hat, and Zoran pats the white blaze on the mare's forehead.

Zoran doesn't know many stories. It's because so many incredible things happen in his own life that he doesn't have to invent anything. He can always tell the tale of his cuckolded father's revenge on Bogoljub Balvan again and again. Sometimes the story takes less than two minutes – there's no Tetris-playing and nothing gets thrown into the river, Zoran's father spends all day polishing his shotgun and weeping over it and then polishing his tears away and weeping and polishing again. That version ends with Zoran on his knees, begging his father to take the barrel of the gun out of his mouth.

Zoran and Musa gravely say goodbye. Zoran shakes hands with me too, nods, and disappears into the shop. I set off for home. A long-distance bus turns the corner behind me, its driver wears a cap. His moustache, his long arms, his long fingers on the steering wheel, the dark hair coming out from under his cap above his ears – just like his son's.

Anywhere there are stories, I'll be right there.

How did Milenko Pavlović, known as Walrus, the three-point shooter once feared for the number of points he scored but not quite such a good shot with a gun, come to be behind that steering wheel? And shouldn't I run straight back to the barber's shop and tell Zoran that his father was back again, not too early this time, more like a year too late?

When something is an event, when it's an experience, how many deaths Comrade Jito died, and how the once famous three-point shooter gets behind the wheel of a Centrotrans bus

It's an event when Mr Fazlagić storms into our classroom. Punctual Mr Fazlagić races up to the board with a dripping-wet sponge as if he weren't a teacher at all, as if he were a firefighter in a hurry to extinguish the board because it's gone up in flames. We have Serbo-Croat lessons every day and Mr Fazlagić is right in there every day to put out the burning board and rescue our spelling with thousands of model sentences. As a teacher Mr Fazlagić may be a good firefighter, it's hard to tell for certain because his rescue attempts have no effect on most of us. In spite of all the Mr Fazlagićs of this world, we'll never be able to tell *ć* and *č* apart, and the board has never burned down either.

Edin and I have tried to burn it down several times. First with maths books, then with half a Coca-Cola bottle of petrol that Edin pinched from his mother's garage. I was sceptical: these school boards aren't made of wood, and how much petrol do you need to set a brass board alight? You could pour the contents of a whole fuel station on brass and the brass still wouldn't burn, I said, and I repeated the word *brass* until Edin held the Coke bottle of petrol up to the light, examined it through narrowed eyes, and nodded: yes, I see your point. You can cut glass with brass, and glass doesn't burn either, so why would brass burn? Let's sell the stuff to Čika Spok or set fire to a frog with it.

Petrol is alcohol, and Čika Spok is a drunk. Every town has to have one. Čika Spok phones the stars far into the night, with his thumb to his ear and his little finger on his lips. He sweet-talks the Great Bear: one of these days, he promises, I'll have a great, proud weapon, I'll lay you low with it and make myself a Great Bearskin cap.

Well, perhaps those aren't his exact words, but whenever his shouts wake me up I wish he'd explain the Bear's fate to him more soberly, and not keep shouting abuse and accusing him: those are my stars you're carrying off, you thieving animal! Or throwing bottles around the place night and day, and letting fly with curses about the Bear's mother and how he's going to skin him. And I wish he wouldn't puke on the park benches where he sleeps and then go to sleep in his puke.

Edin and I decided on the frog and not Čika Spok because Čika Spok was sleeping so peacefully, sitting up straight with his back to the mosque wall. It was two hours before we could catch a frog. I lit a match, and then a second match. As I did so the frog must have been reflecting on its present life and the whole stupid situation it had got itself into. Instead of puffing out its cheeks on the river bank and darting its tongue into the air to catch flies, here it was, sitting in a cardboard box and being doused with petrol, while two dark-haired heads above it threw burning sticks at its back, waiting for a spectacular explosion. The fourth and fifth matches went out too. The petrol smelled of fermented apple juice.

If you keep throwing lighted matches at a frog sitting motionless and thinking about its fate, you soon begin to feel very sorry for its captive frogginess, but still you try one more match. Only then do you let the frog have its pond back, throw the empty Coca-Cola bottle in after it, and set fire to the cardboard box.

It was also an event when our Serbo-Croat teacher climbed a ladder on the first day of the new school year and took Comrade Tito's picture down from the wall. He clutched it to himself and announced in a solemn voice to Tito's big face, Tito's epaulettes, and Tito's officer's stripes: from now on you children will stop calling me Comrade Teacher and call me Mr Fazlagić instead. Is that clear?

After the silence observed by grown-ups when they've just made a solemn announcement, I clicked my fingers and stood up, like we'd been told to do when we have anything to say. Mr Fazlagić, not-Comrade-Teacher-now, how filthy is not-Comrade-Tito-now, then?

I thoughtfully placed my thumb under my chin and laid my forefinger on my pursed lips, observing the silence that suggests that the next thing you say will begin with the words: let us suppose that . . .

Let us suppose that Tito isn't totally filthy dirty, then you wouldn't have to take him down. We, I said, his Comrade Pioneers, and here I spread my arms out like a folk singer, we can scrub our former President clean in the toilets in no time at all!

I could positively hear the eyes of those Pioneers rolling in an uncomradely way, so I scored more points on the eccentricity scale, where I was already well ahead of the class. Edin swallowed a raw egg during break every day, collected insect legs and did ballet dancing, but all the same he was way behind me. Even Edin's physical appearance scored him points: slight, bony, pale, with little blue veins showing at his temples, and eyes that bulged like a horse's. None of his movements was ever fluent, I had no idea what he learned in ballet classes – he darted jerkily along like someone made entirely of secrets, looking to the left, to the right, up at the sky, all because he wanted to be a special agent. Aleksandar, women always fall for 007, and I can imitate any sound except the sound of a heartbeat. Sure enough, sounds of some kind were emerging from Edin's mouth all the time – even when he was standing still he wasn't silent; he was whistling, breathing heavily, yapping and twittering, but always so softly that you wouldn't notice unless you put your ear quite close to his mouth. When the two of us were on our own he stopped all that stealthy darting about, he looked healthier, spoke more slowly, and knew a lot about biology and the female body. For instance, he knew it had a wound that bled every thirty days, which could be really dangerous if, for some reason, the earth took it into its head to turn thirty times faster than usual.

Mr Fazlagić was still looking at me. And the class was still looking at me, so they wanted me to go on. The Party Committee would certainly approve of scrubbing Tito clean too, that is if the Party Committee still existed, I said, encouraged by all the attention. And I'll ask my Granny to lend us one of her tapestry pictures while Mr Broz, not-Comrade-Tito-now, is absent from school. There's a really nice one with a ship in a storm. It would look better than the mark on the wall.

Vukoje Worm, who was proud of having broken his nose three times, threw a crumpled-up death threat which hit me on the back of the head. It listed the various tortures waiting for me after school and called me a *smahrt aleck* and a *Commie swein*.

My crumpled-up reply just missed him.

Strictly speaking, Tito hadn't left any mark behind on that first day of the school year. Marks are dirty, but the wall behind Tito's back was clean – a white rectangle surrounded by the rest of the wall, which was beige. Tito had been protecting the paler bit, that's how it had stayed clean.

And Tito protected us too, his Pioneers.

Well, that's what they say, although Tito never actually stood in front of us dealing out Bruce Lee kicks to any dissidents with a grudge against us or the Red Star. He thought young people were progressive in the cause of progress and the well-being of Yugoslavia, he even moved his official birthday to the Day of Youth. He was often to be seen with Pioneers in photos, he was laughing and the Pioneers were laughing, and the caption under the picture told you that Tito and the Pioneers were enjoying a joke.

I once met Tito, but it hardly counts because I was still a baby at the time, and a meeting you can't remember isn't much of a meeting. Tito was visiting Višegrad, and when his white open-top Mercedes drove by he waved to me, or so Grandpa Slavko claimed. He also claimed to have spent an hour arguing with Tito about the closure of the railway line, but even he was powerless against Tito. Soon no more trains came through our town and Grandpa Rafik lost his job.

When I'm as old as Tito I'll have a white limousine too, the kind where you can stand up in the back. Edin will be my driver, my loyal Party Secretary and best friend and special agent, responsible for bird imitations and also for the Ministry of Biology because he knows so much about the female body.

Our framed Comrade wasn't cleaned up at all. Everyone understood that, even people whose mothers were not former political advisers to the local committee of the Communist League of Yugoslavia and whose grandpas couldn't explain everything. Something else happened to our Comrade Tito. Our Comrade Tito died. Again. Josip Broz Tito died for the third time when his pictures were taken down from classrooms.

Edin tapped me on the shoulder. Psst . . . Aleks, what did you write to Vukoje Worm?

Nothing. I was only correcting his spelling.

Tito died his first death at five past three in the afternoon of 4 May 1980. But it was only his body that died, and year after year everyone in the world and in space would stand still to remember Tito at five past three on the afternoon of 4 May, except in America and the Soviet Union and on Jupiter, because no life is possible on Jupiter. Sirens would howl and cars stop, while I searched my memory for a suitably sad quotation from Marx with which to conclude the minute of silence and impress someone, anyone. I never managed to find my quotation.

Karl Marx never wrote a single sad thing in his life.

After his first death, Tito moved into our hearts with a little briefcase full of speeches and articles and built himself a magnificent villa there out of ideas. Grandpa Slavko described the villa like this: the walls are made of economic projects, the house is roofed with messages of peace, and you look out through the red windows at a garden full of poppies, flowering slogans about the future, and a well from which endless credit can be drawn. As the years went on, more and more people did as they liked and took less and less interest in Tito's ideas, and when no one is interested in an idea any more that idea is dead.

So Tito died for the second time.

But he lived on in poems and newspaper articles and books.

Soon, however, it was correct not to own those books and not to have read the poems. Then it was even more correct to put books on your shelves that used to be banned, and the time came when the most correct thing of all was to write newspaper articles and books yourself of the kind that would once have been banned. After Grandpa died it was my mother who told me all these things. She was a political scientist and knew what she was talking about. Grandpa called her a Marxist, and was pleased about it. She wasn't too pleased herself. In the old days when people asked what my mother did for a living, I didn't hesitate for a moment. I used to say, at Auntie-Typhoon-speed: political adviser to the local committee of the Communist League of Yugoslavia! She writes speeches for those dimwits the secretaries and president of the local committee. I didn't say *those dimwits* out loud, but I knew that's what they were, because my mother had moaned and groaned over and over again about their many kinds of dimness. Their empty heads, their poor memories, the gulf between what they promised and what they did, the holes in their purses, and moreover, she would say: they can drink like a fish, all of them, but they can't get a reasonable sentence down on paper.

If people ask me now what my mother does for a living I usually say: she's tired. You get to be especially tired if you're always working too hard and always talking about how you're always working too hard. Working makes you old. My parents come home from work and talk about work. Father takes off his shirt and washes his feet in the bathroom. He works in a factory that makes wooden furniture, but he's not a woodworker, he sits in a room with pocket calculators and a desk diary and he wears a shirt. At home he never wears shirts and he works in his studio, but he doesn't call that work. He says he can't abide figures any more than he can abide our government. Father cleans his glasses and makes a face when he's looking closely for marks on the lenses. When I'm his age, I'll have hair that's going grey at the temples myself. When I'm my mother's age, I'll be able to talk about troubles for an hour on end, all by myself without stopping, but the troubles won't be my own. Mother would really have liked to be a figure skater. Now

60

she races around our local law court all day until she's tired. She says: this legislation is so clumsy you almost grow fond of it. In the evening she makes sandwiches for work. I'll make the sandwiches for work – she always says this in just the same words, it's like Father washing his feet. I wonder why she doesn't make the sandwiches for herself and Father – work doesn't have to eat, I once pointed out, and my mother replied: oh yes, it does, my work is eating me up day after day.

I always preferred talking to Grandpa about putting Marxist ideology into practice, Socialist self-government, Tito's foreign policy, or the best way to gut a fish. Conversations like that are very difficult with my father. He is inclined – if he feels like talking to me at all – to think up all kinds of ways of not revealing his incompetence on such subjects. He will talk not about Yugoslavia but some unnamed kingdom where there are words for things that don't exist, and things for which there can't be any words.

You inherit the ability to tell good stories, but it sometimes skips a generation.

Tito lived on longest in our school textbooks. History, Serbo-Croat, even maths couldn't get along without him. The distance from Jajce to Bihać is 160 kilometres. A Yugo drives from Jajce to Bihać at a speed of 80 kph. At the same time Josip Broz Tito is walking from Bihać to Jajce at a steady speed of 10 kph. At how many kilometres from Jajce will they meet?

To conceal my total ignorance of the calculation, I protested that obviously you couldn't have a Yugo and a Tito on the same road at all, because if our President had wanted to go for a walk, the road would have been closed to everyone else. As a safety precaution, I added, and I for one would have welcomed it.

But maths teachers are unrelenting about such things.

A new teacher once got so angry about Tito's life as told in the history textbook that he could be heard from the corridor, shouting away in the headmaster's office. I'm a historian, he shouted, not the presenter of a children's story hour on TV!

I told Grandpa Slavko about the historian, and next day Grandpa came to school with his glasses on, in his overcoat, carrying the walking stick he didn't need, and wearing a hat and all his Party decorations. Out in the corridor, we were able to hear my grandpa's voice, but not the historian's.

Tito lived his third life on TV too. Partisan films were shown so often that I could act along with the dialogue of some of them. My favourite film is called *Battle on the Neretva*. The Neretva isn't quite as green as the Drina, and the finest bridge over it, in Mostar, has ten arches fewer than ours. I went to Mostar with my class last year. Men were jumping off the fairly high bridge into the Neretva, and everyone clapped. In the film a whole army of people sick with typhoid jump into the river. Their leader cries: follow me, all of you typhoid sufferers, over the river to freedom! Then he drowns. Another saying from *Battle* is: our people sing even when they're killed. If Marx had seen that film, maybe he would have thought of something sad to say.

I wash my hands before meals so as not to get typhoid.

In my second-favourite film, miners blow up an incredible number of Nazis with an incredible number of dynamite sticks. Colliers are left lying in the mine like sailors on the seabed, says one of the miners. A German soldier gazes into the distance and says: we are to blame for being naive and weak. The weak have no place in history. I'm only sorry that I shall die a soldier and not a miner, he says.

Tito also lived on at commemoration ceremonies, rallies, and holiday celebrations. At dismal meetings of elderly men with un-ironed shirts and women with dyed perms in smoky back rooms, where I spent endless hours in my mother's company. They ate ham and grumbled: in the old days, ah, the old days, well, those were the old days. Even Grandpa Slavko turned quarrelsome there, complaining of this and that, and his bad-tempered carping made him seem ten years greyer than usual. I coughed and had red eyes the next morning.

Last summer, two weeks after Grandpa's death, was the first time I refused to go with my mother to a meeting of former something-or-others in the basement of the municipal library. Grandpa doesn't have to go any more either! I said. I stuck to my guns, and Mother didn't look disappointed, she looked frightened. She changed her clothes, painted her fingernails red in front of the bedroom mirror, and then closed the bedroom door. When she kissed me goodbye her breath smelled of wine. I painted our flag with the five-pointed star and kept thinking of Mother's red nails the whole time. After a while I couldn't hold out any longer. I knocked on the studio door until my father admitted to being at home and agreed to go and fetch Mother with me.

The Yugoslavian flag was hanging from a central heating pipe in the library cellar, and a man with glasses perched on the end of his nose was reading aloud from a gigantic tome. But no one turned the gramophone off. There were toothpicks bearing small home-made flags with Tito's portrait on them stuck into cubes of cheese on plates. My mother was tapping her red fingernails in time with the music. She was the only woman in the room and the only person there under sixty. On the way from home she'd had her hair done differently. Father stopped in the doorway, playing with the car key. When Mama saw us she slowly stood up and reached for her bag. She didn't say goodbye to anyone. No one said goodbye to her. One man coughed, another stood up and turned the record over. That was the last meeting Mother went to. I couldn't tell if she was particularly happy about it or particularly sad, she just stopped going, the way I suppose I'll stop growing some day. And her hair hadn't really been done differently. My mother just looked different in the smoky light.

Pictures upon pictures of Tito were still around too – in offices, in shop windows, in living rooms next to family portraits, in schools. Tito on a yacht, Tito standing on a speaker's podium, Tito with a girl handing him flowers. You could get a jigsaw puzzle of Tito and ET holding hands. So when those pictures were removed from the classrooms, Tito died for the third time. Comrade Jelenić, known to us as Fizo, was still a Comrade and the only teacher to leave Tito's portrait hanging on the wall that first day of the school year – Tito in his admiral's uniform with a German shepherd dog. Fizo placed himself behind his desk without a word of greeting, put on his glasses, and entered something in the register. You'd better all invest in a workbook and a formula book, said the strictest teacher in our school without looking up, you have a hard year's work ahead of you.

That day Mr Fazlagić, not-Comrade-Teacher-now, didn't just take away Tito's steely brow in its gilded frame, he also took the red flag carried at the head of the procession in every school parade out of its glass case. When I'd asked whether we Pioneers couldn't clean Tito up he embarked very seriously on a long and serious speech: this is a serious matter, Aleksandar Krsmanović, and your irony is wholly misplaced! Serious changes to the system are in progress. The new forms of address and the abolition of all remnants of any personality cult are constituent parts of the process of democratisation and should be taken seriously! The teacher's lips went on moving, the teacher's mouth produced one long sentence after another. Mr Fazlagić put the picture down several times and shook his arms about. But instead of leaving the picture on the floor, he kept picking it up again, and went on talking to us until break.

To show that I'd understood how serious the whole business was – the system, new forms of address, the personality cult – I came to school the next day in my dark blue Pioneer uniform, which was much too small for me, but I thought it still looked smart. I sat down in the front row of Mr Fazlagić's class, my back straight and Socialist as Grandpa always demanded. I'd even scrubbed my fingernails clean. I spread my fingers out on the table in front of me as we used to do in the old days when a hygiene supervisor came to inspect the class. At the first question Mr Fazlagić asked us, I sprang to my feet and said: now let's consider what's left of labour products. There's nothing left except the same old eerie realism, just a jellified mass of indistinguishable human labour, that's to say the expense of the labour force without any thought for what it's expended on.

Three hours' detention. Three teachers invigilated, their grim expressions speaking volumes about the social and political shift in ideology, otherwise known as radical change. If you don't see sense, they threatened me, you'll be here after school every day.

Students are left lying in school like sailors on the bottom of the sea, I said, drawing two diagonal lines in red felt pen on my cheeks, I'm only sorry that I shall die a student and not a miner.

After that there was another voluble and angry exchange, but then I was allowed to go home, because even teachers have a private life. I decided to take a closer look at the meaning of the expressions *provocation, family brainwashing,* and *political shifts in ideology otherwise known as radical change.* I knew the meaning of irony by now. Irony is when you ask a question and you don't get an answer, you just get trouble instead.

Edin turns to me and says: Jasna's shirt. Edin, Comrade-in-Chief of human biology, explains what's making Jasna's shirt swell out like bodywork that has to be flattened when a car's been in an accident. Friday, third lesson, Mr Fazlagić wipes the board clean with such vigour that water drips off the sponge and runs up his sleeve. Edin and I quickly agree that Edin's explanation is not quite the right way to describe those swellings, because what's suddenly appeared under Jasna's shirt has nothing to do with car-repair workshops. Nor is Jasna's red shirt in any way connected with bent axles. It is rather clearer to Edin than to me why, when he and I come anywhere near her, we act as if she were both the most important and the most unimportant thing in the world. Kneading bread, stroking a dog, trying to find a radio station, that's the best way to work on those non-technological swellings under Jasna's shirt, Edin explains. You have to be gentle and precise. You have to master the art of touching and do it perfectly or girls will run away from you, whispers the Comrade-in-Chief of biology, and he looks dreamily at Jasna. If I could touch her just once, he sighs, then I would die happy.

I've never heard the word 'precise' in Edin's mouth before, and when his voice rises a little on the word 'perfectly', Mr Fazlagić flings his bunch of keys down on the teacher's desk with full force. Silence. All of a sudden. Precisely.

The bunch of keys is an experience. For Edin, for me, for Jasna too. Because Edin, Jasna and I are personally responsible for Mr Fazlagić's irritation. The former Comrade Teacher is unbeatable in the irritation line anyway. At least once a week he predicts in a shaking voice: you lot will have me in Sokolac yet! By 'you lot' he means us when, for instance, he catches us trying to set fire to the board, or when we've all ganged up to write the first school essay of the year in the Cyrillic alphabet, although express orders went out after Tito's third death: no more writing in Cyrillic characters. And there's a lunatic asylum at Sokolac. It's where Adolf Hitlers and people who think they're chairs go. Mr Fazlagić might make it to the asylum too. And when his nerves are reaching Sokolac-point, he likes to bang things down on his desk. The flat of his hand, the register, the map of Turkey – a country that Mr Fazlagić has recently taken to holding up as an example for this, that and the other. Today it's his bunch of keys, which must weigh fourteen kilos. All Yugoslavia and half of Turkey could probably be opened up with those keys. The echo of the bang hasn't quite died away when he shouts: perfectly? Do what perfectly, Edin? And just what do you want to touch? Your marks are far from perfect, so you might touch your books for a change!

The noise and the shouting alarm Edin; he jumps up from his chair, performs a pirouette, thrusts his chest out, spreads his arms wide and cries: I don't want to touch anything! And when I said perfectly I was talking about our move, my mother and I are moving away, Aleksandar said he'd help and I said with him we'll do it all perfectly.

Edin isn't moving away at all, but the move is a good excuse, because Mr Fazlagić asks no more questions, he just says: you can leave discussion of that question until break.

These first warm weeks of the year are going-away time. There's a general mood of departure, as infectious as a cold in spring. Whole families get itchy feet, you can hardly see the cars under so much baggage. People are leaving town in such a hurry, they're so intent on getting away, they can't even find time to say goodbye to the people staying behind. They're setting off in frantic haste, as if

66

to save their carpets and their sofas from a flood. I like the idea of loading cars up with sofas. When I go to see Granny I always sit on Grandpa Slavko's sofa. When I'm watching TV, when I'm eating, when I'm sleeping, when I want to listen to my heart to find out if it's stopped. The Ladas and Yugos are so heavily laden that their floors scrape the bulging asphalt of the petrol station. This road will take them to Titovo Užice, perhaps even Belgrade or Bulgaria, or if they turn off the main road a little sooner, they'll reach Veletovo. But something tells me no one wants to go there. Edin and Zoran don't know where all these people are going, my parents don't know either, and yesterday after school when I asked Kostina the care-taker where people were off to on holiday, he laughed nervously as if he was scared of me.

Yesterday Edin and I spent all afternoon at the petrol station. Everyone in Višegrad knows that road and its bumps: if you take your foot off the accelerator your exhaust will stay put. But yester-day it seemed as if the drivers had forgotten what their own roads were like; they raced over the bumps and the floors of their cars protested so loudly that an old lady in the house opposite the petrol station put a cushion on her window sill and leaned out of the window so as not to miss a thing. By early evening, cars with cases on the roof had stopped driving past. A woodpecker flew by, and I thought of the various different kinds of birds. Some birds spend the winter here in spite of the cold, others fly to warmer places. Do birds of the first kind sit on the overhead wires to watch the other birds leave, the way we watched the cars? Do they get an uncomfortable feeling when the other birds sing about places in the south? Quick, off we fly to the sun to build nests in coconut palms and eat mandarins all day! Do they roll their eyes and twitter: oh, you conceited formation flyers! It doesn't bother the birds who fly away that the other lot are staying, they couldn't care less what the other birds think: you could come too instead of freezing your beaks off.

Can birds actually roll their eyes? I asked Edin.

Danilo Gorki's Golf approached the petrol station so fast that Edin and I jumped up from the side of the road and took a few steps back. Danilo is our neighbour, old Mirela's son, and a waiter at the Estuary Restaurant. He's a young man known to half the town because his last girlfriend wrote him a letter after she dumped him. Her letter consisted of a single sentence, and she wrote it in spray paint on the road under Danilo's window.

The floor of Danilo's Golf crashed over the biggest bump. He stopped and kicked the exhaust, which wasn't attached to his Golf any more. Edin and I congratulated each other as if we and the road had just succeeded in some great mission. The furious Danilo was cursing the road, mentioning pig's guts, cunt, grape must and mothers in the course of his tirade. We greeted him with extravagant enthusiasm as he walked into the petrol station, dragging the exhaust behind him. Old Mirela got out of the car, stood at the roadside and looked back at the town as if waiting for someone. An hour later, she and her son were able to drive on again.

Edin spat through his teeth, watched Danilo's Golf chugging away and said, looking in the direction of Titovo Užice, in the direction of Belgrade, in the direction of Bulgaria: hey, Aleks, I think they're all clearing out of here.

I didn't argue with him. The twittering of weary birds surrounded us in the dusk. They're running away, said Edin more quietly, picking pebbles off the palm of his hands. He'd been leaning his hands on the ground, and the little stones had stuck to them.

But why? I asked.

Danilo, everything about you, from your brain to your prick, is tiny!

Mr Fazlagić turns away, he's satisfied with Edin's answer. Get your exercise books out, he says, I hope you were listening properly yesterday when I explained the difference between an event and an experience, because today you are going to write an essay on the subject of 'A Wonderful Trip'.

Well, it makes a change from 'My Native Land' and 'Why the View of My Town from My Window Makes Me Proud and Happy', or 'Why the Day of the Republic is My Day Too'.

A wonderful trip, and it has to be an experience – not just an event! Mr Fazlagić looks at us. Vukoje, I shall stop reading after the twentieth spelling mistake. Faruk, anything illegible will lose you marks. And Aleksandar, I don't want to know anything about your Great-Grandma uprooting oaks, or inauguration parties for the family loo, or your Auntie Whirlwind running a race with Carl Lewis over the bridge and ending up in Tokyo. You've wandered off the subject in every essay you've written this year, so kindly restrain your imagination! Mr Fazlagić comes up to my desk and bends down towards me. And we use quotation marks for direct speech, he says, leaning his fists on the desk top, you know that, I don't have to explain it to you every time. Now, you all have an hour!

Mr Fazlagić sounds cross. When he was still Comrade Teacher he once gave me punishment because I did restrain my imagination, and my essay on 'My Native Land' was seven pages of geographical and economic statistics about Yugoslavia that I'd learnt by heart. We were given 'My Native Land' for an essay at least twice a year. So I wrote a footnote referring to my previous essays on the subject, and added that, despite inflation, I hadn't changed my mind and wasn't likely to change it in a hurry. In a second footnote, I suggested to Mr Fazlagić that he might like to look at my poetry collection, particularly the poems '8 March 1989, or I Send My Political Adviser Whole Spruce Woods Full of Motherly Love'; '1 May 1989, or The Chick in the Pioneer's Hand'; and 'Comrade Tito, In My Heart You Will Never Die'.

Grandpa Slavko had liked my inappropriate choice of subjects, Mother wasn't quite so keen on my bad marks, and Father didn't think school mattered much. Just don't get into fights, he said.

I open my exercise book at the first blank page. 'A Wonderful Trip'. I go to the Adriatic every summer, always to Igalo. It's organised by the workers' syndicate at Varda, the firm where my father wears a shirt and tie. Hundreds of the people of Višegrad who work for Varda pack their cases, gather their families together and tell them: we're being put up in this hotel, though we'd rather have the one where we stayed in '86. All Varda goes to Igalo, its people are moved from a little town without any seaside to a little town by the sea for one month. I know my way around Igalo as well as I know my way around Višegrad, and not just because of the annual trip there, it's also because the hotel beds and shelves, in fact all the furniture, even the wooden floorboards and the wooden panelling, are made by Varda, exactly the same as we have in our bedrooms and on our walls at home. So if you want to write about a wonderful trip you don't write about Igalo.

Thinking about Igalo, I've drawn a head in one corner of the sheet of paper. The corners of its mouth are turned down, I give it a moustache. Now the head gets two long arms instead of ears. Walrus. A wonderful trip for Zoran's father Milenko Pavlović, the three-point shooter once feared for the number he shot, but not quite such a good shot with a gun! Walrus's wonderful trip to a new wife and new happiness!

Secure in the knowledge that a good story is never an inappropriate subject, I write the title:

What Milenko Pavlović, known as Walrus, brings back from his wonderful trip, how the station-master's leg loses control of itself, what the French are good for, and why we don't need quotation marks

. . . the reason being that anyone can say anything, or think it and not say it, and what would be the point of quotation marks round thoughts you don't say, or something you do say that's a lie, or thoughts that aren't important enough to be said out loud, or something said out loud that *is* important but no one hears it?

Drunk and deceived as he was, Milenko Pavlović, known as Walrus, had taken his son aside and said: Zoran, I'm going away now, I have to get everything new for us: *Das Kapital* for me and a new mother for you. He had got into his car and driven out of town, hooting the horn. No one knew where he was going.

Yesterday, one year later, Walrus came back. He drove into town still hooting, just as he had left, but this time at the wheel of a Centrotrans bus. These days everyone was leaving town, no one knew where they were going, only Walrus came proudly back, no one knew where from, and the first thing he said when his shoes touched the ground of Višegrad was:

Anyone want to buy a bus?

You won't sell a bus like that in a hurry, I told Walrus, breathlessly. I'd run after the bus as it drove down the streets at a slow and victorious speed. I wanted to see what Walrus had brought back from his journey.

That bus isn't quite straight, said Armin the bus station-master, scratching his head under his station-master's cap. He didn't mean the bus itself, he meant the way Walrus had parked it – with the front right-hand side up on the pavement. Armin crouched down, his knees creaking, he looked underneath the bus, he ran his finger

71

over rusty metal, opened the baggage space and kicked the tyres. Nodded three times and said: a good bus, I know this bus, you can't sell it to us, it's ours already.

Of course you know it, said Walrus, throwing his hands up jubilantly in the air, but are you and the bus related? I'm not selling you your uncle, and the days when you could only sell what's yours were over in this country long ago.

A young woman appeared in the doorway of the bus behind the grinning Walrus. He forgot about doing any kind of deal and tucked his shirt into his trousers. Red hair with black slides in it, a red scarf with black stripes, red high-heeled shoes with black buckles, size four at the most; a low-cut blouse and a miniskirt with a pattern of red and black dots too. The ladybird laughed, and it was a great relief to see that her teeth were plain white.

Walrus offered the redhead his arm, which she took with a smile. Her red shoes hardly touched the cracked asphalt. Batting her eyelashes and practically hovering in the air, the young woman looked at the little group that had gathered to welcome the miracle of Walrus's return, and insofar as it consisted of men, the group lowered its eyes, and insofar as it was wearing a cap it took the cap off.

Wouldn't you like to sell *her*? was the thought that shot through Armin's mind, or at least he was staring at Walrus's new girlfriend in a greedy way that suggested it. As if she were a Sunday evening Western that had never been shown before. Armin whistled through his teeth, barely but still audibly, the way you whistle at the sight of something really expensive. The redhead's eyes, bright blue in the middle of all that red and black, had something to do with Armin's whistle. And her long, slender neck! Armin kicked the hot right-hand front tyre for about the twentieth time; he didn't have that leg under control any more.

This is my Milica! said Walrus, introducing his Milica in a voice as solemn as if he were really announcing: listen, all of you, I want everyone to know that this is my Milica! Milenko's beautiful Milica!

Everyone knew about Walrus's misfortunes, everyone had heard how he'd been cuckolded before the eyes of his only son, and how a tobacconist had humiliated and soiled his bookcase along with *Das Kapital*. All the same, no one applauded when the ladybird tripped along beside Walrus. We weren't impressed by all that red and black, the bus station isn't a cinema, and from a purely medicinal viewpoint such a heavy dose of lipstick can't be good for anyone's mouth.

Walrus put Milica's baggage down carefully and flung his own sports bag on to the pavement, sending dust flying up. He handed Armin the key of the bus as if it were the station-master's birthday, and there was nothing Armin could do but thank him and finally stop kicking the tyres. Walrus's new girlfriend put her scarf around her slender neck, and I'd never seen such a tiny handbag as hers, her lipstick might fit into it but then there'd be no room left for her headache tablets.

Where's the driver? I asked Walrus after he'd shaken hands with everyone present the way presidents do at airports, clasping their hosts' hands in both their own.

Picking mushrooms on the Romanija, replied Walrus, punching my forearm in a way I liked. And where's my son, you young rascal?

Sweeping up hair for Maestro Stankovski, I replied, dancing about in front of Walrus like Muhammad Ali, I've just come from there. He's still wearing your jacket.

Ah, my jacket, nodded Walrus, and the palm of his hand sketched a straight right and an uppercut. Then today's the last time he'll wear that old thing, no one wears denim jackets in Trieste, and I've bought him everything new.

Milica pushed her sunglasses down from her hair to her face and ran her eyes over the little bus station, frowning. The pale bushes around it, all pale green like that, could hardly appeal to anyone so dotted. And probably nor did the oil stains on the asphalt, or the pack of dogs lying there dozing, or the holes in the rusty fence, or Armin the tyre expert scratching his belly under his shirt. Milica concluded her inspection over the top of her sunglasses with me. What was wrong about me? I had big ears, but normally women of marriageable age liked that. I had a wonky haircut, but that was

Maestro Stankovski's fault, not mine. Milica slowly opened her lips, showing her teeth, she had about forty more of them than most people, and a diamond sparkled on one of her twelve incisors. Those teeth could be giving a kind of smile, I thought, and sure enough, there was something she liked about me! She clasped her hands in front of her breasts with delight, her disappointment at the sight of the shabby bus station gone. She pinched my cheeks with both hands and an incredibly sweet perfume hit me in the face. Look, if there's one thing, I cried, wiping my cheeks with my sleeve, if there's one thing that I personally find distressing it's having fingers jabbed in my face!

'I personally' is what my mother said when she wanted to disagree with something, and 'distressing' was what she said when she was very upset.

Just hark at him talking! cried the delighted Milica, clapping her hands. Her voice sounded like the last piano key on the right. And see the funny way he opens and closes his mouth! She took a step back from me as if admiring a picture in a gallery. Walrus was pleased because his Milica was pleased, he wanted to hug her, but by now he was so laden with cases and bags and carriers that he couldn't really move at all.

How old are you, darling? Milica took another step closer. I took three steps back.

There are various rumours, I muttered, ranging from eight to fourteen, it all depends, but too old to have my cheeks pinched anyway. To avoid any more questions I followed Walrus, who had set off in the direction of the town centre, walking heavily. Out of the corner of my eye I saw Armin reversing the bus, he couldn't have the right-hand side of one of his buses trespassing on the pavement. I kept my eye on the ladybird. Goodness knew what else someone who wore tights like cobwebs would be capable of.

Čika Walrus, where have you been all this time?

On my travels – all over the place. Across the Pannonian plain, over the Dinarides, to the coast, all the way to Italy. Not a bad trip. I didn't have much money, so I used five sentences of French from the Marseillaise and my recipe for leg of lamb Breton style to make out I was Jacques, and I introduced my Milica to everyone as Mademoiselle Bretagne. The French always make our sort happy because, like us, they know how to love, they're just as good at playing the accordion, and they've made a real art of their inability to bake proper bread. As Jacques and Mademoiselle Bretagne we always had enough to eat, and a bed to sleep in, where we could get to know each other better. Everywhere we went people told us why Yugoslavia had been such a fine country, it sounded as if they were talking about someone dead. Our act worked until we met a real Frenchman. We got drunk with him on French rosé and then he confessed that he'd just been speaking Macedonian with a French accent and the wine was local wine cut with schnapps. Then he had too much of his local wine as well, and he wept in Milica's lap, telling us how he'd saved up for years to buy a motorbike to impress the most beautiful woman in the village, but the most beautiful woman in the village had gone and married someone who didn't even have a pushbike.

On our way through Višegrad on 2 April 1992 Walrus said: it would be a good thing if everyone had trained to be on the road, same as me. Because everyone will soon have to go on a long trip. But I'm staying put, come what may.

On the way past the fire station Walrus turned serious and said: Milica and I will be happy here.

On the way past the mosque Walrus stopped and drank water from the tap in the wall.

On his way, and it wasn't far enough for him to tell me all the things he could have told me, Milenko was glad to see every passerby who recognised him and stopped to say hello, because then he could put the heavy bags down. Many of them welcomed him warmly, for one thing because they were glad to see one more person back in the town, which was shrinking daily.

Musa, said Walrus to Musa Hasanagić, who was leading his mare Cauliflower along by her reins, Musa, brother, shall we stick together?

Always, said Musa, and Cauliflower nodded the way horses do.

On the way to his son, and it was much too long since he'd seen

75

him, and on the way to saying: I'm back and the war is hard on my heels, Walrus told me about his trip, the last trip, he said, to be made in this country for a long time by someone so full of care and yet so carefree.

Where bad taste in music gets you, what the three-dot-ellipsis man denounces, and how fast war moves once it really gets going

My car broke down on the Romanija, would you believe it? Right where my son Zoran and I once stopped for a pee, the engine gave out. Mist like cement, same as before. So off I go on foot, and then the bus comes along. The driver's switched some music on. My head's going round and round. I tell him: you're not on your own here. He laughs at me: no, I'm not, but I'm driving you, and as long as I'm driving you the volume of the music is my business and sitting there is yours. He's right. I admit it. I have no quarrel with that. But not only does the music stay as loud, it also gets worse. It gets revolting. He's put a cassette in and is singing along with it, something about sharp swords by the bloodstained river Drina. I speak up again: right, the volume and the radio and the steering wheel and the speed and the hairs in your nostrils are your business, but these ears are mine. And I'm not happy with the insult to my ears and my river Drina, I don't approve of it at all. And since you're singing along – here I tap him on the shoulder – I'm not happy with you either, I don't approve of you at all. Not as a driver or a human being, if you know such garbage by heart. Switch it off or I'll shoot your balls off! However, he turns round, ready to fight. Into battle, heroes all! he shouted at me, and I thought we were going to come off the road any minute, and the last thing I'd hear in my life was this Greater Serbian donkey braying. He couldn't sing at all, or he wouldn't have been a bus driver.

I have a headache and my life is not the easiest of lives at this moment, I whispered in the donkey's ear. And I may be Serbian but I'm ashamed to hear this kind of stuff. There's nothing more dangerous than a cuckold with a headache who feels ashamed of himself and has a loaded gun in his bag. Aleksandar, promise me

77

that *you* will never hold a gun before a bus driver's eyes, throw him out of his bus, give him a good kicking and shoot his cassette player!

Word of Pioneer's honour!

There aren't any Pioneers now, you young rascal.

Once a Pioneer always a Pioneer.

Walrus nodded, satisfied. Right, so now I'm in charge of the bus, I told the passengers, and you can have it any way you like. I'll take you home or anywhere you say, you've paid your fares. Anyone who doesn't fancy travelling with a headache like mine and a gun like this can get off the bus, I won't take offence.

So there were these faces, men and women, gaping at me, all rather concerned, all black-haired − except for my Milica, she was red-haired, she was sitting on the fifth seat at the back painting her mouth. Aah! I realised at once that I hadn't really meant it, or not entirely, when I said I'd let *anyone* out. Because a girl like that doesn't get away from me.

Milica smiled and lowered her eyes. Walrus put the bags down, took her waist in his big basketball player's hand, and traced circles on her red and black blouse.

Three people got out at once, said Walrus, raising three fingers, and a fourth − Walrus wiggled his little finger − stood up. A tiny old man with a hat much too big for him, long locks of hair at his temples, and a shabby frock coat. So tiny I hadn't seen him at all behind the seat that was hiding him. Everything about him was either small and short or large and long. He had to climb on the arm of the seat to get his bag down from the baggage rack. He was a grouch, you could see his honesty and his grief on his lips. Still standing on the arm of the seat he put a small pair of glasses in front of his enormous eyes and made a speech in his own three-dot language: to think we always have to settle things by violence . . . we always have to . . . it upsets me . . . it upsets me . . . weapons . . . fighting . . . even with words . . . fighting . . . vulgar abuse . . . spitting . . . cursing . . . like the old days . . . again and again . . . and it's only . . . you just wait . . . this is a land of thugs . . . it never stops . . . it never ends . . .

78

Aleksandar, you never saw such a long beard as that beard with the three-dot-ellipsis man grouching away into it! He wore it combed down past his bow tie, in two long waterfalls of beard. So there he was, standing in front of me, I can still repeat everything he said: senseless . . . senseless . . . do we always have to keep on this way . . . it could be much easier . . . like back then . . . boots on the ice . . . the lake frozen over . . . so cold . . . even the smallest nail they . . . it's just fifty years ago . . . someone gave me food . . . I wanted to go to God . . . so hungry . . . the priests, the kind priests . . . faith or food . . . young man, young man . . . you can go blind with cold . . . I saved nothing . . . nothing . . . that's what wars are like . . . that's how it was back then . . . I saved nothing . . . the loneliest people love only themselves . . .

All this was exactly what the three-dot-ellipsis man said, you can't forget a thing like that. Then he lay down in the front row of seats and went on muttering into his beard. You never saw such a long beard, really, you never saw one like it.

You never saw one like it, repeated Milica.

You never did, I agreed, and after a pause, quietly and squinting at the ladybird, I said: so why did you bring her back?

No one brought me anywhere! Milica said indignantly, I came here because I wanted to. I'm impressed by men with opinions, large hands, a headache, a gun, and – here she looked over at Walrus – and an arse like that in their trousers. Oops! Are you allowed to use such words here?

Like *impressed*? I'm a Yugoslavian!

Walrus laughed, and Milica laughed. She wasn't like the Više-grad women. She was always searching her surroundings with her eyes as if expecting someone, even when she was talking, even when she was laughing. She concentrated entirely on Walrus. She was going to have a tough time here.

I never did get another copy of *Das Kapital*, said Walrus, I used to read my old one at night when I couldn't sleep, and I swear I didn't understand a word of it. I understood my Milica very well. She and the three-dot-ellipsis man were the last passengers left after I'd taken all the others home. The three-dot-ellipsis man told us how his home and his synagogue and his memory of how to end sentences had all been looted. He had nothing left but his hat, his case, his beard and his bow tie. Tarirara, that's what you could . . . that's my . . . I'm called . . . But Tarirara wasn't his real name, they'd taken his real name away as well. Tarirara was his song. Deep in thought, he scratched the strip of rubber under the bus window with his fingernail, tarirara, tarirara, he sang. He drove around with us for two months. I let him take the wheel so that I could get to know my Milica better on the back row of seats.

Once, at night, we're somewhere in the high mountains of Slovenia and I'm just getting to know Milica's neck better, when there's a big bang! The bus has gone right through the crash barrier on the left, it careers downhill through undergrowth in a way liable to rearrange all your bones, then all of a sudden it comes to rest at the bottom, I'm only just able to hang on to Milica.

Not bad . . . calls the three-dot-ellipsis man from the front, waving goodbye to a hub-cap. All around us there's wind and a huge, empty surface. The three-dot-ellipsis man takes a couple of steps and almost tumbles over. He says: that was . . . that was . . . I couldn't save anything . . . so many years have . . . but now . . .

We're on ice, Aleksandar! The bus is standing on ice. On a frozen lake. Nothing but the dark blue of the lake as far as the eye can see. My Milica and I dance a polka on the ice. I get to know her ice-blue eyes in the beam of the headlights. The three-dot-ellipsis man takes a pair of skates out of his little case and tells us his story. He tells it fluently – he's been cured of those three dots!

Skating on ice by night, said Milica, and the three-dot-ellipsis man skates into the darkness, tarirara, tarirara.

I switched off the lights, and Milica and I finally got to know each other really well. Next morning we drove over the lake, our faithful bus performed several pirouettes, no one in the world was ever as happy as us with our bus. Until we heard about Croatia on the radio. We must go to Osijek, cried Milica at once, my father!

Do you know about Osijek, you young rascal?

I did know about Osijek.

Well, just you remember Osijek!

I knew about Osijek from TV. Osijek was burning, and there were things you saw there and couldn't understand, you saw them again and again, lying under blankets or sheets in the street, in farmyards. Boots. Forearms. Grandpa Slavko wasn't there to confirm that what I saw was what I was afraid of. My parents said it was a long way off.

In Osijek I kissed Milica's father on the left cheek and the right cheek, and I told him at once, I told him straight. Milica, I said, it's Milica or no one for me!

Don't make life hard for her, then, he said, and he gave me his watch, his bedside table and his caramels. Then we philosophised for a bit. About women, marriage, tobacconists, wood-chopping, life and its heavy weight. That was me philosophising. He philosophised too: life weighed heaviest in the summer of '43. Running away from the Italians. Nothing to eat all day long. Nothing to drink. A sky like blue lava. Sets the hair of your head on fire. A farmyard. Nobody there. A shed. Nobody there. Only hams and yet more hams. Hams in brine. Smoked hams. We ate ham straight off the beam where it was hanging. Licked the salt off it. And forgot about water. No one had any water. Too much salt, too much sun. And the Italians sunning themselves around the village well. Three times as many of them. Life weighed heavy then. We mowed them down. Tactics and good order. Every shot went home. None of us were killed. And then the well was empty. The empty well. Ah, life weighed heavy then.

I told him a joke: the Italians and the Partisans are fighting day and night in a forest, then along comes the forester and throws both sides out.

Milica's father didn't laugh. He had taken off his undershirt and poured us more sauerkraut juice when we heard the first shots outside. We were only talking about it, that's all, what the hell's going on now? he shouted. Milica took her father with one hand and me with the other. Papa, you must go. Milenko, you must drive him. I'm staying here or they'll take the whole house apart.

You're coming with us!

I'm not leaving the house alone!

I'm not leaving you alone!

Then prove it and come straight back to me!

And as my Milica stood there, a truly commanding woman, I vowed all my love to her. Milenko, this isn't the time for it, she said. Her father protested, but we got his undershirt back on him. Off to Zagreb – no checkpoints, we were in luck. I went straight back, I got there in the middle of the night. Sheer hell. Coming from the west you could still get in, but sheer hell! The street lights smashed, houses in darkness or in flames. People everywhere, none of them happy. I left the bus in a yard, goodbye bus! I thought. I almost couldn't find the house again. A candle in the window. Milica was sitting in the kitchen peeling a potato very slowly. With an ancient TV programme on in front of her. She was crying.

I thought you were – Milica interrupted him.

But I wasn't, he said, and Milica kissed his shoulder.

Out of here and off to the sun, off to Italy. The bus was still there, it was even intact. Milica got behind the wheel because she knew her way around the town. But the soldiers knew their way around it too: this is a roadblock, get out, they say, this bus is being commandeered for military purposes. But this is a peace-loving bus, I said. And that's how I got *this* – Walrus bent down, Milica pushed the hair back from his forehead. There was a scar running along Walrus's parting. I didn't lose consciousness, he said, I'm proud of that. Then Milica said: let's see which can go faster, our bus or your war. She stepped on the accelerator and off we went, right through the roadblock. There was still a soldier in the bus, my gun was in the bus too, he lost his balance, I didn't, and then there was no soldier in the bus any more.

And I never took my foot off the pedal until we reached the Piazza Verdi in Trieste, said Milica, stopping to look in a shop window.

What about the war? I asked.

The war was hard on our heels all the way, but it didn't have a visa for Italy, said Walrus.

Does it have a visa for Višegrad?

Walrus stopped and looked around. We'd reached Liberation

Square. This was where Maestro Stankovski had his barber's shop. Zoran was nowhere to be seen. Walrus put the bags down and gave me a hug. How brave are you, Aleksandar? he asked seriously.

I lose my head rather easily, I said, but that's when I notice things best.

Just hark at him talking, said Milica, but this time she said it in a firmer voice.

You'll manage. Walrus stroked both sides of his moustache and went up to the road junction. Cars stopped, no one hooted. He climbed up on the bonnet of a red Mercedes, made his hands into a trumpet round his mouth and shouted: Višegrad! Hey, I'm back, with the war hard on my heels! Višegrad! he shouted, Višegrad, Walrus is back! Zoran! he shouted, here's your father. Zoran! The war is hard on my heels, but we're a family and no one can harm us!

. . .

First some came, then others, the first of them wondering how we really felt about synagogues, they salted cucumbers and ate breakfast on the Torah shrine and they gathered to discuss the situation in the *schtiebel*, the prayer room, they couldn't make up their minds, then they moved on and the hard winter came, everything froze, the blood in my veins and the tears on my face, because when the others came they didn't wonder about anything, they pushed me over in the snow so that they could go about their work in peace; it's all made of stone, one of them shouted, but we can get at the books; the priests heard that, they went on their knees to the soldiers, fat-bellied priests with girls' eyes lovingly caressed the soldiers' boots, they prayed and begged for mercy for the building and the books and me, but the soldiers had longer beards than the priests, very well, said the drunkest soldier among them, we won't burn anything, we'll take it all out on the lake; the priests thanked them and you could hear the organ playing music in their church, the bass went down low while the synagogue was gutted, they carted everything out on to the frozen lake, the Torah scrolls, my tefillin, my kippa, the Talmud, the old, old books, and when the synagogue was as empty as their hearts they dragged me over the snow and ice by my legs and tied me to the Torah shrine in the middle of the lake, don't you worry, Jew, spring will come soon, they laughed, and they called to me from the bank to make sure that I could see every girl before they flung her into the synagogue, so that I'd have seen her alive before they brought her out to me, dead, hours or days later; we'll spend the winter here, they sang, they slaughtered pigs in front of the bima, they posted guards by the lake so that I couldn't escape and so that they'd be told when the ice began to give way; the priests fed me with bread, they cleaned me up, it grew warmer every day, the snow melted, the full moon was never redder at

Pessach, I could see the flowers coming up on the bank, and I heard the thin ice creak under the priests' quick footsteps; the soldiers didn't want to move on until I and the sacred objects had sunk, the war wasn't going to run away from them; the sun came and went, the ice held, and the soldiers, getting impatient, threatened my neck with their knives, but they threatened from the bank because they didn't trust themselves on the ice any more, the youngest of them, wanting to prove himself, had to be rescued, he went in right beside the bank, and I knew: this ice will hold out through the summer if it has to, hunger will kill me before the lake does, for I believe with all the faith in me that the Creator, praise be to his name, does good to all who obey his commandments and evil to all who break them; they shot at me a few times and hit the shrine, I remembered the priests in my prayers to the very last when I fell asleep with no strength left, I was only skin and bone, as light as a song in the morning; the priests woke me, Rabbi Avram, they've gone! they cried happily across the ice, Rabbi Avram? they cried in alarm, because I didn't move; but I stood up, the ropes had worked loose long ago, I walked over the ice on my shaking legs, hunger guided them, I thought of nothing but food, of chewing and tasting it, surely the priests will be able to find something kosher in a hurry, I thought, I was thinking of food and not the Torah scrolls, not the Talmud, not the venerable old books, I brought nothing with me, I went over the lake empty-handed, and the ice broke in the tracks behind me, as if my weight were stepping on it just a little late; I didn't turn round, and when the priests helped me up on to the bank the holes left by my footsteps joined into a single mighty crack in the ice, there was a deafening crash, and now more and more cracks began to split the ice, running into each other and meeting in the middle of the lake, under the Torah shrine which disappeared first, only seconds before everything else sank into the depths, I saved nothing, it was all gone: my name, my dignity, my breath for saying long sentences, my self-respect, my confidence, but as the priests gave me water I knew one thing, I knew that the whole world is only a very short bridge, and we need have no fear of the depths below it.

What we play in the cellar, what the peas taste like, why silence bares its fangs, who has the right sort of name, what a bridge will bear, why Asija cries, how Asija smiles

The mothers have only just called us, in a whisper, to come for supper when soldiers storm the building, asking what's on the menu; they sit down with us at the plywood tables in the cellar. They bring their own spoons, they wear gloves without fingertips. The soldiers insist on joining us, just as they insist on knowing everyone's name, they insist on shooting at the ceiling, they insist on pushing Čika Hasan and Čika Sead downstairs to the cellar and taking them over to someone who wears a headband. But he dunks bread in the pea soup, saying: we needn't insist on that just now. Come quick and sit down, soldiers, supper will get cold, was not what the mothers called. There isn't any room for rucksacks and guns and helmets on the little tables, but Zoran and I are more than ready to make way for the Kalashnikov. What are your names? We have good names, that's why we can wear helmets. I don't know how a helmet can smell of pea soup.

Before the soldiers arrived everything was the way it had been all the time recently. I wasn't allowed out of the cellar after nine-thirty, I wasn't allowed to pull Marija's braids, but I pulled them all the same, I had to eat peas although these peas tasted of beans. And at nine-thirty on the dot this morning, the same as every morning over the last nine days, the noise began. Heavy guns, people said, nodding, and they named them by their letters and numbers, VS-128; T84. Čika Sead and Čika Hasan argued about which letter and number was shooting where, and whether it had scored a hit. In theory, they said. When the department store opposite was hit they said: in practice, and laughed. Čika Sead and Čika Hasan are widowers, both pensioners, always arguing, always laying bets, you seldom see one without the other but you never see the two of them sharing an opinion. The sound of the heavy guns, said Čika Hasan this morning, is coming from Panos; no, said Čika Sead, polishing his glasses with a small cloth, the guns are stationed on Lower Lijeska.

We children like the term 'artillery' better than 'heavy guns'. Edin is best at imitating the sound of the artillery scoring a hit and the machine guns yapping. That's why every team always wants him when we play at artillery in the cellar. Three against three, no bombs allowed, no, Marija, you can't join in, prisoners can be tickled, unlimited ammunition, it's an armistice at the way out to the stairwell. When Edin goes ta-ta-ta-ta-ta he purses his lips and shakes like crazy! The side which has Edin on it nearly always wins. No wonder, what with the salvos he fires and the way he shakes about.

There was a skirmish this afternoon too, even Zoran joined in, as commander of course. Edin was on the other side. Before the first shot was fired the two teams usually ran off in opposite directions to hide in dark corners of the cellar and lie in wait: who's going to leave his position first and storm into the attack? Sometimes no one stormed into the attack, and it got boring – we'd begin playing marbles and forget that there was a war on. Easy prey for the enemy if he happens to overrun you when your only weapon is a small glass globe held between thumb and forefinger, although mine has a quadruple spiral inside it.

Today we secretly followed the others instead of hiding. They barricaded themselves behind two tubs of sauerkraut and a rusty old bedstead. Zoran peered around the corner, and Nešo took his Winchester repeating rifle off his shoulder. That Winchester won't do, we'd told Nešo about a hundred times: an old thing like that is out of place here with its engraved bison and its twelve shots. He might as well bring a bow and arrow, we told him, I shoot more accurately with this, he said. He didn't shoot accurately at all, he just looked peculiar. Before he went to bed in the evening and after he got up in the morning his mother stuck his jug ears to his head with heavy-duty parcel tape. The grey strips of sticky tape always reminded us to tease him, I've no idea what she had against big ears.

Zoran waved at us to come on. Edin and his two companions, Enver and Safet, the watchmaker's sons who always arrived late, were crouching down with their backs to us, drawing women's breasts on the sauerkraut tubs. Zoran put his finger to his lips and went ahead, ducking low, me after him, clutching my gun firmly. It wasn't a quiet approach, I stepped on some pebbles, they made a grinding sound on the rough cellar floor, little explosions, I thought, then Zoran stormed forward. Hurrrraaah! I called, raising my gun. Surprised and alarmed, the defenders retreated before us, groping for their weapons, only Edin stood his ground, turned his head to me, dropped his chalk and raised his machine gun. Before he could purse his lips and begin shaking, I flung myself on him. Did he jump aside? Did he duck? Was he trying to avoid me? I don't know, I couldn't see. We fell to the ground and rolled about together. I shot him in the side, bang bang, you're dead, I shouted, trrrr, trrr, trrr! He said: hang on a minute, I'm bleeding, stood up, put his cupped hand under his nose as if to drink from it, and showed me the blood in the hollow of his hand. It's bleeding, he said, your knee caught me. The blood was running around his mouth and on to his sleeve. How much blood is there in a nose? he asked, and I said: enough to fill four litre bottles.

Nešo looked at his Winchester and shook his head: wow, won't I be glad when we can get out of here and kick a ball about – it's jammed again.

When Edin's mother saw the blood she put her hand in front of her mouth, opened her eyes wide, and dived headlong at her son. Tip your head back, what happened?

Aleks's . . . knee . . . murmured Edin.

Knee! she cried, grabbing Edin by the ear, as if his ear had started the nosebleed, not my knee. She hauled him to the stairs with her, but turned in the doorway as if she'd forgotten something, and so she had – me. It was no use Edin saying it was unintention-al, her fury was now directed at my ear too, and she shook me by it until it made a cracking sound.

Soldiers shot the men in the stomach. They fell over forwards, like when you get hit there in volleyball – just like that. I saw it from the upstairs window, Edin fantasised when he came back. He was whispering and holding a towel to his nose. I didn't believe a word he said, but I didn't say anything, and anyway, what soldiers? Čika Aziz, the only man with a gun anywhere nearby was playing Ghostbusters on his C-64 console at that moment with his mouth wide open, the neighbours were watching him and smoking, and Walrus told him, sounding bored: you've flattened them good and proper, my turn now.

I was planning to show Edin what I thought of his fairy-tale soldiers, but not until his nose had stopped bleeding and his mother wasn't around any more. Edin folded up the towel and showed me how much blood he'd lost. It was a lot, maybe enough for two litre bottles, but I knew you could grow more blood. Edin's mother shook her head. She put her hands on her hips and paced up and down in front of me. She was jingling all over. All that jewellery. She frowned, and wagged her forefinger in front of my nose. Her bracelets jangled vigorously. Just you wait! she said through her teeth. But I wasn't ashamed of my knee and I wasn't afraid of her – Edin and I had made it up by now. Just you wait! I waited, and soon she jingled away to join the other mothers and the pans on the stove.

The peas were simmering away on the thank-God-we-still-have-power. Less and less light was falling through the ventilation grille. You could hear occasional shots, now and then a salvo, then silence, then a distant explosion, then rattling again. The noise came from the streets, it wasn't coming from the hills any more. Around seven it was so calm outside that our mothers warned us, keep-quiet-now-keep-quiet! although we weren't saying anything at all. It was all just as usual, except that the silence seemed to weigh down louder. Why was everyone listening to the silence?

The silence is baring its fangs, whispered Walrus. He usually said that about the sun in April when it shines without warming you. Even when the mothers called: supper-time! it sounded as if they were whispering.

The grandfathers put their heads together over a little transistor radio. I wished Grandpa Slavko was among them. What would he say now that everything had turned to untold silence? It was a long time since there'd been any music on the radio, it was all talk now. At that moment someone with a hoarse voice was saying that our troops were withdrawing from their positions in order to regroup. In silence, the grandfathers propped their elbows on their knees and their heads on their hands, or they got to their feet and leaned on their sticks, shaking their heads. Everyone was feverishly following our troops and their positions, even though no one knew exactly who these troops of ours were, and what kind of important positions had to be abandoned. Only when the hoarse voice mentioned a town with exactly the same name as ours did everyone know something. Even I knew a little – the hoarse voice said 'Višegrad' like something you wouldn't be safe from wherever you hid. So this was the knowledge baring its fangs in the silence. I arranged the marbles from my pockets side by side on the floor, running from light to dark, then trod on them. Every single marble had to crunch.

The mothers told us what else we should know. Drink only boiled water, be in the cellar from nine-thirty onwards, don't go breaking Čika Aziz's C-64 records when he's got his gun around. When the hoarse voice on the radio said Višegrad, and I wondered: how can a town fall, wouldn't there have to be an earthquake? even the mothers didn't know what to do. They salted the peas and stirred the pan.

Outside, a wedding party broke the silence, hooting horns. Zoran, Edin and I slipped out of the cellars – first into the stairway, for a cautious look out of the window, then into the yard, then into the street. No one stopped us, but we could already hear the mothers calling behind us. What was all this about? Bearded bridegrooms in camouflage jackets and tracksuit trousers drove past. Cross-country vehicles hooted, heavy trucks hooted. An army of bearded bridegrooms drove by, shooting at the sky to celebrate taking their bride, our town. Bridegrooms on the roofs and bonnets of the vehicles swayed in time to the potholes in the roads that they'd made themselves from nine-thirty in the morning onwards, every day for nine whole days. They shielded their eyes with their hands, they squinted out from under them, avoiding the setting sun. Legs in green and brown hung out of the backs of trailers, dangling like decorations.

The first tanks chugged up the street. Their tracks scored white grooves in the asphalt and turned concrete to gravel where they drove over the pavement. There was no holding us now: who oils those, then, why do they squeal like that? I shouted, and we were running towards the tanks – we could run faster than anyone! The mothers held on to their long skirts and wailed after us, we were running so fast towards the tanks. Who's driving them, what does the steering wheel look like, can we come too? Clattering past the gardens, clattering past the yards where there are cases standing ready and people desperately cramming them into car boots and stacking them on car roofs. What a whimpering and trilling sound there was under those metal fists, forefingers outstretched! Even the bridge sagged under those toothed gearwheels, the arches of the bridge will break, Granny Katarina's china is nothing to that. We stopped in the little park by the bridge where the statue of Ivo Andrić used to stand before it was torn down. We wanted to hear how loud the bridge would sound when it broke.

The mothers raced up to us, mine gave me a slap in the face, and she really meant it. She knew I'd have followed the tanks right over to the other side. The slap was still making my head ring, like the tiled roofs vibrating as the tanks passed. I put my hand to my cheek and listened to the steel centipedes grating the street into dust.

The bridge held.

Our mothers dragged us back to the cellar, Edin by his ear, me by my sleeve.

Asija, my Asija, hadn't run after the vehicles with us. She was sitting on the bottom step of the stairs where you go when you've run out of ammunition. That's in the rules of the game: the way out to the stairs means an armistice. I sat down beside her, rubbed my smarting cheek, she rubbed her eyes. I said: gun barrels. I said: camouflage colours. I said: faster than Edin. Asija got up and ran up the stairs, crying.

Asija had cried once before, two days ago. She had cried until she fell asleep with her hand in mine. Asija's Uncle Ibrahim had been shot when he went to shave in Čika Hasan's bathroom and moved his head close to the mirror. He was shot in the neck through the little bathroom window, and his chin was grazed too. And I could hear it through the door, Čika Hasan told the others, Ibrahim struggled for air for minutes on end, fought for air as if he were trying to take a never-ending breath and tell us about all the things that lie ahead. But I didn't have any air to give Ibrahim, said Čika Hasan, lowering his voice, and he climbed down to death without beginning his story. Čika Hasan showed us how he'd raised his hands, because everyone else was just standing around Ibrahim, and Hasan told us how he'd closed Ibrahim's eyes, because there was blood everywhere sticking to Ibrahim's head and the tiles and the mirror. Blood everywhere, he said – blood the colour of cherries everywhere, that's how I imagined it dripping off the fingers that had been digging into Ibrahim's throat so that he could get some air.

I would have run straight after Asija if the mothers hadn't called us to supper for the second time, and if there hadn't been the sound of breaking glass in the stairwell, and all the silence vanished because of the shots and shouting and cursing. Asija is crying because soldiers' fists smell of iron, never of soap. Because the soldiers' guns are hanging around their necks, and doors give way when they kick them in as if there were no locks on them at all. Asija is crying because that's the way soldiers kicked in the doors in her village too, she's crying, and she'll be hiding in the storeroom where we chase mice, where there's dust on the glass cases, and bikes stand about getting rusty. I'll go and find my Asija there any moment now.

Here in the cellar the mothers are ladling out peas for us and the soldiers. The one with the black headband breaks the bread and hands it round – I'm not going to touch that bread with the dirt from under his nails on it.

The hoarse voice on the radio says: Višegrad.

The soldier with the headband says: OK, we heard, and stands up.

The voice on the radio says: fallen after a bitter struggle.

The soldier scratches himself under his headband: all right, that'll do. And he gets ready to take a run at it.

The voice on the radio rises: but our troops are regrouping!

The soldier murmurs: hm, interesting, but somehow kind of . . . irresponsible. Or do you lot want another punch in the gob? He kicks the little black box, hard, and the voice on the radio says nothing more. The soldier throws the bent aerial and one of the knobs at the grandfathers' feet: something for the do-it-yourself lot, if any of you can repair it I'll buy it off him. And he sits down again. And you there! More bacon in the peas! I'll never get a bellyful this way! Life would be a poor thing without bacon. You – yes, you over there – you go and cut me some bacon. And he points his spoon at Amela from the second floor. Amela with the long black braids lays strips of raw meat over the soldier's hand, trying to cover it. Hey, did you make that dress yourself? the soldier asks Amela, licking the meat, say yes and I'll kiss your clever fingers. Don't even think of saying no.

Amela bakes the best bread in the world. She says nothing. Čika Hasan and Čika Sead, who are twisting their caps in their hands as they stand in front of the plywood tables, can't answer any of the soldier's questions either.

Eci-peci-pec . . . The soldier with the headband recites a counting-out rhyme, and ends with his finger pointing at Čika Sead, takes his glasses off him and breathes on the lenses. A man wearing a stocking mask ties Čika Sead's hands behind his back with wire.

Please, Čika Sead begs the soldiers, please don't . . . but the headband puts the glasses on himself.

Another shot in the stairwell; the echo mingles with anxious people's voices. The rushing sound of the voices comes down to the

93

cellar, like when you hold a seashell to your ear. I don't hear Asija's voice, I must find Asija. I catch up with the soldiers who are taking Čika Sead away, I'm still the fastest in the stairwell. The soldiers are chasing up and down in camouflage colours, bawling: get down! Get out! No! Papers! No! Hands up! What? Papers! What's your name? What's your name? Taking three steps or seven steps at once. Going into living rooms that smell of apple compote. Rummaging around in white bedrooms. Rocking the wardrobes, drawers, chests. Smearing the doors with their words, with crosses and double-headed birds, out out out, everybody out! I keep hearing soldiers' orders through the seashell. Faces are pushed up against the wall, arms are pushed up above heads against the cracked plaster. The soldiers call out a name, the person they're looking for. I don't know these soldiers, but I know the name very well – Aziz.

When soldiers curse, the stairwell whimpers. When they get noisy, when they bellow, when they break things, when they hit people, when they shout abuse, when they call for Aziz, Aziz, you fucking bastard! the seashell in the stairwell begs: please stop! I count the steps up to the loft out loud, as loud as I can, but I still hear it all. I see. I see Čika Muharem on the second floor, Čika Husein and Čika Fadil on the third floor, their heads pushed hard against the banisters of the stairs by the soldiers. The backs of their necks are pushed from above with rifle butts, from the side with boots. Čika Fasil's cap is lying on the floor. I run past, I don't say hello to the neighbours, I go on counting, counting. No one is pushing Mr Popović the music teacher's head against anything. Mr Popović wears a suit and a bow tie, his wife Lena has a pearl necklace over her black blouse. Arms crossed over his chest, Mr Popović asks one of the soldiers: what do you want, gentlemen? We're all honest folk here.

We want you to keep your mouth shut! Shut your gob and nothing will happen. And Mr Popović the music teacher keeps his mouth shut.

I just want to find Asija, and I keep my mouth shut too so that nothing will happen. I want to get to Asija as fast as I can, she'll be frightened, she'll be crying again, I'll find her in the attic with all the brooms and cobwebs in among the empty bottles and the mice that you never get to see but you always hear. I burst through the attic door, Asija gives a start and stands back against the wall. It's you, it's you! Quick, close the door, quick or they'll find us! Tell me, will they find us? Asija puts her arms out to me and asks, sobbing: did you see my mama and my papa with the soldiers? Did my mama and papa maybe come back with those stupid soldiers? They took them away because they have the wrong sort of name. Asija doesn't know where her parents would be coming back from: no one knows, she whispers, and no one must know we're here! If the soldiers find you they'll take your papers, and if you have the wrong sort of name they'll drive you away in the truck with the green tarpaulin. Like Mama and Papa. Oh, perhaps, says Asija, suddenly raising her head from my hands and calling out, amidst still more tears, perhaps the soldiers will take me to Mama and Papa if I tell them my name, do you think? Perhaps it would be good for me to have the wrong sort of name just now, do you hear what I'm saying?

I hear what she's saying – and I hear footsteps coming closer. I hear heavy boots, and I know I have the right sort of name. And although the soldier with the yellow beard is grinning, although he doesn't smell of sweat and schnapps like the others, although he only wants us to go back into the stairwell, I shout at him: my name is Aleksandar and this is my sister Katarina, this is Katarina, she's only my sister Katarina!

My granny's name can't be wrong, I'm sure of that. The soldier looks round the attic, the floorboards whimper under his boots. Out of here, you two! He speaks quietly, his fingers are working away in his beard, a thick yellow beard eating its way over his face. Asija hesitates. The soldier crouches down in front of her, his beard touches her cheek. She turns her head away. The soldier breathes into her girlish face. The soldier whispers: stand up! I think: stand up, oh please, stand up! Slowly Asija stands up and leaves the loft. I follow her, the soldier closes the door, you two don't move from this spot, understand?

We're in the fifth-floor corridor and we don't move from the

95

spot. Asija rubs her cheek. My mother calls my name up the stairs. Aleksandar, come down at once!

You two stay here, the soldier orders.

It's not the mothers telling us what we need to know now, it's the soldiers. I call back: Katarina is with me.

Mother asks no more questions.

We wait. Everyone is waiting. How long and what for no one knows. Grown-ups and older kids won't let go of the really tiny children. They are rocked back and forth in the crook of an arm, they whine. Ssh is the answer they get to everything. A fat soldier looks at us as if we've stolen something. Shots are heard somewhere close by, there you go, says the fat soldier. We nod and sit down beside Čika Hasan, who is tied up.

Night hangs in the window at the end of the corridor. Engines are revving and soldiers are singing outside. Čika Hasan says: they're going on west, further into the interior, in theory. Čika Sead isn't there to contradict him.

The bridegrooms in our building aren't in a mood to celebrate any more. They wearily walk up and down above us and among us and under us. One of them sings a sad song, they all know it, he sings alone and falls asleep singing. Two more soldiers come up to our floor with a plastic bag and a pan, one of them shows his crooked teeth and puts his finger in the sleeping singer's ear. He takes bread, salt and beer out of the bag. He unwraps the aluminium foil from two roast chickens. The pan is steaming; boiled potatoes. Large knives with jagged blades and notched handles; they don't need plates.

All the doors on the fifth floor are either open or lying flat – you have to walk over the doors to get into an apartment. Two soldiers are going into the one where Čika Sead used to live. Table legs scrape over the wooden floor but the table won't fit through the door frame. So the soldiers stand around, two inside, one outside, now what? The hungriest of them is already gnawing a chicken leg as he stands there. The two who are inside Čika Sead's apartment sit down at one side of the table and the other one sits down at it out in the corridor. That's the way to do it. Soldiers dig their fingers into the chicken meat, pick it up with their jagged knives, eat the chicken off the points of their knives.

Every couple of minutes the light in the stairwell goes off. We wait enveloped in darkness for seconds on end. Not enough time to get used to seeing outlines in the dark. Someone switches the light straight back on again. Each moment of darkness is a small disappearance, a small convalescence. In one of those dark moments Asija whispers: don't forget me! The forgetting tickles my earlobe, I don't know why she says that, why she says it just now, I don't know what to answer. The light comes back to life, Asija is winding hair around her finger. Tears have drawn dirty veins on her cheeks.

Every time the neon tubes come on there's a powerful blinking, but nothing really wakes up. The soldiers don't go away, they take off their boots and look at their toes. The waiting never comes to an end.

Asija and I are thirsty, they let us into Čika Sead's apartment. Nothing in it is closed, no door, no window, no cupboard, no dresser, no drawer – there's not a single secret left in here. Knives and forks and plates and cups and seasonings are lying on the carpet, and a single large shoe. Someone's poured milk into it.

I wash Asija's face.

Asija washes my face.

When we're back in the stairwell a woman soldier with a delicate nose, green eyes and bright red hair is standing where we were before, beside Čika Hasan, reading a book. The moments when the light goes off annoy the beautiful soldier and she hits the light switch. She pushes a sofa out of an apartment into the corridor and sits down right below the switch.

Once, just after the red-haired soldier has switched the light on, Asija nods in her direction and begins counting in a whisper. At a hundred and seventeen the light goes off. The redhead hits the switch. Next time we'll be faster, whispers Asija, and she glances at the switch on our side and begins counting again. Surely we just have to be ready for our switch to be faster, but we count, and later we can have a wish for every time we whisper the number at the same time the light goes off. At a hundred we put our hands behind our backs and on our switch, I never take my eye off the redhead on the other side of the corridor, at a hundred and five there's a burst of gunfire outside, at a hundred and eleven I whisper: we can't forget each other as long as we don't lose one another, at a hundred and seventeen the redhead laughs out loud, then darkness catches up with her laughter, I take Asija's hand, we press our switch together. In this victory, which makes her clap her hands in delight, Asija's smile is brighter than any light.

Quiet over there! The woman soldier with the red hair wants to read.

*How the soldier repairs the gramophone, what
connoisseurs drink, how we're doing in written Russian,
why chub eat spit, and how a town can break into splinters*

The mothers pour water into the hollows they've made in the flour,
the soldiers shake hands saying goodbye, one soldier, with a gold
canine tooth, asks: why don't we all wait for the warm bread?,
another says no, adding, to us: we're posting guards, I don't want
anyone leaving this building after eight, don't make the street your
grave, there are better graves to be found. Tired soldiers thump
sleeping soldiers on the shoulder, nudge their noses with the sights
of their rifles, up, up, time to march away, get up! The man with
the gold tooth doesn't want to march away, he wants warm bread.
But hands can't form the dough any more firmly, fingers can't
knead it any faster, doesn't he know that? He doesn't know it, and
it's no help when he asks Amela for soap, rubs the soapy water into
his hands with a metal scourer, and buries his own fingers in the
dough. He puts his arms around Amela's waist, he clasps her hands
in his fists and kneads the dough that way. Amela with her hair in
braids, some strands falling over her face too. With flour on her
cheek and now an anxiously furrowed brow as the soldier listens to
the nape of her neck, puts his ear against it, and from under
Amela's braided hair tells the other women: you go out and close
the door behind you – all of you, now! They close the door, lean
against the wall, give each other cigarettes, spit on their forefingers,
put the spit on the cigarette ends and wipe the tears from their
cheeks. Amela, they whisper, Amela, Amela.

The soldiers were with us for an evening and a night, they
stormed the building and then went straight off to see what they
could find in cupboards and drawers. They drove everyone into the
stairwell, shooting as they yawned, yelling: what idiot has to go on
shooting now? The small children were crying all the time anyway,

99

what with the noise in the stairwell and the plaster crumbling off the ceiling. The little ones cried for their mothers even though they were lying in their arms, were sitting on their laps, were already hugging them. Yells and fine plaster dust. And for Čika Hasan, ropes tying him to the banisters and a rifle butt at his neck: where's your son, old man, where's that misbegotten bastard?

The soldiers were with us through a twilit evening and an unquiet sleep; they slept on our beds, we slept in the stairwell. The guards woke us in the middle of the night, they were playing in the corridor with a chicken bone, two of them against two others. They had parked their tanks in the yard, their dogs had no names and were bad-tempered and fond of children.

The victors march away while the mothers bake bread. One of them comes out of Čika Sead's apartment, ducks his head under the door frame, no helmet in the world would fit that head, it's the biggest head ever, it would need a tub to cover it. A victor's skull like that must weigh as much as two stone slabs, and when the victor blinks a rockfall rolls out of his eyes. The victor shouts at his men and the red-haired woman soldier: there's some fun coming now, men, time to enjoy yourselves.

He's dragging a gramophone along behind him, he's taken hold of it by its horn and lifts it over the threshold as if taking a goose to be slaughtered. The gramophone is toy-sized in his great paw. Any moment now, men! He has Čika Sead's gramophone in his left hand, his shiny, polished Kalashnikov in his right. Any moment now, now, now . . . his voice echoes in the stairwell, and the armed men and people who've been tied up listen. The victor with the biggest head in the world puts the pick-up arm on the record, but nothing happens. Don't you dare! he shouts, hitting and kicking the gramophone. Right, men, I'll get it working in a minute! and he pulls at the knobs, works the switch, shakes the pick-up arm, looks hard at the record, thinks it over and sticks the barrel of his gun in the horn.

If only I were a magician who could make things possible.

There's a crackling from the gramophone. When a hawk kisses a sparrow carefully so as not to hurt it, there must be a tiny sound like that. The needle engages in the groove: accordion! The tune is lurching along too fast, but now the victor adjusts the controls. It's the song everyone knows – nothing can stop you, you have to hug straight away. Normally you have to cling to each other, here and now while the music plays, holding each other tight as you keep in step! But no one moves, only the soldiers raise their guns above their heads and howl along with their dogs. Wailing and rejoicing: yoohooo! Shrill whistles, shouting in competition, yoohoo, louder, rata-rata-rata-ta. Soldiers take each other tenderly around the waist, two steps to the right, one to the left, yoohoo! The victor takes the beautiful redhead by the shoulders, shoots a question mark in the ceiling above her head – they all shoot in answer along with the refrain, and yoohoo! – in wild enthusiasm for the song. They're already swaying in a semicircle, four of them, five of them. Holding on to waists and shoulders: two steps to the right, one to the left, seven of them dancing down the narrow corridor. Two steps to the right – yoohoo! – one to the left, past Čika Hasan, who whispers, sitting tied up there: what times are these when you have to fear dancing and close your ears to songs and music?

The accordion draws the soldiers further into their furious dance, caps are thrown on the floor – yoohoo! – now the voice of the woman singer is briefly heard and the soldiers join in: we're the voice! We're the gramophone! No one can hear the small children crying any more – a whimpering among the throaty, thunderous sound of the army singing along, raging with joy.

The army sings, no one stops them, they sing two to the right and one to the left:

Niška Banja, topla voca, za Nišlije živa zgoda
Sve od Niša pa do Banje, idu cure na kumpanje,
Mi Nišlije meraklije ne možemo bez rakije,
Bez rakije šljivovice i bez mlade cigančice

Isn't that true, men? sings the dance song. Isn't that just the way it is? Girls take a hot bath, we connoisseurs drink slivowitz, we men can't do without slivowitz. The soldier with the gold tooth sings along too, the one who wanted warm bread, the one who held

Amela's hands in his and dipped them in the dough. He comes out of Amela's apartment, the song on his lips, his shirt unbuttoned. Amela is kneeling behind him with a veil of wet hair over her face. The hungry soldier sings louder than any of them: we connoisseurs can't do without a young gypsy girl. There's yellow dough on his fingers and his knuckles and under his nails. He unscrews his hip flask and puts it to his sore lips. Isn't that so, men? We can't do without schnapps and gypsy girls!

If only I were a magician who could make things possible. I'd give objects the gift of defiance; banisters, gramophones, guns, the napes of necks, braided hair.

Fish bite best early in the morning. I gave the worms coffee grounds, I tell Edin, now they're all on a high like Auntie Typhoon. Let's go down to the Rzav to catch some chub first, then we can go to school and see if the place is still standing.

We spit down from the bridge into the little tributary of the Drina. The chub come close to the surface of the water and lick it from below with their fishy lips. Edin spits again, says: a school like ours isn't wrecked so easily, why do you think fish eat spit?

It's going to rain any minute, I say. Maybe this is the last time we'll cross this bridge. Why don't they build a bridge like the one over the Drina? That stands up to anything.

This one will make it, says Edin, it stood up to the tanks.

Want to bet it'll be gone by the day after tomorrow at the latest?

Living at the mouth of two rivers. Learning to swim well and early, learning to fish well and early, learning early how to pump meltwater out of flooded cellars. Last night was a non-stop cloud-burst – the soldiers gave us blankets, but the walls of the stairwell breathed out the cold of cement, and I woke up several times. Light fell into the corridor from Čika Sead's apartment, I made bird shadows fly over the wall with my fingers, and hoped real thunder would break the constant rushing of the rain, but there was only the thunder of explosions in the distance. Grandpa Slavko had shown me how to train the shadow animals you make with your fingers.

Long ago I'd magically given the birds the power to fly my sleep-lessness away to the south. The rain didn't stop until morning, just before the dancing, singing soldiers left the building, but the clouds didn't clear.

If our mothers find out we've gone, I say, you can bet we won't be allowed down to the Rzav when the floods carry the bridge away. What are they afraid of? If their own soldiers are in our town they can't shoot at it.

Edin shrugs his shoulders. Raindrops are making the first ripples on the river. We go and stand under the bridge. I put a worm on my hook and cast it out. Edin pokes around in the mud with a stick for a while, imitating the noise of the rain falling on the river. Our floats drift with the current, it rains harder, and the soldiers ask: are they biting? Three bearded men and the victorious soldier with the biggest head in the world. Where did they spring from?

No. Only minnows. Too much noise for the fish these last few days. They go down into deeper water.

Ah, yes. Hiding. Let's see how well they hide.

The hand grenade sinks at once. The soldiers are wearing rain-coats, they bend forward as they speak. It's bucketing down, it's raining in torrents, more rivers are raining on the river, and now the rain is falling on the fish scales and fish bellies drifting downstream too. No use trying to collect them, the Rzav is too deep here and too fast, still too cold in April as well, and a catch like that would definitely not taste good.

A mongrel emerges from the undergrowth on the opposite bank, drinks from the river.

Want to bet, boys?

No!

The first volley doesn't hit the dog. The dog starts, jumps up, dances sideways, stops and raises its pointed muzzle. Has it caught the scent of the bet?

Bet you fifty I get it this time, says the victor to the bearded men, one of them spits in his hand and shakes on it. How can a head be so big and a bet smell of schnapps and earth?

The second volley of shots.

It must have been a catfish! A hundred kilos, maybe two hundred, Edin guesses on the way to school, spreading his arms wide as if hugging someone: it must have been that big, at least that big!

I know about catfish and I don't believe a word of it. Another reason why your line can break is if the hook gets caught somewhere at the bottom, and catfish are conceited anyway, they're not going to bother with a little river like the Rzav. We've caught two chub, and I wish I knew who's stirring up the clouds like that – the rain has soaked us to the skin.

Soldiers on the porches of buildings, soldiers behind sandbags, soldiers in bars acting as landlords and guests combined. Outside the biggest department store in town we ask: are we allowed in? The soldier clambers out of the display window, says: mind the broken glass, and straps a TV set into his passenger seat. We avoid the splintered glass, although it makes a good crunching noise. We're out shopping, the soldiers, Edin and I. We two take as many pencils and exercise books as we can carry. By the time we get to school they're all wet. We stack the limp paper on the radiators, but what are we going to do with five hundred pencil sharpeners? The way our school looks, we won't be needing those again. We lay a trail of pencil sharpeners down the dark corridors, over splintered glass and rubble, through devastated classrooms. There isn't an intact window in the staffroom, there are towers of tables and a tangle of chair legs in front of the broken windows, and ten thousand empty cartridge cases among a hundred thousand splinters of glass. Our trail of pencil sharpeners meets a trail of blood. Edin and I follow it to a large window and look out at the town in the rain; still no thunder. In the middle of the room there's a mountain of red volumes, shabby class registers. Some teachers asked questions in alphabetical order, others opened at a random page.

Want to see how we're doing in oral Russian? I ask, but there's a huge pile of dried shit on top of the mountain, with two flies making rectangles above it, so we content ourselves with knowing that our mark for written Russian is four, which is kind of alright.

Hey, Edin, why did they shoot the dog like that?

Edin shrugs his shoulders, picks up several cartridge cases and throws them through the broken window one by one. Last summer, he says, I drew a goal down there on the front of the building. With red chalk, standing on tiptoe. The crossbar was so high that I had to lower my arm twice and shake the stiffness out of it. I'd just finished when Kostina the caretaker came out and asked: what's that supposed to be? A goal, of course, I said. Wipe it off, he said, it'll be detention for you.

Didn't you get to shoot at it even once? I ask.

Not once, says Edin, unwedging a couple of chairs. Well, I could have broken a window.

In the lab, our physics teacher Fizo is kneeling in front of another carpet of fragments, and when we get down on the floor beside him he says: there'll be lessons, we just have to clear up first. I've found three intact measuring beakers and two burners. All the pinhole cameras but two are broken, the spring pendulum's all right, most of the light bulbs aren't. Put gloves on and be careful of the glass. Don't touch anything with blood on it.

We have to leave most of it lying there. Fizo removes his glasses, takes a handkerchief out of his shirt pocket, wipes first his eyes and then the glasses. Edin finds an unbroken pipette, holds it up, says good-good-good, and laughs. Fizo nods, yes, good, and gets the broom. We'll go on with lessons in a minute, do you have your exercise books with you? I want to dictate some formulas to you. After that you can go home, right?

Nothing in the lab is in its usual place except for Tito over the board. The more quietly I try to put my feet down, the louder the glass crunches under them. Tito's white admiral's uniform. Tito's German shepherd dog. Tito's right eye: a bullet hole in it. Tito has died yet again, for the fourth time. Shot dead this time.

Trite symbolism, says Fizo.

I can't really take anything seriously under Tito's one-eyed corpse, in a school that isn't a school any more, or if so it's only Fizo's school, the school of his resistance, his energy, his power. I'll look up 'symbolism' later, but only because the word annoys me. I want to know whether one-eyed people would rather be blind in the left eye or the right eye, I want to know how much blood we really have in us, and I want to know if every shot to the throat is fatal. I want to know how many deaths Tito still has to die.

Nothing in the lab is in its proper place. I stand there.

Krsmanović, calls Fizo, aren't you going to help us?

I don't know how, Comrade Jelenić.

I clean the board with the dry sponge. If I were a magician who could make things possible, then glass could decide for itself whether it broke, and Fizo, who is the strictest teacher in the school, would say: good.

Good, says the soldier with the gold tooth when Edin and I turn into our street with the fishing rods, the fish, and the exercise books from the department store. Perhaps our mothers won't have noticed that we were gone, and anyway, we've been to school, that's not a lie. So we just have to get rid of the fish. The first thing we do is hide the rods in the yard.

Good, but what are those fish doing on the roof? asks the soldier as I put the bag with our catch on the roof of the tobacconist's just as he's coming out of the shop, doing up his zip, bread dough on his hands.

They're for the cat, says Edin. A dead loss for humans.

Right, says the soldier, a dead loss, everything's a dead loss, all battles are a dead loss, all my poor corns are a dead loss if I don't find my Emina. Do you two know Emina? Amela isn't my Emina.

I remember Great-Grandpa's song at the harvest festival, I remember vain Emina and her hyacinthine hair. The soldier sits down on the pavement beside a sparse-haired man who wears a flowing white garment. The man's hands are inside a black top hat up to the wrists, and he's fidgeting nervously with it. It's only by his top hat that I recognise the man, his face is so swollen, and he's sitting there so bent over. It's Musa Hasanagić, but where's his mare, Cauliflower?

Please, Musa begs the soldier, please tell me what will happen to her!

106

I feel sorry for horses, says the soldier, licking his cigarette paper, now which war has been the worst for horses? Which war is this one? Nineteen fourteen, nineteen forty-two, nineteen ninety-two . . . once it was horses that died like flies. Now humans are dying like that, but the horses have forgotten how to be free.

Edin digs his elbow into my ribs: let's go! But I can't move, I can't leave while the soldier is talking in that tone, telling stories in that tone. He puts Musa's hat on Musa's head and pushes the cigarette between Musa's lips. He takes a loaf from his rucksack and breaks off large chunks, feeds the old man. Amela's bread. Musa chews toothlessly, handcuffs rattle on his hands.

I've tumbled many girls, says the soldier, and I left only one of them unkissed: my Emina. How she'd eat cherries from my hand! How she'd tickle my wrist with her chin! The soldier bows his head awkwardly and scrapes dough out from under his nails.

Emina escaped you! She escaped you! cries Musa, and his eyes are shining.

There you are, there you are! My mother runs to meet me as Edin and I come into the yard. Listen, Aleksandar, we're leaving. Pack your things. Hurry. A couple of days and we'll be out.

The stairwell's almost empty. Čika Milomir is sweeping the corridor, smoking, dropping ash and sweeping it away again. The doors of most of the apartments are open, our neighbours are clearing up in silence. There's glass everywhere.

Granny Katarina is standing at the open window. Granny?

Edin and I go and stand beside her. Granny?

Four bearded soldiers are trying to throw a horse off the bridge and into the river. They are leading it by the reins. The horse and the soldiers look down into the river over the railings of the bridge. The soldiers are pushing hard. The horse stands there. It's not going to clamber over the railings by itself, I'm sick and tired of this obstinate nag, shouts one of the bearded men like someone who's hard of hearing, and he holds his pistol to the white blaze on the horse's forehead. The soldiers smoke. The soldiers pat the horse's nostrils. The soldiers lead the horse off the bridge and back to the bank.

Oh, just shoot it for Christ's sake, a soldier with sunglasses calls to them. He's playing with a Gameboy on his tank, which is wet after the rain.

You shoot horses when they can't work any more, cries the man with the reins in his hand, leading the horse into deeper water, we want to see it drown.

Cauliflower likes to eat cauliflower, says Granny. Wherever else would you hear of a horse with a name like that?

Musa Hasanagić used to wear the top hat when he trained his mare Cauliflower. Edin and I often watched. The gramophone played *Boléro* and the mare would walk around in time to the music, trotting with her head held high. Half-pass! cried Musa, tapping his top hat. Passage, he cried. He clicked his fingers, and Cauliflower would turn round on the spot.

A shot rings out, the horse shies, Granny jumps. Oh, if my Slavko had seen this, she whispers behind her hand, his heart wouldn't have stopped, it would have broken into ten thousand pieces.

The soldier with dough on his hands is walking in a leisurely way across the street, Musa's hat on his head, carrying the bag with our fish in it. I press my face into Granny's side. She ought to send Edin and me away from the window, she ought to close the window. She whispers: Cauliflower, what an ugly name for such a beautiful creature.

The beautiful creature shies, the beautiful creature bucks, the beautiful creature kicks out at the soldiers with her forelegs, the beautiful creature tears free, the beautiful creature races through the water towards the bank. Three bearded soldiers are standing on the bank smoking, look-no-hands, their guns raised to fire.

Trembling, I step back from the window and put my hands over my ears. I stumble backwards out of the room, I pack my rucksack. Edin helps, silent and serious. I quickly get three last pictures of unfinished things down on paper and hide them behind Granny Katarina's wardrobe with the rest – ninety-nine in all. Pictures of

Emina far away from the soldier with the gold tooth. Of Cauliflower galloping off, no fences in sight. Of pistols that were never loaded.

I meet my father in the stairwell, he's racing upstairs, nods to me as if he were a mere acquaintance. There are damp patches under his arms. I call Asija's name on every floor, but get no answer. I stuff my things into the heap on the back seat of our heavily laden Yugo, which now looks like the other cars that have given up on Višegrad these last few days. Nena, do you have enough air back there? Nena Fatima smiles at me, and the bag with my painting things falls into her lap. I want to take my football, Mother shakes her head, so I pass it to Edin. Father and Granny come out of the building, Granny, in tears. She kisses her women neighbours, they're in tears too, then stops in front of one of the soldiers on guard. She looks him up and down, she stands on tiptoe to hiss something into his ear. The soldier gives a nasty grin and shrugs. Granny squeezes herself into the back seat beside Nena Fatima.

Edin has stopped the ball with the sole of his foot. He takes a piece of chalk out of his trouser pocket and twirls it in his fingers. He jiggles up and down on the bent garage door that a tank smashed yesterday when it was trying to park. A soldier climbed out, examined the damage, cursing, wiped his sleeve over the metalwork and drove away. The door fell off its hinges and the little panes in it broke. Edin imitates the sound of the door breaking and stirs the fragments with the toe of his shoe. One way or another, he says, the whole town is breaking up into splinters. Are you going now too?

Only for a little while, I say, and I have to swallow.

So we never will cross the bridge again together. I bet you, he calls, already waving, there won't be another flood this year. It can't come, he shouts, there can't be one, not another flood, he weeps, how could there be? A town without its people or its bridges, bridges with us standing on them to feed fish with our spit, how could there be? he says – or perhaps he says it, because I can't hear him any more, I look in the rear-view mirror and I can see him drawing the goalposts with his chalk, the crossbar so high that he has to give his hand a good shaking twice. He sends the ball flying, top left, stops the ball in mid-turn, a bouncing ball, going halfway up to the right – every shot a goal, until rain washes the chalk away.

Emina carried through her village in my arms

I carried Emina through her village in my arms, says the soldier with gold in his mouth and dough on his hands, I carried Emina's weight from house to house, gravely and saying little. Her arms around my neck so that she wouldn't fall. Kicking wardrobe doors open with my boots, looking at thousands of dresses, touching hundreds of fabrics, until at last I found the right one for my Emina in a chest made of the darkest cherry-wood. Softer than silk, white as snow for Emina's white skin and her black hair. I carried that wonderfully beautiful material and my wonderfully beautiful gypsy girl to the village square. My comrades gave the thirsty villagers water and herded them into the trucks.

What are you doing? I shouted to my companions. You can't do that yet! I need a dressmaker, I need someone to play music for me and my bride! I sang the song, and the company, all in chorus, agreed that I was right. I told dressmakers to feel the material, holding the end of it well above the ground, no dirt was to get on it except the dirt of these hands of mine. I told musicians to rescue their instruments from the flames: who's lighting fires now? We're going to have a wedding here at first light! Are you the accordionist, old man, is it your fast fingers they all talk about? Dressmaker, can you make this material into a dress for Emina, a finer dress than anyone ever wore? Old man, good dressmaker, do you want to save your lives?

Just let my daughter and my grandson live, begged the old man. Just let my sister and her little ones live, whispered the dressmaker, and she kissed the white fabric. The trucks drove away, and as soon as they had left the village the guns began chattering.

Why all that shooting? I cried when my comrades came back five minutes later, hitting the driver's ear with the flat of my hand, don't do that again! Don't you ever do that again! Drive them further into the forest!

You idiot, said the driver flatteringly, hitting me back, get your gun, you idiot! We're under attack! And then there's shooting and standing firm and securing the bridge and ten on our flank and get away from the flames and there's the radio operator and where are the heavy machine guns and Vladimir cries no and runs and Mayday, Mayday, please come in we're under fire there's explosions and Vladimir and Dule on the ground with Vladimir twitching and get back and stay close together men get back and there are hits and rubble and blood trickling through fingers just leave him there – don't leave me here – we retreat and when night falls and the battle's over I call Emina's name into the dark and there's no answer. Has she taken the dress material with her? Is she wandering through the burning countryside with the dressmaker and the old musician? We abandoned the village and I've been looking for my Emina ever since, I can never rest.

The soldier picked dry bread dough off his fingers. He sat there with his wet, bare torso beside old Musa, playing with Musa's handcuffs. Emina, Emina, he whispered, Emina.

26 April 1992

Dear Asija,
If my Grandpa Slavko were still alive, I'd ask him what we ought to be most ashamed of now.

I'm writing to you because I couldn't find you, I was ashamed of the earth itself for carrying the tanks that came to meet us on the road to Belgrade. My father hooted at every tank, every jeep and every truck. If you don't hoot, they stop you.

They did stop us at the Serbian border. A soldier with a crooked nose asked if we had any weapons in the car. Father said: yes, petrol and matches. The two of them laughed and we were allowed to drive on. I didn't see what was so funny about that, and my mother said: I'm the weapon they're looking for. I asked: why are we driving into the enemy's arms? and then I had to promise not to ask any more questions for the next ten years.

The rain never stopped, the road was jammed, we kept coming to a halt. Once, armed men wearing masks and white gloves were walking along behind two other men, beside the column of vehicles. The men were gagged, their eyes were blindfolded, and I wanted to promise to wipe that memory out for the next ten years, but Granny Katarina wasn't in favour of forgetting. To Granny, the past is a summer-house with a garden full of twittering thrushes and twittering women neighbours, and you can draw coffee from a well while Grandpa Slavko and his friends play hide and seek. And the present is a road that leads away from the summer-house, swarming with tank tracks, smelling of heavy smoke, killing horses, dogs, horses, people. You have to remember them both, Granny whispers to me from the back seat, the time when everything was all right and the time when nothing's all right.

We got away, Asija, and our acquaintances in Belgrade embraced us, first as if we were oak trees, then as if we were the most fragile glass, and I hope all of you in Višegrad can get away and be hugged too.

Višegrad was on the TV straight away but the people who are defenders on our TV at home are the aggressors here, and the town didn't fall, it was liberated, because a madman and not a hero was trying to blow up the dam. The newsreader said: schools and factories have gone back to work. But not the people at the telephone exchange, apparently – we only ever get the engaged signal.

Nena Fatima cast the beans for Granny Katarina, and read Granny Katarina's future from them without words. I asked my deaf mute Granny what she really wants. Nena took no notice of me. I said: not telling me now could mean traumas for me with far-reaching consequences later. When Mother asked me where I got that from I told her: no idea.

Asija, can you read the beans?

Granny Katarina wants to go back to her home and her friends in Višegrad. Father didn't try to persuade her not to, Mother shouted when she heard that Father was keeping quiet about it.

Father wants to keep quiet about it.

Mother wants to shout.

I wonder what Uncle Miki wants. No one knows where he is.

I want to listen to a story from another world or another time, but everyone just keeps talking about now and asking: now what? If I were to tell a story of this time and this world, after I'd told it, I'd have to promise never to do such a thing again for the next ten years. It would begin like this: no sooner have the mothers called us in to supper in whispering voices than soldiers storm the building, they ask what's for supper, they sit down beside us at the plywood tables in the cellars.

I don't have to invent anything to tell a story of another world and another time.

Tonight I heard Mother sighing in her sleep, she woke up with congealed blood under her nose. There are problems with the neighbours because we're living so close to them and they don't like us living close. If they'd been given a war too, they'd have shot us at once. Religion is not the opium of the people but their downfall. So Father says, anyway. A boy in the street called me a bastard. My Serbian blood was contaminated by my Bosniak mother, he said. I didn't know whether to hit him for that or be defiant and proud. I was neither defiant nor proud, and I was the one who got hit.

I'm sending you a picture with this, Asija. It's you in the picture. I'm afraid I can't get any paint as beautiful as the colour of your hair, so you may not recognise yourself. It's my last picture of something unfinished. It's unfinished because you're alone in it. I used to like unfinished things.

With love from
Aleksandar

Dear Asija,

I wanted to write to you from the Lake Wörther – trains have names in Germany – but the Lake Wörther went so fast that my eyes couldn't keep up with the landscape, and I felt slightly unwell with so many quick fields and houses and a packet of round chocolate-covered biscuits that I also polished off too quickly. For the last two weeks we've been living with my Uncle Bora and my Auntie Typhoon in a city called Essen, right next to a motorway. Granny Katarina has gone back to Višegrad. I want to be near my husband, she said.

Where he is he doesn't need anyone, said my father.

Everyone needs someone, and the dead are the loneliest of all, I said, and I had to go out of the room. We still haven't heard from Granny. Getting through on the phone is difficult.

Nena Fatima has had a secret ever since we left Belgrade. She's writing something all the time, but she hides it under her headscarf. If I could choose a voice for Nena Fatima, it would be the voice of a superior kind of witch who has something to laugh about before the fairy tale ends happily: a little rough, self-confident and full of plans. Would my Nena say clever things if she were to speak? What would her singing sound like?

New Year's Eve was a disaster. I got a pair of jeans as a present. Uncle Bora bought rockets and bangers, and we put coloured hats on and turned up our music louder than usual. My mother said: whatever I cook, it doesn't taste right. My father said: whatever I drink, it doesn't help, and he buried his face in his hands. This was just before midnight. At twelve everyone hugged everyone else, then Uncle Bora and I let the fireworks off, and little Ema the baby typhoon woke up and yelled.

What was it like for you? Do you have snow there? We do here, but only for five minutes, and it looks as if it got dirty even while it was falling, it's already brown when it lands on the ground.

Tomorrow I start at a German school. I'm going to try not to be a deaf mute like Nena Fatima, so I've learnt the first ten pages of the dictionary by heart. Uncle Bora says I'm three years ahead of the Germans in maths. Subtract my lack of talent for maths from that and I'm still one year ahead. School marks work the wrong way round here, and there's almost no one but Turks in our part of town. You can play Nintendo in the department stores; I haven't yet managed to get locked into one and be forgotten overnight, but I'm working on it. My mother didn't feel well last week, but she couldn't tell the doctor what her pain was like, so she came back feeling even worse.

Five or six other families from Bosnia live in this building with us, twenty-five people on two floors. It's very crowded, there's always someone else in the bathrooms, and I can switch off Čika Zahid's TV set with my uncle's remote control, it sends him mad. He believes in Nazi ghosts. There's a little railway station very close, and Čika Zahid waits for the green light to cross the rails there. I go bobsleighing under the motorway bridge on sofa cushions with his son Sabahudin. After he arrived, Sabahudin cleaned his teeth with shaving foam for the first three days.

Yesterday we got a permit to be in Germany. We waited at the letter K for three hours, in a big office with a hundred doors. The people waiting spoke our language, which we're not to call Serbo-Croat any more. They gathered around the ashtrays and left slush on the floor and the marks of the soles of their shoes on the walls. Mrs Foß was looking after us Ks. She smiled wearily, had little dimples, and a pink brooch that had bitten into the collar of her pink blouse. A mouse called Diddl grinned out at us from postcards all over the K room. Mrs Foß was the friendliest, most patient person in the world, she smiled like her mouse and gave my mother a handkerchief. We couldn't say much but we didn't have to, Mrs Foß knew what to do with us. We got our passports stamped because Mrs Foß agreed to having us here. 'ß' is my favourite letter of the alphabet now and a very good invention, because it has two letter 's's in it I'd like to be called Alekßandar Krßmanović. As I went out I said to Mrs Foß: A, aardvark, aback, abacus, abandon, abase, abash, abate, abbey, abbreviate, abdicate, abdomen, abduct, aberration, abhor, thank you. I knew 'thank you' even though I hadn't got that far in the dictionary yet.

We all sleep in this little room, Asija, and we're all a little angrier than we were at home, even in our dreams. Sometimes I wake up and make bird shadows on the wall with my fingers; a street light outside the window looks sternly in at us as if it were keeping watch, and Uncle Bora promised he'd knock that filthy glaring bastard down. There's no financial priority for curtains, or for a canvas and paints for Father, but Mother and he are looking for work.

Last night Auntie Typhoon woke up for a moment beside me. She's slower now, my beautiful speedy fair-haired aunt who has tears in her eyes full of love for her daughter Ema and a thousand good wishes to spare for everyone. In the bright light coming from outside I counted the weariness in her face, all the lines and shadows. She smiled at me and whispered: Aleks, no one else has a head like yours, my sunshine, don't be afraid.

Don't be afraid, Asija! I wish so much that I had more memories of you, I wish I had memories of you as long as a journey from Essen to Višegrad and back. You'd be coming back with me this time.

Coot is the funniest word I've learnt here in Germany so far.

With love from
Aleksandar

17 July 1993

Dear Asija,

I know from Granny Katarina that you got away to Sarajevo last winter. She gave me this address too. She couldn't tell me whether you got my first two letters, she said hardly any post was arriving, and no parcels, but letters were disappearing without trace as well.

SO I AM SENDING 17 MARKS 20 PFENNIGS IN THIS LETTER, IT'S ALL I HAVE. DEAR WHOEVER-OPENS-THIS-LETTER, KEEP THE MONEY, BUT PLEASE IN RETURN SEAL THE ENVELOPE UP AGAIN AND SEND IT ON. THERE'S NOTHING BUT WORDS IN IT, AND SOMEONE MISSING SOMEONE ELSE, AND IT DOESN'T GIVE MILITARY SECRETS AWAY BECAUSE I'M ONLY 1 METRE 60 TALL, SO NO ONE EVER TELLS ME ANY MILITARY SECRETS. BUT I WOULD LIKE TO SAY SOMETHING VERY IMPORTANT TO SOMEONE VERY IMPORTANT, AND I DON'T MIND IF YOU READ THE REST OF IT JUST AS LONG AS YOU DON'T THROW THE LETTER AWAY AFTERWARDS. THANK YOU VERY MUCH!

Dear Asija, my mother is working in a laundry and has less time to be unwell now. She says it's so hot in that hellish laundry that her brain boils. Mother has lost the ability to see things in a good light. She's chain-smoking, she smokes like the chimneys of Essen. Father is working in the same place as Uncle Bora. They're both out and about all day. They're working in the black economy. That means doing work that breaks your back and at the same time it makes you a criminal, even though you're not really stealing anything.

Nena Fatima fits in best. She cooks for us all, she takes long baths, and I can't see any sorrow in her face. Once I caught her whistling, and it sounded amazingly beautiful, considering that she doesn't really make any sounds at all. She's made friends with the girls at the supermarket and takes them coffee at their cash desks every day. In return, she can pinch things that cost less than five marks and the girls at the cash desks pretend not to notice.

I still haven't found out her secret, she writes and writes, the paper is scribbled all over, right to the edges. When my parents are talking about things we don't have, like health and money and our home in Višegrad, I always have to go out of the room, and Nena Fatima stands guard at the doorway to make sure I don't listen. The things I'm not allowed to hear are the worst of all.

If I'm asked where I come from, I say that's a difficult question, because I come from a country that doesn't exist any more, not where I used to live. Here they call us Yugos, they call Albanians and Bulgarians Yugos too, it's simpler for everyone.

I've had my first school report, still without any marks except in maths, and that's not worth mentioning. It's enough to say that my head start over the others disappeared very quickly. In German we had to write an essay on the subject of 'Essen, I love you', and I wrote about how we make börek at home. We all had to read our essays aloud, and when it was my turn the class laughed itself silly. To understand that, you have to know that in German *Essen* means *hrana*, food. I knew that, but because I don't like the city of Essen, I thought I'd write about börek made with minced meat and yufka dough. And that was quite difficult, because I didn't know the German for minced meat, and just try explaining minced meat to someone if you don't know the word for it. The other Bosnians in the class copied down the recipe and took it home, because they thought there ought not to be onions in börek, and you should use flaky pastry. Josip and Tomislav, two boys from Croatia, said there wasn't any börek where they came from. Can you imagine that, Asija? A country without any börek?

I miss the moody Drina, Asija, apparently there's a river here, it's called the Ruhr, but I don't think just any watercourse that happen to flow along deserves the name of a river.

Yesterday I was playing the city-country-river game with Philipp, Sebastian and Susanne, and I didn't come last with Duisburg,

Denmark, Drina, day-lily, dentist and Dalmatian. I'm not sure how to explain a day-lily to you, and yesterday for the first time I couldn't remember a Bosnian word, the word for a birch tree, I had to look it up: 'breza'. There are birch trees in a park here called the Kruppwald. All Essen is really one huge garage, you have to be grateful to the weeds between the paving stones for growing at all.

Birch trees and day-lilies and water milfoil and gentian and the Ruhr. I'm noticing everything, Asija. I'm collecting words in my new language. Collecting helps to make up for the hard answers and sad thoughts I have when I think of Višegrad. I can't put them all into stories without having Grandpa Slavko near me, but I'm trying. You didn't know Grandpa Slavko, he was the only person who could have explained your hair.

On the morning of her return to Višegrad, my granny gave me an empty book. She had written on the first page herself. Together with the story by Andrić in which Aska dances with the wolf until the wolf is dizzy, and so escapes alive, I treasure that one page by my granny more than anything I've ever read.

Asija, I don't remember the birch trees. I feel as if one Aleksandar stayed behind in Višegrad and Veletovo by the Drina, and there's another Aleksandar living in Essen and thinking of going fishing in the Ruhr some time. In Višegrad, back there with his unfinished pictures, there's an Aleksandar who began and never finished. I'm not Comrade-in-Chief of the unfinished any more, the unfinished is Comrade-in-Chief of me. I don't paint any more unfinished pictures. I'm writing stories in Granny's book about the time when everything was all right, so that later I can't complain of having forgotten it. If I were a magician who could make things possible, Asija, good memories would have a taste. The best of them would taste the way Stela ice cream tasted back then. Do you remember me?

Aleksandar

8 January 1994

Dear Asija,
Nancy Kerrigan's knee got injured with an iron bar in figure-skating practice. Her rival Tonya Harding had something to do with the attack. It was on the news just now, and my mother left the living room in a temper. After that news item Somalia was next. Somalia and Bosnia, they come to the same thing these days, except that we don't have any black children with short hair and guns over their shoulders. We don't have any oil either, says Uncle Bora, that's why the Americans aren't helping.

My mother has bought herself 'Ice Magic 1–6', six video cassettes of figure-skating championships and Olympic events, Sarajevo among them. In the evening we sit in front of the TV set murmuring: loop, salchow, lutz and toe loop, double and triple. Sometimes Nena Fatima switches the TV off and hides the cassette. And Mother still sits there saying: axel, flip. Her hands are so wrecked by the laundry that wrecked is the only word I can find for them.

We have a new apartment, just for our family. The police came to the old one three times. The police wear green here, and they're different from ours in other ways too; they put their hands on their pistol grips and they don't want a schnapps. They don't just look serious, they are serious too, and they twist your arm behind your back if you get close to them too quickly, like Čika Zahid did. We were given extended deadlines and let them run out because we didn't know where to go. On the morning when the police came for the last time, more of them than usual, and didn't ring the doorbell but knocked hard instead, my father said: we're moving. He finished eating his slice of bread, and we packed. I've found us somewhere, he said, the landlord just wants to take his sofa out and then we can move in.

We have much more space in the new apartment, and we're away from all the dirt and gossip and noise and the screeching sound of the motorway and the feeling that you could never, ever, be further away from a real home. Where's your home, Asija? I've no idea where you are. Are there still any addresses in Sarajevo?

I've phoned Višegrad. I couldn't reach anyone except Granny Katarina and Zoran. Granny Katarina talks about the old days a lot. We listen to her and we don't contradict anything she remembers, we say: that's right, Granny.

Do you remember Zoran? A friend of mine from Višegrad, a silent rebel. He says the town is full of Serbian refugees. They're living in the school, or else they've simply taken over the empty buildings and the apartments of the Bosniaks who were driven out. And maybe those Bosniaks are living in Serbian apartments now. In the end no one will be where they were before. There's a family living in what was once our home too. Granny says that's all right because they have small children. Zoran says the Višegrad people can't stand the newcomers, he hates them himself. I never heard Zoran talk so much before. Zoran's hatred is enormous.

Schalke 04 is my favourite football team, I have a fishing licence and my best friend here, Philipp, has lent me the Sensible Soccer game. I listen to Nirvana and I dream in German. I dream of having a PC so that I can play Sensible Soccer properly and I won't have to tell Philipp lies about the number of goals I've scored against Brazil.

I'm letting my hair grow.

With love from
Aleksandar

Hi. Who? Aleksandar! Hey, where are you calling from?
Oh, not bad! Well, lousy really, how about you?

. . . and I hate the water being turned off at midday, and the street lights not working, and power cuts all the time, and the rubbish not being taken away, and what I hate most of all is the way it has to be so cold. The soldiers burnt both mosques down, and danced around the ruins, and now there's supposed to be a park there, only it isn't a park, it's a dismal empty space with four benches in it, and I hate everyone who sits on them, and now and then someone comes along with a watering can, but nothing will grow there. You'd say it was a gaping wound and nothing can grow from a wound. Then you'd go invoking some kind of magical nonsense, but you'd need a hell of a powerful magic spell to make things any better here. I hate school, I hate the teachers there, I hate having fifty-four of us in a class, I hate having to stand in line for everything because there's not enough of anything to go round except people and death. I hate my father, I hate his pride and defiance and his principles. For the last six months Milica and I have been trying to persuade him to leave this horrible place, and I hate the way he won't hear of it; I hate it that he's opened a tobacconist's exactly where Bogoljub had his own tobacconist's shop, but what else can he do? Basketball referees are the last thing anyone needs around here, no one plays anything any more, the gym is crammed full of people, I don't even know if they're prisoners or refugees. I hate the soldiers. I hate the People's Army. I hate the White Eagles. I hate the Green Berets. I hate death. I'm reading, Aleksandar. I like to read. Death is a German champion and a Bosnian outright world champion. I hate the bridge. I hate the shots in the night and the bodies in the river, and I hate the way you don't hear the water when a body hits it, I hate being so far away from everything, from strength and from courage; I hate myself for hiding out up at our old school, and I hate my eyes because they can't see exactly who's being pushed into the deep water and shot there, or maybe even shot while falling. Others are killed up on the bridge, and the women kneel there in the morning, scrubbing the blood away. I hate the man from the dam in Barjina Bašta who complains because they throw so many people into the river all at once that it blocks the outlets. I hate what they're doing to the girls in the hotels – Vilina Vlas and Bikavac – I hate the fire station, I hate the police station, I hate trucks full of girls and women driving to the Vilina Vlas and Bikavac, I hate burning buildings and burning windows with burning people jumping out of them to face the guns, and I hate the way the workers work, the teachers teach, the pigeons fly up in the air, and most of all I hate the snow, the filthy, hypocritical snow, because it doesn't cover up anything, anything, anything, but we're so good at covering our eyes it's as if we'd learnt nothing else in all those years of neighbourliness and fraternity and unity. I hate the way everyone condemns everything, and the way everyone's so good at hating, me too, I hate being good at hating even more than I hate the snow and the bronze soldier. I hate myself for not daring to ask the sculptor why the soldier on his monument is carrying a sword and not a bloody knife. And I hate you. I hate you because you've gone, I hate myself because I have to stay here, where even the gypsies don't think it's a good idea to pitch their tents, where dogs form into packs and no one goes swimming in the Drina. You once told me you'd been talking to the Drina. I wonder what tales it would tell now if it could. What would it taste if it had a sense of taste? What does a dead body taste like? Can a river hate too, do you think?

My hatred is endless, Aleksandar. It's there even when I close my eyes.

16 December 1995

Dear Asija,

Uncle Miki is alive! He's back home in Višegrad again, he's even living in our old building. For three years no one knew how he was, but then he sent Granny a letter. He was well, he said, he was coming back soon. Granny read the letter aloud to us over the phone. He didn't say where he was coming back from. Granny told us Miki had been seen in Višegrad in '92.

In the Hotel Bikavac? Father raised his voice, thinking of the stories. Heaven forbid!

No one shakes their heads any more over Granny Katarina and our phone conversations with her. Father once said down the phone: I don't know, I just don't know. He pressed his lips together and pinched the bridge of his nose with his thumb and forefinger. Granny Katarina doesn't live in the present any longer and has made up a past of her own for each of us. I'm paying back the credit that time granted me, she explains. In the Granny-version, we're all overtaken by our own past. Six months ago she was diagnosed with astronomically high blood-sugar levels, and the insulin treatment has turned her life into a rollercoaster ride. The days when she sounds worried and thoughtful on the phone are followed by calls to the whole family when she's in tremendous high spirits. Auntie Typhoon thinks we're exaggerating, we take it all much too seriously, after all, she says, it's nice to know what you used to be like. Since Auntie Typhoon had a call of her own from Granny she hasn't said any more on the subject.

There was a party yesterday. Uncle Bora called it The Dayton Peace Agreement Party and wrote a speech full of jokes about war, peace, vegetarians and my long hair. I can braid it now. My father said: there's no need to make jokes about Dayton, Dayton itself is the biggest joke ever. A peace agreement giving political accreditation to ethnic cleansing! Father will say almost anything and almost never do anything all his life. We're very alike in that respect, Father and I, only I say rather more than he does, and I do even less.

I imagine there's even more rejoicing over the peace agreement where you are. To be honest: I'm very glad of it, but now I'm afraid of what will happen to us. It looks as if we'll have to go back to Bosnia. But I don't want to go back to the town after everyone was driven out of it. Not wanting to go back is the one point on which my parents and I agree. When they were talking to Uncle Bora and Auntie Typhoon about it, and Mother said: I'd sooner die than look those murderers in the face, Nena Fatima stood up, wrote 'Thank you and goodbye' on the low-cut bosom of the woman on the cover of the TV magazine, tore the piece of paper off and stuck it on her forehead.

Nena Fatima only wears her headscarf when it's drizzling out of doors now, but it's always drizzling in Essen. She's made a huge garden in the middle of the inner courtyard. Tomatoes and cucumbers and peppers. The caretaker came to look, and so did the police, they looked at Nena's garden, and we're all expecting to be reported to the authorities. Nena Fatima is the only one in my family that I get on well with. All the neighbourhood terriers shit in the garden, and I don't eat lettuce any more these days.

I was sitting in the garden with Nena when she told me her secret. She reached under her headscarf and put a limp, torn piece of paper down between us. She handed me a comb and turned round. Nena's long hair. I combed it. When I'd finished she stood up and left the note there.

With love from
Aleksandar

what I really want

i want to talk again i want to talk
i want to talk i want to talk again but i need a reason
it has to be a good reason and that's a fact

i want to see everything
even in the grave i want to go on seeing i'd like to go on seeing even
in my sleep
i need a good reason not to see and death isn't a good reason
i want to see what i'm cooking

i want to go into the world that's what i want
the filthy war came just at the right time for me
there was nothing to be done with my husband not with rafik
he carried his crooked back around in his head his whole life was
crooked he ducked down low there was nothing to be done with
him
i want to be young still for a while i'm not all that old i could only
be old with rafik i had to stay at home he was working and i was at
home and he didn't want men to see what beautiful hair i have

i want to have beautiful hair always it takes a lot of caring for

i want to go out in the world that's why i've gone away from rafik
because he had principles all the way from the drina to china

i want to be friendly
i want an unmasked sun but who can stop the clouds coming

if i were a magician like you rain and progress would all be different and the megdan would spit fire we'd have quite different worries from the ones we have now

i want to be a bit useful to you all for a while yet but i want to be useful to myself even more

i don't want to be kind to everyone all the time i'd rather wait

i want to know what you'll be like at twenty and what you'll know your grandpa was that age when i had to marry him
there was a walnut tree in my village it snowed under that tree in summer about as often as you found unmarried girls there
i want to find another husband or maybe not

i never want to herd cattle again or look after courteous birds

i want to be proud of breaking something

i don't want to die of loneliness or guilt or a fishbone or a river i want to have the feeling when i'm dying that i'm wearing a lot of jewellery that's how it is

i want to fly some day and climb a volcano and throw a stone into it.

nena fatima

1 May 1999

Dear Asija,

Forgive me for not writing for so long. Do you ever get my letters? Are you still there? I go on writing, I'm alone a lot just now anyway, but I don't mind that.

My parents have been living in the USA for a year. In Florida. They've gone there for good, they say. Father picked a coconut and painted his first picture for seven years. He calls it 'Self-Portrait with Coconut', and the colours he calls a duet of ochre and brown on a lush green summer meadow. Mother started work in an attorney's office, she says it's not difficult, the laws there are a lot easier to understand than ours. She's bought skates, she goes to the ice rink every Sunday, and she'd like to watch a football game in the stadium, without my father. She thinks the footballers' kit fits them nicely.

If they hadn't emigrated, she'd have been sent back to Bosnia. It's called voluntary repatriation. I don't think something you're told to do can be voluntary, and you can't really be repatriated to a place where half the original population is missing. It's a new place, you're not returning to it, you're going there for the first time. I can't even imagine what it would be like, going to school in Bosnia now. All I see is my old classroom and Edin on the bench behind me. Tito's picture is still hanging on the wall. I was allowed to stay here because of school. My parents thought it was sensible for me to take my final exams in Germany. Mother wrote down eleven recipes for me, ten easy ones plus the recipe for minced-meat-and-plum schnitzel. She explained how to boil clothes that need it before you wash them.

The last year in Essen was a little better for us. Mother gave notice to the laundry. She signed on for a course in German and studied every day for three months. After that she wrote seventy job applications. In the seventy-first, she didn't mention that she came from Bosnia and she got a job as a cashier.

I talked to Father so little here that I was sometimes surprised to hear him speak my name. Mother fell sick and then got better, Father got quiet and then grew older, and now he's sitting in the sun, painting still lifes again, and even selling them.

You see, Asija, I haven't gone to any trouble. All this time I haven't gone to the trouble of wondering or maybe even asking what my parents think or what they want or how I can help them so that we'd feel better here. It was embarrassing for me to go to their interviews with them; it was embarrassing for me to translate the question they were asked: how good is your German? I was never ashamed of my deaf mute Nena Fatima, although she laughed at jokes and talked in her sleep. She had more friends here than I'll ever make. She listened to her women friends when they were talking, they asked her opinion, she would nod or shake her head. But then she'd sit out on the pavement in front of the building cutting her toenails. She was happiest of all about Florida. She gets up early and swims in the neighbours' pool, one more length every day.

I sometimes wish my name was spelled Alexander and I often wish people would just leave me alone. For a long time I thought I was just playing at being a teenager so as not to make my parents anxious. But a time came when I really didn't want to see war or know about suffering and flight any more.

Today is the first of May, and Granny Katarina wants to send me a package from Višegrad. Granny Katarina always wants to send me a package on the first of May. Photos of Tito, Grandpa's speeches and decorations, my Pioneer uniform. Every year at this time Granny tells me how I especially liked wearing the uniform on church feast days, how I knew whole passages of *Das Kapital* off by heart, and understood what they meant.

Now my father buys himself chewing tobacco and says: coconuts! I'm the first Bosnian to know how to chew tobacco and Mother says: the Jacksonville Jaguars have a good team this season. In the evening, they invite other Bosnians, they grill home-made čevapčići and supermarket hamburgers on the veranda, and the crickets chirp, the asphalt cools down and smells of cinnamon. A man called Dino Safirović tells them how he and his troop played football against the Serbs in the trenches, and how he stopped the shot that would have decided the game with his face, but ever since then there are certain sounds at the ends of words that he can't pronounce properly. He tells them how he was going to light a fire in a hollow tree trunk where a hand grenade was lying. My mother says she misses me. She buys Slovenian wine, and Father thinks our crickets would knock the stuffing out of the American kind.

I tried looking for your name on the Internet, Asija, and then I realised that I'm not at all sure of your surname, even though I always write one on the envelopes. I read pages full of lists of missing persons, an Asija was mentioned twice, but that doesn't mean anything. At least I found out what your name means.

If I look for my own name I get a single hit: *Midsummer Night's Dream* in the school theatre. I played Puck. Puck is an elf whose king gives him the job of finding a special flower; if its nectar is put on a sleeping person's eyes, the sleeper will fall in love with the first living creature he or she sees on waking up. Not a great story, but Puck can work magic. At some point in the play everyone gets to be loved, even a man with a donkey's head, and it all has to be a dream because that's what the audience decides in the end.

Asija, I can make Nazis think I'm from Bavaria just by using the words Bavarians like. I can make Frisian jokes, they're a bit like Montenegrin jokes at home – if the Frisians' flies aren't open today they'll wait until tomorrow to pee. I back five national teams. If anyone says I'm a good example of integration, it really freaks me out.

Asiya (Asija), f.
1. As Arab, name: healing, tending the sick; peacemaker.
2. Traditionally the name of Pharaoh's devout wife who rescued Moses from the Nile.

My father asks if I knew that more people are killed by coconuts than sharks every year. Coconuts are murderers, he says.

I decide to have dreamed everything.

With love from
Aleksandar

Aleksandar, I really, really want to send you this package

I packed it up myself – for you. Karl and Friedrich and Clara and Tito. The whole bunch of them are in it. Do you remember? You liked Karl. And I really, really want to send you Slavko's Party book. His speeches on special occasions. His articles. What picturesque handwriting your grandpa had! Capital letters twining like tendrils! No one writes by hand any more. I'm sure you type everything too. It's not right! How do you find out who you're dealing with through a machine? I mean, do you want to kiss only a girl's lipstick and not the girl?

I really do want to send you some newspaper articles about Grandpa! You used to sit on his lap and do crossword puzzles with him! Oh, Slavko and his crossword puzzles! What else? You really must have the photos of Vladimir Ilyitch and the photos of Tito! What have I got here? 'The Mission of Revolutionary Youth'? Yes, wonderful! You're the youth in the title! Oh, your grandpa's handwriting in those crossword puzzles! Oh, Tito's uniform, and we thought we had it so good back then, sheep that we were! I couldn't stand all the fuss they made. I didn't marry my Slavko for his minutes of Party meetings and his reports. Politics and kissing don't go together. What am I supposed to do now with workers' songs and Clara Zetkin postage stamps and leaflets explaining how people have to act when Tito comes to town? Point One: we're to decorate our front gardens and put out as many green plants as possible! Everything except the green plants – for instance underpants, bedclothes, etc. – is to be taken out of the front gardens! Did you ever hear of such a thing? Then there's Point Four, that's a good one too: everyone must bring at least one flower to throw into the street a hundred metres in front of the first car in Tito's column. Whatever happens, nothing must be thrown at Comrade Tito's own car! I could never be doing with any of that, Aleksandar, but I expect you still have ambitions of that kind. You and Slavko may never have got beyond the chapter on goods and commodities in *Das Kapital* without nodding off, but you could quote whole passages by heart. And you wore your blue cap and red cravat of your own free will even when it wasn't a festival day. Even when wearing the Pioneer uniform wasn't a duty any more, hands clasped behind your back the way your grandpa always clasped his. At the end-of-year celebrations in Class Four you carried the flag. Half the school marched behind you and the Red Flag. Your ears were glowing with happiness and excitement. The flag was huge. During a break in the marching, a poem was recited about some commandant or other, and you sat down and laid the flag on the ground. There's a photo of you resting in front of the flag. I really do want to send you that photo. Tell me, do the Germans still open all packages from Yugoslavia? Are they still keeping tabs on us? I wouldn't like to put you in the awkward position of having to explain why you need these things. Slavko would have made a speech at the Ninth Congress of the Communist League of Yugoslavia. That was in nineteen seventy and quite something. But then unfortunately none of the speakers fell ill, so no substitute was required. I really would like to send that speech − it's for you. The Role and Perspectives of Marriage and the Family in the Proletariat! Oh, Slavko and his perspectives! The maternity question! The education question! The sexual question! All so topical! Slavko was annoyed by hypocritical bourgeois virtues! And I . . . I was his proud Comrade! Oh, my Slavko . . . Aleksandar, when are you finally going to get married?

When Everything Was All Right

Aleksandar Krsmanović

with a foreword by Granny Katarina
and an essay for Mr Fazlagić

For my Grandpa Slavko

Contents

Aleksandar,

You were four years old. You were sleeping with us, in bed between Grandpa and me. That's the way you liked it best. Grandpa had to go out early. A Party Committee meeting. You were whining, you wanted to go too. He whispered something to you. You quietened down. You laughed, yes, you laughed. Your mother came to our place later, wanting to take you to the barber's. She knew Grandpa wasn't there. He usually took you to the barber's with him, nothing came off. When people are deep thinkers their hair falls over their foreheads, that's how it was with your grandpa. Mama and I went for a coffee nearby, at Amela's. Waste of time, you said. You stayed behind and sorted out your little cars. You never really played with them, just changed the places where you'd parked them. You made up a story about each car. Where it came from, where it was going. The problems of the driver's prim and proper wife. The exhaust of the Porsche was belting out Partisan songs.

We came back an hour later. The cars hadn't been put in any order, they were just lying there. You were lying there too, in front of Slavko's sofa. You were watching TV. The volume was turned down, then you switched the TV off. You pushed your hair back from your forehead. The cars were just lying around. I noticed the vase at once, I noticed that it wasn't on the window-sill. Or anywhere else. You hadn't got the Hoover out because you were scared of vacuum cleaners. Washing machines too. Those tiny little pieces on the carpet.

You never said anything about the vase afterwards; I never said anything about the vase afterwards. And Grandpa probably never noticed the vase. I mean, that it wasn't there any more. Even though it had been his present. You knew that. He had spent three days picking flowers for me. He had filled the whole apartment with flowers. I'd never seen so many flowers at once, either before or afterwards. And there'd been red poppies in the vase.

The cars lay there. You dressed yourself. I watched you. You said the two of you would go to the barber's now. Your mother was surprised, I didn't say anything. I didn't kiss you on the forehead. I didn't tell you there'd be hot milk in the evening. You always used to wait exactly twelve minutes before you drank the milk while it was still warm. I didn't tell you it was all right. I didn't tell you you were only a child. I didn't tell you that you were our sunshine, and there was no need for you to feel scared over a few bits of broken china. I didn't tell you how much I liked it when you slept between Grandpa and me. And I didn't tell you how much I liked the way you began every day with five questions. Five questions before saying good morning. Whatever had you been doing in your dreams? I didn't tell you everything was all right. The two of you went out. I put the milk on the stove. I rearranged your little cars. The Ferrari in front. It had a driver who's a desert nomad with a very sick grandfather lying in a tent in a non-aligned African state. He tells his grandson in a faint voice: my boy, you're my sunshine, I'm going to die soon, but I have one last wish. There's a place far away where the water is solid. You can throw it like a stone. If you hold the stone in your hand long enough it turns to cold, soft water. I want to drink a stone like that before I die. Bring it to me, my sunshine. And ever since then the young nomad has been roaming the world in his Ferrari, looking for a way to bring the stony water to his grandpa in the desert. That was your story, the story you told at a time when no one thought anything was wrong. A time when everything was all right.

With love from
Granny Katarina

Ice cream

There's always ice cream, but there isn't always this particular ice cream, it's my favourite and its name is a favourite name of mine: Stela.

If I have a little sister, I tell my mother, digging the little blue plastic spoon into the ice cream carton, we'll call her Stela, OK?

Have I been putting on weight? asks my mother in alarm, and I say: no, but I've a right to join in family decisions, haven't I?

My father slept all through my birth, and my mother fainted immediately after it, she couldn't stand the sight of so much blood and shit all at once, so the only person present who was still conscious, my Uncle Bora, had a perfect right to say at once: ugly little dirtbag, we'll call him Aleksandar.

It's true that I was still very small at the time, but you never forget a remark like that.

My favourite Stela ice cream is vanilla flavour. It comes in a blue carton. There are little coloured spoons in a plastic bag in the ice cream vendor's fridge. If you buy a Stela ice cream you can have a little coloured spoon for free. Blue is my favourite. Stela is a pregnant ice cream with a secret inside it. Buried somewhere in the vanilla ice, sometimes near the top, sometimes in the middle, sometimes at the bottom, an icy, dark red, sour cherry lies hidden.

Wish

My parents don't know anything about it. I'm in the mosque. I know what to do: you get down on your knees and think of something nice that hasn't come true yet. You wish for the nice thing every time you bow down. Make it come true! There are coloured rugs spread on the floor of the mosque, from the outside it looks like a rocket, on the inside it's a belly. I'm afraid. I'm out of the ordinary here, because I'm the only one wearing shoes. It isn't April in the mosque, it isn't spring. I bow down and bow down and bow down.

Dear Mosque, let Red Star win the championship. Dear Mosque, let Red Star win the championship. Dear Mosque, let Red Star win the championship.

Dear Mosque, let Mama forget how to sigh.

Parade

I wear my Pioneer cap tilted sideways. I'm a wild Pioneer. I sit in front of the Red Flag, exhausted and content. The choir sings the Internationale.

1 May 1989, or, The Chick in the Pioneer's Hand

I climb up on the armchair, push my hair back from my forehead
and clear my throat:

It is the First of May
the wind caresses the red flags
fluttering your name: Tito.

The mother bird lays an egg
in our nest of brotherly love,
she lays it in my hand.

The chick slips out in the Pioneer's hand
at once it's as muscular as Rambo I
with red white and blue feathers and Adriatic eyes.

It's a dove of peace
it's an eagle in war
it's a chicken for lunch.

It's a dinosaur for the children
the dinosaur sings the Internationale
for Tito and the working class.

The bird eats up the first of May
and because the first of May is the future
the bird grows big and full of the future
like our country Yugoslavia.

I read, pull the hair back from my forehead, thank the audience,
and climb down to Grandpa Slavko's applause.

There are no Partisans now. There are commissars. There are uniforms with soldiers inside them and machine guns and generals in front of them. There's the five-pointed red star. There are parades, there's the National Liberation War, there are records of Partisan songs that everyone knows by heart. There's black bread, people stand in line for the black bread, and there's Grandpa who helped the Partisans to liberate everything possible and impossible. There are the Pioneer caps that look like Partisan caps except that they're blue, and I wear mine even when I don't need to. There's white chocolate with nuts in it, there's the big orange gas bottle in the kitchen, we play basketball, the ring for the gas bottle is the basket, I'm Dražen Petrović and I always score three-point shots. Granny is boiling milk on the stove. I always wait exactly twelve minutes and drink the milk warm. Granny is boiling sheets on the other gas ring. There's plasters in the bathroom, there's a gigantic rubbish bin in the yard that isn't often emptied, there are American Indians, there are bikers in leather jackets who sometimes stop off in our town and look at the girls the same way our own boys do. There's the green building with the peculiar roof around the corner from us. There are the Japanese, the only Japanese who ever lost their way and came to our town, they went into the green house with the peculiar roof and nobody saw if they ever came out again. There are swastikas drawn in secret, so strictly forbidden that every piece of paper with a scribbled swastika on it is crumpled up and thrown into the rubbish. There's the river Drina. There's hours and hours of sitting by the Drina fishing. There are catfish in the Drina, I know one with whiskers and a pair of glasses. There are computer games called Silent Service, Space Invaders and Moon Patrol, I break all the records. There's a bicycle for my birthday, my first: a Pony, green and fast. I ride in circles, I'm a sprinter with muscular legs and a close-fitting jersey. I get laughed at for the jersey, but what do ignorant people know about aerodynamics? There are plastic bags. My Granny never throws plastic bags away, she washes them out if whey has run into them from the sheep's milk cheese, she keeps them in a bottomless space called the špajz. She keeps everything, she says: you never know what times are coming. That gives my father an idea, he says: I'll open a shop selling artists' equipment. There's the artists' equipment, there's the Sunday afternoon in the megdan cemetery behind a gravestone when Nešo's sister Elvira showed me what the difference between me and her looks like.

It doesn't look good.

There's me, acting as if I hadn't known all about it for ages.

There's a Partisan on the gravestone, in a small round photo frame, looking serious and wearing the cap with the five-pointed star.

But there are no Partisans any more.

I go to Igalo with my parents every summer. The entire factory where my father works goes to Igalo. The syndicate moves people from a small town without any seaside to stay for a month in a small town that does have a seaside. There's an artists' colony in Igalo, so the only person who looks forward to going to Igalo is my father. The men and women in the artists' colony wear their hair long and nothing else, and Father is depressed when he has to put a tie on again at home. It's hard to say whether my mother looks forward to Igalo, or anything else at all.

'Right, family this year we're going to . . .' cried my father last week in the tones of an enthusiastic TV presenter, waving the hotel prospectuses.

'Oh, Papa, you're only talking like that because I'm supposed to show Mr Fazlagić, not-Comrade-Teacher-now, that I know how to use inverted commas.'

'Yes, and what's more I never talk like an enthusiastic TV presenter.'

'Igalo-o!' said my mother with the voice of a weary TV presenter announcing misery to come, and unable to do anything about it, she went to pack.

It might really have been a wonderful trip that year if Mr Spok had come with us. A nice trip for Mr Spok, Comrade-in-Chief of the town drunks, who never goes away anywhere. When I see Mr Spok staggering across the street I can't help thinking of my Grandpa Rafik, which isn't easy, because I don't remember his face, all I know is a story about a drowned man. I feel sorry for a frog because it doesn't realise we're about to set it alight, I feel sorry for Uncle Bora because he makes himself do knee-bends but can never manage it, I feel sorry for you, Mr Fazlagić, because you'll soon forget how to laugh if you don't stop looking so grim. And I feel sorry for Mr Spok, who says: 'I'm worse off than a mongrel dog, I don't even have a pack of other dogs to run with. Everything around me is made of stone – streets, mountains, hearts. I'm never near the sea.'

I wanted to give Mr Spok the sea, that would be the most wonderful trip imaginable for him. I wrote 'Prize-winner!' on a picture postcard, and 'Mr Spok', and 'Igalo'. I congratulated Mr Spok, but I didn't shake hands with him. That was the most difficult bit. I invited Mr Spok to our place so that he could shower and comb his hair. After the first shower, I asked him to shower again. I asked the now showered and combed Mr Spok if he knew how to shave, but he didn't. As part of the prize I gave him one of the two suits in my father's wardrobe and four ties, because I knew how much Father hated ties. I put on the trousers that my parents thought were my best pair. Thus prepared, showered, combed and sober, Mr Spok and I waited in my parents' living room. I asked Mr Spok if he could cry at will.

My mother came home first, and she just asked if Mr Spok was a vegetarian. 'I eat anything,' he said, so I gave him an apple, two slices of bread and two eggs, he could cook those for himself later, there wasn't any time now, Father was already coming through the door. I called out in a TV presenter's voice, 'Family, we're going to Igalo this year, and we're going wi-i-ith . . .' I pointed to Mr Spok, who began to cry dreadfully. I raised my eyebrows, pleading, and hugged my father, which certainly struck both of us as odd.

'Aleksandar, go to my studio!' he ordered, and Mr Spok stopped crying. 'This is really a social question,' he told me. 'The fact is, I'm afraid that only family members can benefit from the syndicate's offers. Mr Spoković can't come too. I'm sorry.'

'Couldn't you and Mama adopt Mr Spok? That would solve two problems at once. He could come to Igalo with us, and I wouldn't be an only child any more.'

'Those aren't real problems, son.'

'This isn't a real conversation, Father.'

'Give my regards to Mr Fazlagić.'

'I will.'

'All the same, you haven't written about a wonderful trip.'
'But technically speaking I've done everything right.'

Aleksandar Krsmanović

A wall has fallen down in the better part of Germany, and now only the not-so-good part of Germany is left. The wall was bound to come down sooner or later, that's what everyone says. Uncle Bora the guest-worker, every family should have one, says the not-so-good part of Germany is better from his point of view because it pays him, and because there are a hundred houses all the same in a row there, no one feels envious, and there's traffic rules you can understand, and the traffic lights don't just stick like ours, they really can go green, and there's Lothar Matthäus, and there are tampons for Auntie Typhoon. Tampons are little cotton-wool sticks, Auntie Typhoon puts them inside her to slow her down a bit. We can sometimes get tampons here too, but maybe they don't work with people who move really fast, I'm not sure about that.

Now that the business about the wall has been settled, we have AIDS here and a power failure. Happy people are waving black, dark grey and pale grey flags on top of the high wall, which doesn't look at all as if it has fallen over. While they're having a good time up there, other people are still working down below, knocking little stones out of the wall. My Uncle Bora says: the Germans work the whole time.

Germany looks very congested, people everywhere, you can't even see the street any more.

Here comes the newsreader with the neat and tidy hair again. Epidemic, he says; USA, he says; sexually transmitted diseases, he says; another four cases confirmed in Yugoslavia, he says. AIDS, he says, raising an eyebrow. Astronauts are looking through little telescopes now, and someone says: *virus* and *blood* and *fatal*.

Now that the wall has fallen over in the better part of Germany, all the bad things are coming our way! The power failure comes our way too – Granny is alarmed, there's no sound, the TV set just crackles and goes black. It must be something like this when you're alive and then suddenly you're not alive any more. You feel a bit frightened, and then someone lights a candle. Grandpa does that here, and in the candlelight the faces around the table turn the colour of baked potato halves suffering from AIDS.

On a single evening I learn how walls fall down, how people fall down, how even the light falls down; a sickness is always to blame, and once things fall down they disappear. The better part of Germany fell sick and disappeared. I understand about disappearing. AIDS is a proud sickness, it doesn't even recognise small letters, it doesn't bother with anything like coughing and patting the dog. It wants our blood.

I lie on the carpet. Lying on the carpet I can't fall down or cut my finger and get AIDS. All the same, I wait while Grandpa Slavko, Granny Katarina, Auntie Typhoon and Uncle Bora play rummy in the candlelight; I'm waiting to disappear.

Bikers zoom through Višegrad. Austrians, Swiss, Italians. The Germans have the biggest motorbikes. Michael rides a Kawasaki, Jürgen rides a Honda. Čika Doctor says: Germany and Japan have always been good friends, they just don't like to remember it.

Sometimes there are two of them entirely encased in leather, on one motorbike. The leather bikers drink lemonade in the Estuary Restaurant and say they like our rivers. Čika Doctor – we call him that because he once cut the calf of someone's leg open – winks at us, meaning: it's more than just ordinary lemonade I serve the bikers. If Čika Doctor has no customers to serve, and nothing to do, he sits in the hotel garden, snaps his pocket-knife open and shut, and sleeps in the sun.

We've counted fifteen bikers since June, but we aren't always standing there counting the bikers.

There's something of myself in it, says Čika Doctor, letting us into the secret of his lemonade. He doesn't say which part of himself, and anyway, we'd never be able to give the secret away to the leather Germans, because for ideological reasons words where they live are not the same as here, where no one rides a motorbike like theirs because no one would venture out into the street in that weird leather gear.

Edin and I are sharing a lemonade at Čika Doctor's hotel, sitting there with our legs wide apart and acting as if we were Germans. Hans kugel kluf nust lust bayern meinen danke danke. We do it so that maybe Čika Doctor will tell us which part of himself he adds to the Germans' lemonade.

Why Vukoje Worm whose nose has been broken three times doesn't break mine

Tito was taken down from the classrooms today, and Vukoje Worm swore he'd take me apart after school.

The bell rings for the end of the last lesson. Everyone storms out of the classroom. Vukoje points at me and draws his thumb across his throat. Edin shrugs. I'm right in there with you, he says, that way he'll have to try thumping both of us at once and he'll get tired more quickly.

Edin has some excellent ideas.

Vukoje Worm, whose nose has been broken three times, is waiting in the school yard. He's not alone. Hi, Vukoje, old friend, how are you? I call. Vukoje takes off his jacket, ties his bootlaces, shoves me several times and asks if I'd rather have kicks, punches or throttles. A crowd of schoolchildren surrounds us at once.

Throttles, I say, because there's no such thing.

Good answer, says a tall young man who walks out of the crowd of kids and plants himself in front of Vukoje. Push off, he tells Vukoje, or my forehead will make mush of yours.

Vukoje stays there, puts his hands on his hips. There's a little line of freckles on his nose. He spits out a thin sideways stream of saliva and wags a finger at me menacingly. Only when Vukoje and his friends jog slowly off do I recognise my rescuer, Damir Kičić. Damir is considered to be the finest footballer our town has ever produced, he even went to our school.

Thanks, I say after the other kids have started off home, looking disappointed.

I wouldn't have minded seeing it, really, says Damir.

Edin goes Cuckoo!, folds his hands and cracks his knuckles. Vukoje wouldn't have stood a chance against us, he says.

Damir, what are you doing in our town? I ask. I thought you played in Sarajevo now.

Damir laughs. Call me Kiko, he says.

Kiko, is it true what people say about you being able to knock the ball up into the air with your head as often as you like? asks Edin. Aren't they exaggerating?

We could always have a bet on it . . . Kiko scratches his forehead, and the bet is one we can't possibly lose. Kiko laughs, the Adam's apple under the skin of his throat jumps up and down, and we shake hands on the deal.

Twelve noon on Sunday. The school yard's empty except for a little girl who is carefully riding round on her bike for the very first time, with her mother holding on to the saddle.

Edin brings the ball with him. We shoot at goal a couple of times.

Do you think he'll come? asks Edin.

Of course he'll come. Got the money?

You know it's summer when the ball bounces and it's so hot that the heat is a space, the leather smacks down on the concrete inside that space and it echoes. If I were a magician who could make things possible, then winter and autumn would be two special days some time in November, spring would be another word for April, and the rest of the year would be summer, with life echoing, asphalt melting, and Mother putting yoghurt on my sunburn.

Here he is. Give me the money.

Hi, boys!

Hi!

Nice and hot, eh?

Yes.

Got the cash?

You don't need to count it, I say, handing Kiko the bundle of notes. He licks his thumb and forefinger and sorts out the crumpled notes in his hand. Gives me his stake. You'd better count it, he says.

All present and correct, I say.

Then let's start.

Just a moment! Edin has a ruler in his hand. He puts it against Kiko's foot and works his way up his leg to his thigh, over his hip and up to his head. He has to stretch a good way for the last bit. The little girl's mother has let go of her, she's screeching and wobbling as she rides the bike, she slows down and falls forward, braking with her feet. The mother claps, the little girl shouts at her: you didn't hold on to me, you let go, she screeches, again, again! she demands.

Edin says: a hundred and ninety-two.

Grown four centimetres since last week, not bad going, grins Kiko, taking off his shirt and throwing up the ball. One, two, counts Edin, three, four, and the heat is a little girl screeching on a bike, five, six, he counts, and late summer is a bet one hundred and ninety-two centimetres high, seven, eight, he counts, and the girl shouts: look, Mama, I'm riding, I'm riding my bike, I can do it! nine, ten, we count, and at ten Kiko begins to whistle, eleven, twelve, he stands there hardly moving, only ducking his head slightly before the ball touches his forehead each time, at thirteen he heads it high into the air, it's unlucky not to do that, he calls, and the ball flies and flies, and Edin says: fourteen, fifteen, sixteen, seventeen, eighteen, nineteen, twenty, twenty-one, twenty-two, twenty-three, twenty-four, twenty-five, twenty-six, twenty-seven, twenty-eight, twenty-nine, thirty, thirty-one, thirty-two, thirty-three, thirty-four, thirty-five, thirty-six, thirty-seven, thirty-eight, thirty-nine, forty, forty-one, forty-two, forty-three, forty-four, forty-five, forty-six, forty-seven, forty-eight, forty-nine, fifty, fifty-one, fifty-two, fifty-three, fifty-four, fifty-five, fifty-six, fifty-seven, fifty-eight, fifty-nine, sixty, sixty-one, sixty-two, sixty-three, sixty-four, sixty-five, sixty-six, sixty-seven, sixty-eight, sixty-nine, seventy, seventy-one, seventy-two, seventy-three, seventy-four, seventy-five, seventy-six, seventy-seven, seventy-eight, seventy-nine, eighty, eighty-one, eighty-two, eighty-three, eighty-four, eighty-five, eighty-six, eighty-seven, eighty-eight, eighty-nine, ninety, ninety-one, ninety-two, ninety-three, ninety-four, ninety-five, ninety-six, ninety-seven, ninety-eight, ninety-nine, a hundred, a hundred and one, a hundred and two, a hundred and three, a hundred and four, a hundred and five, a hundred and six, a hundred and seven, a hundred and eight, a hundred and nine, a hundred and ten, a hundred and eleven, a hundred and twelve, a hundred and thirteen, a hundred and fourteen, a hundred and fifteen, a hundred and sixteen, a hundred and seventeen, a hundred and eighteen, a hundred and nineteen, a hundred and twenty, a hundred and twenty-one, a hundred and twenty-two, a hundred and twenty-three, a hundred and twenty-four, a hundred and twenty-five, a hundred and twenty-six, a hundred and twenty-seven, a hundred and twenty-eight, a hundred and twenty-nine, a hundred and thirty, a hundred and thirty-one, a hundred and thirty-two, a hundred and thirty-three, a hundred and thirty-four, a hundred and thirty-five, a hundred and thirty-six, a hundred and thirty-seven, a hundred and thirty-eight, a hundred and thirty-nine, a hundred and forty, a hundred and forty-one, a hundred and forty-two, a hundred and forty-three, a hundred and forty-four, a hundred and forty-five, a hundred and forty-six, a hundred and forty-seven, a hundred and forty-eight, a hundred and forty-nine, a hundred and fifty, a hundred and fifty-one, a hundred and fifty-two, a hundred and fifty-three, a hundred and fifty-four, a hundred and fifty-five, a hundred and fifty-six, a hundred and fifty-seven, a hundred and fifty-eight, a hundred and fifty-nine, a hundred and sixty, a hundred and sixty-one, a hundred and sixty-two, a hundred and sixty-three, a hundred and sixty-four, a hundred and sixty-five, a hundred and sixty-six, a hundred and sixty-seven, a hundred and sixty-eight, a hundred and sixty-nine, a hundred and seventy, a hundred and seventy-one, a hundred and seventy-two, a hundred and seventy-three, a hundred and seventy-four, a hundred and seventy-five, a hundred and seventy-six, a hundred and seventy-seven, a hundred and seventy-eight, a hundred and seventy-nine, a hundred and eighty, a hundred and eighty-one, a hundred and eighty-two, a hundred and eighty-three, a hundred and eighty-four, a hundred and eighty-five, a hundred and eighty-six, a hundred and eighty-seven, a hundred and eighty-eight, a hundred and eighty-nine, a hundred and ninety, a hundred and ninety-one, a hundred and ninety-two.

Why Čika Hasan and Čika Sead are inseparable, and what even those who know most about catfish can't count on

Čika Hasan and Čika Sead don't go fishing for fun, they don't go fishing because they enjoy a struggle against the fish, they don't go fishing because they want peace and quiet, they don't go fishing because you can't have bad thoughts while you're fishing in the Drina. Hasan goes fishing because he wants to catch more fish than Sead, and Sead goes fishing because he wants to catch more fish than Hasan. I'm the one who goes fishing for those other reasons, also because I like fried fish, but all the same I catch more than the two of them put together.

When Hasan first gave blood after his wife's death in an accident, Sead did the same a few days later. And so it went on. Recently Hasan was letting everyone know that he was way ahead of his friend: he'd chalked up eighty-two litres of blood to Sead's fifty-three.

I stand by the bridge fishing for catfish with leeches. In the early summer heat the path taken by Hasan and Sead on their way from the bridge to me is one long argument. I don't hear exactly what the two of them are arguing about, but judging by their vigorous gestures and the scraps of conversation I catch, the subjects are life, death and cucumber salad. Nice clear water, Aleksandar!

They interrupt their quarrelling to set up shop: a three-legged stool and a four-legged stool, a white tackle box and a black tackle box, grasshoppers and worms. As soon as their floats are in the water they start accusing each other of casting them out too close. Even the daftest Danube salmon is not going to believe in grasshoppers and worms who go for a swim together, says Hasan, shaking his head.

Normally sounds other than those made by the river itself bother me when I'm fishing, but I can listen to those two carrying on, they're funny, they need a referee, so I have to keep laughing and I'm always being asked to adjudicate, which I don't mind at all. I never decide it's a draw. That would probably make them shut up and do nothing but fish, and neither they, nor I, nor the fish fancy that idea.

And just as I'm being asked whether I agree with Sead, who says vegetarians are useless, or with Hasan, who says oh, they're not that bad and anyway, you never get a fish without bones or a human being without faults, my float is tugged so violently under the surface that I pull hard without thinking about it. The float doesn't come up again, the resistance is strong, the line stretches taut, and Hasan cries: oh, it's a great big 'un . . . He realises I can't stand up to such a strong tug in the opposite direction, I'm being pulled along and slipping into the water, clutching my rod as it arches over, Sead grabs clumsily for the rod, his glasses fly off his nose and land in the river. He immediately lets go and plunges his arms in the water, groping for them. I finally give the frantic monster fish more line, more room. You can swim a little longer, just a little longer, but soon I'll get my breath back, my beauty.

A fish is always bigger in a story than it is in the hands of the angler telling his story, says Grandpa Slavko, interrupting my tale.

My fish is a catfish and it is exactly as big now as it was on the hook, I say, going back to the story just as Grandpa has taught me. We know it's a catfish when it shows itself above the water for the first time fifteen minutes later, two whole metres of beautiful catfish! And as strong as a Hasan and an Aleksandar put together, or a Sead and an Aleksandar, but never as strong as a Hasan and a Sead – that won't do because it would lead straight to a fight in which the fishing rod would be forgotten.

Half an hour later I still haven't got the catfish, but the catfish hasn't got me either, and Sead hasn't got his glasses. The fish has tired us out, instead of the other way around – as soon as we get him closer to the bank he lashes his mighty tail, he tugs at the line to right and to left, like a dog, dives down suddenly so that the rod bends dangerously and the line is about to snap. Sead is more and more silent now and suggests giving up. Hasan is more and more talkative, and now that Sead wants to give up he takes off his shirt and trousers, does five knee-bends, and jumps into the river. The sun is high in the sky, it's hot, Hasan comes up. Now then, give it all you've got, boy, we'll get him yet!

I reel in the line until I can feel the weight, the catfish feels mine, he pulls left, you won't do it this time, I pull against the fish, how it must hurt him! You won't do it this time, thinks the catfish again, swimming strongly right into the current, I take two steps forward, brace my foot against a stone. Sead leaps to my aid. Don't do that, I say, hauling on the rod until it traces a letter 'C' in the air, this is personal now – he deserves it, I groan. Striking out powerfully with his arms, Hasan comes closer to the place where the line emerges from the river. My arms are quivering, the rod is quivering, every time I turn the reel I wait for the ratcheting sound. I feel my heart racing, I don't let the fish gain a centimetre. As if signalling the last round, the catfish flings himself out of the river. With the light scars on his smooth black back, with the height of his leaps, with his yellow, challenging eyes he declares: I have a scholar's beauty, and this isn't the only fight I'll have won. He is counting on knowing me and all my tricks, but he hasn't reckoned on that crazy couple from Višegrad. With the last of my strength I keep him at the surface, everything's about to break, the rod, the line, my arms, Hasan dives down, and with him the river dives into a great silence.

Nothing to be seen. No Hasan, no catfish. The line loses tension, traces a curve on the surface. It's over, I think, he's gone. But suddenly the catfish swerves, pulls on the line again, braces himself against me, takes me by surprise – I don't let go, I fall, I cut my head open, the handle of the reel slips away from me, there's blood dripping from my chin, and in the river, in the cold Drina not far from the bank, Hasan and the catfish are wrestling on the surface, the pair of them striking out and splashing and swirling and writhing. As I lie there I snatch up my rod, I'm pulled into the river on my belly, Sead grabs my legs, urges me on. Now, get him out of there, boy! I go on reeling in the line under water, there's only weight on it now, nothing's pulling the hook the other way,

Sead gets me up on the bank, and before our eyes what little hair Hasan has left emerges from the water first, then his face covered with waterweed, and then finally, in his embrace, the catfish. The catfish with whiskers, and with Sead's horn-rimmed glasses on its nose.

I lie there laughing, laughing and bleeding, Hasan laughs and spits out water and mud. Got me right down to the bottom, he says. Sead laughs loudest of all: O learned scholar! Those glasses suit you much better than me. He wipes the catfish's glasses clean. I put my hand on the fish's big, cool head, I stroke the tired scholar's back and long ventral fin, I wonder what I could keep to remember him by, he doesn't have scales and he hasn't brought any memento with him.

Do we let him go? I ask.

And for the first time ever Hasan and Sead agree.

So what did you keep of him? Grandpa asks.

I kept that day, I say, looking at him.

How the game of chess relates to world politics, why Grandpa Slavko knows revolutions may come tomorrow, and how things can sometimes be so difficult to say

Grandpa Slavko and I start by pushing some sleeping cows over, then we play chess on one of the fallen cows until the queen strikes the king sharply and runs away with the black pawn on a white knight to Bulgaria, home of the black knight on the Black Sea. So much black and white!

That is because of the way Propaganda paints everything black and white in international politics. Checkmate! says Grandpa, and he opens a newspaper that will be printed in thirty years' time. Meanwhile I'm helping Great-Granny with an oak tree. She carries the oak tree on her shoulders and makes oak broth. Soil drops off the roots. I plant minced-meat plums among it.

Is Propaganda a painter on the side, then? I call from the river Drina as I wrestle with a catfish. The catfish has whiskers and a pair of glasses, and Grandpa says: Propaganda is the name of a teller of fairy tales.

Aleksandar, why do you keep talking to the Drina? Grandpa puts on Johann Sebastian's wig and looks at the sports section to check where Red Star stands at the top of the league championship.

I whisper it to him and kiss his hair, as if he were the grandson. Grandpa smells of crossword puzzles on fresh newsprint, he hands me a pack of Stela ice cream.

Sheep aren't really clouds that have fallen to earth, I say, and I introduce Grandpa to the voice of the Drina. Its voice is so cold, flowing from my hand, that Grandpa and I swim indoors and make up a bed with Turkisms: jastuk, jorgan, čaršaf – pillows, blanket, sheets. The Turks brought us their language, says Grandpa, waving to Marica Popović as she flies past the window, and when people are together a great deal, the time comes when they begin to talk like each other.

People say I talk like my Grandpa. There couldn't be a greater compliment.

Tonsils are the worst kind of physical propaganda! I lie down in the freshly made bed and cough. I have tonsillitis and spread spit over my face so people will think it's more tears than anyone has ever shed before, then they won't give me penicillin injections.

Vinegar and potato compresses really do lower my temperature. Grandpa brings me mandarins and minced meat with plums in bed, and explains: your fever is hungry, it's walking down to your calves.

Walrus says: the only compresses that really work are schnapps compresses on the feet, but you're too young for that. Nothing's worse than getting drunk through the soles of your feet.

Get dressed, we're off, Father tells me.

Artists have the most uncompromising sort of profession on the side.

On our way to hospital we stop at the bridge, because Ivo Andrić is trying to jump the river Drina on a horse. All Višegrad is there, dancing. Auntie Typhoon and Carl Lewis run a race across the bridge to open the programme. Andrić the Nobel Prize Winner gives the horse some wine as they come running up.

I never tire of watching Grandpa shave. I hold on to the wash basin and get gooseflesh on my head, Grandpa and I are standing so still.

There are hoof-beats on the asphalt, and Ivo Andrić takes off.

Do you think he'll make it? Grandpa asks, and he picks Granny flowers for three days running.

Hard to say.

*The promise a dam must keep, what the most beautiful
language in the world sounds like, and how often a heart
must beat to beat shame*

Francesco rented a room from old Mirela and moved in opposite,
and old Mirela unpacked her dusty make-up, saw that the powder
was crumbly and the lipstick no use any more, bought herself new
make-up that very same day, and fiddled around with the tomatoes
in her garden, her cheeks all rosy. You could get a good view into
Francesco's room from the garden. On warm summer evenings
Francesco would sit on the veranda, armed with a gigantic pair of
compasses as he pored over plans of our dam; he wore an undershirt, and from the garden you had a good view of the veranda too.
The women in our street and later of the whole town dropped by to
help old Mirela with the grass, the carrots, the cucumbers and the
cherry tree. The transformation of that little patch of grey-green
ground within six months was a botanical miracle. Edin and I called
Mirela's garden a jungle, and Edin swore he'd seen a golden horned
viper sitting on a pumpkin there. My mother peered out from
behind the net curtains before she went to work because Francesco
did pull-ups on the cherry tree in Mirela's garden before *he* went to
work. The cherries and my mother's cheeks bloomed as seldom
before, so I decided either to make friends with Francesco or chase
him away.

One evening I stood by the fence and stared at Francesco's back
so hard that my gaze climbed up his backbone all the way into his
head, and Francesco had to look round. I didn't understand him, he
didn't understand me. I pointed to the ball and then to him, and
said: Dino Zoff. It was a simple bet: if Francesco kept out at least
three of my five shots he could stay. If he kept out two or only one
I'd have to burn his plans and bury his compasses and his undershirt
among the strawberries in the garden, and then put frogs, pigeons

and cats in his room – I'd have no problem with any of that. But if he let a single shot at goal through on purpose, then I'd tell our butcher Mislav Sakić, also known as Massacre, that his wife had been wearing a scanty summer dress under the cherry tree recently, and playing about with her hair, and laughing a lot before she said goodbye to Francesco's undershirt.

So Francesco and I made friends. The tireless gardening ladies and the sweet cake-baking ladies weren't interested in weaning Francesco off Italian – far from it – so I taught him some words that very first evening, after he'd easily kept all my shots out. He could already say, 'My name is', and 'I am an engineer on the dam', and 'no thank you, I really couldn't eat another thing'. I opened his dictionary and pointed to the words for 'marriage', 'a bit', 'baroque' and 'eyebrow'. Then I pointed to my ears and said: sympatico, which wasn't a lie and sounded Italian. Francesco repeated after me: I. Am. A bit. Married. But. My wife. Doesn't. Have. Anything. Like. Such. Baroque. Eyebrows. Or. Such. Sympatico. Big. Ears. As. You.

You say that, I told Francesco, if you like the look of a woman – I pointed to my eyes and sculpted the figure of a woman with a broad behind in the air, the way men do when they've eaten a lot of smoked meat. And you must tell my mother and any ugly women: I am very much married although you are extremely friendly. After all, I hadn't come to Francesco's veranda to drink lemonade – there was family business to be done. When old Mirela brought us home-made cherry cake on the veranda, Francesco said to her: although extremely friendly. He had understood it all. After she had gone he pointed to the words 'ugly', 'woman' and 'no', in his dictionary, then to 'man', 'boy' and 'not', and finally to his eye and the word 'learn'. Francesco couldn't just build dams, he was Comrade-in-Chief of love.

After that evening I often went to see him. The dictionary lay on the table between us, Francesco drew, I did my homework, drank lemonade or read the *Encyclopedia of World Music*. Francesco explained that Italy was a boot, I painted a sandal half-standing in the Adriatic and gave it to him. My first sentences in Italian went like this: Bella sinjorina! Mi kjamo Alessandro. Posso offrirti una limonata? I said that to Edin, putting my hand on my heart. Edin looked at me as if I were an opera singer or a Japanese tourist in Višegrad and went away without a word, slowly, shaking his head a great deal. I'm only rehearsing for Jasna, I called after him.

I tried to explain to Francesco that Italians and Yugoslavians were more than just neighbours, because people who share something beautiful like a sea, and something dreadful like a Second World War, ought to sing together more. I don't know if he understood, at the word Mussolini he cried: nonono! I liked the way he ran his pencil along the ruler with great concentration, I liked to see the thin lines he closed up into rectangles, or how he could feed numbers into his pocket calculator for hours murmuring under his breath 'kvatro' or 'činkve' or 'čentomila'. I liked the 'mila' part best, and said: there, you see, Francesco, the sea, the war and we have the word mila too! Though to us it means nice.

The rains came in the middle of August. Short, violent and predictable, even the grasshoppers didn't sound surprised when raindrops drummed down on the veranda roof. We were quiet even though we talked a lot – our voice was the pages of the dictionary, we pointed to the words and formed sentences with gaps in them all the way to Italy.

And there were evenings when we didn't say anything in either our own voices or the voice of the dictionary. On one of these evenings I wrote Grandpa Slavko a long letter applying for the post in the Party of Magicians Who Could Make Things Possible. I attached a list of the possibilities that still had to be magicked into existence. Francesco drank wine and drew on his plans. He always sniffed the wine before putting the glass to his lips, and when he had finished work he massaged his temples, which made me feel tired and content.

Another time Francesco took me out to a meadow on the Drina, unpacked some shining silver balls from a black leather bag and began throwing them around. Boća, he said. He taught me the rules and told me you said boća but you wrote it 'boccia'. I tried to explain that we Yugoslavians saved whenever we could, and two letter 'c's side by side was one 'c' too many. Next evening Walrus played too, and a week later there were six of us, then eight. Francesco polished the balls, and Massacre the butcher said things like 'pallino' and 'volo'. If Francesco had had more than sixteen balls the whole town would soon have been playing boccia. I always played, that was what Francesco had decided, and once I didn't even come last by so very much.

I put Nivea cream on my hair so that it would be arranged in the same gleaming way as Francesco's, and I learned the names of the Italian national football team by heart. He was still keeping out all my penalty shots. Italian music was slow and the singers did a lot of suffering. I discovered that not all Italians have black hair, and I let Francesco know that not all Yugoslavians like börek. Francesco never smelled of sweat or detergent but always of the same lemony perfume. When I was as old as Francesco, I decided I wanted to wear shirts with an alligator on them too, and shoes that were always shiny, I wanted to smell of lemon from a world where every word ends in 'i'.

And one evening Čika Sefer, a small, elegant man in a suit who was deputy Comrade-in-Chief of the dam, or something like that, visited us at home and said that Francesco loved men.

I switched off the TV.

Everything was different now, and the difference had something to do with Francesco. I listened to Čika Sefer and didn't understand. Čika Sefer was keen on something that he called propriety and something else that he called the climate of work. And that, he said, is really not right or proper. Čika was amused by Francesco's tidy hair, and my mother echoed Čika Sefer: it really isn't right or proper, she said; I'd never have thought of such a thing.

What was 'such a thing' and what would 'never have been thought of' in the rocking chair where Francesco sat to read old Italian newspapers? What was 'such a thing' and what would 'never have been thought of' in our street, where my mother stood with the other women who lived nearby the next day, casting surreptitious glances at Francesco's veranda? Just what would she 'never have thought of'?

Soon everyone was whispering about Francesco, not only the women. That kind of thing was sick, said people, shaking their heads, and I discovered that there is love and love, and not every kind of love is good. Francesco went on going to work punctually with his hair combed back, he understood all this even less than I did, or else he didn't mind, and it made me furious. He read something from his newspaper aloud to me, in a good humour, and brooded as usual over his silly plans, even after he found the scratch on his car door one morning, a scratch that looked to be both intentional and the work of a spanner. Only Walrus still played boccia with us now. The other men sat on the benches on the river bank, eating pumpkin seeds and looking at the river.

I was furious because I didn't have to protect my mother from Francesco's undershirt any more, instead my mother told my father that I had to be protected from the Italian – look at the way they talk together. I was furious because our dictionary didn't know the words for 'I would never have thought of such a thing'.

A week after Čika Sefer's visit I was sitting on the veranda with Francesco. There was no lemonade and the cake had been baked the day before yesterday. I coughed, I sat down in the rocking chair in the corner, then at the table again, then on the veranda steps. I pulled up grass and rubbed it between the palms of my hands, and I shrugged my shoulders when Francesco pointed to 'what' and 'happened' in his dictionary. Ke kose sućesso, Alessandro?

I leafed through the dictionary to 'I'm sorry'.

Old Mirela came out on the veranda kneading a checked tea-cloth in her hands and asked me to translate for her; Francesco was to move out next week at the latest, she said. I shrugged and strung a few Italian-sounding syllables together. Confused, Francesco asked again: ke kose sućesso?

I said: sućesso kvatromila much, and to Mirela I said: he would like to stay for two weeks and then he's going anyway.

Mirela thought about it. But not a day longer, she said, taking away her lemonade carafe, her cake tin, and her coffee service. As she went out she whispered to me: it's late, you ought to be home by now.

My fury had turned into something with a muzzle and fangs and claws, and it was stuck in my throat, rocking back and forth.

Francesco had written down the date when he was leaving for me on one of our nicest evenings on the veranda, when nothing had sućesso yet; he had shown me photos, including one of the badly built tower. I put my finger on it and asked: tu . . . engineer? and we laughed.

Pisa, said Francesco, my Višegrad! Several black and white pictures showed a particularly large dam. Francesco turned serious and pointed to the lake: Lago di Vajont. The dam rose to an alarming height in the sky. I knew that in my next dream about falling I'd be up there on it. Francesco narrowed his eyes and leafed on – to a village under water. Then he went back to the gigantic dam with gigantic amounts of water foaming over it, water that must have hit the village and its people. Francesco tapped the dam and said, mio papà.

On the evening when old Mirela gave Francesco notice to leave I slipped away from the veranda without an arrivederci. I sat down in front of the bookshelf and read *Das Kapital*. But I wasn't really reading. I thought of Francesco's lemon scent, I thought of lemonade and the summer wind in the garden humming with insects, and the night when Francesco had pointed to that slice of bread hanging in the sky between the branches of the cherry tree and said: la luna è molto bella!

I lay flat on the floor so as to disappear.

There are no ugly women, only men who never learned to look at women properly when they were boys! Francesco had tried to explain to me that first evening. There was nothing in any encyclopedia about men loving men. In the school yard we called the weakest, palest boys 'queer', but that was all. I'd call people I hated the same in a fight, except that I hated being thumped even more than calling people names, so it never happened. The next morning I waited until Francesco went to work and then climbed the fence into Mirela's garden. Francesco's drawing instruments were lying on the veranda table. I weighed the compasses in my hand; the metal was cool. I dug a hole.

I didn't visit Francesco any more, and I avoided going out into the street when he was sitting on the veranda. I was ashamed of myself. Shame has a heartbeat of its own. Everything people said about Francesco and everything I thought made the heart of my shame beat louder.

After a week Francesco rang our bell. He'd never done that before. I was in my room. Father came out of his studio and opened the door to him. I listened with my door just a crack open, my ears and my whole head felt coloured, and no colour weighs you down as heavily as red. Alessandro, kalćio? Francesco asked, and my father said: no, no.

On the day he was leaving, Francesco leaned on the fence with his foot on the ball. He was waiting for me to come back from school, waiting for a last penalty shoot-out. I had turned into the street, seen him, and hidden. Like a thief, I pressed close to the wall of a building and went the long way home through the plum orchards. I peered out of the kitchen window: school kids were running past Francesco, ciao Francesco! they called, he passed them the ball, laughing, ciao ragazzi! I went to my room and went on with the list of possibilities to be magicked into existence. There was a ring at the door. Mother called my name. I thought something was being stolen from me. I didn't reply.

Oh, there you are, she said when I left my room that evening, feeling hungry. There was a package on the table. From the Italian, said my mother, who had taken to calling Francesco only by his nationality. I ate beans, it was always beans when I was feeling wretched.

If I were a magician who could make things possible, I'd have lemonade that always tasted the way it did on the evening when Francesco explained how right it was for the Italian moon to be a feminine moon. If I were a magician who could make things possible, we'd be able to understand all languages every evening between eight and nine. If I were a magician who could make things possible, every dam in the world would keep its promises. If I were a magician who could make things possible, there'd be kvatromila ways out of any miserable mood. If I were a magician who could make things possible, we'd be really brave.

The package was very heavy. It had my name on it, and underneath: Francesco Ballo. The package had a metal sound. Bocce. I undid the string and lifted the lid. On top was a photo of the big dam on the Lago di Vajont. I'll never know if Francesco's papa was the engineer or one of the villagers.

Mama, quanto costa un biglietto per Pisa? I asked, and Mother put her nose close to my throat: mm, young man, you smell nice.

I know, I said, because I did know, really nice, I said, and I leafed through the little dictionary. I pointed my fingertip at 'grazie', I pointed my fingertip at 'di', I pointed my fingertip, now wet with tears, at 'tutto'.

Mio caro amico Alessandro,
Puoi dirti fortunato to be boy in such nice town. Drina make eyes at everyone. Ground grow cherries, plums and clear water per la limonata. I let walrus win boccia. Your dam never go wrong now. Your papa e mamma et tu e tutto – safe. But no one say arrivederci. So Francesco say: arrivederci allora e a presto!

Presents per te, mio caro mago: bocce, perfume with lemon, dictionari, azzurri jersey! e cartina di Višegrad. I draw! Your house e house di good old Mirela! La vita, mio Alessandro, è solo questione di fortuna. We remember us well, please, and veranda and silence and jungle with horned viper and baroque girls under la luna!

Grazie quattromila!
Francesco

Why houses are sympathetic and unselfish, what music they make, and why I want them to stay sympathetic and unselfish, and above all to stand firm

Buildings are sympathetic and unselfish and they can't play musical instruments, which is a pity. If buildings were people they would be vegetarians or vegans or vgtnrs or just vgs. If you are a vg you don't eat or drink anything that might have a heartbeat, even just theoretically, which means not even water, because Grandpa told me that South American Indians believe there can be a whole god swimming in a river like the Amazon, or at least a whole religious faith.

If there were a god in the Drina too, I once asked Grandpa, would the catfish be fish-priests?

Or fish-hodjas, said Grandpa, nodding.

If I were a magician who could make things possible, there'd be houses making music, houses as musically gifted as Johann Sebastian Bach – I know about his merits and his wonderful wig from the *Encyclopedia of Music* that Mr Popović the music teacher gave me, a grandpa who is friends with Grandpa Slavko. You can look up the meaning of the word 'baroque' in the encyclopaedia too, I learned it by heart; for quite a while 'baroque' was my main term of approval, it's only recently been replaced by 'exquisite'.

The house would play songs for a grandmother living alone and watching TV and watering flowers and giving them fertiliser and waiting for someone to come through the door; a grandmother who's always cooked too much to eat because she can't get used to being on her own; it would play songs from a time that was much quieter, because there were more cows chewing the cud, and not so many car exhausts and vacuum cleaners.

My Serbo-Croat teacher Mr Fazlagić's house would make a sound like the sea, because that lowers your blood pressure.

My family's house would have a repertoire as wide and un-predictable as the many different moods living under our roof and inside us. Our kitchen would play The Doors because Jim Morrison turns my mother's anxious look into a wistful expression. There'd be French chansons when my father disappears into his studio. Johann Sebastian when Uncle Miki and my father are watching politics and Father shouts: no, we are not quarrelling, we are just raising our voices in a discussion!

When Father, whistling French songs, takes Mother to supper in the Estuary Restaurant there'd be Pink Floyd. Mr Floyd makes you feel grown-up and nice and tingly. I sip Father's cognac and watch the TV with the sound muted.

There'd be the last three minutes of Ravel's *Boléro* at full volume when Auntie Typhoon comes to visit.

The sunflowers in Nena Fatima's garden by the Drina would play the songs Nena sang when she was a girl, she still knows them all by heart. Nena would hum along silently, and when her tears came – because knowing something by heart can sometimes be the saddest thing in the universe – the clever chimney would play a medley. Tears and medleys don't go together. The really special thing about my musical houses would be that even someone as deaf as a post could hear them.

My own house would sing in Great-Grandpa's voice, and once a day it would promise something that would last.

I put the *Encyclopedia of World Music* back on the shelf and ask my mother when she is finally going to make me learn an instrument or three, or the accordion. She is watching the news; barricades and burning flags. I ask the same question again in the same words.

I paint ten soldiers without any weapons.

I paint Mother's face, smiling, happy, carefree.

If I were a magician who could make things possible, then pictures could talk while we painted them.

If I were a magician who could make things possible, then houses could keep their promises. And they would have to promise not to lose their roofs or go up in flames. If I were a magician who could make things possible, the scars made in them by bullet holes would close up again over the years.

What music does a tower block make in war?

What victory is the best, what Grandpa Slavko trusts me to do, and why people act as if your fears are less if you don't talk about them

No one could have guessed that I'd win. Uncle Miki claps me on the back of the head and says: no one could have guessed that you'd win. My mother tucks a strand of my hair back behind my ear, but it falls straight back over my forehead. Really, no one could have guessed it, she says, taking my face between her hands.

The no-one-could-have-guessed-it victory celebrations are just over, the man who came second is at least six times older than me and twice as tall. He shakes hands, our fishing rods cross like swords. Uncle Miki pushes him aside – he doesn't particularly like me, but he likes other people even less, and congratulations that go on too long are always suspect.

My father didn't come with us. He had to finish a picture in his studio. Recently he's been finishing pictures all the time, and as soon as he's through with one he starts two more. There's no room left for them in his studio, they have to go into the bedroom, Mother wakes in the night screaming: faces everywhere!

I look at the river, then at my gold medal, I'm never going to take it off. With that medal I've qualified, and next Saturday everyone who's qualified is to meet in Osijek on the Drau. Among the best anglers in the Republic, says a short, fat man when he hands me the certificate, whereupon Miki shouts at him from the back of the crowd: no need to look so doubtful about it, fatso!

Miki, so close to the water and related to a winner, is all enthusiasm. Apart from me, he's the only one in the family with any idea about fishing. He wasn't allowed to compete today because not so long ago he threw Čika Luka into the Drina when Čika Luka wanted to see Uncle Miki's fishing licence. Miki says he didn't do it: the stupid snooper slipped, he says, and if I hadn't been nearby to pull him out, someone would soon have had a rather ugly catfish on his hook.

With spectacles and whiskers, I finished, as Miki shrugged his shoulders, the picture of innocence. I was on his side, because Čika Luka doesn't like people or fish or even himself – it's through him that I discovered the meaning of the word 'frustrated'.

I won today because of the secret in my bait. Breadcrumbs mixed with water, a little vanilla sugar, small pieces of liver sausage plus the secret. The chub freaked out when I fed them the bait, they jumped out of the water shouting: stop, stop! because my secret mixture tasted so good to them.

I don't have to go to Osijek, I tell Mother, trying to comfort her, you – any of you – really couldn't have guessed that I'd win.

Because Osijek is a problem; no one can drive me there because no one could have guessed that I'd win, so they've all made other plans. So my mother says. She doesn't say: it's because there's shooting in Croatia. She doesn't say: it's because a tank crushed a red car in Osijek. She doesn't say that the final was cancelled long ago for that reason, that is, if anyone can even stop to think of cancelling things.

I'm scared myself.

Number Three, my starting number, is still sticking there in the bank. Today at noon I landed sunbleak after sunbleak, several enthusiastic chub, and even a small Danube salmon. That one got away because Uncle Miki shouted behind me: what are you doing, you fool, don't let go, are you crazy?

I make sure that no one is watching, I crouch down and pass the back of my hand over the surface of the water. What does your heartbeat sound like?

I keep my medal on at home too. My mother calls down to the cellar: we're back, Picasso, come on up, there's something you've got to see here.

Uncle Miki flings himself down on the sofa and switches the TV on. The coffee starts to brew, my father comes into the living room whistling, rubbing his hands on a cloth.

You smell of fish, he says, about to pat me on the head.

You smell of acetone, I say, ducking out of the way.

He taps my medal. Not bad!

Yes, I say, it's good, but Father isn't looking at me any more, he's looking at his brother's feet on the sofa. He pushes them roughly off and sits down beside him.

Coffee and a rainstorm. That's how it is on August afternoons. Osijek comes on screen, even the Drau is shown. It may be very beautiful, but if there are houses burning all around you being beautiful is difficult.

The war is switched off when Grandpa Slavko comes in and sits down opposite me. He looks at the certificate and the medal. I guessed it, he says, or no, I knew it.

No one else could have guessed it, Grandpa, what do you mean, you knew it?

Grandpa raises his eyebrows. I was watching you at the bridge last week and the estuary yesterday.

I never noticed you.

I can watch very quietly.

And how could you tell that I was going to win?

I could see that you were happy. I saw your mouth moving although you were alone.

I had to learn a poem by heart.

I think you were talking to someone.

I was alone, Grandpa.

Grandpa Slavko leans over to me and whispers: I don't think you were alone, I think the river was there with you.

Grandpa!

Aleksandar!

We both lean back, resting against the backs of our chairs like two boxers between rounds, except that boxers don't often smile at each other. Grandpa's hair is thick and strong and grey at the sides, like Father's hair, like my hair will be in thirty years' time, he sticks his thumbs in the braces over his chest, we both shake our heads. I'd like to be a grandpa who's friends with my grandpa, we'd talk to our grandsons in riddles and go out walking every evening with our shared memories and old arguments clasped behind our backs.

Would you have won in Osijek too? Grandpa asks, knowing that I'll never go to Osijek now.

No.

Why not?

I lean forward now and whisper: it's not my river there.

Do you know, says Grandpa, that there are people who don't have any games where there's a winner at the end?

People in Amazonia?

More or less.

We lean back and look at each other contentedly. Only now do I realise that no one else has said anything all this time. Mother is standing in the doorway, and she has no worry lines today. Miki and Father are both kneading something in their hands. Granny is making plates clink softly, I look at my family as if we've all succeeded at something.

Shall we watch Carl Lewis tomorrow? I ask Grandpa. I'll catch fish for our supper, you can fry it, then we'll watch Carl to see if he can stay under ten seconds, right?

Later, when everyone has gone and I'm in bed, my mother asks what I'd like if I could have a wish. She calls me her Comrade-Angler-in-Chief. She knows I like the term comrade-in-chief. People treat tired winners gently.

I'd wish for everything to be all right for ever, I say.

What do you call all right? asks Mother, sitting down on the edge of the bed.

It's all right when you make me sandwiches this evening for tomorrow, and I can go fishing tomorrow and you don't worry about where I am, and Grandpa lives for ever, and you all live for ever, and the fish don't stop being in the river and Osijek stops burning and Red Star win the European Cup again next year and Granny Katarina never runs out of coffee and neighbours, and Nena Fatima can really hear everything, even though she's deaf, and the houses play music, and no one has to bother about Croatia any more, starting now, and there are little boxes containing tastes so that we can swap them with each other, and we don't forget how to hug, and . . .

My mother's lips are trembling. That's fine, she says, and for the first time since there have been first times she doesn't say: but don't go too far.

I choose the fattest worms. They wriggle. I make holes in the jam jar lid with a screwdriver. Along the Drina on my bike, two hours through the morning mist, through villages without any names. Go fishing, catch fish, swim, talk to the river, tell it everything, eat my sandwiches. Smoked ham on kaymak. Plum jam on plum jam. Let the Danube salmon go. Laugh out loud because I know the Drina likes winners to laugh like that. Let the Danube salmon go. I laugh out loud, and the Drina says: I knew it all along.

How the bold river Drina is feeling, how the lipless Drina is really feeling, what she thinks of little Mr Rzav, and how little you need to be as happy as a falcon

My town of Višegrad has grown into the mountains in all directions. My Višegrad rises from two rivers, they've made a date here, the Drina and the Rzav, an endless date, going on for ever, every second. Who was here first? I call from the estuary. And what did they look like and what did they sound like: those last ten seconds when the water was still on its way and then – suddenly? – they met?

The mountains accompany the Drina, they fold her in between steep rocks, making what I say echo. The higher the rocks, the deeper the river, it seems to me, and the more lost you are, whether you're in a boat or here on the bank.

Yesterday no one could have guessed I was going to win, today I ride my bike along the Drina and I just want to go fishing. It's early morning, it's Sunday, the mist whistles around my ears, it's chilly. My mother has made sandwiches and put two apples in my rucksack. You can get some on the way, said my father, taking the apples out again and down to the studio with him. 'Still Life of a Shipwrecked Regime and a Yugo Broken Down on a Stony Road' is the name of the picture he's been working on for weeks.

Smoked ham, kaymak, plum jam spread thickly on rye bread. My two rods stick out of my rucksack. Two years ago Uncle Miki promised to give me an even better one every birthday. Uncle Miki is someone who has almost as good an idea of fishing as me, and not a man to break his promises.

I want to live to be a hundred and thirty years old beside the Drina.

I've never been this far on my own before. The fact that it's early morning and a Sunday doesn't stop the farmers from working in the narrow fields. Three women with headscarves holding hoes in their big hands straighten up and watch me go by. The rocks and the river hem the earth in, the fields are long and narrow. So is the apple orchard where, on my father's instructions, I steal apples, two red and two yellow: an unfenced strip of land between the rocks and the water. I'm just about to get back on my bike when the sun breaks through the mist, breaks so abruptly through the still thick swathes of it that its light is splintered, the splinters fall on the river and cut into the rippling surface, glittering. Almost hidden by the long-haired branches of two weeping willows and the towering white cliffs, it sparkles brightest in a little bay beyond the orchard. From now on its name will be the Lagoon of Light, because unusual places need a name, it's the same as with stars. I lean the bike against the rickety fence, a lizard immediately climbs on to the handlebars and darts its tongue out at me. I tap my forehead and go through the arch of exuberant willow branches to the water, which is still racing with splinters of sun. A moss-grown tree trunk lies across the bay, rimmed on the left by rocks with peaks that you can only guess at in the misty air. A hawk takes off from the tree trunk, its slate-blue feathers disappear into the mist, the tail feathers are red; kyu, cries the hawk, ket-ket, it cries, turning head over heels in the air as if this is all great fun. The fluttering of its pointed wings dies away slowly, then there's no sound but the wind in the willow trees. The silence leans forward. I look around, from here I can't see the fence any more, or the apple trees or the road; I'm in a room, a lagoon of light.

I unpack my rods and sit down on a stone by the water. Here the river swerves into a branching embrace, I'm sitting in the crook of its elbow. Grandpa Slavko says the Drina is a bold river. That's why I don't mind when grown-ups call me bold. I think being bold is a good thing, and I shout at the water: you bold – you beautiful – bold – river – beautiful river. The canyon echoes, kyu, ket-ket, replies the hawk, and something large throws up foam in the river; perhaps the falcon has dropped a stone. But the splashing is deeper and lasts longer than the usual meeting of stone and water. I can't see rings or ripples anywhere, it can't have been a stone, perhaps it was the Drina herself, clearing her throat. The wind grows stronger, the Drina takes a breath and asks: what do you mean, bold?

I scrape up some of the earth from the bank with the toe of my shoe and tread on it, because that's such a nice feeling under your sole. I don't know, I say, perhaps because you're unapproachably muddied and fast in autumn, you don't freeze over in winter, you flood everything in spring, and you drowned my Grandpa Rafik like a kitten in summer.

I wait. The Drina is silent. The rocks aren't silent. Stones come away and tumble into the river. The Lagoon of Light grows darker. There's a rumble further up the mountains. The Drina does not reply. I get my can of bait and my rods out of the rucksack. Kyu. Ket-ket. I get angry because the Drina is silent. Aren't you going to say something? Don't you even remember Grandpa Rafik?

I push the ball of bait down below the surface, briefly, then angrily I throw it out. Breadcrumbs, gingerbread and ground liquorice, oat flakes, chopped maggots. The ball lands with a hollow splash, and where it falls the Drina asks: what did your grandpa look like?

You should know better than I do, I say, dipping my hands in to wash them. You saw him last, and I was still very little.

I'm sorry.

Well, I *was* very little.

Would you like to swim?

Thanks, but not so soon after talking about death.

I decide on a plain hook, size six. Do the fish-hooks hurt you? I ask.

Why don't you ask the fish?

I put the first worm on the hook and cast it out. The float moves slowly with the current.

What does it feel like, fish swimming about in you?

It tickles when they jump.

I pass my hand over the surface. Does it tickle when someone throws an old washing machine into you too?

Those bastards!

I straighten up and pull the line in. The worm is still on the hook. I cast again, a little further to the left, closer to the rocks. Drina? How come you don't speak in dialect?

Do you?

I look at the float and don't answer. If I say no, the river will reply: well, then! Perhaps if I don't say anything she will go on of her own accord, telling me what good friends she really is with the Rzav, how much the dam bothers her, and whether rivers feel afraid too. I don't say how much I envy her because she can see so much, from her source to the river Save, up to the sky, down into the ground, right, left, it's quite a view.

The Rzav is a fine gentleman, she says, he plays around the rocks like a good colleague, although he has his fits of anger every spring and bursts his banks. And the dam closes her mouth, flowing fast is like shouting out loud. Yes, she admits, she does feel fear. She defies the winter cold, the autumn rains don't bother her, but she's afraid the shooting will infect us with war too. Up against the rocks she complains, she's been through countless wars, each more dreadful than the last. She has had to carry away so many corpses, so many blown-up bridges lie at rest on her bed. I must believe her, she says, her waters are murky by the bank, nothing in the world suffers like the stones of a bridge without their bridge. And she has never been able to hide, or close her eyes to crimes, she says, foaming angrily, I don't even have eyelids! I know no sleep, I can't save anyone, I can't prevent anything. I want to cling to the bank, but I can't hold fast to anything, I'm a horrible state of aggregation! Look, no hands, not in all my long life! When I fall in love I can't kiss, when I'm happy I can't strike the accordion keys. Yes, Aleksandar, I have a wonderful view, a wonderful view and all for nothing.

Once or twice the float jerks, I stand up, I guess at a third bite, the float goes right down, I pull in and immediately feel the weight on the rod, I give out a little more line, pull it in again – and I know I have him. He tires quickly, a young Danube salmon, I give him back to the Drina, and she lets him leap above the surface.

Drina, I need a bigger one. If Grandpa Slavko is going to cook, we need a proper fish. What do you think, will Carl Lewis win the hundred metres? I ask, casting again, but the river gives no more answers. The wind blows more strongly, or is it a sobbing from the ravine, or would the mist like to say something too? It disperses, and now the sun is there for the lagoon again, the grasshoppers are there for the lagoon, ket-ket, calls the hawk, plunging into the ravine, ket-ket, and I wonder if the Drina has gooseflesh at this moment – look at the ripples on the surface – ket-ket, kyu, ket-ket.

11 February 2002

Dear Asija,

Did I make you up? Did I guide our hands to the light switch together because of some touching story about children in wartime? You never told me your surname, but all the same I've addressed every letter as if I knew it. I remember the morning of the soldiers' dance. The architecture of the town was rain clouds, camouflage colours and splintered glass. Edin and I wanted to do something completely normal, we wanted to feel something as simple as the weight of a fish on the line. You don't come into that part of the story. You don't come into it, frightened on the stairway, or throwing stones into the river, I don't see your beautiful hair among the soldiers looting at their leisure. You didn't come with me, we never said goodbye, Asija.

No more letters. I'm getting drunk and calling Bosnia, so forgive the theatricality. The clock on my laptop says: 23:23 Monday, 11 February 2002. What day was it when we switched the light on? No more letters, Asija, did you ever really exist?

I'm Asija. They took Mama and Papa away with them.
My name has a meaning. Your pictures are horrible

I run the cursor over the clock. '23:23 Monday, 11 February 2002'. I click, the Properties window comes up showing the date and time. What day did we switch the light on, what day was 6 April 1992? I turn the date back ten years. Any moment now there'll be a flash, and my father will put a book on my head and mark my height on the door frame with a pencil. Any moment now there'll be a flash, and I'll be 1.53 metres tall, and . . .

Father is waking me up: Aleksandar, there's no school today, we're going to Granny's, get dressed, I'll tell you what to take.

People grow in their sleep.

Any moment now there'll be a flash. I wait to be turned back to a day – and yes, the computer shows it; a Monday – when I'll be afraid of my father. Afraid of his list of things I'm to pack, afraid of his warning: only what you need. Afraid because he doesn't say why.

What do I need?

Any moment now there'll be a flash, and an almost forgotten feeling will become the sight of cobwebs clogged with dust on the cellar walls as we wait for the next hit. I make a list of all the things I can remember in my grandmother's cellar. Worn-out ironing boards, headless dolls, duffel bags containing shirts that smell of old pumpkin, coal and potatoes and onions, moths and cat's pee. Light bulbs flickering as shells explode. Gooseflesh and yet more goose-flesh. Not because the fear is so great, but because going to sleep in peacetime and waking up at war is so unimaginable.

'7:23 Monday, 6 April 1992'. There's no school today. My mother sits in the living room sewing banknotes into her skirt.

My father will give the signal for everything that was unimaginable before we woke up, both through what he says and through the nervous state he's in. Father's uncertainty and the first shells make everything that was good before the unimaginable happened retreat into the distance. Thinking of setting fire to a frog is further away than Japan; dreams of the curves under Jasna's shirt are so out of place that I feel ashamed of them; plum-picking is suspended for now, the secret signs showing how Edin should run towards the invisible defenders in our games are pointless. What's going to happen is so improbable that there'll be no improbability left for a made-up story.

I make a list of things I was never punished for. Setting fire to the board in school. Putting frogs, pigeons and cats in Čika Veselin's apartment after he called Uncle Bora a steamroller. Looking through the window when Zoran's Aunt Desa visited the tired labourers working on the dam. Throwing snowballs at windscreens. Phoning presidents of the Local Committee and saying in a disguised voice: this is Tito speaking, you're useless. Stealing those pencil sharpeners and exercise books from the department store. Breaking Granny's vase.

Why aren't you at work, Papa?

Father presses the drawing pins on my Red Star poster more firmly into the wall with his thumbs. Pack the biggest rucksack, he says. Seven pairs of underpants. Rainproof jacket. Cap. Stout shoes. Wear your trainers. Two pairs of trousers. A thick pullover, two or three shirts and T-shirts, not too many. Your green fishing jacket, the one with all the pockets. A towel, toothpaste, toothbrush, soap. I've put handkerchiefs and your passport on the table downstairs for you . . . do you have a favourite book?

Yes.

Good, nods Father, he smooths out my no-one-could-have-guessed-you'd-win certificate and doesn't close the door when he goes out.

'7:43 Monday, 6 April 1992'. There'll be a pocket-knife lying beside the handkerchiefs and a notepad with the addresses and phone numbers of all our friends and relations. Father will be in his studio. The canvases, the pictures, the paints, the brushes – he stacks everything in a corner and covers it with blankets. I crouch on the stairs watching. He pushes my old mattress in front of the canvases and puts his beret on top of the lot. He closes the door. We drive to Granny's, the tall apartment block has a large cellar. The sound of the first shell is cramped and polished in the big cellar. That's what I think: cramped and polished. Not like in a film, not exploding seriously, no shaking, nothing trickling down. Something heavy without enough room to break into pieces properly – cramped. And free of any rushing noise, clear, clean, metallically smooth – polished. The cramped thing is injected into the cellar walls and Emilija Slavica Krsmanović burps in the silence after the fiftieth shell.

'0:21 Tuesday, 12 February 2002'. I make a list of Granny's neighbours who have come to shelter in the cellar, like us. I add all the neighbours from our street that I can think of. On another sheet of paper I write: Bars, restaurants, hotels, and under that: Café Galerie. Estuary Restaurant. Hotel Bikavac. Hotel Višegrad. Hotel Vilina Vlas.

I surf through search-engine entries:

'football in the war Sarajevo training shelling'

'višegrad genocide handke shame responsibility'

'victim innocent bombardment of belgrade'

'milošević international interest fades'

I scroll through discussion groups, I read diatribes and nostalgic reveries, click and click and click and note down other people's memories, Montenegrin jokes, cookery recipes, names of heroes and enemies, eyewitness accounts, reports from the front, the Latin names of the fish in the Drina, I download new Bosnian music, I

click on the first link: 'den haag own goal european union srebre-
nica', I read that the war criminal Radovan Karadžić is in Belgrade,
and here my computer crashes. I press the restart key. My face
is reflected in the black screen and I suddenly don't know what
I'm looking for, here in my apartment with a view of the Ruhr,
thousands of kilometres from my river Drina. The screen-saver of
the bridge in Višegrad comes up, but I didn't take even that photo
myself.

'16:14 Thursday, 9 April 1992'. The truck drives up. Six men get out.
Two stay there drinking Coca-Cola. They're wearing boots. Four
peer through the ground-floor windows. They cross the yard.
Krsmanović and Spahić. Two families? Mixed marriage? A case of
sub-letting? The lock gives way. Two of them search the living
room. Two of them go down to the cellar. They shoot the cellar
door open. They pull the blankets away. They tear holes in the still
life entitled 'The Snake and the Optimistic Letter to a Young
Democracy', and 'Portrait of B. as Virtuoso on the Tender Violin'.
They push the old mattress aside. They go to the trouble of
breaking every single brush. They paint each others' faces with
acrylic paint. They kick through the canvases. One of them puts the
beret on his head.

I phone Granny. I wake her up. She sounds worried: why are you
calling so late?

Granny, is the green house with the peculiar roof still there? Is
the gym still in use, what's being played there, what league are we
in?

Aleksandar . . . ?

Granny, it's important. I read about the building in Pionirska
Street in the paper. Has it burned right down? What happened to
Čika Aziz? Did the soldiers ever find him? Are Čika Hasan and
Čika Sead still alive?

I've made lists. Granny doesn't answer.

What about the bridges? Has there been another flood since we
left?

You always used to count your footsteps, says Granny in a calm, sleepy voice. You measured the whole town on your walks.

Two thousand, three hundred and 49 steps from your place to our home, I say, surprised that I still remember that after ten years.

Your legs are longer now, says Granny, come here and walk around again.

I've made lists. I've written about the two mosques, I've written: 'torn down'. Pages full of names, pages full of nicknames, friends and neighbours, lists upon lists, betting on my memory. I don't want it to be torn down too; I've made lists, and now I have to see it all.

You don't have to send me the package, I tell Granny, I'll come and fetch it myself. I'm booking a flight this very evening.

You ought to wait for the plum blossom and come by bus. Granny's voice has none of the crazy light-hearted tone of her earlier phone calls.

Don't expect a holiday, Aleksandar.

Granny?

You're late, and I'll have to tidy up.

I can help.

You've never been here to help me, and soon it will be spring.

I'm so sorry.

We all are.

Granny?

I'm looking forward to it, Aleksandar, I'll fry you minced meat and heat up the milk, I'm really looking forward to it.

'3:13 Tuesday, 12 February 2002'. I am not planning to sleep.

'sniper alley barricades water canister'

'harry hitler potter milošević gotovina delić'

'there is no absolute evil and no absolute memory'

'WHERE WERE YOU ALEKSANDAR KRSMANOVIĆ

'low-cost flights to Sarajevo'

I ring 00 38 733 for Sarajevo, and then add a string of digits at random. I ask for Asija. There's no Asija anywhere, usually I don't even get a connection. Several times I raise voices that are sleepy first, then angry. An answer-phone. Hello? It's me, Aleksandar, I'm coming. Are you there? Are you there, Asija?

'10:09 Saturday, 11 April 1992'. On the fifth day of the siege, shells land in the mountains, sailing down into the town only occasionally. Cows and sheep crowd the yard outside the apartment building, hooves tread the concrete in among the Fiats and the Yugos.

Refugees have moved into the cellar and the stairway overnight. Old people and mothers and babies wrapped up in pieces of cloth like hot rolls. They're looking for shelter in the big building because there are no buildings left to shelter them in their villages – no big ones, no little ones, not one is left intact. Only half-walls, soot and cellars, and what does a cellar look like without a building? With my paper on my knees, I paint an uncracked glass.

Let them stay! The more the merrier! Walrus decides, and his voice echoes right through the stairwell. He's become something like the mayor of the building, second only to President Aziz, who has the right kind of gun to be a president. Walrus wins at Uno against the farmers, I learn the rules by watching.

Our horses have been taken away from us. Our sons would have been taken away from us too if they hadn't already gone to war, sighed the farmers, mourning their horses; they lower their eyes thinking of their sons, they lament for their girls.

They won't stop at our villages, says a man with twirled moustaches, I ask his name, I write 'Ibrahim' on a mug and pour him water. The toothless women chew bread with their mouths open. They smell sour and lie down in the corridor to sleep. You have to climb over them, they wake up and curse you feebly. I don't call them refugees, I say: protégés. They themselves have been protecting a girl with such bright hair that I have to ask my father if there's a colour word to describe such brightness.

He says: beautiful.

I say: beautiful isn't a colour.

Beautiful and her uncle with the twirled moustaches eat in the cellar with us. Ibrahim waits until Beautiful has gone to sleep with her head on his lap, and then he quietly tells us about their flight. He and his niece were weak and hungry when they met the others. The others fed them and put Beautiful, who wasn't well, in a half-Lada that was being pulled by two donkeys. We are the last of our village, says Ibrahim, he thinks for a moment, we are the last of nowhere. Our houses are gone. I'm telling you all this so that you will know who you're dealing with, but first I want to sleep. And then, good people, then I want to shave, my beard is full of memories of the worst night of my life. Ibrahim strokes Beautiful's hair. The child has lost everything, he says, everything and every-one.

He doesn't have to say any more. I'll never let Beautiful out of my sight, I won't let anything happen to her ever again. Beautiful says nothing. Beautiful can sit so still that she's invisible. When Beautiful isn't near me I look for her. Beautiful is clutching a shabby old bag. A dirty, scruffy teddy bear dangles from the strap of the bag.

My name is Aleksandar. I paint unfinished pictures, look, here are books without any dust, there's Yuri Gagarin without Neil Armstrong, there's a dog without a collar. That's Nena Fatima with her hair unbraided. My name is Aleksandar, and there's always something not so beautiful that's left out of the pictures. Do you like boys with big ears?

I'm Asija. They took Mama and Papa away with them. My name means something. Your pictures are horrible.

Where are Asija's parents?

Do I know any of the soldiers out there? Could Uncle Miki be with them?

What do we need? A pocket-knife costing fifty marks and a little luck, is that all?

How heavy do memories weigh in a beard?

'5:09 Tuesday, 12 February 2002'. I've written down all the names of streets in Višegrad, all the children's games, I've made a list of the

193

things that you could find in the school, including the five hundred pencil sharpeners that Edin and I sprinkled over the rubble left by the bombing, like Hansel and Gretel. I want to trace the patterns of the past. There's a box in my grandmother's bedroom containing ninety-nine unfinished pictures. I'll go home and finish painting every one of them.

Out of three hundred and thirty Sarajevo numbers rung at random, about every fifteenth has an answering machine

Good evening, my name is Aleksandar Krsmanović. I'm calling you because I'm trying to find out something about a childhood friend. She escaped from Višegrad to Sarajevo during the civil war. Her name is Asija. I've tried everything I can, the civil service offices, the Internet – no luck. I can't tell you her surname because unfortunately I'm not sure if I've got it right. If you know anything about anyone of that name, please call me on 00 49 1748 526368. Asija is in her early twenties now, and back then she had extremely bright blonde hair. Thank you very much.

Good evening, my name is Aleksandar Krsmanović. I'm calling you because I'm trying to find out something about a childhood friend. She escaped from Višegrad to Sarajevo during the civil war. Her name is Asija. I've tried everything else, the civil service offices, the Internet – no luck. I can't tell you her surname because unfortunately I'm not sure if I've got it right. If you know anything about anyone of that name, please call me on 00 49 1748 526368. Asija is in her early twenties now, and back then she had extremely bright blonde hair. Thank you very much.

Hello? Mr Sutijan? I hope I'm pronouncing your name correctly – I called your number at random because I'm so disappointed by my efforts to date. My name is Aleksandar and I'm calling from Germany, where I've been living since our war. Do you happen to know a woman called Asija? It's not a common name, maybe you've heard it and could give me a clue where to find her. The name means bringer of peace, I'm looking for my own Asija and I can't be at peace until I know what's happened to her. That may sound naff and drunk, and so it is too. Mr Sutijan, if anything occurs to you, my number is: 00 49 1748 526368.

Hello, Asija, this is Aleksandar. You're not there. I've just booked a flight to Sarajevo. I'm arriving on Monday. I'd like it if we could meet. You can reach me on: 00 49 1748 526368.

Hello, this is Aleksandar Krsmanović. Asija? It would be nice if we could meet, I'm arriving on the twenty-fifth. There won't be any ripe elderberries and plums and quinces yet, but there'll be stair-wells around smelling delicious. You can call me if you like on 00 49 1748 526368.

Asija? This is Aleksandar. Aleksandar with the big ears from Višegrad. The boy in the cellar. The one who called you Beautiful because there wasn't any better word to describe the colour of your hair. Aleksandar who was your brother for a day. Let's meet in Sarajevo or Višegrad and remember what we went through to-gether. 00 49 1748 526368.

Asija? Hi, Aleksandar here. Mondays are the best days to begin something. It's almost ten years since we last met. That makes about five hundred and twenty Mondays, which doesn't sound like much. But if you think about it carefully, it's a whole lot of Mondays when something new could have begun. I'd like to know all the things you've begun in your life. I'm going to spend a few days where I once came to the end of something. 00 49 1748 526368.

I've written six letters, Asija, and I thought up a different surname for you for each envelope, but I always wrote the same one in the end. Bosnia is boundless compared to just six letters. In my ima-gination I see you as a violinist. You have tough, hardened skin on your fingertips and you wear yourself out at every concert. If someone asks how you're doing, you hardly know where to begin for pride. You run five kilometres every day, you speak French, but you couldn't care less about France. I'll be in Bosnia from Monday, please call me: 00 49 1748 526368.

Good evening, this is Aleksandar. Asija . . . ? Are you there . . . ? Please pick up the phone . . . I miss you, you see, and if you pick up the phone maybe I can tell you what exactly it is I miss about you. Things build up over ten years. How do you do your hair now? Do you like minced meat? I love minced meat. I'll be in Sarajevo on Monday, for three days. 00 49 1748 526368.

I'm sorry to trouble you. Once upon a time there was a blonde girl with the Arabic name of Asija and a dark-haired boy with the far from Arabic name of Aleksandar. There was a definite chance of a love story there: their parents might have come over all religious and opposed the connection, convention opposes it anyway, and war makes all those objections even stronger. Terrible, because the heart has its reasons and so on and so forth. I have to disappoint you. Asija and Aleksandar were too young for a love story. They didn't yet have any sense of the tragic potential of their happiness and possible unhappiness. Asija who was protected! Aleksandar who protected her! Ha! The two of them held hands and switched the light on at a time when only lunatics thought of being light-hearted. 00 49 1748 526368. That's my number, in case you'd like to know more. Sorry to trouble you.

My cases are packed. The wine tastes good. The plums that grow in Višegrad are better than any others. 00 49 1748 526368. You can reach me at any time, any time over the last ten years, so to speak. I'm writing a portrait of Višegrad in thirty lists. Bur first I'm coming to see you, Asija.

Hello, good evening. I'm nothing special. My story is nothing special. Good evening. I arrive too late for everything. I arrive too late to be special. I'm arriving at the story of my life too late. Good evening, Bosnia, please call back: 00 49 1748 526368.

*

Asija, I'll look for your hair, I'll look on all the faces I see for your forehead. I'll drop your name into every conversation like a seed and hope it will grow into a flower. Dear answering machine, do you know a flower called Asija? If so please call me on: 00 49 1748 526368. Excuse me, please . . .

Hello? Hello? Is there anyone there? I have no idea who you are, I'm Aleksandar Krsmanović, student, grandson, refugee, long hair, big ears, looking for his memory. Looking for a girl. Well, a woman, really. Asija. Do you know Asija? I once met a madman, a soldier looking for a girl called Emina. Do you know a girl called Asija? I'm conducting a methodical search. My method is to gloss over my own story and draw up endless lists. 00 49 1748 526368.

Asija? Asija? Asija? Asija. Asija. Asija.
One day a man who asked good questions asked:
    Who is that, what is that? Forgive me!
    Where is it,
    Where does it come from,
    Where is it going,
    This country
    Of Bosnia?
    Tell me!
    And the man he was addressing swiftly replied:
    There is a country called Bosnia somewhere, forgive me,
    A cold, bleak country,
    Naked and hungry,
    And besides all that,
    Forgive me,
    It is defiant
    With sleep.

This is me, Aleksandar. The poem is by Mak Dizdar. If you pick it up, call me on: 00 49 1748 526368. I'd like to tell you the story of the baker who sprinkled thirty sacks of flour over the streets of Višegrad one summer night in '92, and after that, in her little shop, she . . .

What makes the Wise Guys wise, how much you ought to bet on your own memory, who is found and whose existence is still unfounded

Mesud and Kemo can't remember Kiko's real name. The two men have spent hours, in between coffees, telling me the myths and legendary tales of football in Yugoslavia, Bosnia, Sarajevo. We're sitting in a small betting shop and café above the Old Town, and Mesud says: perhaps he was just called Kiko, same as with the Brazilians.

Kiko, number nine, Kiko of the amazing headers, Kiko the iron skull of the gentle river Drina had scored thirty goals in the last half-season before the war, twenty of them with his head, three with his right foot, the other seven all with his weaker left foot and all of those in his last game, only a few days before the first shots were fired in Sarajevo.

I landed in Sarajevo yesterday, found a room, three days for thirty euros with a young woman who had three daughters. I went to the tram terminus stops, I went out to the grey tower buildings made of prefabricated concrete slabs, I walked through the Old Town, hands clasped behind my back, eyes on the ground, as if I were lost in thought and thus belonged here; tourists are never thoughtful. I wanted to know what people were talking about in the city, but I didn't dare ask. I listened, I wanted to know how you get up on the rooftops, I went to sniff the air in stairwells, at the library they gave me a number belonging to a table with a reading lamp. I saw students studying. *Orpheus and Eurydice* was being performed that evening, I wanted to see what kind of underworld the river god's son goes down into, only to lose the woman he's already lost yet again, but I couldn't get a ticket. I was glad to find that such things were sold out. I was glad of everything that looked like riches rather than ruins or that seemed carefree, although I told myself that being carefree is no good. I climbed to a rooftop. I had the feeling that I'd given something up, I looked down at the city and didn't know what it was. I didn't want to go dancing, I wanted to see people dancing. There was no queue outside the club, but I waited all the same, and then I just bought yesterday's *Süddeutsche Zeitung* at a nearby news-stand. I found a note from my landlady on the bed in my room: there's pita in the oven if you're hungry. I was hungry, the shadow birds my fingers made flew over Bosnian walls again, I slept for three hours.

On the second day I made coffee for my landlady and asked her about Asija. I asked about Asija everywhere I went, I kept looking out for Asija's bright hair. In the trams, at the terminus stops, among the tower buildings and in the cafés of the Old Town. I read names outside doors, I climbed to rooftops and searched the area from above. I dropped her name into every conversation, I tried to convince officials and notaries of the urgency of my search, they let me look at registers of names, statistics about refugees, lists of victims; I was told I'd come very late in the day, and I politely asked people to confine themselves to constructive comments. At the Academy of Music I secretly leafed through the card index of members of the library, still feeling sure that Asija was a violinist. I wasn't allowed to see the records of customers at the video library, but the suntan studio let me see theirs. On the way between those places I read the phone book. I called eight Asijas, apologised to six for disturbing them, two weren't at home, which gave me grounds for some hope.

There's no such street in Sarajevo, said the taxi driver when I gave him the address for Asija that Granny Katarina had given me years ago, but at my insistence he got his central switchboard to confirm it. I asked him to drive me to a street that sounded rather like the address on my note, rang at five doors and read all the names by the doorbells. The sky was cloudy, I reached the end of the street and looked around me. Children were writing their names on the asphalt with coloured chalk. I'm not leaving Sarajevo until I've found something.

I bought a book about the genocide in Višegrad. I was planning to walk through the city until some kind of stray dog met me, or someone who'd fled here from Višegrad recognised me. I watched budgies billing and cooing in a window, and on the sly I asked for plum jam with my čevapčići. Don't you try taking the mickey out of me, replied the waiter. Later on it rained, and instead of going to the driving licence centre, I went into the little betting shop and café with its view of the Old Town.

Mesud, who is fiddling with his moustache, looks hard at me and says: Kiko. Kiko of the gentle river Drina. Like you.

I was going to drink a coffee and wait for the rain to stop. Four TV screens on the walls, teletext on all of them, a billiard table in the middle of the room, ashtrays on the plastic tables. Men in leather jackets or tracksuits poring over tables of numbers with great concentration. I ordered a Turkish coffee. Two older men were reading the paper at a table in front of the broad glass façade, one wore a tracksuit top with the inscription *Rot-Weiss Essen* and the number II on it.

Well, what a coincidence, I said, I live in Essen.

The men lowered their newspapers and looked round. I was standing behind them, coffee cup in hand. They said nothing.

The top, I said, and pointed my cup at the man with the moustache. The other man put sugar in his coffee, sipped cautiously, and devoted himself to his paper again.

Germany, Regional League North, Essen versus Düsseldorf on Sunday, it'll be a draw, said the man in the jacket. His moustache covered his mouth, moving up and down as if the man were chewing.

I'm Aleksandar, is that seat free? I heard myself saying, although the deep voice under the moustache didn't exactly sound inviting.

We're the Wise Guys, said the voice, and the arm pointed to the vacant chair.

What does that mean? I asked, sitting down with them.

It means I'm right when I tell you to put your money on a draw between this Essen of yours and Düsseldorf on Sunday.

The Wise Guys: Mesud with his moustache and the tracksuit top his son-in-law had brought him from Germany years ago, Kemo the diabetic who refused to admit that he had diabetes. Kemo was the quieter of the two. He sat immersed in sporting papers most of the time, writing down numbers and drawing circles, triangles, lightning flashes and yet more numbers beside them. Mesud had countless conversations with the short-haired men who kept coming up to our table and saying things like: under three in the Anderlecht game? With Zidane banned for those yellow cards, a draw? Deportivo away – handicap of two, what do you think, Čika Mesud? He had answers and advice for every gambler; I couldn't see any system behind it.

How often do you bet yourselves? I asked the Wise Guys.

Oh, we don't bet, said Mesud, raising his hands defensively, that's no way to be happy. We're here in case someone doesn't believe the statistics or can't think what to do, that's all.

A lot of people couldn't think what to do and came to our table sooner or later for a chat or to ask a question. A shy man in a suit and bow tie wanted to know what chance Inter had of winning today. I've never been to Milan, said Mesud, hands off Italy. Kemo gave a thumbs-up sign; Inter will make it.

The place filled up, people made out their betting slips against the wall. Music was switched on, a woman was singing about what it's like to be deceived by a man, then a man sang about what it's like to deceive a woman, best friends featured in both songs. Leather jackets gathered in front of the games machines, punched the buttons, they clanged, clanged, clanged. The rain had stopped, but I didn't feel like leaving, I wanted to be taken for a friend of Kemo and Mesud. No one asked me anything, I put ten KM on Essen–Düsseldorf for a draw.

Two boys, ten years old at the most, were knocking the white ball into the cushion of the billiard table with their cues. Kemo fed a coin in for them and ran his hand through the smaller boy's flaxen hair. The balls clattered around on the table, the first live results came through on the teletext, it was getting dark outside. We talked about Red Star, we talked about the national team of ten years ago and more, the national teams of today; if we were still all one country, Mesud said, we'd be unbeatable today. The boy with the flaxen hair sank ball after ball, Benfica, someone suddenly shouted, Benfica are bastards, the whole bunch of them! A chair fell over, at the next table someone was saying his Cousin Husein sent envelopes full of shit to the public prosecutor's offices every day, someone else asked what the postage cost, then I lost track. The boy with flaxen hair was drinking Fanta out of a can and hit the ten, the ten hit the fourteen and the fourteen disappeared into the pocket. A man in a tracksuit asked: do you know this one? and I should simply have waited, but I asked: do I know what one? and the tracksuit told a joke. I wanted to know about everything all at once, but I didn't know what to make of anything.

Mujo and Suljo go for a walk, that was the joke. Suddenly Mujo falls down. Suljo calls the emergency doctor: quick, I think Mujo's dead! The doctor says: take it easy, make sure he's really dead first. There's a brief silence, then a shot is heard. Suljo says over his phone, right, so now what do I do?

The boy with the flaxen hair pointed his cue at the black ball, then at the middle pocket, and after potting the ball he leaned against the bar. His opponent bought him another Fanta and left the café, shaking his head. His own balls were still all on the table. Kemo nodded appreciatively, the boy nodded gravely back.

You'll find two sorts of people here, said Mesud, turning to me: people who miss everything and people who are indignant about everything. Me, I never get indignant about people who miss things and I'll never miss being indignant. He shrugged and grinned. Sixty-two in Chile, he said, the country was doing all right, and when a country is doing all right sport doesn't do badly either. Now it's like this: shit here, shit there. Then we had a semi-final against the Czechs. Back then Pelé said that the best player anywhere, even better than him, was the Yugoslavian Number Ten. He couldn't pronounce the name, so I'm happy to say it myself: Dragoslav Šekularac!

Mesud leaned back and looked at me. The name meant nothing to me. I nodded, said: Dragoslav, that's right.

The best away games were in Split and Rijeka, Kemo put in, and his face lit up too. The Seventies by the Adriatic, ah, my dear fellow! We took Czech girls to the stadium with us! How did those games go? No idea! They wrote to us afterwards, and during the war they sent cigarettes.

Asked who was top of the league table in Bosnia at the moment, Kemo put two piled spoonfuls of sugar in his well-diluted coffee and shook his head: oh, well, as for Bosnia! he said, dismissing the subject. You can lay a bet on the last backwoods dump in Finland, but here in our own league – forget it!

Let's have a little something small, said Mesud, let's have a little something sweet, said Kemo later in the evening, when most of the football games were in progress and everyone was staring at the screens of teletext. I went to get us flatbread stuffed with spinach, kaymak and baklava. When I came back with the food I heard jubilation. Inter was in the lead.

Where do you come from? asked Mesud, his eyes on the warm flatbread.

Višegrad, I said, thinking of Asija again for the first time in hours, thinking of Granny Katarina and my lists. The trip didn't feel like much of a trip at the moment.

Good. Good town. Mesud bit into the flatbread. The Drina is a good river, it never had any good footballers. Except maybe for one. Kemo, can you remember – and now Mesud will say Kiko and remember him. What was his real name, now? Turned pro straight after he came out of the youth teams. Could do header after header. What momentum, Mesud will say with enthusiasm, he didn't have to prop himself up on anything. Wow, you could hear the sound of it up in the stands! Kiko, Mesud is going to say, Kiko from the gentle river Drina. Like you.

The results flicker green and red on the teletext. The old men's hands are rough and dry, coarse and clumsy, covered with scars and bumps. We wish each other success as we say goodbye. The street lights flicker in the Old Town, TVs flicker in dark living rooms. A cold wind rises, there are no stars. I dig my hands into my pockets, turn up the collar of my jacket. Those are my hands in my pockets. Those are my footsteps. This is my key. Here's where I unlock the door. Here's where I tiptoe up the defiantly creaking staircase. This is me being quiet. This is my room. Here's my case. Here are the piles of lists. Here are the piles of streets. Here are the piles of names. This is where I kneel down by my case. This is where I read 'Damir Kičić'. This is where it says 'Damir Kičić – Kiko'.

What they're playing behind God's feet, why Kiko saves the cigarette, where Hollywood is, and how Mickey Mouse learns to answer

At 14.22 hours they radioed a ceasefire through to the Bosnian Territorial Defence trenches. The third this month. At 14.28 hours the ball rose from the Serbian trench on the northern outskirts of the forest and flew through the air, tracing a high arc, towards the clearing that separated the opposing positions by about two hundred metres. The ball bounced twice and rolled in the direction of the two spruce trees, now shot to pieces, that had served as goalposts before, when hostilities were suspended.

The commander of the Territorials, Dino Safirović, nicknamed Dino Zoff, jumped up on the edge of the trench, cupped his hands around his mouth like a megaphone and bent his torso back as he shouted to the other side: how about it, Chetniks, want another hiding? He reached for his crotch and thrust his hips back and forth, back and forth, then went a few metres in the direction of the ball, to the place where Ćora lay with a huge hole in his head.

Mujaheddin cunts, we've already fucked your mothers' arses twice, roared a hoarse voice from the Serbian trench, while Kiko – Kiko number nine, Kiko of the prodigious headers, Kiko the iron brow of the gentle river Drina – joined Dino Zoff, took Ćora by the ankles and dragged him back to the trench. He covered him up with his coat and pulled the bloodstained strands of hair back from his forehead, oh, look at you now, friend Ćora, he whispered, grass and earth everywhere.

Beside him, Meho clicked his tongue, dug the red and white Red Star Belgrade shirt out of his rucksack and put it on over his jacket. He ceremoniously emptied his jacket pockets: a Swiss army knife, a lighter, two hand grenades, an opened can of meat paste. He kissed Audrey Hepburn's photo several times, enraptured, and then put it away again. He grinned in reply to Dino Zoff's enquiring gaze, said: we all have our lucky charms, did you know about Maradona's underpants . . . and then he noticed Kiko, and Ćora's dead body, and stopped short. He shouldn't have gone out, never mind how dark it was, began Meho, both apologetic and accusing, but then he met Kiko's eyes, sighed, and offered him a packet of Drinas. Everyone in the troop knew Meho still had cigarettes, there were even rumours that the packet was half full. Kiko took the last but one. He passed it over his upper lip and breathed in the fragrance

Mirabelles, he murmured, closing his eyes, Hanifa's throat when she's brought me home from training, coffee, real Turkish coffee. That's the way of the world, friend Ćora, you've snuffed it and I get a cigarette. Kiko passed his fingertips over Ćora's eyelids and put the cigarette behind his ear. For after the game, he said with his head bowed.

The Serbs had won the last two ceasefires five-two and two-one. A man called Milan Jevrić, nicknamed Mickey Mouse, had scored three of their five goals in the first match. Mickey Mouse was a farmer's boy aged twenty, two metres six tall and weighing a hundred kilos, maybe as many as thirty of them in the great rock of a head with its projecting nose and sparse tufts of hair all carried on his bull-like neck. He was really an inside defender, and surprised himself more than anyone with his goal-scoring prowess when he stormed ahead at the beginning of the second half, took aim from a distance of thirty metres and hit Dino Zoff right in the face. Dino didn't come round until Marko, one of the Serbian forwards, held some schnapps under his nose, and for the next two hours he spoke nothing but fluent Latin, quoting several Ciceronian maxims. After that direct hit Mickey Mouse played as a midfield attacker, hammering the ball from every conceivable position. When he fired off one of his right-footed shots and the ball made for the goal like a bullet, Dino Zoff regularly threw himself not fearlessly but bravely into its flight path, and was just as regularly floored, lying there dazed, or with his face twisted in pain. Probably because there was no other way of keeping out

Mickey Mouse's mighty shots, or perhaps hoping for the return of Marko's schnapps. There was no art in Mickey Mouse's shots; they didn't spin or come off the outside of his foot, and after the first time they no longer took anyone by surprise. In their lack of finesse and sheer strength they reflected Mickey Mouse's straightforward thinking, which he seldom expressed in words.

There was just one drawback to the force of Mickey Mouse's right foot, and the Territorials mercilessly exploited it. After every shot, the giant gave vent to his delight with a shout that, in musical terms, was somewhere between a bull rutting and a twenty-five-ton truck and trailer braking on a steep downhill slope. Eat your heart out Monika Seleš! cried Kozica with the goatee beard, the Territorials' outside left, after one such cry of exultation, and he roared with laughter.

Hey, is Monika playing with you today? Dino Zoff's men would mock the Serbs after that, or: Monika, Monika, come play on my harmonica! And they groaned out loud whenever Mickey Mouse got the ball. This great mountain of a man, so large that no uniform fitted him and he had to wear his enormous dungarees from home, was thrown off balance by these digs. In the second game he toned down his shouts, and promptly his long-distance shots became less decisive, causing Dino Zoff no more headaches. If an opposing player yodelled near him, Mickey Mouse would jump, his massive head would rock on his comparatively slight shoulders, and his narrow brow would furrow. If he'd been given a little more time, Mickey Mouse would have liked to say what he was thinking, but then play shifted to the other side of the field and his tormentor ran off.

Today, as before, Kozica yelled at the Serbian side during warm-up: what a shame Miss Graf couldn't come to Mount Igman! She's in Wimbledon but she sends Monika her best wishes. Ho, ho, ho, cried Kozica, and his companions joined in.

Two halves of forty minutes each, a Territorial ref for the first half, a Serbian ref for the second – if there was going to be any sharp practice at least it would be fairly distributed. Mickey Mouse tied a rope between the goalposts on the southern end of the clearing to serve as a crossbar. The other goal consisted of the remains of the fence that used to stand beside one of the two cart tracks. The wire netting between the fence posts had been cut and the posts extended using boards up to two and a half metres high. Whoever had control of these cart tracks could reach the mountain more rapidly, no need to forge a path through dense, poorly mapped forests with more mines in the ground than mushrooms. That was what it had all been about here for the last two months: two cart tracks. Lower down the valley one of them turned into a paved road leading to Sarajevo. In normal times, flies flew here in square formation over dried cowpats, but now there were no fresh cowpats; the farm cattle that hadn't been driven higher up into the mountains had been slaughtered long ago, and humans buried their own shit. These days the flies circled above corpses that couldn't always be got into the earth quickly enough.

At sixteen hundred hours the teams met roughly in the middle of the football pitch, the rest of the soldiers sat down in long rows on the grass to form living touchlines. No one was visibly carrying weapons; there were some guns propped against trees. The players passed the ball to each other, warming up in silence. The Serbs won the toss for choice of ends.

Standing a little way from the others, Kiko and Mickey Mouse gave each other a friendly hug. They knew one another from school, where they'd both had to repeat the eighth year twice, which was unusual. It was even more unusual for someone to have had to repeat the first year twice as well, and then the fourth year and the sixth year. Once, in the middle of a maths test, the boy with the ever-open mouth had asked exactly how you set about learning things. His fellow pupils considered him to be a quiet, kindly colossus who, when asked the date of Columbus's discovery of America, had looked out of the window and replied: Colorado beetle. Kiko, on the other hand, was soon among the country's most promising footballers. While the first-division clubs were vying with each other to recruit Kiko, Mickey Mouse was toiling day and night on his parents' farm, and there was nothing to suggest that better days and better nights would ever come for him.

But come they did – with the war. Where's the war? Mickey Mouse had asked. His mother said: still far away, thank God. Good, he said, whose side are we on? You're a Serb, his father told him. So next day there was Mickey Mouse, standing in the doorway with a rucksack that, on his broad back, looked like a make-up bag. He told his father, his father's ten fried eggs, the pale blue tiled kitchen, the notched cherry-wood table, the dusty yard, the stink of muck from the cowsheds, the plough that had strengthened the muscles in his back, and the countless sacks of maize that he kicked hard night after night because he was angry with his father, with the ten fried eggs his father ate every morning, with the table into which he had carved his name, with the yard where his father had knocked him down in the dust and kicked him, with the muck through which he'd waded all his life, with the plough because he wasn't an ox – goodbye, he told them all, goodbye, I'm going away, I'm going to war.

Mickey Mouse walked for five days, asking the way and saying he was Serbian, until he was given a gun. Can I go shooting now? he asked, and he learned how to load the gun and take the safety catch off. He was sent to Mount Igman, where the Serbian troops were preparing for the siege of Sarajevo. Mickey Mouse never complained. He liked these remote places better than his home, although his comrades said God had abandoned them long ago, and a God like that doesn't come back again. This place lies behind God's feet, they said.

Mickey Mouse didn't mind his nickname. I like the duck and the dog too, he said, though Pluto is rather clumsy. He hadn't been called Mickey Mouse at school though, so Kiko still called him Milan.

Milan, said Kiko, putting his hand on Mickey Mouse's upper arm, your lot fucked up Ćora last night.

By way of answer Mickey Mouse raised his eyebrows, ducked his head and took a deep breath. His face lost any kind of symmetry. It looked like unhewn stone, pale and scarred with acne. Kiko was waiting for some kind of response, but Mickey Mouse just breathed out and closed his ever-open mouth.

A shrill whistle signalled the end of warm-up.

Mickey Mouse took Kiko's hand off his arm. Kiko, they told me: Mickey Mouse, you're playing in defence again. He didn't add that he was the only man who had fired a shot that night.

A heavy bird flew up from the woods, and the big man went back to the defenders.

Gavro, the key player on the Serbian side, a black-haired, curly-headed man with a raven tattooed on his shoulder, whistled as the bird flew away. Gavro never stopped whistling or humming tunes except to talk or eat. Even in his sleep he would snore a resonant 'Blue Danube' through his moustache. The bird flew over the clearing and soared south towards the valley beyond the trees. Gavro picked up the ball and went over to the ref, who was gazing at his watch as if spellbound.

Fuck the sun, man, what are you waiting for, a sign from Allah? We don't have all day!

It had been quiet on Mount Igman more frequently over the last few months, particularly at night when the guns in the clearing and the valley fell silent. But there hadn't been such peace and quiet here behind God's feet as there was now, before kick-off, as Gavro began to whistle something that could have been Glenn Miller.

General Mikado, commander of the Serbian unit, slapped the back of the whistling man's head, took the ball away from his foot, whistled shrilly through his own fingers and made the first pass. You can whistle for the end of play seven seconds early, called the sturdy commander with the slanting eyes to which he owed his nickname. He raced past the ref and swerved to the right wing, where he was to set up a score of one-nil to the Serbs less than two minutes later – a ball centred towards the head of the whistling Gavro.

Mickey Mouse made it two-nil to the Serbs with one of his mighty shots. He captured the ball near the corner flag – a gun rammed into the ground – and forged through the enemy ranks accompanied by shouts of derision. He didn't seem to mind the insults this time. He was still in his own half when he aimed for Dino Zoff, his mouth wide open as always. A one-two, a feint, the shot at goal, *uh!*, and Dino Zoff couldn't deflect the ball properly. After kicking the ball Mickey Mouse stopped abruptly and watched it sail through the air with his arm raised, as if waving an old friend off on a long journey.

The Territorials had their one good chance of a goal at the end of the first half, when Kiko finished a solo run through the opposing defenders with a shot that hit the woodwork of the spruce goalpost. Gavro countered this shot by passing to Marko, who then went on the attack, but Meho from the Territorials got to the ball just a tad faster and hammered it with all his might out of their penalty area, off the playing field, out of the clearing and into the forest.

Oh, fuck the forest fairy, said Meho, shaking his head and crouching down as if he wanted to throw up. The referee whistled and pointed first at Meho, then at the forest – a gesture unlikely to be seen in any other football game in the world – meaning: Meho bungled this, so he has to fetch it back. But no one could give him a plan of just where the mines were planted; presumably no such thing existed. The mines, however, most certainly did exist. Even before the front lines were entrenched around the clearing, the Serbs had lost two men in the forest during an attempt to come up on the Territorials from behind, and a third man had lost a leg. That's right, they'd shouted from the Territorial positions at the time, take 'em all back like good lads and don't leave any of them lying around, shame about losing the goats, though.

Dino Zoff took Meho's arms. For God's sake, Meho, he whispered, haven't we been over this a thousand times? A good defender doesn't knock the ball away! Good clearance behind, short passes, it can't be that difficult.

Can't be that difficult, Meho whispered to himself as he arrived at the edge of the forest with two paramedics in attendance. All the players and both touchlines were looking his way. Someone waved and Meho waved back. The ball, about twenty metres inside the forest, was lying peacefully on a bed of moss under a reddish fern. The sun was flooding the woodland with bright light that slanted across the slight rise of the forest floor which concealed dozens of mines from the trembling man in the Red Star shirt. The shirt! In panic, Meho took off the red and white strip of his favourite team, kissed the star, folded it carefully and laid it on the ground.

Hang on, Meho! Marko had followed his opposite number up the slight slope. Here, it's for the ball, said the Serbian striker, winking, and he handed Meho a bullet-proof vest, wrap it up well before you bring it back.

Meho stared at the black vest.

Hey, Meho, what's the idea? Marko picked up Meho's shirt and shook his head. They're from Belgrade, right?

Meho's chin was quivering. The Red-and-Whites for ever! he growled, wiping the sweat from his brow. He put on Marko's bullet-proof vest, said: you better go back, and then added in English without a trace of accent: this could get fucking dangerous!

Marko went back to the others, carrying Meho's shirt. They were all sitting on the grass talking, looking at the trees even after Meho had disappeared under the shade of their canopy. Gavro was scraping dirt out from under his toenails with a wooden splinter, whistling a playful tune. The full tones of his whistling floated past the bare chests of the Serbian eleven and danced before the Territorials' tense faces. A klezmer tune, and they were all listening to the same song, some of them tapping the grass or their thighs in time to it, some not, but that was the only difference. Watching the trees become forest, they listened and waited – for Meho, for another song, or for a bang.

There was a bang when General Mikado hit the back of Gavro's head again. He stopped whistling, and the general asked in a loud voice: so just what are we going to do if we lose the ball because of that idiot?

No one replied.

The two paramedics on the edge of the forest were munching bread and looking at the trees. They wanted to watch Meho's progress as closely as possible so that they could follow his trail and spring into action if he was blown up.

But Meho wasn't blown up, he just shat his trousers, it would wash out. His own side and some of the Serbians applauded as he stalked back into the clearing with the ball under his arm and his head still on his shoulders, looking as if at the very least he'd just scored in extra time in the cup final against Brazil. At close quarters, his pride looked more like anger, at close quarters the arm with the ball under it was trembling, at close quarters Meho's face was grey, a thick blue vein stood out in the middle of his forehead, and he stank to high heaven. At close quarters, he said: here's the ball, OK, let's carry on with the game, I just have to get changed, that's all. And he added, to Marko, now we can swap shirts again, bullet-proof vest for Red Star Belgrade, and let me tell you something, I don't care where the team I support comes from, the lads are only playing football. When I was that big, said Meho, pointing to somewhere level with his waist, they were my heroes. The final against Marseille in '91! That win! That penalty shoot-out! I don't mind you being Serbian either. Just as long as you don't shoot me or sleep with my wife, who cares?

Meho put his shirt back on and stalked over to the trench, which was empty except for Sejo, the fat radio operator, dozing in the sunlight and three wounded men playing dominoes. He washed himself thoroughly with water from a white plastic container, rinsed his arse well and scrubbed the inside of his thigh with the clean trouser-leg.

And as I stood there in that rubbish bin of a trench, friend Ćora, as I stood behind God's fungus-infected feet, my poor friend Ćora, pouring water over my fingers, I kept thinking all the time: don't waste too much water, Meho, use grass and leaves if you must, and while I was wiping away brown drops from between the little hairs on my legs, I suddenly had to weep buckets, I wept buckets, friend Ćora, I thought the tears weren't flowing down my cheeks but bursting in jets straight from my eyes, I really did. Oh, friend Ćora, what a bloody awful day, and I hope you'll understand if I borrow your trousers now, you'll be OK, it's not cold out here, the sun's shining, it showed me just where to tread in the forest, it really did, shining down on the ground! I can't beat the Chetniks naked anyway, we're two-nil down, like I said, a bloody awful day, Ćora, but who am I telling? Meho stroked the dead man's hair and undid his camouflage trousers. Just until the end of the game, Ćora, he said, you'll get them back afterwards, Pioneer's word of honour!

Meho crossed the fifty metres or so back to the pitch at a run. Over the last ten metres he realised that his bloody awful day was far from over. His unit was lined up level with the spruce-tree goalposts, many of them with their hands behind their heads. Some ten Serbs were standing in front of them in a semicircle with machine guns at the ready, while others ran around the clearing, gathering up the remaining weapons. No one was taking any notice of the ball, which lay to one side in the tall grass. Meho blinked and soundlessly moved his lips.

General Mikado mimed an embrace. Ah, he cried, that was the perfect perfume for a Muslim!

While Meho was searched for weapons and then driven over to join the others, a gun at his back, artillery fire could be heard far away. Sporadic salvos, filtered by distance and the sun to a muted, rather weary sound. Fat Sejo the Territorials' radio operator was blundering about on the edge of the trench, a panic-stricken expression on his face, but before he could announce that the ceasefire was over, as everyone had by now deduced, the Serbian goalie fired several shots at him. Sejo collapsed, first to one knee, then right over sideways, and lay there in a curiously distorted position with his knee still braced on the ground.

You fucking bastard, shouted Dino Zoff through the first shots, breaking away from the group of prisoners and imploring, raising his hands in their goalie's gloves, we're surrendering, for God's sake . . . But he got no further. General Mikado caught up with him and put a pistol first to the back of his head and then, pushing him to the ground, against the side of his neck.

That's not the way I see it, you ape! His spit fell on Dino Zoff's cheek and mouth. The way I see it, you lot are fighting back ferociously, the way I see it you're going to fight to the last man! It's sad, but I don't see how a single one of you Mujaheddin is going to survive to tell the tale of your last, glorious battle. General Mikado pushed Dino away and aimed the pistol at his chest. His soldiers were in position in front of the prisoners, a firing squad thirty strong.

OK! Dino flung his arm up above his head. OK, then we *will* fight back, let's play on!

What? General Mikado made a disgusted face.

You want to shoot down unarmed men? I can believe even worse of you, I don't know how I'd have held my own lads back if we'd been quicker getting to our weapons. But the game isn't finished yet! There's the second half still to come! If you're enough of a footballer then let's go on playing. And if we turn the game around, and you're still man enough, then no one here gets executed. If your lot win . . . he said, looking round at his men and straightening up, then you'll stay a fucking miserable murderer all your life!

And Dino Safirović, who had been chucked out of school because Latin and the classics are important in the education of the young but hard drinking is not, pulled his gloves more firmly over his fingers. And Dino Safirović, the lover of Cicero, who had volunteered because he thought alcohol wouldn't be so readily available at the front and he really did want to dry out, clapped his hands so hard that the dust flew. And Dino Safirović, nicknamed Dino Zoff, the cat of Trebević, looked General Mikado in the eye and spat: come on, then, come on!

Kiko made it two-one with a header in the fourth minute of the second half, just as there was a considerable explosion in the valley. He scored with another header five minutes later, but this goal, like its predecessor, was disallowed for allegedly being offside. This head of mine, said Kiko, slapping the back of it, was damn well not offside.

But it was no use. General Mikado had accepted Dino Zoff's challenge with some amusement, on condition that he himself didn't just play but also acted as referee. I don't have any yellow cards on me, he said, so there's only a bullet waiting for anyone who complains.

An obvious foul on the goalkeeper preceded the score of three-nil to General Mikado's team. As a team, the Serbs were playing with such fierce determination that you might have thought their lives, and not their opponents', depended on the result.

Kozica made it three-one with a long shot that sent the ball straight into the goal. A minute later Kozica was being carried off the field with an open wound on his forehead, having been knocked off his legs by one of the touchline soldiers and then beaten with the man's rifle butt. After that the Territorials stopped attacking down the wings.

In the sixtieth minute, Mickey Mouse and Kiko collided. They both fell to the ground and the game went on. Since Mickey Mouse, two metres six tall, had been marking the Territorials' best man, Kiko hadn't had a chance of another header. After the collision they both stayed sitting there, gingerly feeling their chests. Kiko made a face: lucky thing we have ribs, he said, and Mickey Mouse nodded: yes, ribs come in useful. His eyes wandered uneasily over Kiko's face, he took a deep breath and let it out again. The big man was about to stand up, pushing off from the ground with his fist, but Kiko grabbed hold of it and whispered: that's right, Milan, stand up, don't stay down there, don't stay sitting down again.

No? said Mickey Mouse in surprise, opening his mouth wide, and when Kiko next headed the ball he certainly was not sitting, but stood as if rooted to the ground. He didn't leap into the air, the ball bounced and it was three-two.

After this successful shot, with the Territorials now only one down, General Mikado managed to foil all their efforts to get anywhere near his team's goal. Every tackle was said to be a foul, the whistle blew every time there was an attacking pass, every throw-in went to his team, even for obvious clearing kicks that landed out of play.

Two minutes before the end of the game Kiko forced his way through on the inside left, avoiding any kind of physical contact. He swerved, he dodged, he leaped. With the last of his strength he centred the ball in front of the Serbian goal and took a harmless shot at the goalpost. The Serbian defender on the right kicked the air, Mickey Mouse missed the ball on the bounce, the rest of them, friend and foe alike, either slid past the ball or were too surprised to react, and so it rolled to Meho's feet. Meho had done nothing during the second half but wander around the pitch, lost in thought, muttering to himself as if hypnotised: it can't be so difficult, Audrey darling, it can't be so difficult.

So there lay the ball at his feet, but Meho didn't even look at it, he was staring eastward, enraptured. The sound of heavy artillery fire came from the valley, metallic, hollow. Moving in slow motion like an action replay on TV, Meho shifted his weight to the left and easily clipped the ball into the goal with his right leg, acting as if the movement had nothing to do with him. This is for you, he murmured, reaching under his shirt, a goal for you. Eyes shining, he put the photo of Audrey Hepburn to his lips and whispered: hey, real Hollywood stuff, Audrey love, oh, fuck me, what a happy ending!

Meho had been in the States in 1986, the only time he had ever been to the West. He'd saved his wages as a brickie for five years, living with his father and never spending money unnecessarily. Evening after evening he had watched American films, mostly thrillers, horror movies, and films featuring Audrey Hepburn. He learned to swear in English and could order coffee without an accent.

After scoring his goal, Meho wandered over the field with his head tilted back. The game went on, the ball hit him in the back once, but Meho wasn't interested in that, he was interested in the sky. Someone shouted his name. We are the champions, replied Meho in English. Arriving at his team's penalty area he stopped and put out his hand to see if it was raining. Wrinkling his nose, he crossed his arms over his chest, as if rain really were falling and it was cold. Someone fell at his feet, there was excitement, uproar, a whistle, a salvo of gunfire.

A group of players had gathered around General Mikado. Only when someone fired into the air did the men scatter. Penalty! shouted the general, taking the ball. Dino Zoff shook his head, that was never a foul! he protested, and gazed at the ball that was now lying at the requisite point. General Mikado stepped up to take the penalty himself.

You shut your stupid mouth! the Serbian goalie snapped at Dino Zoff from one side. He had run all the way across the pitch from his own penalty area after the alleged foul, got one of the touchline soldiers to give him a pistol, and was now aiming it at Dino from the left-hand spruce tree. Maybe you can stop the penalty, he said, squinting along the pistol, but can you stop a bullet too?

General Mikado grinned, jerked his thumb in his goalie's direction, and took a run up.

Meho had turned his back to the penalty kick by this time and had moved away from the penalty area. He didn't look back. Perhaps they're just shooting in high spirits down there, he told his Audrey, perhaps it's because this filthy war is over and they're celebrating. Audrey looked like a boy with her short hair. She was wearing black and leaning against a white wall. Meho looked up from the photo and glanced absently at the place where some beech trees grew on the edge of the plateau, and the cart track took a sharp curve to the left before beginning the steep descent into the valley. The wind rose in the east and grew stronger. Meho, already near the trees, could see the wind making the leaves tremble. Meho was trembling too, even more than he had trembled in the forest when surrounded by mines. The gust of wind cooled Meho's face amidst the tears that came after a shot rang out behind his back from the Serbian goalie's pistol, followed by a sharp sound like a very loud slap. Oh, fuck these bloody waterworks, muttered Meho, rubbing his eyes, but the tears wouldn't stop.

The crowd was murmuring behind him, then there was a shout of glee, then sounds and cries which the weary Meho probably didn't hear at all, and he could hardly have made any sense of it, just as he wouldn't have been able to tell Serbian from Bosnian jubilation, people cheered in much the same way in this country. And even if he had seen the goal that was greeted with such cheering he couldn't have said for certain from this distance whether the ball had flown sixty, seventy or even eighty metres before going into the Serbian goal. For any moment now Meho would have reached the beeches at the far end of the clearing. He would look down into the valley, although from a height of over a thousand metres it's as difficult to tell war from peace as it is to tell the words and laughter of your friends from the laughter of your enemies. But the view was impressive: indescribably beautiful, Meho whispered to Audrey seconds before he was shot down. The bullets hit the number ten on the red and white shirt. It had been worn by Dejan Savićević on 29 May 1991, when Red Star beat the French champions Olympique Marseille in a penalty shoot-out in the final of the European Cup.

The Serbian goalie had driven tears to Meho's eyes with his first shot and two bullets into his back with two more shots. The first shot was meant for Dino Zoff, but it had missed him by a few centimetres and hit one of the spruce-tree goalposts. The goalie had fired too soon, the noise took General Mikado's mind off his run-up, his penalty shot crashed into the right-hand spruce tree and the ball rebounded straight into the arms of the motionless Dino Zoff. He looked incredulously from one dismayed marksman to the other, then from one goalpost to the other, and last of all to the abandoned goal at the far end of the pitch. Then he kicked the ball with all his might.

Well, hurricanes fuck me! Meho would have greeted the lurching trajectory of the ball that scored this goal with those or similar words. It may even be that the same gust of wind that first dried his tears also gave Dino Zoff's shot the impetus it needed to end up in the Serbian goal. General Mikado froze rigid amidst the cheering of the Territorials, clearly not sure what to do next.

Our ball! Goal kick! he said. No one heard him, so loud were the jubilations over the three-four score. Goal kick, that wasn't a goal! He whistled through his fingers, but only when the Serbian goalkeeper's second two bullets hit Meho did everyone fall silent around him. The general pointed at the Serbian end. No goal! No goal!

Gavro joined in with Mikado's shrill whistling, extended it, raised it to the key of F major, linked it to a series of light, catchy, childish tunes, unexpectedly turned it into a waltz, then suddenly launched into a wild csárdás – and while his composition gained in colour and speed Dejan Gavrilović, known as Gavro, sat down on the grass.

The csárdás stung Mickey Mouse into action. Don't just sit there, he growled at his team-mate who had fetched the ball out of the goal. Mickey Mouse took it from him and marched across the pitch. Don't just sit there, he called rather louder. Two more Serbian players joined Gavro and, like him, gave no sign of wanting to play on.

General Mikado's throat flushed red with fury, and when the general, who was in fact a lieutenant, had spent most of his life laying tiles, and was married with four daughters whose first names all began 'Ma', took aim to hit Gavro on the back of the head for the third time that day, the whistling man's hand seized the tiler's wrist. The csárdás swung into Spanish dance music, don't you ever do that again, said Gavro's eyes, and the flamenco sang the refrain. Gavro whistled, Mickey Mouse marched on, and Marko knocked his own goalie over and took the pistol away from him.

Well, fuck me if it isn't Muhammad Ali! would have been Meho's praise for Marko's simple left hook. As it was, General Mikado was the only one to curse – fuck it all, what the hell's going on? – when his goalie hit the ground and his striker shook the pain out of his hand. What's the big idea? shouted the general, biting Gavro's fingers as they held tight to his wrist, what do you lot want? Goal kick! he ordered Mickey Mouse, who was carrying the ball to the middle of the field. One by one his players sat down.

So it's mutiny, is it? laughed the general. Deserters! He lashed out. I'll have you court-martialled! The men on the touchlines also sat down, although some of the soldiers got their guns ready, not sure whether they ought to aim at their own side too.

Most of the Serbian soldiers just looked at the ground, not as if they were afraid of their commander, but as if they were embarrassed by this angry man with his hairy back. As if they were ashamed of something, as if they had just been asked a very simple question and didn't know the answer. General Mikado's entire neck was now one large red patch. Shoot them all down! he shouted,

Give me my fucking gun! He stepped back and spun round. No one stopped him, no one answered the very simple question. The Territorials stood there too, as if they were merely props on this stage where a short, powerful director with a bare torso was ranting and raging at his actors.

No one could find an answer to the very simple question – except for Mickey Mouse. Most questions had been too hard for him at school, at home his father had beaten exclamation marks into his back with his leather belt, and here behind God's feet there were no questions, only orders. Milan Jevrić, nicknamed Mickey Mouse, put the ball roughly on the kick-off position, placed his foot on it, and thundered the answer above the soldiers' heads, above General Mikado, who had got hold of a gun but hesitated to use it, above the field, above the trenches, above Meho's dead body, above the beech trees, above the wind and above the valley; he answered it in as loud and clear a voice as if, with this one great shout, he was going to give all the answers to all the questions he had never been able to answer before.

It's four-three to them, replied Mickey Mouse, answering the simple question. They're leading, he pointed out, but maybe we can turn it around in extra time, he said thrusting out his lower lip, maybe we can still score.

His words got the Serbian defenders to their feet, the Serbian midfield players rose too, and the Serbian striker poured plum brandy down his throat in such quantities that Dino Zoff looked longingly at him.

Mickey Mouse did the defending by himself, all the rest attacked. Gavro, as the new referee, gave eight minutes' injury time. The Territorials defended with ten men and whacked every ball back into the Serbian half. Not too hard – the mines. The balls promptly came back again, Mickey Mouse persistently kicked them long and high back to the attackers. In the last minute the Territorials counter-attacked, Kiko failed to get past Mickey Mouse, who was everywhere now, even in goal. Mickey Mouse's answer instantly followed, for Mickey Mouse had now learnt the trick of giving answers. He snapped up the ball and dribbled through the Territorial ranks as if he'd grown up with Maradona instead of a muck-fork. The veins on his throat were bulging, he ran down two Bosnian defenders and kicked the ball towards Dino Zoff's goal from a good thirty metres away. The gigantic man put all of his power into this one shot, and the cry he uttered after it sent dozens of birds flying up from the forest. And the ball, that dirty, poorly mended ball, flew across the clearing towards Dino Zoff's goal.

Gavro whistled for the end of play at 17.55 hours. Mickey Mouse's shot was the last in the game. The players dropped to the grass, exhausted. The echo of the whistle died away. No one cheered. Heavy silence welled up from the valley to the plateau. Weapons were quietly picked up. Marko tilted the schnapps bottle over Dino Zoff's mouth until a few drops moistened his lips, mingling with the blood on them.

Ah, slivowitzum bonum deorum donum! Did I keep it out? lisped Dino Zoff, handing Marko a tooth. The sun cast the long shadows of trees on the clearing behind God's feet, behind God's feet in military boots, behind God's feet with the blisters coming up on them, behind God's dribbling feet.

A cat with its tail in the air purrs around my legs in a yard among high-rise buildings on the outskirts of Sarajevo. A young man is getting ready, with his back to me. He removes his jacket. He stretches. He's not very quick about it. There's a ball lying beside him. The cat looks at me. The cat licks its paw. The man throws the ball up in the air. The ball lands on his head. And lands on his head. And lands on his head, four, five, his arms are bent, and every time, seven, eight, the ball lands, nine, ten, he ducks his head, eleven, twelve. A large, shaven, Bosnian head, thirteen, sends the ball up in the air, fourteen, lets it take a quick rest on the flat back of his head, fifteen, sixteen, there's a scar at the nape of his neck. Nineteen, twenty repeated movements of his upper body, twenty-three, twenty-four bouncing balls, the cat mews, the man's crutches slip on the concrete, the muezzin begins chanting at thirty, thirty-one. The man moves his upper body only slightly before making contact with the ball, thirty-five, thirty-six, I don't need to see his face to know I've found him, thirty-eight, thirty-nine, the crutches scrape on the asphalt, forty-four, forty-five. If I'd been a magician who could make things possible on the summer day when Edin and I sweated in the school yard waiting for him, our sweat falling on the asphalt, the asphalt melting in the sun, then I'd have made it impossible for that day ever to end, forty-seven, forty-eight, and I'd have given the little girl on her bicycle the balance of a circus acrobat. Kiko on crutches, Kiko in a white shirt and jeans, the left leg tied together under his stump, Kiko Number Nine, Kiko the iron head of the gentle Drina, fifty, fifty-one . . .

Up in Kiko's small apartment on the fourteenth floor we drink coffee, served by his wife Hanifa in flower-patterned cups and saucers. No crocheted tablecloth, no brightly coloured sofa in front of the TV, no TV, no clock ticking loudly to be heard when we fall silent. A bright, plainly designed apartment with parquet floors and cherry-wood furniture.

Yes, says Kiko, it was my last game as a pro. I'd said I'd kick three goals all with my left foot. The guy let a fourth in so he'd win the bet, but because of that one they went down to relegation position. But no one was relegated that year. Only the country was relegated. Football made no difference.

Then the war broke out and Hanifa went to Austria and studied design.

Then the war broke out and the goalkeeper that Kiko had betted against was on the bench in the Turkish second division.

Then the war broke out and a very popular folk singer gave a concert for the soldiers, the wounded and the politicians. You had to pay to go, and the wounded said later it had been a bloody awful concert: after they'd paid to go in there was no money left for beer and they certainly weren't letting the politicians buy them drinks.

Kiko's son Milan sits down beside me and shows me a very large bogey. Got any chocolate? he asks.

Do you go to nursery school? I ask him.

Hanifa was the first girl I spoke to in Sarajevo and the first girl I ever kissed at all, says Kiko, and he goes into the next room to find photos of the kiss.

And I'm going to be the last too, OK? she calls after him.

Not if our next is a daughter! says Kiko, coming back with photo albums. I volunteered to join up. Thought I could fix it so that I'd stay in the city. That worked for two years. Then I was sent to Mount Igman. We were told: the fate of Sarajevo depends on Mount Igman. I always had a ball with me. Always.

Got any sweets?

Kiko puts the album down on the table in front of me and gets down into a kind of crouching position beside Hanifa, which looks grotesque with one leg – I actually think that, grotesque, although at the same time I'm thinking that such a thought ought not to have crossed my mind.

Then the war broke out and no one called it war. People said:

that. Or: the shit. Or: soon-be-over, like someone trying to make an injection easier for a child. Kiko had told Hanifa, you go away, and she said: I'll be back when it's over. Let's hope the shit will soon be over, thought Kiko, and he was sent to Mount Igman.

So there I was in the worst *vukojebina* anyone can imagine. Kiko shows me his beautiful Hanifa on the back seat of a moped in the photo album. He's sitting on the front seat without a helmet on. That was in the autumn of '91, he says. My moped! My pride and joy!

He leafs on through the album. Milan whines, rubbing his eyes.

Hanifa says: I learned a little German during those three years in Graz. But I couldn't translate *vukojebina*. Do you know *vukojebina*?

Where wolves . . . er . . . with each other . . . I say cautiously, with an eye on Milan.

Behind God's feet, Kiko says, I saw a horse throw itself into a ravine because it didn't have the strength to go on hauling our artillery up and down the mountain, along paths that weren't paths. It killed itself . . . Lost in thought, Kiko goes on leafing through the album. Here he is standing beside a giant of a man. The giant wears dungarees and a cap that looks lost on his massive head. They are both armed. Kiko has the lily of the Bosnian army on his breast pocket, the big man has the Serbian double eagle cockade on his cap. They have their arms round each other's shoulders and are looking grimly straight ahead. The bleak rocks tower grimly up behind them too.

Who's that? Kiko asks his son, pointing to the man in dungarees. The little boy stuffs half his fist into his mouth. Milan, who's that? Kiko repeats.

Čika Mickey Mouse! cries Milan happily, as if naming someone who always brings chocolate and sweeties when he visits, and Hanifa says: yes, there's really no translating *vukojebina*.

There's no need to. Kiko puts Milan on his lap. No language but ours has a word to describe such a place, he says.

The soldier beside Kiko has his mouth open as if gasping for air. How did you come to have this photo taken? I ask.

A ceasefire. The man beside me is Milan Jevrić, says Kiko, and his son shouts: Mickey Mouse! Kiko kisses the back of his head. It's because of him my Milan has a Serbian name. Kiko leafs on. A photo of him in a trench, ankle-deep in murky water. Mount Igman, behind God's feet, he says, and goes on turning the pages. The one in the green beret is Meho. A lunatic. A lunatic because he had too big a heart. And here am I giving cigarettes to the prisoners. Here's Hanifa and me in Mostar. My Milan after he was born, he weighed three and a half kilos. We must sort these photos out some time, says Kiko, leafing through them, and the last one shows a ball, a worn old football lying in long grass.

I get on the one p.m. bus for Višegrad. Three other men are already sitting there, one of them is reading a newspaper, one is asleep, one is looking at me. I sit in the back row, the seats are patterned brown and yellow, the head-rests have a greasy shine. One p.m. comes. Five past one comes. Outside the door a man with thinning hair and lines under his eyes smokes a cigarette, then another; after the third he climbs in and gets behind the wheel. Just before the engine starts, the bus sighs. I can understand how it feels, it doesn't have an easy time on these roads at this time of its life, I go to sleep with my head against the vibrating window.

The Drina wakes me. I open my eyes when the bus turns into a little village with a name I can't remember, driving down the road to Višegrad parallel with the river. A great many tunnels keep cutting off the daylight, only a few of them are lit at all. I move over to the window on the right-hand side; large rocks are piled up on the left, covered with thin moss and sparse plants struggling to survive. My river flows on the right. I confirm that thought to myself: my river, the deep green Drina, calm and immaculately clean. The anglers, the rocks, the many shades of green.

We approach the town along the winding road, past the dam. Driftwood and plastic has collected close to it. The valley widens out, we'll soon be able to see the bridge. Can you stop here, please, calls a young man who must have got in during the journey, and the bus groans.

When the view of the bridge comes in sight after a sharp bend I am surprised, although I was fully expecting to find everything the way it always was. I resist the reflex action of counting the arches; the bridge is complete. The driver puts a cassette in, and I think of Walrus and my promise never to shoot a music cassette. It's Madonna singing.

Hey, Boris, with all due respect, do you have to play that every time? asks the man with the newspaper. The driver turns up the volume, *like a virgin*, he sings, tapping the steering wheel in time.

To me, the bus station looks smaller than it used to but just as shabby. Boris makes for one of the five parking slots, four dilapidated old buses parked over to one side, including – I recognise it at once – the bus in which Walrus drove through half of Yugoslavia. The bodywork is in a bad way, rust is baring its teeth, grey weeds grow through the windows from inside, cover the wheel rims.

Where are you going, young man? Boris calls, but I act as if he didn't mean me and go into the small waiting room in the station. There's no door any more, the smell of urine rises to my nostrils, the ticket window is deserted, the paint on the walls, some kind of colour between beige and yellow, is flaking.

Hello? I call. There's an echo. I'd like to see Armin, the station-master with the uncontrollable leg, he's on one of my lists. Is he in the town at all? Was Armin a Muslim?

Who are you looking for? Boris is standing behind me smoking, one hand playing with the key in his trouser pocket.

Armin the station-master, I say, turning to go, but Boris bars my way, draws on his cigarette and says: there was never any Armin here.

Ah, I say, looking past Boris. The other passengers have disappeared. Boris, five buses, four of them wrecks with rusty wheel rims, and I, have to sort it out between us.

Where do you want to go? he asks, pointing his cigarette at my bag.

A man who listens to Madonna can't be dangerous, it occurs to me, and I say as casually as possible: oh, I'm visiting my grandmother.

Boris frowns, holds his cigarette between thumb and forefinger when he draws on it. What's her name?

Katarina, I say, louder than I intended, Katarina Krsmanović, it's her blood-sugar and diabetes, I say, stammering, she can't do much these days, I try to explain, but then I see a change come over the bus driver's face. His expression changes from pestering to curious. He lets me finish and after one last short pull on his cigarette, he puts it out with the sole of his shoe.

Do you know Miki Krsmanović? he asks.

Yes, he's my uncle.

Your uncle, is he? Boris looks around, hitches up his trousers and puts on a huge pair of sunglasses. He reaches for my bag, I withdraw my hand and take a step into the waiting room. We're going the same way, he says.

Don't you have to drive any further?

Yes, he says, but I don't like driving on an empty stomach. Come on, I'll help you with your bag.

That's all right, it's not heavy, I say, taking it from him. Do you know my uncle?

No, he says, spitting through his teeth, no, I don't know him, thank God.

I've made lists. Nicknames. The man with the uncontrollable leg. Top Hat. My sad man. The three-dot-ellipsis man. Typhoon. The man who climbed the mountains singing and never came back. Walrus and Ladybird. Potato Aziz. Massacre. The soldier with gold in his mouth.

Boris and I pass the football stadium. Young men are training, doing headers, I think of Kiko's head. A man with a long braid throws them balls to be headed into the net. The man wears a suit and a silk scarf. There's no one in goal. Boris and I walk side by side in silence, the slap of the ball against the woodwork behind us. Boris shrugs. We cross the bridge over the Rzav where Edin and I fed the fish with spit on the day when the soldiers sang and danced.

The river is shallow, white islands of foam drift with the current. I spit. The bridge has stood up to all high tides.

I've made lists. Barbel, chub, roach, gudgeon, dace, Danube salmon, carp, sunbleak, catfish with spectacles and a moustache.

We say no more about Uncle Miki. When I ask a question, Boris waves it away and brings up other subjects. He distracts me from the smells and colours of the town, asks how old I was back then, where exactly I've been living in Germany, whether I can get him a visa, what I think of the rumours about Madonna and Guy Ritchie. As we part outside the tower block where Granny Katarina is living, he says: don't take offence, but it's like this. If you don't know anything you're an idiot. If you know a lot and admit it you're a dangerous idiot. Višegrad always knows just how much it may know and how much it should tell.

In the yard outside the tower block six black-haired boys are playing football, using their school satchels as goalposts, the ball rolls to my feet; I put my bag down. After a moment's shyness they join in, who's on my side? I call, who's on my side? One of them runs clear on the left, Čiko! he calls, I pass it to him running, he has only the goalie ahead of him and feints.

There's no light in the stairwell, the light switches have been torn out, wires stick out of the holes, thin red and blue necks without any heads. The corridors are narrower and the flights of steps shorter than they used to be, the air smells as overpoweringly of bread as if everyone in the building were baking at the same time. No name by the bell where Teta Amela, the best baker in the world, used to live. My granny coughs behind the closed door with the name 'Slavko Krsmanović' beside the bell. The bell doesn't ring, no power, I knock.

I've made lists. The mosques. One of them is supposed to be being rebuilt. There are concrete plans for it, and concrete protests against it. Death notices still hang on the chestnut trees not far from the square where the minaret of the larger mosque once pointed to the sky. The ones with green rims are in Arabic letters, the ones with black rims have the cross on them. It's fourteen to one for the dead Christians. Very few Muslims have come home.

Aleksandar, says Granny Katarina, I've been baking bread, I'll put the milk on in a minute.

Our hug is a brief one. Granny comes up to my throat, she kisses me on the throat, I'm horrified by her and horrified by myself because I'm slightly repelled by her moist mouth and the tickling little hairs on her top lip. Come on, she says, you're tired, let's have a look at you. Oh yes, your grandpa.

Granny's hair is dyed black, white roots show, she has a sourish smell like damp maize and is trying to pick up my bag. Do you drink coffee these days? she asks.

Leave that to me, I say, taking my bag into the bedroom. I can see the mark on the door frame telling me how tall I was on 6 April 1992: 1.53 metres. As the first shells were exploding, my father sharpened his pencil and called to me. Still time for this, stand here. Today I measure myself and cheat by standing on tiptoe, just as I cheated Father back then by two or three centimetres. I mark the wood of the door frame with a pencil line just above my hair. I smell milk in the kitchen. I wait, 1.80 metres tall, twelve minutes, and I drink the milk still warm.

I've made lists. The green house with the peculiar roof is still a green house with a peculiar roof. A bonsai in the single large window. A satellite dish on the peculiar roof. The roof slopes steeply almost all the way down to the ground. I peer through the window. A young woman is sitting cross-legged on a bamboo mat in the middle of the small room. She has closed her eyes. Her hands are resting on her knees, palms upwards. Her thumbs and middle fingers are touching.

The old locomotive stands in the little park near the building. It's been restored and repainted, I pass my hand over the front of it: smooth, cool iron. Grandpa Rafik, grey, railway engine. An elderly couple of tourists ask me to take a picture of them in front of the engine. They wear panama hats. They're buying souvenirs made of wood, the bridge and the mosque as pendants, a mini Ivo Andrić; there are no limits to my imagination.

I unpack diabetic cherry jam. Granny Katarina laughs heartily, I don't eat any jam I haven't made myself! She wraps the jam up again and asks me to put it away in the špajz.

List of smells: the cellar smells of peas and coal. The graveyard in Veletovo: freshly mown grass. Zoran's sweet Aunt Desa: honey. Soldiers: iron and schnapps. The Drina: the Drina. The špajz, the larder: sourbread and rotten wood – and in it the bread-box, cans, sugar, flour, bags inside more bags, moths, bottomless boxes and rusty mousetraps. My fishing rod has been lying behind a shelf ever since we left. I'll have to oil the spool, the hook is rusty. Granny, I call from the little room, since when have mice eaten corks?

We go everywhere now to drink coffee, says Granny, leaving the apartment. I respect a clever mouse, I call from the stairs.

To Granny coffee isn't just a drink: coffee is praising her neighbour's white net curtains to the skies because they're so well washed. I drink the first coffee of my life with my grandmother at Teta Magda's on the fourth floor, I've made lists. People living in the tower block. Legend has it that I took my first steps in Magda's arms. Neither sweets nor plums nor minced meat were necessary on that occasion. With her long neck and long nose Magda looks like a stork. Magda from the fourth floor is now a weary and mythical figure, she has to prop her head up because it can't hold itself straight any more. She puts her hand under it, which makes her look dreamy and exhausted at the same time. Her cheeks are hollow, her thin hair is strands of silvery lead. Oh, Katarina dear, says Magda, I could sleep and sleep until the cows come home. You've grown, Aleksandar. She examines me with her green eyes.

You're looking well, I say, not sure what I mean by that.

Yes, yes, says Magda, pulling a leaden strand back from her forehead. Back then, but you won't remember it any more, she says, and Granny and I lean back, because now the legend is about to be sung in her worn old voice, back then you walked into my arms, tottered over to me without holding on to anything, a smile on your face, your conquests were just beginning, hello big world, I'm ready for you now, you were enchanted by your own strength, you'd found your sense of balance there in my arms.

Milomir from the first floor makes strong coffee. During the war, he says, my main worry was whether a grenade or a sniper would get me; now I have so many worries I don't know which is the main one. Pock-marked, arthritic, holding a lit cigarette behind his back, he bows and kisses my grandmother's hand as we leave. Katarina, he says to the hand, come and see me again soon.

After two sips you came to the coffee grounds.

I've made lists. Bars, restaurants, hotels. The Estuary Restaurant where the Rzav and the Drina meet, with a view of both rivers. I remember the domed building with its large terrace, I remember the rare evenings with mosquito bites and the sleepy croaking of the frogs when Father, Mother and I, just the three of us, sat in the Estuary and musicians came to our table. Father would fold a banknote and put it in the accordion, and the accordionist would grin and bow in my mother's direction.

Rubble, stones, iron bars, rusty beams and broken boards are woven into the round foundations of the Estuary to make a wreath. I'm standing in the middle of it now, looking at the Drina on my left and the Rzav on my right. The shards of a salt-shaker crunch under my feet. The frogs are croaking.

Granny Katarina and I sit in the living room watching *Isabella*. I've drunk so much coffee today that I'm shaking and I can't imagine ever being able to sleep again. That's not really the name of the soap opera, Isabella is the beautiful heroine, always suffering a little but good at heart. Granny watches three soaps a day: one at four in the afternoon, another at seven in the evening, and *Isabella* at nine. She injects insulin during the ads. I can't watch. She pushes up her blouse and tells me about a bomb that exploded under a newly married couple's table just as the bridegroom was cutting the cake. The bride and a dog that was asleep under the table at the

233

bridegroom's feet died. They made the dog a little golden coffin and threw it into the Drina. The bride was buried in her wedding dress, but without her shoes, because they were only borrowed.

Granny injects insulin and breathes loudly through her mouth. I can't watch. I can't listen. The more stories I know, I say, turning up the volume on the TV, the less I know about myself.

Granny looks straight at the TV set. Isabella, she says, pressing her forefinger and middle finger to the place where the needle went in, ought not to trust her stepmother so blindly.

Someone, I write later in the when-everything-was-all-right book, which I'm going to give back to Granny before I leave, someone ought to invent a tool, a kind of plane to shave the lies away from stories and deception away from memories. I'm a collector of shavings.

I've made lists. Mr Popović the music teacher. I ring at the door on the fourth floor, his wife Lena opens it, an elaborately dressed lady with her hair pinned up, gold earrings and a musky perfume, she's ready to go out though she doesn't go anywhere. I don't have to explain anything to her. Katarina told me you were here, she says, smiling, come on in!

Mr Popović turns the TV off and gets to his feet when I come into the living room. He looks at me curiously and gives me his hand. He doesn't remember me until his wife introduces me. Aleksandar! What a surprise! Sit down, my boy, sit down. To be honest, I'd hardly have recognised you. Mrs Popović disappears into the kitchen and comes back a minute later to offer us a plate piled high with cheese, a beer for me, and for her husband water and two red pills on a silver salver.

Oh yes, says Mr Popović, I remember. I was friends with your grandfather when we were studying, and political friends later too. Slavko was a good speaker, very few in the Party understood his ideas and almost no one thought they were any good. Which means they were excellent ideas.

I nod, enjoying the old man's deep, thoughtful voice, the calm I see in his bright eyes, which widen as he talks. His wife sits opposite us, folds her hands in her lap and watches him as attentively as if he were the guest.

But for Slavko, Mr Popović goes on with his little speech, the library, for instance, would never have been extended, and to this day the schools and indeed the whole town feel the benefit of it. How long ago that was . . .

I spear a cube of cheese on a toothpick, the cheese is very cold and tastes of paprika. There are cupboards and chests of drawers adorned with flowers in the apartment, a large *art nouveau* lamp, a desk made of dark wood, Tito's portrait over it. Sheet music and records on shelves, on the floor, everywhere. The piano in a corner, a gramophone beside it. I look at Mr Popović again, he has narrowed his eyes and is offering me his hand. I'm Professor Petar Popović, and you are . . . ?

What did you say?

Mrs Popović clears her throat. Petar, she says, this is Aleksandar, Slavko's grandson.

Slavko Krsmanović? cries Mr Popović, and his face brightens, what a nice surprise! You've changed a great deal, Aleksandar! Do you know, your grandfather often used to bring you with him to see us. We got on very well, the Cicero of Višegrad and I. You'd have been . . . Well, at the time I'd say you were at the most . . . Mr Popović becomes thoughtful again, rests his chin on his hand. I look at his wife, who is still smiling. You'll remember, Petar, she says quietly, you'll remember, just take it slowly.

Mr Popović frowns. Lena, he asks his wife, who is this gentleman?

Aleksandar Krsmanović, I say myself this time, I stand up and once again shake hands with the old man wearing a tank top, his hair accurately parted. I'm visiting my grandmother. You once gave me an encyclopedia of music for my birthday.

Mr Popović laughs, stands up too and clasps my hand warmly between both of his. Of course, he cries, the *Encyclopedia of World Music*. So you're Slavko's grandson. Sit down, sit down, and bring us a beer, please, Lena. I expect you drink beer?

Yes, indeed, I say, and Mr Popović looks at me with a friendly expression, a smiling old gentleman among his records and books of musical scores. Grandpa Slavko always spoke highly of his piano playing and described him as the only real intellectual in our town. After his wife has disappeared into the kitchen Mr Popović presses my hand more firmly and whispers in confidential tones: all my life I've treated my wife's beauty and kindness carelessly, otherwise it's only history and death I treat that way.

Mr Popović drinks a sip of water and looks closely at his glass; it is cloudy with condensation. Mr Popović undoes the cuffs of his shirt. They're not real, he says, pointing to the gold cufflinks with the silver treble clef on them.

His kind and beautiful wife comes back into the living room with the beers just in time to see her husband offering me his hand again and saying: I'm Petar Popović, and whom do I have the honour of . . . ?

After I've introduced myself he stands up. A little music, Mr Krsmanović? You look to me as if you'd know the value of Johann Sebastian, who is underestimated in this country. 'I will not let thee go except thou bless me,' he suggests. I am glad, he sings, to cast off the misery of these times today. Pam-ta-tam, he sings, and he stops by the gramophone and stays there.

Maybe it's for the best, says Mrs Popović, taking a sip of beer from the bottle, he can hide from memory and not suffer the horrors of the present day by day.

Mr Popović turns away from the gramophone and goes over to his bookshelf. After a moment's thought he takes out one of the scores and leafs through it as if looking for a certain passage, pam-ta-tam, he sings.

The way from our home to Granny Katarina's: 2,349 steps. I've made lists: distances in footsteps. Home is on the other side of the Drina. Granny is still asleep, snoring peacefully, I could wake her to ask who lives there now, but I don't know how she likes to be woken, and I don't like not knowing the answer to the question myself.

It's 2,250 steps today, and the name by the door says Miki. I stand on concrete, the garden has had concrete put down over it, how are the worms doing? I don't ring the bell. It says just Miki.

I've made lists. Our street. I go from building to building, I know this balcony, I know that swing in the yard made from an old tyre, I know the taste of mirabelles pinched from that garden, I don't know a single name on the letter boxes except the name of Danilo Gorki.

Danilo and I sit on his veranda, the table and rocking chair just as I remember them from Francesco's time. The garden is neglected, the cherry tree has been cut down, old Mirela, Danilo's mother, is dead. Danilo lives alone in the big house, gets up at five every day, goes fishing, and if he can't sell his catch he eats it himself. His freezer is stuffed full of fish. Better fish all day and get nothing on your hook, he says, than toil all day and get nothing in your pocket. A lot of people these days think you can't be happy unless you have a job, it doesn't even have to be a paid job. To hell with that kind of happiness, I say.

I ask Danilo if he knows where his colleague from the Estuary Restaurant went, the man we children called Čika Doctor. List: myths and legends. I tell the tale of the lemonade for the leather-clad biker.

Danilo says yes, he knows. I wait for him to go on, and when he doesn't, I ask: where?

I was in the same unit as your uncle, he says, laying the table. That's why you're here, right?

Čika Doctor, who cut a man's calf open because the man had compared his sister's teeth with the teeth of a horse.

What with all the fish, says Danilo, you don't even smell fish any more.

The muted cries of children playing make their way in to us from outside. Danilo asks if I'm married, pours oil into the pan and puts two fish in.

Just as well, he says, women are devils with pretty skin. Oh yes, says Danilo Gorki, opening the window that looks out on the street, I ought to know.

*

From home to school: 1,803 steps, counted on the day of a maths test for which I'd revised heroically, and even so I handed it in without a single correct answer. Today it's 1,731. The students are standing about in small groups, all talking together in loud voices. I pace out the penalty area of the little football field, which has lost its goals. This is where Kiko won the bet with me and Edin. I go across the yard to see Kostina the caretaker. The thin man in his blue dungarees with a pencil behind his ear is leaning against the wall.

Mr Kostina, I say, the goals have gone.

The goals have gone, he repeats, scratching the thick veins on his forearm. Laughing girls' voices in the yard.

What would you think if I drew a goal on the wall?

Not much, mutters Mr Kostina.

A bell rings, slowly, clattering. Like saucepans clashing, I think. The children wash around us, a torrent of brightly coloured back-packs streaming noisily into the building.

New bells? I ask, since there's nothing to say but the obvious.

The same we've had these thirty years, just a bit slower. The caretaker speaks slowly, he's as durable as the bells.

The school hall always smelled of damp cardboard and nougat. I stop at the entrance.

Mr Kostina, is Fizo still here?

Home-comer, are you? He never came back after break one Monday. Mr Kostina pushes himself away from the wall with an effort and slouches into the building. The yard is quiet now, except for a boy anxious not to be late racing across the goalless football field.

I've made lists. I'm sitting on the fifth floor with Radovan Bunda while his wife gives me the first coffee of my second day in Višegrad. It's early morning, I had to make an appointment, seven in the morning was the only time he had free. Bursting with vigour, never ill in his life and never at a loss for a curse, Radovan Bunda used to be a welcome guest at my great-grandparents' parties in Veletovo. In the winter of '91 he left his village, where they were afraid of electricity, blue denim and the full moon, and moved to Višegrad. On his first day in town he sold his sheep and rented the fifth-floor apartment. He couldn't get his two cows up the stairs, so he sold them too. With the money from the cows he bought a chair, a table, his first vacuum cleaner, his first fridge, and his first carbonated mineral water. He raised chickens on the roof, his rooster crowed even before the muezzin and woke the entire building. But then, on the first day of the skirmishing around Višegrad, a shell fell from above, and none of the chickens ever cackled again. When Radovan saw his silent hens, he decided to leave town. He loaded his chickens into the fridge, and the fridge on to his back, and left. He couldn't think of a safer place than his old village, he tells me, adding sweetener to his coffee. Eyes on his cup, he says: but my village wasn't a village any more. You need people for a village. I went from door to door, all the locks were broken off, and they weren't asleep in the bedrooms, they just lay there dead. In bed, on red pillows. All of them Serbs, except for one house we'd all been Serbs. Revenge on revenge. Back and forth. That was good old Mehmed's house. I knocked, he opened the door, he said: Radovan, old friend. He showed me his hands and embraced me like a brother.

Radovan pauses, stirs his coffee, takes a sip. The hum of car engines rises from the street, calls, a whistle. A terrible night, says Radovan, pressing his lips together, Mehmed told me they poured petrol over the dogs, tied them up and set fire to them. My grandmother was a poor sleeper and used to sit wearily on the swing on the veranda every night, they hung her next to the swing. All the others had been shot, but she was still dangling there. Was it supposed to look like suicide? She'd never have thought of such a thing of her own free will, a stupid thing to do, she'd have said, I've only got this one life!

Radovan Bunda buried the village and set off with the chickens to take his own revenge. On the way, he collected fourteen sharp stones for each of the fourteen victims, and he wept for seven days. He didn't close an eye for six nights, and on the seventh he admitted to himself that he couldn't be a killer. I know about hatred, not bloodshed. I'll get rich, I told myself, and then we'll see. I moved back in here and kept well clear of all of it, that's what I did. I learned to write from Mr Popović the music teacher, and to speak better, to think faster, I learned the art of sweet-talking from him too, I took lessons from Mr Popović every day for a year, in the end he was always playing the piano. Then he forgot Mozart, then he forgot Brahms, then he forgot Vivaldi, in the end there was only Johann Sebastian left. If you want to get rich, Radovan, you have to master rhetoric, that's what the music teacher told me when he was still all right.

Radovan sold everything except the chickens. With the money he invited smugglers and thieves to dinner, he listened when politicians and loudmouths were talking, he watched a doctor playing poker with three of the United Nations blue helmets and gave the doctor secret signs.

And when I'd found out enough about the way things were going, says Radovan, spreading his arms wide, I stopped a truck and had a little argument with its driver, nothing too bad. The thing was stuffed full of medicinal drugs, it was on its way to a mayor who was going to sell them on. I left the truck with one of my smuggler friends and told the poker-playing doctor: over to you now.

Today Radovan's fridge is the kind a large American family would have. A walk-in fridge, extra living space. His blonde wife has 'Princess Bitch' in silver glitter on her close-fitting top. A second woman comes in, a redhead, and kisses Radovan on the mouth. I'll have to think about these complicated relationships. Radovan introduces both women to me by their first names, they both end with a 'y' sound, he pats both their bottoms. Princess Bitch and the redhead smoke by the window, leaning out into the Višegrad morning.

They wiped out my whole village, says Radovan, but I can assure you I still had a life! I invested in medicinal drugs, then in scrap. But a time came when everything was scrap, the town, the whole fucking country was scrap, and scrap wasn't worth a thing any more. I rented a room, sold coffee and grilled meat and called the whole operation 'McRadovan's'. One bar among many, but it was the first where you could lay bets. They all came, my doctors, my blue helmets, my refugees, my politicians, my inventors, my smugglers. But I was the outright winner, me, Radovan Bunda.

Radovan is a sturdy man, well shaved, suntanned. All that remains of his dialect is the way he tends to emphasise long words on the first syllable. His hair-oil smells of apples. Radovan doesn't smoke, and when he talks about money he mimes a circle in the air with his hands, fingers spread wide. He owns the whole fifth floor of the building. He's demolished partitions, combined apartments into large rooms, and glazed the whole façade that looks out on to the street. He's put in offices, a grand bedroom with a four-poster bed and gilded mirrors, and there are two guest-rooms. You can't expect anyone to stay in our hotels, says Radovan Bunda. He shows me everything, he thinks the pictures in the offices are kitsch, but his colleagues like them.

Radovan smiles. My girls sing, he says.

They're not making music now, but there's a video. He plays it for me, Princess Bitch and the redhead dancing. Radovan features in it, Radovan in a hat.

The loft where Asija hid is a lumber room now. Radovan opens the skylight to the roof, and I immediately hear chickens cackling.

They got over the shock in the end, he says, scattering a handful of grain. Radovan Bunda goes to the edge of the tower-block roof and looks out at the town waking up.

I've made lists. Zoran Pavlović. My friend Zoran. Walrus's Zoran. Owner of Maestro Stankovski's barber's shop. I sit on the old barber-shop chair, Zoran stands behind me, a hair grip in his left hand, a large pair of scissors in his right. Zoran's long hair, Zoran's narrow lips, Zoran's serious, immobile expression.

Where did you train? I ask, passing my hand through my hair.

Here and there, mostly with Stankovski. I'll start now, OK? You want it all off?

Yes, all of it. I remove my hand and hide it under the smock. Zoran clamps my hair back with the grip and applies the scissors.

Aleks?

Yes?

Oh, wow, man . . .

What is it?

I mean, look at us! Look in the mirror!

Zoran has my long hair held back, our glances meet. If it's a problem . . . ? I say.

Oh, come on, what do you mean, a problem? You want it all off?

Get on with it or I might change my mind.

My Zoran. Walrus's Zoran. The scissors snip, he shows me the bunch of hair. We say nothing while the Panesamig razor hums away. I am Zoran's last customer. He closes the shop and turns up the collar of his jacket. You'll eat with us this evening, he says. I run my hand over my head. Zoran puts his hands in his pockets, hunches his shoulders in the cool evening air, it's windy and there are no stars.

The red façade and black window frames were Milica's idea, of course, and immediately after Walrus's house had been renovated hardly anyone could pass it without laughing or standing there shaking his head. I had to paint over the shame, the big man told everyone who asked about it, we've decorated inside too. Zoran, his father and his stepmother moved into the house when Walrus threw Desa's seasonal workers out on the very first day he was back. As we ate the moussaka with egg to which Zoran had invited me, Milica said, smiling: Desa did act up a bit, but then I had a word with her. Milica is wearing a red and black lumberjack shirt, black jeans, and there still isn't a single line under her big blue eyes.

It's all new, you young rascal, Walrus tells me. He stands up, still chewing, and spreads his arms wide in the middle of the living room. My Milica and I turned the whole house upside down in three months. Walrus has shaved off his moustache, I stare at what's gone from between his nose and his upper lip, I can hardly say a word.

Zoran spent those three months in prison in Graz, waiting to be deported after he'd tried to cross the Austrian border one misty March morning. Walrus tells the story while Zoran salts potatoes, eyes bent on his plate the whole time. Walrus tells me how thick the mist in which his son tried to hide was, how very nearly Zoran had given the border guard the slip, how bad the food was in prison. That mist, he says, mopping his mouth with bread, there's always mist in our stories.

Mist like cement, Zoran murmurs, putting his half-sister Eliza on his lap. Eliza is two years old and already has her father's drooping cheeks. Milica looks me over, crosses her legs, jiggles her foot up and down. Zoran is helping Eliza with her jigsaw puzzle.

You won't believe this, you young rascal, says Walrus, but do you remember Francesco? The gay Italian I took apart at boccia? Well, just wait for this!

He goes to a biscuit tin full of photos – I catch a quick glance of a basketball game, and Walrus and Milica in front of their bus – and takes out a letter. Half a page in Francesco's broken Serbo-Croat. Is Walrus well, Francesco has been worried, he's kept sending food and medicine to Višegrad, has any of it arrived? My name comes up in Francesco's hopes too. A photo came with the letter. It shows Francesco, a young woman and a little girl on a dam. Would you believe it? says Walrus, tapping the photo. On the back it says 'My wife Kristina and my daughter Drina'.

Austria . . . says Zoran when we go out into the cold late that evening and put our caps on. Ankica never wanted to go with me, I frightened her too much.

The night smells of burnt coal, I try to find something reasonably sensible to say to Zoran, you can always come visit me in Germany, I say, and Zoran takes a deep breath and claps me on the back.

Café Galerie. My list: bars, restaurants, hotels. Turbo-folk and Eminem and the boy with the side parting and a flaking scar on his chin. He puts a fabric heart on every table, and under the heart a handwritten explanation of his disability. There are red hearts and pink hearts. The boy doesn't look anyone in the eye, he's almost invisible amid the drunken singing. They know the songs by heart in the Café Galerie, and the boy collects his fabric hearts with as much concentration as if he were clearing an empty room. It's hot, the café is too full, the window panes are clouded with condensation.

It's odd, I say to Zoran, this is the first time I've been out in Višegrad.

They have teletext screens here too, with results coming in live. Essen versus Düsseldorf, one-all. I've won.

Zoran says: you don't miss much.

We're sitting opposite each other in the far corner of the café, I can hardly hear him, the speaker is right above our heads. Zoran keeps silent most of the time, I ask questions and seldom get more than a shake of his head in return. Sitting in silence with Zoran was never really uncomfortable, it was more of a feeling that I didn't know what to say to get the words out of him. It's much the same this evening: never mind if I talk about the war, the time after the war, women, studies, football − nothing in Zoran reacts, his answers are brief, mostly no more than gestures. After the third beer, I give up shouting remarks on these subjects into Zoran's ear like a journalist, I lean back in my chair and nod in time to the music. Zoran orders two beers and then waves to me as if calling me in from another room. He comes quite close to my ear and shouts, so loud that it makes me jump: look around you, Aleks! Just look around you! Do you know anyone here? You don't even know me! You're a stranger, Aleksandar! Zoran stares at me at close quarters. You'd better be glad of it!

I say, as an aside: I only want to compare my memories with here and now.

Zoran's eyes are red, he doesn't blink. I'll tell you something by way of comparison! he shouts, sounding angry, and not just because his voice is raised.

aleksandar?
    Hello?
aleksandar?
    Who's there? I can't hear you at all well!
it's me it's me the trees are so tall here so healthy it's lovely trees so tall

Nena? Nena Fatima, is that you?

i saw it in the moonlight on my way it has such a slender neck i want to go up it tomorrow i want to

Nena, where are you, what . . .

two black people are putting my tent up they're polite but i can't sleep there it's far too cold

tomorrow we'll take the way with the strongest wind

i'll be sitting by the crater at midday

What? Does Mama know?

oh dear boy why should I wait any longer yes it's me here

snow will lie on mount st helens they say

i want to be proud of something no one would believe of me

Nena, please put Mama on the line, is she there?

you really can't be happy in silence for ever my boy i have a good reason now i've oh yes dear boy i've flown and i had to strap myself in but i didn't

Nena . . .

aleksandar i was never happier i'm going to throw a stone into a volcano

Will you call Mama, please, will you call her now?

don't worry she'll understand

the black people don't understand me i want to sleep in the hut i'm going in there now oh dear boy dear boy such tall trees and such space to breathe and an unmasked moon

Nena . . . Will you do me a favour?

you have rafik's voice my boy

Will you throw a stone in for me too?

i will dear boy i'll throw a whole mountain in

i'm there now.

Nena Fatima giggles. Nena Fatima's laughter is the laughter of a boy.

I try to be as quiet as possible, the garden gate squeals, I sit down at a small table that wasn't here before. The gate doesn't belong to us, nor does the garden or the table. Only what was here before still belongs to us, Nena and me; the sunflowers in my Nena's garden used to turn her way when she braided her hair.

Nothing moves inside the house. The view of the Drina doesn't belong to us either: when the poplars and chestnuts were blossoming it used to snow in summer on the river banks outside the house. Nena stood under the trees letting her hair down. A rope hung from one of the chestnuts, a tyre dangled from the rope, a boy dangled from the tyre, trembling with cold and pleasure as the leaping wind sowed flower-flakes.

The view of the bridge doesn't belong to us. I held tight to the soapy stone of the fifth arch of the bridge, feeling furious with Grandpa Slavko for the first and only time. He had made me swim through the arches, but it was too cold for me, the current was too strong, I was scared and I didn't want to disappoint him. I swam again and again, upstream through the arches, downstream through the arches, until the Drina received me with casual persistence, as if my body belonged to the river. The light breaking through the surface of the water, seen from below, was uncanny when it began to burn in my head behind my nose. Grandpa reached for me, slipping away, disappearing, dragged me coughing and protesting to the bank, said: you'll soon be seven, you must be able to swim through all the arches by then.

The poplars and chestnuts have gone for firewood. A dog is rummaging in the rubbish on the bare slope. An angler stands near the drainpipe feeding bread to the fish. I never did swim through all the arches, Grandpa, but Nena will throw a stone into the magma for me.

Aleksandar, I know what skin looks like when the person it belongs to is tied behind a cart and dragged through the town for hours. Back and forth, Zoran shouts through the music. Do you remember Čika Sead? People say they impaled him and roasted him like a lamb somewhere near the Sarajevo road. If you remember Čika Sead you'll remember Čika Hasan. He gave eighty-two litres of blood before the war, he was always boasting about it. They took Čika Hasan to the bridge every day to throw the bodies of the people they'd executed into the river. Hasan spread the arms of the dead wide, he supported their bodies with his own, he let them rest against him before he let them go. He buried eighty-two of the dead in the river Drina. And when they ordered him to throw in the eighty-third he climbed on the railings and spread his own arms out. That's all, they say he said, I don't want any more.

I've made lists. Čika Hasan and Čika Sead.

Pokor isn't on any of the lists. On the way back from Nena Fatima's house – 986 steps – I meet a policeman trying to stuff an enormous net bag of onions through the door of his police car. When he takes his cap off in his struggle with the onions I recognise him by his untidy red hair. Pokor was a policeman before the war too, I often met his son out fishing, we were good at keeping quiet with each other. Later, the rumour that Pokor had been promoted – from easy-going policeman to leader of a violent band of irregulars – reached us even in Germany. Pokor was nicknamed Mr Pokolj, and it was said that Mr Blood-Bath often ordered his men to live up to his name.

Mr Pokolj is in Liberation Square, which isn't called that any more now, it bears the name of some Serbian king or hero, Pokor is only Pokor again and wears his blue police uniform. He struggles with the net of onions, but it won't go through the door. The whole car is full of onions, their skins peel off and drift out into the street. Other cars drive slowly around the blue Golf, and I stop. Pokor throws the net bag on the ground and kicks it several times, snorting with rage. Breathing heavily, he looks around and hitches up his trousers, which are slipping down over the crack between his buttocks. There are onions in his trouser pockets too. He jerks his head challengingly at me: what's the matter? What are you gaping at?

Can I help you? I ask.

So whose are you? replies Pokor.

I don't understand the question at once, no one's asked me that for so many years; only gradually does it dawn on me that by 'whose' he means who are my parents – it's a question you ask children who have lost their way. I tell him my father's first name and surname.

You're Aleksandar, right? He repeats my father's first name, and speaks my mother's too, he says it twice, the second time it's a question. I ought to repeat her name immediately in a firm voice, I ought to confirm my mother's beautiful Arabic name proudly and tell Pokor that it means ship, or spring, or pleasure. And I ought to tell Pokor to his face that it is monstrous for murderers to be able to go around freely in this country, and not just that, but wearing a police uniform too. However, I hesitate, I look past the man in his grubby blue uniform at the onions filling the whole car. I hesitate, and swallow, and pretend not to have heard the question. I can't swallow the shame rising inside me.

Pokor gives himself a little shake as if he were cold. Miki's in town, is he? he asks, and when I don't reply he squeezes himself, without a word of goodbye, into the car, which is much too small for such a man and such a quantity of onions.

Here I am, afraid of a Serbian policeman described as a 'presumed war criminal', and people say 'there are plenty of witnesses to that'. Perhaps it's a groundless fear, but it's enough to make me disown my mother to the little policeman Pokor who has put on thirty kilos in the last ten years and is now surrounded by a strong smell of onions. He leaves that last net bag lying on the asphalt. And fails to give way to another driver as he turns into the street that – like the square where I stand rooted to the spot by shame – now has a new name. The name of a king or a hero.

I've made lists, but that's not the point.

I've made lists. Girls. Elvira. Danijela. Jasna. Nataša. Asija. No, Marija, you can't join in. Marija was too young and too girlie for just about everything we wanted to do.

Her mother opens the door, a dark-haired woman with rosy cheeks, Marija's curls, and floury handprints on her apron. She points apologetically to the apron and goes into the kitchen. Come on in, Aleks! she cries – in German. Pots and pans clatter, oil hisses, you're looking well, she cries, your granny said you were coming to visit. Want to see Marija? She's downstairs.

Yes, I'd like to say hello, I reply, also in German, relieved by this uncomplicated encounter.

She's in the cellar, says Marija's mother, peering out of the kitchen. There'll be schnitzels in a moment.

Down on the ground floor a cat startles me, hissing and jumping up. I stop, the cat stops and circles around me. Music drifts up from the cellar, light casts the shadow of the banisters on the wall, I follow the grey cat down, what's Marija doing here? The music gets louder, I'm not going back down the steps of my memory, I'm going down into a cellar, it's only a cellar.

This is where my parents quarrelled.

This is where I was the fastest.

This is where frightened Asija sat.

This is where a soldier passed the butt of his rifle over the posts of the banisters, clack-clack-clack-clack-clack.

It's only a cellar. I've gone around in enough circles these last few days, I'd like to be a pigeon, pigeons never do anything but what they always do. There's a small CD player on the floor, I know the playful beat. 'Swayzak.'

Swayzak, a young woman says on the other side of the room reading my thoughts, I met James Taylor in Munich, he told me that whatever he dreams, there are always dogs in it, barking at him. It felt so strange that he got himself a Dobermann and slept in the same bed with it, and the dream dogs shut up. Hello! says Marija in her wraparound skirt made of a scarf with another scarf in her hair to keep her curls off her forehead. She hands me a spatula thin as the edge of a screwdriver, points to a small wound on her thumb, says: the bloody cat scared me. Marija's eyes are yellowy green in the dim light, she bows her head, dust over her eyebrows, lips pressed to the wound.

Hello, I say, it's Aleksandar.

Are we going to introduce ourselves to each other, shaking hands and all that? says Marija, smiling.

I look for a handkerchief for her thumb although I know I don't have one, I'm thinking: what a green those eyes are! I'm thinking: after all, I've made lists. Marija switches the music off, yes, I'll show you around, she says, but let's eat first, you will eat with us, won't you? Good.

The schnitzels are coated with egg and breadcrumbs, Marija and her mother describe Munich to me. Marija says: the Starnberger See, says: you just automatically support FC Bayern, says: of course I'm going back there, I'm getting ready to go, says: I can't manage without good music. The two of them have been living near Munich for eight years, they came back because Marija's grandfather died and her grandmother fell sick – she's sitting at the table with us, rocking back and forth and smiling whenever her name is spoken. I tell them what I like about Essen, I defend the Ruhr when Marija says it's a dreary dump; we talk about dialects and mentalities, we talk about Germany, no I say, really, Sylt is better than its reputation. Marija asks if I've ever pushed a sleeping cow over, laughs, and puts her hand in front of her mouth as if to catch her laughter.

Marija, you can't play, she says later in the evening, of course I still remember that, you bet!

The second glass of wine tastes of caramel, we lie on yellow loungers in the cellar. Marija is studying art in Belgrade, sculpture, it's her second year. She calls what she's doing here her first serious work, she doesn't think too much about things that are larger or more abstract than the seasons, so she makes plaster models of ordinary people and puts tennis socks on them, or ear muffs with rabbit ears, or a T-shirt with an ad for an arthritis remedy. She's hung wall coverings in the two largest rooms in the cellar, aluminium spirals hang from the ceiling, plastic bows, coloured glass mosaics, papier mâché dolls, and there's a landscape painting in the middle of the room: conceptualist, says Marija, and Provence! A generator gives a little light, the rough, grey walls of the past seem to me as improbable as

the plywood tables by the longer wall,
our mothers' anxious voices,
the stove in the corner,

Čika Aziz's C-64 around which we gathered while the town took a beating outside,

the yellow begonias under the ventilation grating where Marija now stores her scrapers, knives and files. She's made casting boxes out of the plywood table tops, square frames covered with veneer.

My last boyfriend was the Serbian taekwondo number two, she says. We were together for twelve hours, then he told me he was the Serbian taekwondo number two. Marija pauses. Are you really all right, Aleksandar?

Not always, I say, raising my glass, but I am now.

To the people we knew, she says, drinking. Have you ever heard from Edin?

He's in Spain.

And?

I examine the colour of the wine closely. Blackcurrant colour. To be honest, I don't know any more. All I know is that he is or was in Spain. I called him once but he was out. I left my number on the answering machine.

And that's all? I don't believe it, Aleks! You two were inseparable! A single phone call . . .

I've called Sarajevo three hundred times, I say.

Marija waits for me to go on. Are you doing all right? I ask. It's colder now, we've nearly finished the wine, and this evening I don't want to remember anything that's more than three hours old.

I put boxer shorts on little plaster men, says Marija, finishing her wine. Shall we have breakfast together tomorrow? Will you fetch me? she asks, writes down my phone number, pulls off her headscarf and takes the cellar stairs two at a time.

I switch off the music, the generator hums. I breathe in deeply. Plaster. I sit down on the stairs.

There are the loungers.

There are the wall hangings.

There are the empty wine bottles.

There's a priest with a Tarzan apron frying a fish.

There's a boy in a tanga buttering bread.

There's the grey cat asleep.

Here am I. The rules of the game say it's an armistice at the bottom of the stairs. Here on the steps, Asija sat beside me, crying. Here am I, the person who didn't mean to remember anything else this evening.

Here was Uncle Bora chain-smoking at one of the plywood tables, telling us he'd vowed to give up smoking the day before, Pioneer's word of honour! The plywood tables were put together so that we could eat and play dominoes more easily. I learned the word 'provisional' and two men carried a stove into the cellar. The stove isn't here any more, but a man in flip-flops is mowing the lawn over there, and my uncle swore he meant his vow seriously, Sundays are the best days to give something up, and Mondays are the best days to start something. Just before midnight, he said, he'd smoked his last packet, and then he began constructing famous buildings with matches: the Eiffel Tower, the Egyptian pyramids, the Berlin Wall. When the first of those cramped, polished things fell on Višegrad in the morning, one of them hit the roof of Uncle Bora' s house. Auntie Typhoon dropped the breakfast tray in fright, the two coffee cups lost their handles, and my uncle praised his glue in glowing terms: the Berlin Wall stood firm where the tiles of his roof and the breakfast china hadn't.

Since Bora, Typhoon and their little Ema moved into Granny's cellar, Uncle Bora has been smoking again, describing what it sounded like, and how everything shook when the shell took the tiles off his roof. He balances a small square clump of matches on his knees, pointing to it every time he says, 'The Berlin Wall'.

Auntie Typhoon sits opposite him, breast-feeding little Ema. I can hear my mother say to Granny Katarina: Gordana looks so pale.

That upsets me. Not because Auntie Typhoon is pale, or so unusually quiet, but because my mother calls her by her proper name. I paint a camomile flower without a stalk and give it to my aunt because I know that camomile tea is soothing. Ema reaches for the paper. Her whole hand fits in my fist.

After the fiftieth hit I stop counting – I'd rather count the kittens. A grey mother cat is washing her four grey kittens in the far corner of the cellar. Uncle Bora has told everyone present the tale of the coffee cups, the roof, and the glue twice over, that means he's uttered the word 'handles' about sixty times, he has said, 'The GDR was just a joke' about twenty times, and he's asked, 'My God, what's going on here?' exactly three times.

The cellar is large enough, three hundred footsteps from corner to corner and corner to corner. No one sends us out to play, although everything is said in whispers as if we ought not to hear it. We're beginning to get bored, Marija is blindfolded and can't find anyone, she wanders down the corridors, groping her way. Nešo is here, Edin is here. When I talk to Marija I always look at her hair. Marija has curlier hair than anyone else I know. I have to look at her dimples too because they make little whirlpools in her cheeks when she laughs. And at her eyes, because they're yellow and green. In the cellar Marija spends most of her time playing alone under the begonias in the ventilation shaft, she makes little pans and spoons and a table out of plasticine, and drinks invisible coffee with invisible guests out of plasticine cups.

More and more people who don't live in the building stream into the cellar. I'm particularly glad to see Walrus and Zoran. And Milica the ladybird trips her way down to us too. Walrus has brought a bag full of fruit. There's a lot of firing in the mountains, he says, it nearly got the green house with the peculiar roof, the one where the Japanese disappeared, and the vegetable shop on the corner. But I left money on the counter, honest I did. We need vitamins. He breaks an apple in two and gives Zoran half of it.

Do mosquitoes really suck the vitamins from our blood?

Milica sits down beside Auntie Typhoon in her red and black outfit. Lovely, she says to Ema's downy hair and to the rest of us all around, I hope it's all right for us to stay until this is over.

I started liking Milica long ago.

I don't ask the following questions:

Who's firing?

Who are they firing at?

Why?

When will it be over?

Will roofs burn in Višegrad like the roofs burning in Osijek?

Will the football season go ahead?

Will school go ahead?

Who's defending us?

When will it be over?

Suppose a shell hits Grandpa Slavko's grave?

Why doesn't Auntie Typhoon stand up, run off and disarm them all before they can reload?

Will the building fall on us if one of those cramped, polished things hits it?

Is it all the same as usual for the fish now?

What do we need?

What is the pocket-knife for?

What are the fifty marks for, and what exactly does it mean when someone says: in case we get separated?

My God, what's going on here?

When will it be over?

Where is Nena Fatima?

My mother! screams my mother, rushing out of the cellar. Father catches up with her halfway up the stairs, has she gone out of her mind, my mother cries oh, wait! I forgot my mother, is she deaf, oh, let me go! can't she hear what's going on outside, that's why, just let me go!

But Father doesn't let her go, he has one arm around her.

I have to go to her, says Mother, a little more calmly, trying to twist out of his grasp. Father takes her by the shoulders, tries to force her down the stairs again, there's a silent tussle, Mother moans.

I feel embarrassed by my parents. I don't like to think they forgot Nena, and now everyone is staring at them. I sit there, wondering to myself in Uncle Bora's voice: my God, what's going on here? It's shell-firing time, and my parents look as if they're about to fight each other. Mother isn't fighting back so hard now, I forgot her, she says, my own mother, she wails, pressing the balls of her hands to her eyes. Milica comforts her, it will be all right, he'll be with her in a moment. By 'he' she means my father. No one stops him halfway up the stairs.

My God, what's going on here?

My God, what's going on here?

My God, what's going on here?

Čika Aziz, known to us as Potato Aziz because of his large toes, first tied a white scarf around his forehead as a headband, then he plugged in his C-64 down in the cellar, and now he is making a speech. Gun in the crook of his arm, barrel pointing at the ceiling, sunglasses in his shirt pocket, toothpick in the corner of his mouth; everyone come over here!

Everyone goes over there. When I'm as old as Aziz I'll have side-whiskers too and I'll be Comrade-in-Chief of the Cowboys' Defence. I'll use any number of toothpicks and call loud and clear: everyone come over here!

Aziz, by your mother's life, tell us, what's going on? says Čika Milomir from the first floor. Milomir must go on smoking even in his sleep, he smells so strongly of cigarettes. Aziz looks past him, looks past us all, tightens his belt by one notch. With his khaki trousers and his open shirt over a white undershirt Aziz is a provisional soldier but also the only person in sight with a real weapon, even Walrus doesn't have his shotgun with him. Aziz lives on the third floor and has the most amazing games on his C-64. He says to the air above our heads: now, everyone step back. However, those prepared to face the aggressor in defence of this building and the persons inside it come with me.

Who's the aggressor?

Why is he aggressing?

How many cramped, polished things will a dam stand up to?

Can Aziz save us?

Which is worse: if a bullet hits you and comes out again through your ribs, or if a bullet hits you and stays there, for instance in the neck, or if thirty cramped, polished items hit the dam and there's a flood?

Will Višegrad look like the village below Francesco's Lago di Vajont?

255

What's the technique for shifting a toothpick from one corner of your mouth to the other so fast?

Nena Fatima sows sunflowers in her garden. Nena Fatima is as deaf as a post, so she doesn't hear the guns sowing shells over our town. I don't believe my Nena is deaf at all. She always looks at me as if she understands every word, and knows clever answers to every question, and once, after they said what the fourth number in the lottery was, she ran out of the kitchen into the living room and she had all four numbers. You can't see the TV set from the kitchen.

But then a shell hits the mountain above Nena's little house and all she does is – she goes on just as usual, loosening the earth with a hoe and sowing sunflower seeds. Gunfire, flames, sirens, and Nena Fatima connects the hose to the tap outside the house and waters the ground.

My Nena went deaf the day Grandpa Rafik married the river Drina, face down. The marriage was legal because Nena and Grandpa Rafik had been divorced for years, something unusual in our town. After Grandpa Rafik was buried, they say she said at his graveside: I haven't cooked anything, I haven't brought anything, I haven't put on black clothes, but I have a whole book full of things to forgive. They say she took out a stack of notes and began reading aloud from them. They say she stood there for a day and a night, and word by word, sentence by sentence, page by page she forgave him. After that she said no more, and she never reacted to any kind of question again.

Nena Fatima has eyes as keen as a hawk's, kyu, ket-ket, she recognises me before I turn into her street, and she wears head-scarves. Nena's hair is a secret – long and red and beautiful, she gives the secret away to me as we sit outside her little house eating börek in summer and feeding the Drina with minced meat. Cold yoghurt, salted onions, the warmth of Nena rocking silently as she sits cross-legged. The dough is shiny with good fat. Nena rocks back and forth and lights a cigarette when I've had enough. I am the quietest grandson in the world, so as not to disturb her stillness and our sunset. Sultry heat gathers over the river and looks attentively at Nena Fatima, who is humming as she plaits her secret into a long braid. I don't laugh with anyone as softly as with my Nena, I laugh with her until I'm exhausted, I don't comb anyone else's hair.

Nena Fatima comes down into the cellar with my father. She stops on the bottom step of the stairs, like Aziz making his speech. She straightens her headscarf, leaving an earth mark on her forehead. She was in the garden, says Father. Mother hugs Nena Fatima, furious and glad, as if Nena were her daughter and had run away. Nena points to her mouth with her thumb: I'm thirsty. I write 'Fatima' on a mug. All the mugs have our names. I've called one 'Slavko', another 'Johann Sebastian', a third 'Herpes', and a fourth 'Jürgen the biker'. Milica thought that was incredibly funny, and wrote 'Ladybird' on hers. Nena drinks the mug of water. She washes her hands with water from the second mugful. Everyone is looking at her. She opens her mouth, taking a deep breath as if to explain herself. But then she just yawns, smacks her lips with relish, and kisses Ema on the forehead.

Ema is a depository for kisses.

Nena, I whisper, cheer up!

If you hear that racket all day long, and then it stops, you wonder: where has the noise gone? Is it coming closer so as to score hits more accurately? Has the ammunition run out? Don't soldiers work in shifts? Or is it all over? In spite of this nocturnal calm I have to sleep on the floor, rule number one is to keep away from the windows, says my mother. I sleep under the coffee table, Mother has stuck a pillow to the bottom of the table above my head, so that I don't hurt myself if I wake and sit up suddenly. She covers me up.

A tower block, and everyone's sleeping on the floor because you'd be closer to the window on a bed. Everyone watches TV from the floor. There's nothing but news and press conferences and pictures of people in long lines. I learn what 'organised resistance' means, who the Territorial Defence are, and what barricades are for.

I close my eyes and hear Grandpa Slavko's voice. In the living room and in the cushion above my head and outside the window. I concentrate on it so hard, trying to make out where the voice is coming from, that I don't understand a word of it. Grandpa has come back to life for the first time since he died, and I've missed out. I haven't a hope of going to sleep now, I get a toothpick from the kitchen and break rule number one: someone is crossing the road junction outside the building with a fridge on his back. It's Radovan Bunda from the fifth floor, he never once puts the fridge down, and goes on along the road into the dark. I lie down under the table again, waiting for Grandpa's voice to come back. By midnight I can shift the toothpick from one corner of my mouth to the other very fast. Next morning my father wakes me.

Here, Aleksandar. Your uncle left you the Wall.

Where's he gone?

Hm.

Uncle Bora, Auntie Typhoon and Ema left the town overnight. No one thought it was a good idea, no one thought it wasn't a good idea, no one stopped them.

If I were a magician who could make things possible, we'd all be as fast on our feet as Auntie Typhoon so that we could avoid every bullet. And the clouds would cling together like cobwebs so that the shells would stick to them. The gunfire would have its own opinion, it could decide whether to fire or not.

I paint a campfire without any smoke. I paint a baked bean casserole without any beans. I paint a sniper's gun without any sniper. I paint a sheet of paper without a crease in it.

My mother is very keen not to forget any more family members today; after the second detonation she hauls me away from the door where I'm listening to Father and Mr Popović the music teacher. He may be up there now, says Father to Mr Popović, and what will he do if they order him: shoot, Miki! What will he do then?

He'll refuse, replies the distinguished old gentleman. Miki is a good boy. He'll have made his way to safety long before then. He's a clever lad.

The light in the stairwell flickers when a third explosion comes, one of those cramped, polished items quite close. People run down the corridors to the cellar in their pyjamas. Teta Magda serves the coffee on a large tray. She curses roundly and kicks the door of Teta Amela's apartment several times with the toe of her shoe, Amela-a, bring some sugar with you if God gives you luck, Amela-a!

Aziz waves us through like a traffic cop, I stop and ask: Čika Aziz, isn't it a bit dangerous, sleeping with a toothpick in your mouth? And as I ask my question I shift my own toothpick from left to right.

After shaving, Aziz doesn't look so much like a soldier.

Strangers at the plywood tables in the cellar. They don't ask if they can stay, which is a good thing, because it seems to me that of course they can. Milica looks after them, talks to everyone, takes off her red high-heeled shoes, is barefoot as she helps them to sort out their baggage.

Zoran says: come on, no, Marija, you can't join in.

With everyone's united strength, the ventilator grating is raised and pushed to one side. Are you lot scared? Zoran asks. Who'd admit it now? We're already outside, crossing the yard. We stop outside the kiosk in Tito Street. No one in sight. Explosions in the distance.

Hey, not bad, says Zoran, showing us the blonde wearing green camouflage trousers and nothing else on Page Four. He puts the stone he's used to break the tobacconist's window in his trouser pocket. Tobacconists watch out when there's a Walrus about!

Edin reads the front page of yesterday's newspaper. Nothing about war, he says, just barricades and sport. We could do with a time machine, there's a flash and we go back to last week and warn everyone. And no one believes us because we don't even know what the barricades are there for.

I do, I say, but before I can explain there's a shrill whistling over our heads, there's a genuine flash, glass breaks, a shove in my back pushes me to the ground. I shield my face with my hands, splinters fall on me, a shower of glass like hail, someone shouts.

Smoke rises from the asphalt. Zoran and Nešo are lying in the street, stretched flat. Edin is still standing there with the newspaper in his shaking hands. Edin is pale, so pale, with blood running from his nose, that I feel as if all his blood is draining out of his face through his nostrils.

259

Oh, go fuck the sailor-woman, spits Zoran, frantically shoving the section of the paper with unusual careers for women under his shirt. Nešo slowly gets to his feet. His hand is bleeding, he counts his fingers. The blast caught all the windows in the building opposite, including the big display window of the shoe shop on the ground floor. Edin says: I'm hearing everything and nothing at the same time. He licks blood from his upper lip with his tongue. The tobacconist's window behind him is full of holes, cracks have sucked their way into the glass, splaying out.

I get to my knees, Zoran gives me a hand.

A large triangle of glass, pointy end down, comes away from the window frame rather late in the day and breaks on the pavement, a starting shot: we run for it, four Carl Lewises, two in pyjamas, two bleeding. Were you scared? Zoran asks again, and in spite of everything we're not going to admit it in front of Zoran.

Is there any glass in my back? I ask.

Edin taps his forehead with his finger: I can hear a kind of note, he says, a very, very shrill kind of note.

The Berlin Wall in my trouser pocket is still in one piece.

Is Ema safe? is what I don't ask after we've stolen back to the cellar as if nothing had happened.

My hand shaking, I paint a slim Uncle Bora.

Am I bleeding?

I paint a wound without any blood.

Suppose that man really does blow up our dam the way he swears he will on the radio, cursing, although the other man tells him: with all due respect, please don't do that! The man at the dam has wrecked Ivo Andrić's statue in the park by the bridge too, with a sledgehammer. He's capable of anything.

I paint a lizard with a tail.

Suppose someone finds out we broke into the tobacconist's?

How much dynamite does it take to blow up a dam like that, and what would the river Drina and the fish think?

I paint a moment of peace.

Over there a baby in a military tunic is reading the newspaper.

Over there a boy with a gold tooth is putting on a Rolex.

Over there a one-eyed giant with a cross on a string around his neck and a crescent moon on his armband is stirring a pot.

Over there a dentist in a miniskirt is busy doing something with a drill.

Here am I on the steps down to the cellar. Here is Asija beside me. Asija's long fingernails.

Over there a woman in an apron is feeding a dog with miniatures of a woman in an apron.

Over there a still unhewn figure is hoovering; here, Asija is saying: your pictures are horrible, twisting her hair round her finger. I'm Asija, she says. They took Mama and Papa away. My name has a meaning. A man once came to our village to answer all our questions. He was as thin as a rake, with only one ear, and you had to shout into it so that he would understand the question. Everyone in the village could ask the one-eared man a question, and in return for the answer they gave him a box with ten chicks inside, or a bottle of schnapps, or an envelope. The one-eared man had a one-eared horse that pulled a cart. The cart was piled high with presents. I showed the man a piece of wood with my name scratched into the bark. What does Asija mean? I shouted in his ear. No idea, the one-eared man shouted back, why do you ask? He had such a strong smell of new wine and horses that I had to wash my face in our stream. A year later the soldiers lined up everyone from the village. Uncle Ibrahim and I managed to hide in the forest. A soldier read the names on our papers out loud. Another soldier crossed himself and poured petrol over the door of our house.

Over there a gentleman with a monocle is cleaning his teeth.

Over there a woman with a top hat is shaving her legs.

Rules of the game: the place at the bottom of the stairs means memories. I stand up and switch the generator off. The light goes out. A list: silences. Silence of those dark seconds with Asija in the stairwell before we press the light switch. Silence baring its fangs. My father. Silence after Kamenko fires his shot. Francesco and the silence of the veranda. My silent Nena Fatima. The silence of my last ten years.

The box is still behind the wardrobe in Granny's bedroom. I lay the pictures out on the floor. I lay the pictures out on the chest of drawers, I lay the pictures out on the beds. I lay the pictures out on the window-sill, on the table, under the table. Ninety-nine pictures of unfinished things, with writing on the back, I'm going to finish painting every one of them now. There isn't a picture of an unfinished childhood among them. I'll begin with the hawk diving through the air, the hawk I painted that day in the Lagoon of Light, I am still the . . .

Comrade-in-Chief of all that's unfinished

A hawk diving through the air.

Our Yugo on the road to Veletovo without its exhaust.

Yugoslavia with Slovenia and Croatia.

Nena Fatima's hair, unbraided.

The river Drina without the ugly new bridge.

The young river Drina without the dam.

A pumpkin not cut up.

Tito in a T-shirt.

Tito with untidy hair.

Tito without a hole shot in his eye.

An open window on a sunny day.

Father's 'Portrait of B. as Virtuoso on the Gentle Violin' without the silly violin.

Grandpa Rafik without a cognac bottle.

Going barefoot.

Shadows of people under a street lamp without any people there.

Candle without a wick.

Friday afternoon, Saturday and Sunday without Monday, Tuesday, Wednesday, Thursday and Friday morning.

Edin's goal chalked on the front of the school, without the care-taker.

A lizard with a tail.

The straight nose of my classmate Vukoje Worm, who tried to break mine four times, but something always happened to prevent it. Painted by Vukoje himself in an unexpectedly gentle moment.

Van Gogh, Father's great example, with both his ears (very large).

Books with no dust on them.

Sunrise (very red).

A cow who has fallen over. Grandpa Slavko and I are playing chess on her.

Yugoslavian flag before the star disappeared.

A shower of rain with no clouds in the sky.

Statue of Ivo Andrić with Ivo Andrić's head still on it.

Beach in the sun at Igalo without the people of Višegrad.

Milenko's Milica in black and white, without make-up.

Veletovo graveyard without Grandpa Slavko's gravestone.

Carl Lewis without his gold medal.

Emina far away from the soldier with the gold tooth.

A börek, uneaten.

Unfinished jigsaw: Tito shaking hands with ET.

Starless starry sky.

Airplane with no vapour coming from its tail.

Cauliflower galloping far and wide without a bridle.

Gramophone without soldiers dancing near it.

Wound without blood.

Hammer without sickle.

Plums without stones, coated with minced meat.

Ten sleeping soldiers.

Ten unarmed soldiers.

Dog without collar.

The beautiful big Kawasaki without Jürgen in his leathers.

Moment of peace.

Johann Sebastian's wig. Without Johann Sebastian.

Mama's face, smiling, cheerful, carefree.

Campfire without smoke.

Party without pistols.

Unloaded pistol.

Catfish with moustache and spectacles leaping out of the Drina at the highest point of its flight, four metres above the surface.

Palm of a hand without lines of fate.

Great-Grandpa radiantly young: with ravines of wrinkles, bushes in his ears, a thicket of beard, hair like a meadow, eyes like lakes, and a little plough under his arm.

Yuri Gagarin without Neil Armstrong.

Neil Armstrong without the moon.

Radovan Bunda's cows on the first floor.

A sniper's gun without any sniper.

Football game, whistle for the start of play.

Goal shot.

Throwing a basketball.

Magic Johnson without AIDS.

Dražen Petrović scoring a three-point shot without car accident.

League table of the year 1989. Red Star still in the lead.

Cheese without holes.

My answer to Francesco's goodbye letter.

Čika Spok without a hip flask to his lips.

One-pot dish without beans.

The hurricane called Walrus sweeping through Bogoljub Balvan's tobacconist's shop.

Railway engine without carriages.

Game of rummy, all cards in the hand.

Bread without breadbin.

Uncle Bora, slim.

Coat-hanger without shirt.

Čika Hasan and Čika Sead arguing.

Sheet of paper without a crease.

Tank without gearwheels.

Rambo 1.

Karl Marx before shaving.

Half-moon.

Comrade Fazlagić, not Mr Fazlagić yet.

Signpost with no writing on it.

Penicillin injection with no needle.

School yard before rain.

Flowers without weeds.

Teta Desa naked, without the men from the dam.

Shooting, but no one lies down, there's no blood in sight.

Milk not yet cold (12 minutes).

Snow without footprints.

Dough on the hands of Teta Amela, who bakes the best bread in the world.

Francesco before saying goodbye.

Glass without a crack.

Hands on a light switch.

Self-portrait with both Grandpas.

Reflection.

When everything was all right.

Blank sheet of paper.

Defiant gramophone gone wrong.

Asija.

It's late evening, and I still haven't finished most of the pictures. It took me a long time to think how to shave Marx, or what it was I liked about a starry sky with no stars in it, what the blank sheet of paper meant, and where Radovan's cows should go. Now Emina lies in front of me, the sketch of a woman's face.

Aleksandar? Granny Katarina knocks and comes in. Are you hungry?

I'm nearly through, Granny.

Soon would be better than nearly, she says, and turns to go, but she stops in the doorway, running her fingers over the height markings. Tomorrow is requiem mass day, she says, we're going to see Grandpa in Veletovo.

This is the first time she's mentioned Grandpa Slavko. How often do you visit his grave? I ask.

Whenever I can. The road is all overgrown now, and it's a long way on foot. Great-Grandpa and Great-Granny look after the grave. Do you remember the day Slavko was buried? I pulled you away from the pit in the ground and asked what you thought Grandpa would want me to do now.

What did I say?

I don't know, says Granny, that's the trouble. So you'll come with me, won't you?

You mustn't forget him. And you must notice everything: what's in the paper, what people are saying, what you see, what you hear. And then you must go to see him with me every Sunday, telling him everything at your leisure. He ought to know what's going on, even without the newspaper and his glasses and going for a walk. You'll tell him how it really is. Then you'll go away and leave us alone for a little while. I'll take over the stories.

Granny wakes me by pulling at the sheet underneath me as if she wanted to shake it out while I'm still on it. The alarm clock says six o'clock and Miki is standing beside Granny. Good morning, Aleksandar.

I've been dreaming of a woman who's a cross between Asija and Marija, with bright curls. I took Asijamarija breakfast in bed, an omelette. Good morning, Uncle, I say, losing my battle for the blanket, so there I lie in my underpants in front of Granny in her black dress and my broad-shouldered uncle in his black suit. Miki turns his face to the window, bump on his nose, high-arched eyebrows, it's still early, he says, we boys will go for a spin. My Grandpa's profile, his beautiful mouth.

Miki starts the car, I get in, we don't talk. How are you doing, Uncle? I ask after a while. Miki looks straight ahead, no one on the street, we'll be there in a moment, he says. He drives to the bridge with me. We get out. I follow him, he goes to the middle of the bridge and looks down into the Drina. There's a cold wind blowing through the valley, clouds race across the sky.

Miki drives to a building in Pionirska Street with me. It has a new yellow façade, which makes it stand out from the dirty houses next to it. The wind rises higher. An old man wearing a hat is sitting on the bench under the window, walking stick on his lap. What are you going to do when you finish your studies? Miki asks me. The old man spits his chewing gum out into his hand and packs it into its foil with shaking fingers. It takes him a long time, and when he's done it, Miki takes the little pellet from him. You OK? he shouts into the old man's ear.

K-k-k, says the old man, fn, fn.

Miki drives me to the Hotel Bikavac, which isn't a hotel any more. The dilapidated little bungalows are now inhabited by people who can't afford anything else.

Do you have a girlfriend? asks Miki, looking up at the sky. It smells like rain, he says, and then: when are you planning to have children? He knocks at several doors, one is opened, a pale woman with her face still crumpled from sleep asks in surly tones what we want.

Just saying good morning, says Miki.

Miki drives me to the Hotel Vilina Vlas. About halfway there, in Kosovo Polje, we stop by a burnt-out ruin. Miki picks up a stone and rubs his thumb over the soot on it. In the car park outside the Vilina Vlas he offers me a cigarette and when I don't take one he throws the packet away, half full.

On the way back through town he turns off at the police station. The police officers greet him as Miki, all of them. He goes into a small office without knocking. Pokor immediately takes his feet off the desk and puts the newspaper down. Keys, says my uncle, and Pokor hands him a large bunch of them.

Everything OK, Miki? But my uncle doesn't deign to give him another glance.

There's no one in the cells. Miki opens the door of the largest cell and places the sooty stone from Kosovo Polje on the narrow bed, says: get your studies over with quickly and see about making some cash.

Miki's made lists. Miki drives me to the fire station. He crouches down outside the garage gate. The two large red fire engines used to stand behind it. I couldn't summon up any childish enthusiasm for them. Miki folds his hands in his lap and looks up at me from below. I crouch down too, but he keeps his eyes on where my head was a moment ago. Your father and Bora, he says, breathing in sharply, don't think it necessary to visit their own mother. Perhaps they think sending money is enough. But it's not enough. She's our mother, without me she'd be all alone. And these are not good times to be alone. Miki speaks calmly, his hands part and then come together again. Your father and Bora have a problem with me. It's just between the three of us, it has nothing to do with our mother. Tell them that.

Father said they were planning . . . I begin, but Miki interrupts me, and his eyes suddenly meet mine: your father hasn't spoken a word to me for seven years. Your father sends money, and photos of a swimming pool and your mother in a bathing costume. As far as your father's concerned I'm worth less than a spat-out piece of chewing gum. Miki speaks calmly, I look at the ground. But that won't do! he suddenly shouts, it won't do, that's not right! he shouts and shouts and shouts, that won't do, it won't do! Miki hammers on the gate behind which the fire engines stand with his fist, a single blow.

I do not deprive my body of the readiness to protest, but I don't trust my mouth to ask questions, I don't let any challenging look come into my eyes, I permit myself no stern expression, I will not let my hands clench in anger. I'm outstandingly good at describing gestures.

Miki drives home with me. Granny is drinking coffee with her women neighbours. Mrs Popović and Teta Magda are wearing black and criticising the gathering clouds. Mrs Popović thanks me for dropping in, I ask why, she says her husband has been playing the piano all morning, rainy pieces, I say: that's none of my doing – nor mine, she says.

Granny would like to sit in the front of the car, Miki pulls out, she says: Slavko once filled the apartment with flowers for me, once he gave the Central Committee his own version of Little Red Riding Hood instead of a speech, once he prophesied: it can't turn out well, we all just have ideals but no alternatives to those ideals, and once he thought of being unfaithful to me, I could taste it in his kisses.

Just after we leave the paved road, we can drive no further. There we are, says Miki, putting the handbrake on. There are so many potholes in the ground, and they're so deep, that even walking is difficult. Brambles and rampant undergrowth reach out to us from the sides of the road, thorny shoots, even rose-bushes, there's only a narrow track left, with young oaks crossing their branches above it. It soon gets hot inside this tunnel of vegetation, the wind carries a sweetish scent of decay. The clouds overhead come together, forming a grey mosaic heavy with rain.

It's incredible, I say, hitting out at the buzzing around my head, all these insects in March.

Yes, incredible, gasps Granny Katarina, pointing to the bushes ahead of us. I stop. Suspended in the undergrowth two or three metres above us is the bodywork of a yellow Yugo. Granny and my uncle walk past the stranded car, which is held aloft only by tendrils, branches and creepers. I cautiously approach the Yugo entwined there in prickly shoots, and am left with a bleeding scratch on my forearm when I push a couple of branches aside to get a look at the registration. Our old Yugo which always, without fail, broke down on this stretch of the road, the donkey, the idiot, the cretin of a car, as Father used to call it, has found its final parking place. The car is in love with this path – I can't explain what I see here in any other way.

The track through the vegetation leads to a meadow, this is where the path ends, it never went any further, dew lies on the ground here, snow lies on the mountain peaks.

We go uphill through the plum orchard to my great-grandparents' house. It's a long time since the trunks of the plum trees were smoothed down, scab and moss have eaten into their bark, fungi sprout at their feet. What are we all thinking? I wonder as Granny, my uncle and I stroke the bark of one of the trees in turn.

There's a table out in the yard between the sheds and the house, the white tablecloth weighted down with stones. At the head of the table Great-Grandpa Nikola is holding on to his long hair. The wind, children, the wind, he sings, taking my chin and then my head between his bony fingers. Aleksandar, my sunshine, he sings hoarsely, Miki, come here, hold me tight, he wails.

Great-Grandpa has grown strangely elongated, he is barefoot, trying to stand upright on damp grass, fighting the wind. His overcoat, stained and crumpled, hardly covers his hips, his dark face is overgrown by moss and fungus – or no, they're only shadows. He sings out a welcome to us, but it refuses to turn into a song. Great-Grandpa's voice is a hoarse file scraping the strength away from his words.

Great-Granny has braided her hair and wound the braids into a dark silver crown around her head. She sits there in her sheepskin coat, flowered overall and woolly stockings above gumboots, sits there with her legs apart on the large stone by the empty pigsty. She stays sitting there when I greet her, she stays sitting when I hug her, she's all soft, I hold her close, how do you hug someone who's as light as a feather and as old as the hills, how tight can you hold her?

Great-Granny? I touch her shoulder. Great-Granny? Glued to her rock, my great-granny is chewing some invisible morsel with her mouth open, scratching the rock with her fingernails, her big brown eyes seeing through everything.

Still Marshall Rooster to you! she'll cry, putting her eye-patch on, if I turn my back to her. I turn my back to her, and thunder rolls above the mountains.

There's some kind of smoked meat in thick, jagged slices, there's crusted sheep's milk cheese, there's the bread, the bread is warm and soft and sweet, there's cloudy plum juice, there's kaymak.

Granny Katarina washes the cutlery again and then we eat with our fingers after all; there are boiled potatoes, there are bits of peel left on the boiled potatoes, there are seven toothpicks. Uncle Miki cuts the bread, Granny takes the knife from his hand. There's dripping with bits of crackling in it, there's salt, there are two onions, there are peppers stuffed with minced meat, there are pickled gherkins, there's the diabetic jam from Germany, there's schnapps and sweet wine, it would restore sight to the blind, says Great-Grandpa hoarsely, raising his glass. To my Slavko, he says, drinking, and stays on his feet. Great-Grandpa stands at the head of the table the whole time, and Great-Granny eats on her rock with the plate on her lap. How are the Ischias, Father? Granny asks; what's that? says Great-Grandpa, and have I ever told you, he asked, how I was a bridge against the Austrians in 1914? There's boiled celery, there's a hunger I can't satisfy, there are no neighbours here feeding each other, says Great-Grandpa, and letting their illnesses tell them where they're head-up and where they're arse-down. There are cracks on the façade, there's no grunting from the pigsty, Petak's grave is in the middle of the yard.

My Mileva and I will survive the sky above, says Great-Grandpa.

We go off to the little graveyard with the food in baskets. You eat twice on the day of a requiem mass, Granny tells me, first without the dead person, then with him, there's wine with the food.

Grandpa wouldn't have thought much of such customs, I say.

The cloud cover hangs heavy and black over the plum trees, their thin branches reach out to the lightning. It's about being with each other, says Granny.

Great-Grandpa's white hair is like a veil in the wind. I catch up with him, I ask what's the matter with Great-Granny, she wasn't to be prised away from her rock.

My Mileva has the lightest head in the world, he says, suddenly leaping aside, striking out around him with his hands and bending his arm as if to take something in a headlock, whereupon the wind suddenly drops. My Mileva, he says breathlessly, wrestling with some large thing under his arm, gets off that rock only when there's something important to be done, or it's night and time to sleep.

The boards in the graveyard fence are crooked, the wood is rotting and cracked, the nails eaten away by rust. There's constant lightning, thunder rolls as if the clouds must be torn apart before it begins to rain. Miki shakes his head and laughs, although no one has said anything. The first heavy drops fall.

Grandpa's grave is clean and solid, the only white patch anywhere around. I put down the potatoes, the schnapps, the wine, the glasses, the marble gravestone is already shining in the rain. There are no Partisans any more, I tell Miki. He isn't listening.

There's an oval picture framed in the stone: my Grandpa in black and white looks at me, looks inside me, listens with his eyes, and he already knows how everything will turn out.

Granny digs a hole in the earth with a spoon at the place where I imagine Grandpa's head must be, and sticks a cigarette into the hole.

But Grandpa didn't smoke, I say.

He did in secret, says Granny, and Miki lights his father's cigarette and his own.

The grave is a festive table, it's raining more and more heavily, we sit on the edge of the grave and eat for the second time. The ash on Grandpa's cigarette curls and bends over. Rain falls on the onions, falls on the potatoes, hits the lid of the pan of peppers. I eat as if I've gone hungry for days, sometimes someone puts something down on the grave, a gherkin, a slice of bread and dripping, I salt the bread and salt the earth too, I dig a hole myself and fill it with schnapps. Yes, this is good, four of the Krsmanović family in the same place, says Great-Grandpa, looking up at the sky. Rain, you idiot, do you know who you've picked a quarrel with?

The rain doesn't know, it sweeps over us in waves, and when Granny says: oh, how much luck my husband deserved! and I say: oh, how many stories my Grandpa gave me! and Great-Grandpa says: how much schnapps is left? and Miki feeds Grandpa some damp bread and says: there's nothing we'd be proud of together, Father, there's nothing we blame ourselves for together, when we say all this no one can know who will shed tears, or just how hard. And I don't know when Great-Granny joined us, I only see her kneeling on the gravestone and kissing Grandpa's photo, kissing each eye once.

My child, my child, if I'd borne a thousand children no heart would have been as close to me as yours. Great-Granny kisses the damp grave and then, with earth on her mouth, she kisses her husband, who is getting taller and taller in the rain. Standing on tiptoe, she can only kiss his shoulder. She combs his wet hair with her wooden comb, she keeps combing its strands, they're tangled in the wind.

I eat and drink and eat and drink and eat, rain runs down the back of my neck, Grandpa's cigarette is smoked to the end. Great-Granny hands me my magic wand and hat. The hat still fits me, the wand, like the whole world, is smaller than I remember it. Miki grins at me, I go over to him, our ribcages touch, I can see the pores of his cheeks, I take the hat off and try to put it on Miki, he knocks my hand away, someone pushes someone else, the hat and wand land in the mud. There's thunder above me and behind me and to the left and the right all at once, shut up, will you? Great-Grandpa sings, shaking his fist at the clouds. Great-Granny puts her eye-patch on, Miki loosens his tie.

Grandpa, I haven't remembered all your stories, but I've written a few of my own and as soon as the rain stops I'll read them to you. I got the idea from Nena Fatima, from the voice of Grandpa Rafik, from the book I'm reading, from Granny, from the veins on your son's upper arms, he's painting coconuts now, from my mother's melancholy. I don't have all the things I'd need to tell my story as one of us: I don't have the courage of the river Drina, of the voice of the hawk, of the rock-hard backbone of our mountains, of Walrus's infallibility and the enthusiasm of the man who misses, but honourably. And I don't have Armin the station-master, Čika Hasan and Čika Sead in their eternal argument, Kiko's leg, Edin who forgets he's imitating a wolf and takes fright at the sound of his own voice, Cauliflower, the names of trees, a stomach for schnapps, the goals scored in the school yard. I miss you. And most of all I miss the truth, the truth in which we are no longer listeners or storytellers, but we give and forgive. Now I'm breaking my promise to you to go on telling stories.

A good story, you'd have said, is like our river Drina: never a calm little channel, it doesn't trickle along, it is rough and broad, tributaries flow in to enrich it, it rises above its banks, it bubbles and roars, here and there it flows into shallows but then it comes to rapids again, preludes to the depths where there's no splashing. But one thing neither the Drina nor the stories can do: there's no going back for any of them. The water can't turn back and choose another bed, just as promises cannot now be kept after all. No drowned man comes up again asking for a towel, no love is found again, no tobacconist fails to be born in the first place, no bullet shoots out of a neck and back into the gun, the dam will hold or will not hold. The Drina has no delta.

And because nothing can be reversed, you'd have thought up yourself and us sitting on you eating, you'd have thought up pictures for the rain, and Granny putting a second cigarette in your earthen mouth, and then Great-Granny challenging me to a duel, let's see if you're finally my equal after ten years in the Wild West.

The rain is heavy and cold. Drenched to the skin, we carry the dishes and the soggy bread back to the house. I feel dizzy, there's no sky left. Great-Grandpa can't hold on to the wind any more, it escapes, it grows stronger, in the yard one of the stones rolls off the table, the white cloth comes loose and takes off. Great-Granny stands still, not the good sheet, she murmurs, oh, not the good sheet. Great-Grandpa puts a hand to his back and laughs with the pain. The sheet flies through the rain, how can it fly when it's so wet, I wonder, but now it's landed at Great-Granny's feet, she wraps it round Miki.

My phone rings. Great-Grandpa bends over with his hand on his back as if to pick something up, and I answer the phone: there's whistling and rushing and a woman's voice. What? I shout, no reply. The rushing becomes a rainstorm of voices, it's as if I were listening to two million phone calls at once, I can't follow any of them, feedback, the voices are gone. Great-Granny rolls Miki under the table, covers him up. I put my other hand over my other ear and go out on the veranda, the roof over my head suddenly cuts off all the noises on the phone. I step back into the rain, crackling, I walk over the yard, slide down the slope, there's the woman's voice. Asija? I ask, softly at first, then louder: Asija? The answer, if it is an answer, comes blurred by rushing noises: Aleksandar. Who is it? I ask, and my voice whistles, who's there? The echo comes back, I have to sit down, I've eaten and drunk incredible amounts, twice, I can't take any more, I let myself drop, I lie there among the sweet humming of a rain of voices, where? howl two million voices at once, I feel sick, I can't cope any more, above me the clouds, one or perhaps two metres above me. The rain fills my mouth, voices like flies in my ear. Yes, I say, I'm here now. Aleksandar? says the woman's voice, and it's a river I'm lying in, I have my own rainy river Drina now, and I say: yes, I'm here.

Acknowledgements

My thanks to Katharina Adler, Martina Bachler, Nadja Küchen-meister, Benjamin Lauterbach, Michael Lentz, Thomas Pletzinger, Ilma Rakusa, Simon Roloff and Leipzig for support.

My thanks to Goran Bogdanović, Hamdo Oprašić, Kristina and Petar Stanišić, Mejrema and Hamed Hećimović and Višegrad for the stories.

Without them, Aleksandar's eyes and ears would never have been so wide open.

My thanks to the Künstlerhaus Lukas in Ahrenshoop for peace and quiet, accommodation, and the dunes.

My thanks to the Cultural Department of the city of Munich and the Villa Waldberta for their confidence, for the sporting activities and the Starnberger See.

This book was sponsored by the Crossing Borders Programme of the Robert Bosch Foundation, the Goethe Institute, and English PEN.